THE WIDOW TREE

ALSO BY NICOLE LUNDRIGAN

Glass Boys (2011, Douglas & McIntyre)

The Seary Line (2008, Breakwater Books)

Thaw (2005, Breakwater Books)

Unraveling Arva (2003, Breakwater Books)

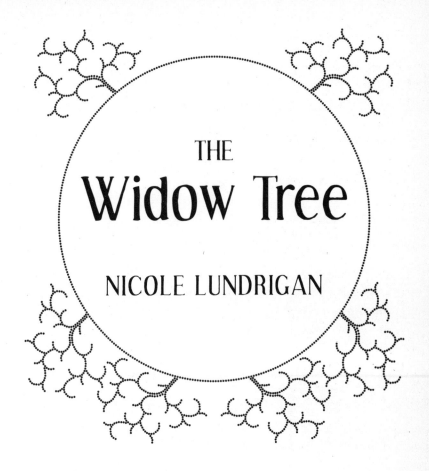

THE
Widow Tree

NICOLE LUNDRIGAN

Douglas & McIntyre

Douglas and McIntyre (2013) Ltd.
P.O. Box 219, Madeira Park, BC, VON 2H0
www.douglas-mcintyre.com

Cataloguing data available from Library and Archives Canada
ISBN 978-1-77100-071-0 (paper)
ISBN 978-1-77100-072-7 (ebook)

Editing by Barbara Berson and Shirarose Wilensky
Copy editing by Maureen Nicholson
Cover design by Carleton Wilson and Anna Comfort O'Keeffe
Cover illustration by Becca Stadtlander
Text design by Carleton Wilson
Printed in Canada

Douglas and McIntyre (2013) Ltd. would like to acknowledge the financial support from the Government of Canada through the Book Publishing Industry Development Program and the Canada Council for the Arts, and from the Province of British Columbia through the BC Arts Council and the Book Publishing Tax Credit.

For
Jozsef Deák
&
For
Aniko Biber

Prologue

AUTUMN, AD 45

PANNONIA, ROMAN EMPIRE

"*DEVI SEPPELLIRE.*" BURY IT.

"I do not understand."

"The trees. The trees are hiding something."

The soldier followed the centurion's gaze but saw nothing in the forest to cause concern. No threat of invasion. Still, he did as he was told, bending and putting the rest of the coins away. A month of wages for the legion. He paused as he picked up the final one, studying the image of a praying mantis, spindly legs, clinging to a shaft of wheat. *You will be a man's future,* he thought, and brought it to his lips and kissed it. Then he took the small clay pot in both hands. As he strode outside, he pressed the pot close to his body. Just a simple clay container, pale brown, covered with loops and whorls from its maker's fingertips.

He found a place between two tents and dropped to his knees. Using his *pugio,* he cut into the soft black earth, forming a deep hole. He gently placed the clay pot at the bottom of the hole, covered it with dirt, pressed it down with the heel of his hand. When he stood, he kicked dry soil over the area to disguise it.

Walking out into the field, he stopped for a moment to watch the trees. Again he could detect nothing, other than the leaves had grown tired and the colour had begun to drain. He did not expect to see them fall, though, as soon they would be moving on. Going home. He would see his young children. The campaign would be behind them and the worry would be over.

As he stood there, the wind lifted, rustling through the forest in a constant drone. The soldier cocked his head and squinted. He did not like it when he could not hear.

:::

WHEN DARKNESS CAME, HE lay down on the floor of a tent, thick stew and sour wine sloshing in his stretched belly. He dreamt of riding toward his village, the hooves of his horse striking the damp ground, muck spattering its legs and underbelly. His *pugio* near his thigh reminding him he was once a fighter. A strong fighter. A pleasant image, and he wore a faint smile as he slept.

He woke in the dead of night, his nose filled with a dense odour, like the stench of yellow wounds that refused to heal. Lying still, he heard a rhythmic shift of fur, squeak of hard leather. Inhalation. Exhalation. Something savage was standing just behind his head.

A gust of wind. The door of the tent flapped open. For an instant, the full moon illuminated the room, and he saw a sudden blur of pelts and greasy skin, limbs scrambling on top of him. Then a foreign eye pressed against his own, and another man's breath entered his lungs. A cudgel hovered above his body, and he raised his hands, fingernails still blackened from his digging. Song of polished wood moved through air, and a bolt of lightning arrived inside his skull. Moments later his ears detected the thunder.

He felt no pain afterwards, just a seeping wetness. Warmth. As though he were floating in the salty sea, swallowed by deep blue. When he breached the surface, he called out instructions to his wife.

She was a hazy form in the distance, like a solitary tree, waving her branches. Two young boys, his sons, dancing in her crooked shadow. He told his widow where to find the clay pot. He tried to wish them a good life with all he had saved over so many years, but the words never left his mouth.

Chapter 1

AS SOON AS THEY left the town of Drobnik, the road turned to dirt. The bus creaked, bouncing from side to side, and in the sunlight Dorján Szabó could see small clouds of dust rising up from invisible holes in the floor. The harsh smell of exhaust filled the bus, and Dorján sipped shallow breaths. Too early in the morning to inhale such fumes, he thought, and his sensitive stomach turned, as it always had with such things since he was a child. He brought his hands to his face, breathing in the chemicals on his skin. Hours ago he had been swimming, and the lingering scent of the pool water was familiar and soothing.

He was seated in the middle of the bus, near the aisle, and had a clear view of his teacher. Gyuri Takáts stood just behind the driver. His arms were up, hands holding the metal racks where travellers might lay their luggage. The temperature was still cool, but Dorján saw the dark rings of underarm sweat already staining Takáts's shirt.

"Remember," Takáts yelled, cutting through the chatter. "I expect hard work. You are not clearing your *nagyanya*'s potato patch today."

They were heading toward a *poljoprivredna zadruga*. A field of to-matoes, potatoes, corn, owned by the government. During the first morning lesson at school, a bell started to clang, over and over again. Dorján's entire class lined up in single file, marched down the hallway, and boarded the waiting buses. He had no idea what was happening or where they were going until Takáts announced they would spend the remainder of the day working in the field harvesting a crop that would later be distributed for sale. In the classroom someone had asked where the money would go, and Takáts replied, "Where it is needed, of course." A snicker, and Takáts spun around, narrowed his eyes, scanned the students. Dorján looked down, swallowed. Not be-cause he had made the sound, but because he knew his best friend, János Kelemen, surely had.

They drove through Bregalnica, the village where Dorján now lived with his grandmother. The place was not much more than a series of narrow streets lined with white stucco homes. Old ladies leaned against the walls, some of them knitting, balls of wool pushed into their armpits. They kept their wrinkled faces lifted toward the morning sun. As they passed, small children in cuffed shorts and long socks jumped up and down, waving at the bus. Most everyone ignored the children, but Dorján noticed Nevena, the Komandant's daughter, three rows ahead, press one white hand against the streaked glass and smile.

Even though their village was small, they still had a proper square. An expanse of cobblestone, circled with stores and stands and a tall church, the largest structure in Bregalnica. On this warm October morning the square was bustling and the buses slowed. Women strolled about with baskets, scarves tied over their heads. Men sat at the small tables, sipping coffee from tiny white cups, laughing with rough voices. Dorján stretched his neck, and sure enough, he located his grandmother. Standing on the stone steps of the church, fanning her neck with her stubby hand. While young people would not cross the threshold, every morning she went into the damp building by herself. She lit a candle, bending on her knees to pray. Dorján once asked why she prayed so much, what did she want, and she replied, "I ask for nothing, *szívem*. I pray only this soil feels no more sorrow."

After his parents had died, Dorján had moved from Drobnik to Bregalnica to live with his *nagyanya*. He fought against it, insisting he could manage on his own. He knew where to buy bread. A quarter loaf. With his mother now gone, that was all he would need. His grandmother was welcome, he told her, to bring him a boiled egg and a bottle of milk on occasion.

Whenever he reflected on this memory, he always felt a wave of love for the old woman. She had not laughed at him when he was that child. Never took his thin wrist in her grip and dragged him out the door. No, she paced the floor, as though she were pondering his ideas. "I see," she had said. "I see you are an independent man." He nodded, and she said, "Today I insist. I have soup. You will insult me if you refuse my soup. Then tomorrow we will see. And each day after. Yes?"

In his child's mind, he had regained control over something uncontrollable. Agreed to her conditions. He took her hand, and together they strode down the dim hallway and out through the door. He promised her he would return to Drobnik the next day. Once the soup pot was empty. But his grandmother made *palacsinta* filled with warm apricot jam. The day after that a flat apple cake. And the day after that biscuits filled with morsels of bacon. "All for you," she had said as time and grief slowly slipped away from him.

On the edge of the square, Dorján noticed Gazda László's wooden cart, laden with a variety of fruits and vegetables. An enormous mound of pointed red peppers shone as though they were greased. Gazda's young grandson, Tibor, who did not attend school, worked there nearly every day, selling whatever Gazda plucked from the vine or pulled from the earth. Dorján knew Tibor was staring at the bus, and Dorján bent his head, examining his knuckles. He could not look at the slow boy's damaged face. It had all started as a joke, a tease, but so quickly had degraded. And then the horrible fight, the flesh on Tibor's cheekbone bursting open.

Out of the corner of his eye, Dorján caught János pushing his face toward the window. János pointed at Tibor and then, putting one finger to his lips, said, *"Kuss,"* in a long, low whisper. Behind a mountain of wild mushrooms, Tibor danced from foot to foot, shaking his hands on limp wrists like a flightless bird. Anger made him do that, not fear. Dorján had seen him doing it before. His muscles twitching with so much frustration and no way to express himself.

When they moved onto a narrow stretch of road, Dorján said, "He couldn't hear you, you know."

"Of course he couldn't." János began to chuckle. "But he knew what I meant."

"We shouldn't bother him anymore."

"So? He shouldn't bother us either."

Dorján rubbed one hand over the other. "Maybe."

"Look. I didn't mean that, you know. I didn't mean for that to happen. But don't blame me. What could I do?"

"I know. You're right. What's the point of it all anyway?"

"I have a point. You just don't know it yet."

When he spoke lately, there was a new coldness in János's tone. Dorján said nothing else. There was no sense attempting to stand against him. They had been friends since they were small boys. He was so young, he could not even remember when they met. Newborns, likely. Dorján's grandmother living next door to János's parents, she would have brought Dorján over, swaddled tightly in cloth. Mother and grandmother comparing them. Dorján's soft folds of fat balanced by János's powerful cry.

Then as they grew, two boys on the floor building with wooden blocks and discs, the women began to call them "the little engineers." Almost as though it were already determined, the status they would attain in adulthood. He and János soon believed it themselves. Agreeing to work side by side, motivating each other, until they achieved this goal. The most highly respected profession in their country.

János had not mentioned their future plans in months. If Dorján brought them up, János simply did not reply. Dorján's grandmother had always said they were two buttons on the same shirt, but Dorján had a frightening awareness that the thread holding them together was working loose.

"Something amusing, boys?" asked Takáts.

Dorján jumped. He had not seen his teacher walking down the aisle or heard his palms slapping the tops of the seats. Takáts stood

beside him now, one leg straight, the knee of the other gently swinging back and forth. Not in time with the jostling of the bus.

"Nothing, sir," János replied.

"Szabó?"

"No, sir," he said. Takáts watched Dorján's mouth as he spoke. "I
was not laughing."

"Do you need to go and sit with Beštić Úr?" Beštić was an over-
weight root growing from Takáts's slender side. Very rarely were they
apart. The only Hungarian teachers among a staff of nearly all Serbians.

"No, sir," they said in unison. Straightening their spines. Beštić
taught mathematics and kept his temper on a weak leash. Last month,
one boy had dozed in his class, and Beštić had noticed his head lolling
forward. With light steps down between the desks, he silently withdrew the left side of his belt from his high-waisted trousers. Managed
to whip it, kiss the boy's cheek with the rounded leather tip. Belt se-
cured, looped through the buckle before the boy even jumped, hand
rising to cover the oozing welt.

"You are boys no longer, you know, but young men. There's a serious difference," Takáts said. Both teachers often lectured about how
their students might become men. Even though there were several
girls in each class, the focus remained on the boys.

"Yes, yes, sir. Yes, sir." Once again, their voices singing together.

"And I expect more from you, Dorján. Your shoulders are built to
work."

Takáts stared at Dorján's broad chest. A swimmer's chest, and Takáts had been his coach for many years. Dorján could remember the
day he learned he was chosen to swim, and if he trained hard enough,
some day he might swim for his country. János stood beside him, and
his friend displayed not a shadow of jealously. Only pride at Dorján's
success. Later on that warm summer night, they had sneaked out
of their houses. Were they only eleven? They tore through the field
behind the village, the smell of earth and crushed grass filling their
nostrils, making them giddy. The square was empty, and they clamoured onto the wall, János standing, his defiant fists striking the black
air. Sitting then, legs dangling, they smoked brown cigarettes Dorján

had stolen from his neighbour. János gripped Dorján's head, hands cupping his ears, "You will be the best, my friend! The very best the country has ever, ever seen!"

"I'll be part of a team," Dorján had corrected. "With the other boys. A team."

But János narrowed his lids, with the tiniest shake of his head. "The best, Dori. Not the other boys. You. I will be right there. You in the water. Me on the side." His eyes glistened with hope. "Come!" he said, leaping off the wall. "Let us work!"

The boys rushed along the streets of the village, coming to a small building surrounded by wire fencing. While Dorján moved slowly, anxious they would be caught, János did not hesitate. Fingers gripping the wire, he scaled the fence, flipping his nimble body over, soles of his feet slapping the concrete as he landed. "Come on, Dori! A legless dog would beat you."

Dorján scaled the fence, easing over, wire digging into his fingers. Dove into the black water and swam. János stood on the concrete edge, urging him forward, encouraging him, trying to arouse a fighter in his soft heart. Those were the words he conjured when Takáts yelled, complained, told Dorján he was useless in the pool. Splashing like an ugly girl. János's voice was louder, sharper. Making him work harder.

Takáts moved past them, wobbling along the aisle of the bus, the back of his hand just grazing Dorján's hair. Dorján did not turn to see where he stopped. There was no need. Takáts knew the history of their country like no other and worked hard to screw it into their skulls. Details of struggle and fighting and seizure. The unknown mounds of dead. While Dorján would notice János clench his jaw, his fists, those lectures had a different effect on him. Made his throat tighten and his toes curl inside his laced shoes. Made him feel shy and cautious. Why did he have to know everything? Could he not simply focus on today, where he and his grandmother had most of what they needed? Of course he could not ask that. He would be ridiculed by Takáts. János, even, would scorn his childishness.

Dorján lowered his head, running a finger over the seam on his thigh. His grandmother had sewn extra fabric to lengthen his shorts, and the difference was obvious. He could feel Takáts watching them now, and he was silently grateful János did not tilt his head, whispering something to force nervous laughter up from Dorján's diaphragm.

As they left the village, the road opened up, wide fields on either side. There were deep grooves in the soft earth, threatening to pinch the rubber tires of the bus. They drove past orchards and solitary homes with steep roofs, smoke trailing from the chimneys. Other *tanya* that had been destroyed, a scattering of stone, bombed and never reconstructed. As they travelled, they slowed for herds of sheep, cart, and horse. Passed an expanse of sunflowers, framed heads nodding, a spray of hungry black birds rising into the air when the second bus backfired.

The bus continued rocking over the narrowing road. Dorján felt his breakfast sloshing around inside his stomach and was relieved when they eventually came to a stop. He stood, stretched, walked off the bus. Drank the dusty air, waited for his weak stomach to strengthen again.

They had parked beside a patch of land, neat rows of vegetables overgrown and drooping in the sunlight. A forest of tall trees bordered the field, leaves revealing just a hint of orange. A breeze lifted and kissed the dried tips of the cornstalks, dancing through the dying leaves. Dorján turned his head and listened, the air weighted by a low drone.

Chapter 2

GITTA KELEMEN WALKED TO the village square in flat black shoes, a long black dress, and a black handkerchief tied over her brown hair. Bright sunshine had long ago burned off the morning dew, and she could feel the rays moving through the fabric. Only a short stroll, but she was already overheated, dizzy.

She placed her basket on the cobblestone, took a clean handkerchief from her purse, and pressed it against the fine hair on her upper lip, then the nape of her neck. This gesture was purely habit, though, a comfort of sorts, as Gitta Kelemen's pores had released no sweat in eight years. Her skin was always dry, as were her palms and armpits and the folds between her legs. It had started when her husband, Imre, died. From that day onward, her body felt as though it were covered with a fine layer of dust. Like something betrayed, discarded. Or abandoned.

She tucked the handkerchief in her pocket, picking up her basket. The square was busy, women milling about, men taking *pálinka* at small tables. The doors of the church were open, and she could see a glow inside, a candle or two burning. But the sight of it gave her no comfort. Hardly anyone went to worship anymore. Unless they were old and set, and had no worry their habits would be noticed.

Or questioned.

Looking about, she saw her neighbour, Zsuzsi Szabó. Like Gitta, she wore a long dull dress, hair covered, and would not disgrace her dead husband by wearing colour. She waved to Gitta, and on aged hips, she wobbled toward her, saying, *"Szervusz, szervusz, Gitta néni."* Hello, hello.

"Szervusz," she replied, and winced slightly as she smiled, corners of her mouth cracking.

"Hogy vagy?" How are you?

"Jól vagyok, köszönöm szépen." I'm fine, thank you very much.

"My pickles are ready," she said, arms flying upward. "The barrel is so stuffed, I hardly had room for the bread."

"Ah, yes." Gitta rubbed her nose. "I can smell them through the fence."

"You can?" The old woman gripped Gitta's wrist with thick fingers and laughed. "I will bring you some."

"That would be nice, Zsuzsi *néni.*"

"János will love them." Zsuzsi gently slapped her stomach, dress billowing with the sudden wind. "Good for the insides."

"I am sure."

"Dorján eats them like there is a thief at the door."

Gitta shook her head. "How do you manage?"

"Manage? Making pickles? Of course my mother taught me."

"No. Everything."

"I manage." She laughed again, eyes wet and happy. "Like you manage. It is what we do. Otherwise we shrivel up and," clap of her hands, "goodbye."

Gitta smiled, gripping the handle of her basket a little tighter.

Zsuzsi checked the watch on her wrist, nearly lost in a fold of fat. "Now, I must run away from you. Komandant Dobrica will be waiting."

"The Komandant?" A slight flush rose up in Gitta's cheeks when she imagined his face. She rarely saw him, but when she did, she could not help but notice that he had barely aged since he was a boy. A handsome boy.

"He is in need of new trousers."

"Ah."

"I will sew anything with pleasure in my heart, except for men's trousers."

Gitta shook her head, and Zsuzsi leaned closer, gesturing toward her hips. "So much measuring." Jiggly laugh that hung in the air even as she walked away.

"Ah," Gitta said again, though no one was there to listen. She watched Zsuzsi leave the square, her short body rolling from side to side. Gitta had thought to visit with her this afternoon but would avoid her home now. The thought of being so close to Dragan Dobrica, the Komandant, made her uncomfortable. They had once cared for each other, maybe even loved each other. But Gitta had married Imre, and shortly after, the Komandant married his wife, Aliz. Still, after all these years, she found it hard to meet his eyes. There was something in his gaze. She could not be certain, but she wondered if it was lingering regret.

Gitta reached over and touched her elbow. She remembered Dragan holding her there all those years ago. Only a girl then, she was eighteen. He had gently guided her through the throngs of people in the square, she leaning her shoulder back, grazing his arm. Their closeness was easy, comfortable. She knew he had the capacity to tease slender roots from her feet, plant them in the soil. He would protect her at all costs. She tried not to consider it, though, as the thought of such stability frightened her. If circumstances shifted, would there not be too much to lose?

The gypsies were there that day. They kept their caravans and tired horses farther up the road but played music in the square. A crowd of them, men and women and children. All with tanned faces and bright black eyes. She remembered a man with an unkempt beard, hat with a chewed brim, playing the violin. His bow jumped up and down, pulling happy music from the strings. Another smacking a tambourine against a wiry thigh.

Was it she who had stopped to watch the gypsies dance? Or had it been Dragan? Sometimes she pondered this single point. It seemed important to understand. Who had slowed their feet, bringing the pair of them to a stop? That short pause in their movements changing everything. If they had rushed past, she would not have noticed Imre. Not had time to watch him. Short and strong and completely at ease.

Of course she had heard of Imre. She knew he was a gymnast, could stay in the rings, body in a taut T, for long minute after long minute. Not a bead of sweat on his forehead. Soon enough the entire country would know who he was, they said. He would make everyone proud.

They also said he would not live in Bregalnica much longer.

Imre had been among the bystanders, but the rhythm wove its arm through the crowd and drew him out. He was not bashful and instead danced among them as though they were family. His arms and legs on strings, a handsome puppet. He glanced at Gitta. Winked. She saw his full face, forehead wide and shiny, heavy brows hiding his eyes from her view. The gypsy women with swishing skirts twisted their hands in the air, dancing around him. The sound of jingling metal mixing with the violin.

She could recall it so clearly. He was flapping his arms and stomping his feet, and in an instant, her picture changed, his feet now replacing his head. As easy as that, he was standing upside down, elbows bent slightly, head pushed outward, then on one hand, stout legs kicking in the air. So foolish and free, and the sight of his shirt falling upward to reveal his flat stomach made her close her hands into loose fists, thumbs hidden.

Coins tumbled from his pockets, rolling over the cobblestone. Children with hair like black wool darted forth, a blur of limbs, and the coins disappeared inside sticky fists. He winked at Gitta again, then lifted a hand and waved at them. Waved at the boys who had stolen his money. He was made of air.

Gitta blushed, could not take her eyes from him. She noticed she was breathing through her mouth. Her tongue was dry. She could hear her throat's struggle as it tried to swallow nothing.

As she stood there, she had not felt Dragan's grip tighten. Only after all these years of remembering did she notice it. Almost a pinch. But perhaps she was making it up. Invented that single detail. All she knew for certain was that when Imre was on his feet again, she had fallen under a gauzy sort of spell, her elbow had a lingering ache, and Dragan Dobrica was gone.

Gitta wandered toward Gazda László's cart. Every morning, the farmer stocked the wooden structure, and his grandson, Tibor, stood behind, selling to customers, mostly local women who needed a little more than what their backyard gardens could offer.

Tibor was skinny with short black hair and a slightly lopsided face. People thought he was mute, but Gitta had heard him make certain guttural sounds. Grunts or wet clicks from the back of his tongue. Gazda László refused to allow this deficiency to diminish his grandson's chance at employment. "Just because his brain is missing does not mean the boy cannot work," he said. "Every man can work. As long as he has a single hand. A few fingers, even." Hammer fist punching open palm of his other hand. "He must be useful. For something."

This morning, Tibor's face was injured. Left eye swollen, and there was a cut on his lip, a raw scrape along his jawline. When she saw him, her mind immediately went to her own son, and her heart seized. She could not imagine seeing János's beautiful face damaged. "Tell me what happened, Tibor. You hurt yourself?"

He would not look up but shook his head back and forth, face a sudden blur.

"An accident then?"

He grimaced, turned his chin toward his shoulder, spat on the cobblestone. She noticed that the hair on the back of his head was missing, rubbed off over time as a baby's might be. She guessed the boy slept fitfully.

He started to wipe his mouth, then stopped, and moved his hand over the vegetables. Glared at her shoulders. *What do you want?*

Gitta touched the scarf covering her head, clearing her throat. She pointed at the red peppers, holding up eight fingers.

He mimicked her, eight fingers. Four of them scratched.

She nodded.

Lips pursed, his bird hands hovered over the mound of peppers, eyes rolled slightly upward. Common knowledge by now dictated that no villager was allowed to touch his fruit or vegetables, not until the money was in his pouch and the produce was in the basket. He picked several from the pile, inspected each one, and placed them gently in the metal dish. Casually, he hooked his finger over the edge of the scale as he waited for the flickering needle to settle.

Only in recent months had she noticed this. His subtle weighting of the scale. At first she thought it an accident, but when it happened again, she understood he was doing it purposefully. Gitta coughed, stared at his finger, and coughed again when he lifted that finger but allowed his wrist to press down on the peppers. Marbled words of irritation or exasperation wedged in his mouth.

Laying the peppers into her basket, he pawed money from her hands. Returned not a single dinar, until she did not waver, staring directly at the buttoned pouch attached to his leather belt. He paused, and when he finally offered her the correct change, she saw a glint in his eyes, a slight downward twist at the corners of his lips. Some sort of calculation revealing itself in his expression. Nothing new, really, only further confirmation of what both she and János had always thought. "He is not as slow as people believe," János had said recently. "He is actually quite clever." Perhaps the façade worked for him, the eye rolling and the snorting. Gave him something he needed. And surely, Gitta thought as she ran a finger over the firm, warm flesh of the peppers, who was she to judge?

She clutched the basket tightly and hurried along the walkway, the odour of warm peppers wafting up toward her. She stayed beneath the shade of the trees, their lower trunks painted white. The morning was passing quickly, and she still had hours of work ahead of her. János would be home in the afternoon, bursting through the door with his hungry demands and his outrageous notions. One she would greet with a pot full of food. And the other, with a heart full of anxiety.

Chapter 3

TWO TRUCKS WERE ALREADY beside the field, tanned men unloading supplies from the backs, dropping items onto the road. As the children filed past them, one of the men pressed a basket into their hands. Hands cupping their mouths, Takáts and Beštić hollered instructions on what to collect and how to collect it. They explained the children were to squeeze the ears of corn with a firm grip. If they felt something substantial inside the husk, pick it, but if the cob was not mature, small and useless, leave it alone. "These men do not want to transfer product they cannot sell," Takáts said. Additionally, he told them, someone would come later to collect leftovers for animal feed.

Dorján and János headed toward the northeast corner of the field, and all the way János kept hissing in a high-pitched voice, "Squeeze your ears, young men, squeeze those ears. Do you have a tall, strong cob? A manly cob?" Once the cornfield had swallowed them, Dorján tried to swat János, but János avoided his swing. "What's wrong, Szabó?" János stern now. "Your cob is too heavy to carry? Shall we find a girl to assist you?"

"Kuss!" Dorján yelled and lunged for János again. A thin root held his foot, making him tumble into a wall of corn. He opened his

mouth to swear, but the words snagged in his throat when he realized Nevena was only a few steps behind them.

She reached them just as Dorján clamoured to his feet, and she stood there, holding her basket close to her stomach. "Did you hurt him, János?"

"Such a foolish question, Neva. Of course not."

"Are you hurt, Dorján?"

He glanced at János, who was inspecting a plant, mumbling "Hmmm," and Dorján shook his head rapidly, heat in his cheeks, coughed, "Tripped."

"All the bickering. I swear you two are more brothers than friends."

Dorján coughed again, looking away, but János blurted, "You've figured it all wrong, Neva. I'm a peaceable man. Now you'll follow us," he announced, ear of corn in his hand poking the air. "And we will work like strong young countrymen."

"I'll believe that when I see it," she said as she strolled past him, bumping him with her hip. "You'll follow me, you mean."

"I'm serious," he said, hurrying behind her. "I can do good things."

"What do you think, Dori?" The words trailed over her shoulder. "Can your dear friend do anything noble?"

Dorján grunted, staring at Nevena's legs. Her skin was pale, and there was a scrape of dried grey muck across the back of her calf. One of her socks had fallen, lay wrinkled near the top of her shoe.

"Ah, silence from your friend," she called. "I can think of no better endorsement, János Kelemen."

János glared at Dorján, lowering his thick eyebrows.

Nevena walked several more yards down a row and stopped in a small clearing. A stretch of plants had been pulled from the earth, compost heaped in a pile. "We'll work here," she said. "The farther we go, the farther we have to carry the corn to the trucks."

Dropping his basket and the lunch satchel he carried over his shoulder, János raised his hands to the sky. "She's brilliant, isn't she?"

Dorján peeked at Nevena to catch her reaction, and he scowled when she blushed.

They worked their way along the row, filling the baskets with ears of corn. When the baskets were half-filled, János plucked one up, dumping the contents into another. "Dori, carry this back to the truck."

Dorján stepped backwards, putting his hand to his eyes. Though the sun had not reached its highest peak, it cut through the dried leaves and shone in his face. "Me?"

"Why not? Take a break."

"Is that all right, Dorján?" Nevena asked. "If János stops, he might never start again."

Dorján shrugged, leaned over, and picked up the basket. Struggled to carry the load down the row. As he stepped along the path, curling leaves brushed against his white shirt, scratching his forearms. The deep basket banged his thighs, and he was happy to see the small incline just ahead of him leading to the road. When he emerged from the row, one of the men grabbed the load from his hands and, with no effort, hoisted the basket up and over, dumping the corn into the bed of the truck. Shoved the basket back toward Dorján, then leaned against the truck, spat in the dirt. Deep voice, "What's your name?"

"Szabó."

"Well, Szabó. You embarrass your family."

Dorján backed up a step. "Yes, sir."

"You play in there," the man said, frowning. "Like a girl. So slow with your skipping." He spat again, a shrivelled mouth, face like a burnt hide. "What? Your father never taught you to work?"

Dorján hurried away. The mention of his father, gone now so many, many years, made his skin itch. He would fill the basket more quickly, show the man his capabilities. He would labour until he felt the burn in his muscles.

He had marched halfway down the row when he paused, feeling a strange static inside his chest. Seconds later, he heard Nevena giggle, and the static sensation moved out through his limbs. Made his fingers tingle. He walked faster, ankles buckling on the uneven earth, and just before he reached them, he hesitated. Though the wind made the top of the field shiver and hum, inside the corn, the air was still.

When he peered through the thick wall of leaves and stalks, he saw János crouching down beside Nevena. One of her hands was on her hip, the other clutched the end of her braid. She had planted her foot on János's bent knee. With delicate fingers, János slowly tugged at the sock that had slid down her calf. Once the sock was in place, he let his fingers linger in the smooth groove just behind her knee. And she never flinched, just stared at the sky, smiling.

"Sorry," Dorján said as he stomped into the clearing. "I thought we were supposed to be doing something."

"We were."

You were. János's use of "we" made Dorján clench his jaw. For years the three of them had been unlikely friends, running through the field or swimming at the pool. The knowledge that Nevena was Serbian, and they were Hungarian, never weighted their interactions. She was only a girl who could run faster than either of them, her round face turned toward them, always full of laughter. Yes, they made a perfect little triangle, each arm the same length. But now János was trying to pull her away. As though those two arms belonged together. Leaving Dorján, a useless base, lying in the grass alone.

"Corn. I meant corn." Dorján drew back his shoe, kicking a heap of decomposing stalks, and a dark rat bolted out from underneath the tangle. Scuttled up and over a mound of dirt and disappeared.

Nevena sucked in air. *"Ju!"* she cried, hands to her neck. "Did you see its tail? Longer than a whip."

"Just another rat," János said, though he stood and looked around. "Always showing up uninvited. My mother sets a small plate at the table."

Nevena giggled, knocking him in his upper arm. "She does not."

Though an occasional rat was common, they had arrived in droves that summer. Sneaking into lofts and barns, hiding in stores of flour and inside trunks of clothes. Dorján's grandmother viewed their arrival as a punishment from God, but Dorján thought the pests were simply displaced. Forced from their home when the abandoned mortuary went up in flames. Nothing left but a weak plaster shell, dirty white, except for the streaks of soot reaching upward through the shattered windows.

János stepped in front of Nevena. "Do it again. Kick it hard."

Foot hauled back, Dorján held his breath, struck the mound with full force, and the compost scattered. No movement, and he said, "It's probably after your lunch." He nudged the satchel to reveal gnawing on a corner. "I can smell it from here."

János sniffed the air, then wandered for a minute until he found a long stick with a forked top. "You're right," he said. "I'll hang it up." He circled, took a couple of steps, and with two hands lifted the stick above his head, piercing the soft soil. Holding the top of the stick, he jumped, putting his weight into it, and the stick slid easily down through a foot of dirt. And then it struck something. János leaned on it, and whatever the stick had struck gave way, and it sank another few inches, striking something else.

János stepped back, stared at the spot where wood met soil. "Something's down there."

"Yes, like a rock."

"It's not a rock."

"You have special vision all of a sudden?" Dorján said, and he glanced at Nevena's shoulders, the front pockets on her blouse. He had hoped she would laugh at his joke, but she did not.

"I don't know," János mumbled. "It felt different."

"I bet your lunch it's just a stupid rock."

"You can have it if you're hungry."

"No," Dorján replied. "Let's make it a bet. I left mine at school, and your food will do fine." He moved the stick in circles, then yanked it from the soil. Dropping to his knees, he wriggled his hand into the narrow hole, pulling out fistfuls of black dirt.

"Watch your fingers," Nevena said. "What if it's a nest? A whole family."

"Shit," Dorján whispered. "Help me."

The other two knelt beside him around the hole, and they started digging. In this moment, they were equal again. Soft black earth working its way underneath fingernails, into cuticles. Staining their palms. Heads lowered, they flung dirt backwards between their bent legs. Mineral smell of the past rising up from the forming hollow.

Chapter 4

IN THE FIELD THE narrow hole deepened, and the three children leaned in closer, forearms occasionally touching, warm breath mingling. For a moment, Dorján felt as though he were suffocating, and he sat back on his feet. He did not like the sight of Nevena's bare knees pushed into the soil and the dirt staining her white hands. Or the sight of János, a sharp stick now appearing in his fist, stabbing it down into the hole. Tip of the stick just missing Nevena's fingers.

"Wait," Dorján whispered.

János looked up, his mouth pulled wide, a smile that was not a smile. He panted slightly. "What if it's a skull?"

"Don't be stupid."

János snorted. "You never know."

Frowning, Nevena reached in and lifted another handful of dirt from the damp hole. Then she paused, stared into her open palm, and plucked something from the clump of soil. Held it up. "No skull here."

"A rock," Dorján said. "Told you so. Your lunch is mine."

János took the piece, wiping away the dirt. "Does this look like a rock?"

"Pottery," Nevena said as she moved her hair with her wrist. "An old piece of an urn or something." She put her hand into the dark hole again, tugging out a second fragment. "Look at this. Top of a jug maybe. The lip?"

Dorján reached in, sifted through dirt with his fingers, and retrieved a small disc, black soil clinging to either side. "This. Ah. Might be something else," he said slowly. And he spat twice on the disc, rubbed the wetness over it, dried it on the band of his brown sock.

The three fell silent, staring at the small item Dorján pinched between his thumb and forefinger. Even though the surface of it was scratched, Dorján could clearly see an image stamped onto the precious piece of metal—a man's profile, strong nose, thick neck, and ring of laurel circling his hair. He turned it over, saw the impression of a single stalk of wheat, and then looking closer he noticed a small insect perched on the side of the plant. A praying mantis.

"Shit!" János's voice warbled as he grabbed it from Dorján. "That's a Roman coin." He lifted it upward, as though the sun overhead might shine through it. "Gold, I think." Exhaling. "It's gold."

"Are you sure?" Nevena asked.

"Yes, yes. Gold. I'm sure."

"How many do you think are down there?"

"I don't know. I don't know."

Dorján reached in again, but János pressed an arm across Dorján's chest. "Stop. Let's be systematic about this. If there are more, we don't want to miss any."

"Right."

Nevena's eyes were wide. "Shouldn't we go and get someone?"

"Like who?"

"*Gospodin* Beštić? *Gospodin* Takáts?"

"Yes, yes, sure. So he can dig this field up and go home with a bagful? Buy himself a house in Drobnik? And all we'll get is a smack over the head for being no better than some filthy dogs, digging holes in the field with our front paws."

"He wouldn't. He really wouldn't. He can't do that."

"Neva—do you want to watch him?"

She nudged János with her elbow. "Why do you always think like that?"

"It's the right way to think."

"Just because your father had troubles with—"

Sudden flash behind his eyes, words through his teeth. "Don't even start." János carefully laid the coin on the ground near his leg. "Not a single word."

"But—"

"You've got no idea, Neva. No idea. I can't even talk about it."

She bent her head slightly, scraped dirt from underneath a thumb-nail.

Dorján cleared his throat. He had never seen János snap at Nevena, but he understood the reason for it. Nevena was a Serb, lived in the largest home in the village. Her father was the Komandant. She had never wanted for a single thing, while János seemed to exist inside a perpetual cylinder of want. Want for a father, want for the freedom to yell his thoughts in the village square, sometimes want for more food, more warmth. "Are you two finished?" Dorján said.

"We're finished. Of course we are finished." Soft again. "Neva, you stand over there and watch out. If you hear anyone or see anyone, let us know. Dorján and I will see what else is down there."

"Fine. If you say so."

"I say so."

Nevena got up, brushed soil from her knees and hands, and walked toward the row of corn. Found a gap and peered through.

"Dori, we'll dig out a bit. See if we can find the edges of whatever this coin was in."

The boys burrowed into the earth, discovered a small pocket of cool air, the curving bottom of a clay pot. Their mouths were open, but they did not speak as they pulled coin after coin from the hole. They recovered thirty-six more pieces of gold, and they laid them, heads up, in three straight rows. Two of twelve, and one of thirteen.

"That's it." János was pale, his shaky voice not more than a squeak. "Thirty-seven."

Nevena stepped closer. "You have to give it to Takáts Úr. You really do."

"Right. Just give me a second."

"No, János. Really." Worry on her face. "You can't keep them."

"And why not?"

She frowned. "It's wrong. Just wrong. If you get caught. *Ju!* If you get caught, no one can save you. You don't know what will happen."

János jumped up, clicking his shoes together, hand to his forehead. "We will not get caught. We will share them—the three of us."

"The two of you, you mean. I don't want any of them."

"But imagine what you can buy."

She paused for a second, staring at the lines of gold. Bit her lip, then shook her head. "No. I…I can't."

János squinted as he stared at her. "Spoken like someone who's never needed anything."

"That's not fair. Do you know how much trouble we would be in? Stealing? Stealing so much. Dori, talk to him so he will listen. This is not a pepper from Tibor's stand."

Dorján heard it first. "Shut it," he whispered. "Both of you." Slow footsteps moving between the rows of corn. A lazy whistle. The three of them stopped breathing, waited, and then two albino hands reached through the thick wall, parting the stalks. Head emerging, Takáts eased his wiry body past the corn, coat buttoned all the way to his neck. János immediately dropped to the ground, closed his legs, and curled his body over the stained earth and bits of pottery and muddy coins.

"You're wasting your time, children? This isn't a picnic, you know."

"No, sir," Dorján replied, standing taller.

"And what's your issue, Kelemen?"

"Dor…Dorján kneed me." Grunts.

"What?"

János moaned and rocked, hands in tight fists. "Kneed me, sir."

"Szabó!"

"Yes, sir!"

"Get your tiny ass back to the bus. You can clean the floor."

"No, no," János said, looking up, waving one hand. "Was my fault, Takáts Úr. Me fooling around. An accident."

Dorján scowled, wiping his dry nose on his forearm.

"Fooling around, hey boys?" Sideways smirk. "Well, then. Watch yourself, Szabó. Watch your feet and your knees and," staring hard at the buckle on Dorján's belt, "your other parts."

"Yes, sir."

"Good boy."

"And you," he said, turning toward Nevena. "I don't know why you spend your time with these two. Does the Komandant know?"

Nevena blushed, clasped her hands behind her back. "I'm doing nothing more than harvesting for the people, Druže Takáts. I can assure you he thinks that's an honourable way to pass my time."

"Of course. Yes, yes. Pass on my regards." He paused. "And I suggest you move several rows to the east. There you'll find some girls who need your help."

"I will, Druže Takáts."

Takáts turned to leave, stopping when Dorján said, "Ah, and sir?"

"Yes, Szabó."

Dorján put his foot up on the rotting hump of stalks. "Beštić Úr was just here. Asking after you."

"Ah, he was, was he?" Takáts touched a lock of his greasy black hair, pressing it back into place.

"Yes, sir. Headed that way." Dorján replied, glancing in the direction the rat had taken just moments earlier.

"Right. All right. Right." Breathy words. He started to step back through the hole in the corn wall, then paused, stern again, said, "No need to wander, boys. Plenty of work right here. Good people are counting on you." And then the corn closed over, light and airy whistling recommencing as he trod along the row.

János burst, hard snorts battering the back of his nose as he rolled onto his back. "*Faszba!* That was close."

"Did you have to say I booted you in the dick? Couldn't you have thought of something else?"

"Played it good, hey?" He stopped laughing, placing his hand on the coins. "Knew it would distract the filthy assplug."

Nevena folded her arms across her beige shirt. "You should've told him."

"Told Takáts? You left your brain on the bus."

"János!"

"Do you know what I will buy for you? Can you guess?"

A faint smile then. Pink in her cheeks. "What?"

"Something. You will see. And you will be happy I did not turn these over."

"Just be careful. Promise me that."

"Of course."

"We'll take them out of here in our pockets and bury them on the hill. Off the path to the park. You know. By Root Rock."

"Ah!" She covered her ears and started to walk away. "Don't tell me anything else. I don't want to know the plan of two thieves."

Once she had gone, János rolled backwards onto the dirt, kicking soil into the hole with the heel of his shoe. "Well, well. We're rich. You know that? We're filthy rich." A wet hiss of words spilling out into the warm space. "Never again will we live under the frog's ass."

Dorján stared down at the thirty-seven dirty heads, could not respond. A slimy block of fear and excitement blocked his throat, and he knew his voice would fail him. He closed his eyes for a moment, imagining how they appeared from above. Two young boys with black hair, one lanky and clumsy, the other stout and nimble, crouched in a vast field of shimmering leaves. Between them, a glint of captured sunlight lying on the earth.

His heart began to drum inside his chest, the pulse moving up through his neck. He felt a hard bubble of gas move through his bowel, and he hunched slightly. "Shit," he finally managed. "Shit." He thought he heard a roll of thunder, but when he checked, there was not a single cloud in the sky.

Chapter 5

ALIZ DOBRICA SAT IN a high-backed chair, a mound of pure white linen in her lap. She was embroidering the edges of the square with a smattering of tiny blue and yellow flowers, and a curling vine of green ivy between them. With a single ply of pale pink thread, she made a tiny loop, then another, pulling gently until the knot sat in the middle of a mess of woollen petals. She held her work aloft.

She knew of no one in Bregalnica, Drobnik even, who did finer crewelwork without pinprick or chalk. Nevena was hopeless. Her sampler was a garbled mess, loose threads and pinched fabric, and eventually Aliz had given up trying teaching her daughter this tradition. Took it upon herself to fashion something fine to cover Nevena's table, years down the road.

When Nevena blew into the room, the needle in Aliz's hand stopped. "Ah! You are such a mess."

Nevena looked at her hands and her knees, skin tight from dried grime. "We were picking corn in the *poljoprivredna zadruga*."

"We?"

"I was with my class."

"Ah. That is the *we*?"

"Yes, well. János and Dorján. I was working. Happened across them."

"Really."

"Yes, really, *Majko*. Where's *Tata*?"

"Out. Where else? With Oficir Račić."

"Why do they spend so much time together?"

"Sometimes old arms have a long reach," Aliz replied.

"Old arms?"

Aliz reached up to touch her hair, the colour of darkened eggplant. "When two men serve together, it creates a strong bond. There is no breaking it."

Nevena frowned.

"No matter. You should wash up. Before he returns."

"Yes, *Majko*."

"Neva?"

"Yes."

"You are getting older now. Too old to play like a child." She watched her daughter tug at the bands of her socks, even though they covered her calves. "Do you like those boys? Well?"

"They're nice. János is funny. He makes me ... He makes everyone laugh."

Aliz was silent, and her daughter stared at the doorway, no doubt wanting to leave the room. After a moment, she said, "Neva, I will tell you something."

Her daughter raised her eyebrows.

"No, no," Aliz said, hand brushing the corner of her mouth. "I shouldn't."

"Please, *Majko*. Tell me." Nevena sat down on the edge of a short tufted stool.

"All right, but quiet, you must promise never to breathe a word about it in this house. Or out of it, for that matter."

"Of course. Promise."

"Once, when I was very young, very, very young, I would take walks with Oficir Račić. We would go to the square, drink lemon soda." And she laughed, shook her head. A flash of gold in her proud smile. "Can you believe? Can you believe I considered him for myself?"

Nevena scowled.

"I see your father now, and I am pleased by my choice. We have so many comforts." Her fingers slid over the fabric arm of the chair. "Sometimes young people think hardship is romantic. Hunger is romantic. But these notions quickly fade when the stomach growls."

"How could you even consider it?"

"Ah. I didn't know myself well. I couldn't think."

"Obviously."

Aliz tightened her mouth, lipstick bleeding into the cracks around her lips. "Don't be harsh, child. He was not unattractive when he was a boy. In fact, he was quite handsome then. Many women sought out his company. He did have some charms."

Eyes wide. "Can you imagine how I'd look if you'd married him?"

"You would look like nothing."

"Sure I would. I'd have a huge head and ears on my neck."

Aliz smiled, reached out, and grabbed her daughter's dry wrist, nails kissing her skin. "No. You'd be no more than a whisper but for your father." She let go of her daughter, then clapped her hands lightly. "Now go and wash the cabbage. Part the leaves. We will make something good together, and eventually you will learn."

:::::

GITTA KELEMEN WASHED HER hands, rinsing the flecks of raw meat and egg into the enamel tub. She dried her hands on a linen cup towel, tucking the towel in the band of her apron. Lifting the lid on the small pot, she saw the tomato juice was beginning to sputter around the stuffed peppers, and she adjusted the heat. So quickly this dish could burn. Entire meal ruined, while the air still smelled sweet.

Sitting down in the chair, she put her fingers to the tip of her nose. Even though the scent of soap was strong, she could still smell the ground meat on her skin. She leaned her head against the wooden back of the chair, closing her eyes. For many years, her husband's palms and wrists had always smelled of spices and smoke and raw meat. She tried not to think about his hands, to think about him, but certain triggers refused to fade. That smell did something to her, iron melded into rough skin. Pushed his absence to the surface, made her heart shrivel. And she placed her hands on her knees, as far away from her nose as possible.

People were not happy when Imre gave up his life as a gymnast. Trading in his hours of training for a family and a home and the wages needed to sustain it. Some said she had tricked him into it, making him turn away from his dreams. Occasionally she caught someone staring at her, an older woman usually, face twisted into a painful scowl. They looked at her as though she had stolen one of their possessions. Removed the best spice from the highest shelf in their kitchens. But that was not the case at all. Imre insisted time and time again that he did not want to continue, that he wanted her, wanted a houseful of happy children. "You are reason enough," he said. Those words made her feel jubilant and sorrowful at the same time.

But she accepted it, never pushed. Only lately, as János's body grew into the sturdy shape of her husband's, was she reminded of Imre's choice. What if she had pushed? Never supported him when he decided to quit. Maybe everything would be different. He might still be alive.

As his dedication to gymnastics dwindled, Imre took a job in a slaughterhouse outside of Bregalnica. Shortly after they married, he began working in a sausage shop in Drobnik. A privilege, he said, to learn the secrets to making perfect sausage from two German brothers. *Schwabs,* they were called. Families of German origin who had lived in the country for generations. "No one else in the entire world is as skilled at preparing so many types," Imre would often say, "as these two men." He was positive about the direction of his life. Told her he was content.

Many evenings, before János was born, he would arrive home with *Würstchen* and cheese, the softest *brotchens,* and a jar of cooked red cabbage. *"Abendessen wird serviert."* "Dinner is served," he would whisper in her ear as he removed the items from his bag and placed them on the small table. Frederic, the elder brother, taught him to speak perfect German, with barely a trace of an accent. And each day, he would practise his new words as he fed her bread and meat and strings of soft cabbage held in his fingers.

She pressed, but he would never divulge the best cuts to use, the right sorts of fat, additives, casings, different types of smoke. Even when he came home with bubbly burns on his wrists, he would not admit to the cause, that he was scalding a particular kind of sausage. At the time, she adored his resolute silence, thinking his secrecy was a sign of respectability. She told herself she was proud to be married to such a man. Even though some part of her detected the tiniest degree of separation—paper thin, but still there. He did not trust her completely. Eventually she realized, sometime closer to the end, that a sausage recipe was not the only knowledge he had concealed.

If only he had told her the truth. Such an insignificant thing to hide. After all, she was his wife and should have known. And look what it drove her to do. Climb the hill in Drobnik, opening her mouth to the *katonai csendőrség*. Once she spoke those tiny lies to the military police, it was too late to go back. She could only step aside then, keep a firm grip on János, and watch their lives crumble.

Gitta stood up, brushed herself off, even though her clothes were free of dust or crumbs. She lifted the lid again and dipped a wooden spoon in the juice, tasting it. *"Guten Appetit,"* she heard him whisper, and she cringed as her own mind betrayed her. Giving life to the kind voice of her husband.

She stepped out the back door. As soon as the door creaked, Buksi began barking in the back garden, a small patch of land filled with cabbages and potatoes, the cement structures that once were home to honeybees. The dog was straining against the chain, she knew. Could tell by the pitch of his yelp. Desperate to escape. A little crazy. A sound she often wished she were permitted to make. Just lean her head backwards, unhinge her mouth, and bawl into the coming dusk.

But surely if she did, someone would hear, and in little time, her front door would bang open, uniformed men would enter, and she would be carted away. Not to the jail where Imre had been. Somewhere else, where *Orvosok* would isolate her, administer drugs, wrap her tightly in fabric and belts. A moaning sort of place where she could rest her chin on a peeling windowsill all day long.

Buksi's wailing continued unabated. "I know," she whispered toward the tall fence. "I know, dog."

She went to the side of the house and stared out into the courtyard. With the exception of a few dried leaves swirling across the stone, it was empty. As she paced back and forth, a familiar feeling of dread began to tickle her ankles, slipping inside the blue veins of her legs, making its way upward. Waiting, waiting, for someone to come home. Food prepared in the kitchen, growing cold and stale. *What if?* She would not allow her mind to go there. Would not, she scolded herself. *He is an errant boy who needs a sharp clap on the back of his neck.* Nothing more. Anger filtered through her and offered some relief. She would wait another hour for János, not more, not more, and then she would take the scraps down to the dog herself.

Chapter 6

A TRODDEN-DOWN TRAIL LED through the woods, connecting the village to a park bordering the town. Unlike the parks in Drobnik, this one contained no fountain or brick walkway or leering metal dragon turned pale green from years of rainfall. No. Simply stunted grass and scattered oaks and broken bottles, and up on a distant hill, Dorján could see the gently curving stone wall with its neat stone cap. Drobnik just on the other side. Once when Dorján told this to János, János unbuttoned his trousers, reached in, biting his bottom lip as his urine arced upward and spattered the grass. "Who needs a fountain?" he said. "I have one built in."

This afternoon, they started down the trail, passing underneath the old willows, but did not come out the other side. Dorján was relieved that they met no one, only a young mother with a flushed and sweating face, carrying a flailing child. When they reached the fattest oak, they both turned and stepped into the underbrush. Feet disappearing as they picked their way through fading shrubs and low-lying vines.

Eventually they reached their destination. Root Rock was the name they had given a large boulder in the middle of the woods. The boulder was pressed against a trunk, tough roots snaking up and over the smooth stone surface. Each year, as the roots spread like a web, it appeared that the stone was working its way into the flesh of the tree. And the boys liked that, the dead sucked into the living.

When Dorján lifted and dropped his legs, a faint jingle could be heard, and the band of his shorts strained against his narrow hips with the weight of the gold. János plopped down on Root Rock and Dorján sat on a carpet of dried leaves. They removed all the coins from their pockets and laid them on the ground. Counted again. Thirty-seven.

"I thought I was going to shit my trousers when we sat on the bus."

"Me, too," Dorján said. The sight of the coins in front of him made his heart start banging again. If they were caught, there was no telling what would happen to them. "Yes. Takáts was staring at us."

"That boxful of pus? He's always staring at us."

Dorján laughed, though he did not find it funny. He folded his arms across his chest. The wind had lifted, and the grid of branches above him moved like nervous fingers. He wished his sweater was not so thin.

"You know we can do whatever we want now," János said.

"We will hide it for a long time, yes? Once we are finished our schooling, we will make a decision." Inside his mind, Dorján could see his grandmother's face. She would be so proud when he completed his degree.

"Engineers."

"Yes." *We are still the little engineers, you and I. We will work together.*

"Dori."

There was a hint of sadness in János's tone, and Dorján lowered his head, letting his palm hover over the coins. A lingering warmth drawn from his own flesh rose up from the metal. "Do you know they call us *bolha*?"

"Fleas? Who does?"

"The boys from Drobnik call all of us *bolha*. No better than dirt."

János spat. "Like I give the last shit from a dead horse. Whores for mothers, all of them. You know what I say? Come talk to me after you shoot yourself." Two fingers to his temple.

Dorján shook his head, laughing for real this time. János knew how to talk, had since he was two. Cursing in their mother tongue, or Serbian. German, even.

"You weren't always a flea," János said, as he reached down, took a coin, and flipped it in the air. "You were the dog."

He frowned, not appreciating the reminder. As a young boy, Dorján had lived in Drobnik with his mother and father. When he thought of it, he could see very little. Instead his mind filled with noises. High-pitched squeals from the sky, radio static, intermittent voices issuing warnings, children laughing and racing up and down the mound of dirt. And then the explosion. It had moved through him with such force, he believed his chattering teeth had loosened. "I don't remember living there," he lied. "Don't remember a thing."

"No?"

"I'm not a fucking flea or a fucking dog." He lit a cigarette, pulling smoke through it hard and fast, burning his lungs. "Now we should put this away. I don't like everything out in the open."

János dipped his arm behind the stone, into the narrow space they had carved away a year ago. He tugged out a blue and silver tin container with a hinged lid, laying it on the ground. Popping the lid open, he pointed to the contents. Some change, some bills. "Can you believe we went through all that trouble for practically nothing?"

Foot reaching, Dorján tapped the tin with the tip of his shoe. He did not like to see the money. Even though it was such a small amount. Pocket change, almost, but still it made him feel guilty. "Doesn't seem like much, does it?"

"It would've taken us forever to get anywhere at that rate. With that cow's ass."

"We can give it back, now. We have the coins."

János struck his head with the heel of his hand. "Is your dick out? Can't you think straight? We'll need money for travelling."

The cigarette dropped from Dorján's lip, and he stood up, stomping on it with his left foot. "What? Travelling where? The city is only a train ride. That's where we will study."

One by one, János picked up the coins and placed them gently in the tin container. Without glancing upward, he said, "I'm going to marry her, you know. I'm going to buy her a ring."

"What are you talking about? What fucking game is this?" Dorján took a step toward János.

Even though there was no sunlight, János narrowed his eyes, two lazy crescents, "You always act like you don't hear shit. But you heard me. I'm going to marry Nevena. I am. As soon as I have a few things figured out, I'm leaving and taking her with me."

"You—what's that supposed to mean?" He shook his head. "I thought we were saving to move to the city."

"My ideas have changed, Dori." Rapid eye roll. "What is there for me? Nothing. More of the same."

"But, we—"

"Stuttgart sounds so much better. We'll sell our share." He plucked up another coin, pressed it to his lips, then dropped it. "Get us started."

"Germany?" Flat tone.

"Yes. You know my uncle lives there. He'll help me. Help us. I know he will."

Dorján began to pace, crunching back and forth in the tiny space. Hands plunged into empty pockets. He kicked Root Rock and winced as he felt his toenail lift inside his shoe. "How are you going to get out? Your brain's soaked in piss if you think they'll just let you across at the border. Bloody dickhead. Not after your uncle took off and never came back. Who chooses to leave their whole fucking family?"

János stood up, sticking out his jaw. "He did what he had to do."

"Do you think he just vanished, and no one was questioned? Do you think his family never paid a price?"

"The price was already paid. Already paid in full, if you ask me. You do not even know. Why are you riding my ass?"

"I'm not riding shit." Dorján glanced behind János, seeing the slightly darker shade of green that outlined their path. "I'm just saying you can't go far. You can't ever leave our country."

"Like hell I can't. Crawl over a fucking mountain if I have to."

Dorján felt a cool sadness pressing out from inside his chest. They had never spoken to each other like this, and he sensed something was buckling between them. Metal bending back and forth, ready to softly break. Barely a sigh to accompany the destruction. Several deep breaths, and he mumbled, "What about me? What about our plans? Were we not to study together, graduate together? Work together? We decided this, didn't we?" As soon as he said those words, he wished he could take them back. The weight of his neediness hanging between them.

János backed down, words of encouragement replacing his vitriol. "I'm sorry, my friend. I just don't know anymore. I don't know."

"My friend, my friend. What has happened? Tell me."

János clenched his jaw, brought his fist to his forehead, and pressed. Then he looked at Dorján. "You come, too, Dori. We'll all go. Nothing we can't do. The three of us. Open a store or something."

"I can't leave. My *nagyanya*. It would ruin her."

"Come on. She'd survive."

"Besides, we need to finish school. That's what we want. Right? Right?"

"There are other things we can do. Open your mind. Just see, Dori. Just see."

"We're going to rebuild. That's what we want to do, yes? We decided when we were boys. Don't you remember?"

János lifted a foot onto Root Rock, patience disintegrated. "Rebuild? Dori. Who gives a shit about that? It's not like you can share your ideas. Unless they fit neatly into theirs. And let me tell you, mine don't. They will turn on us. The people. The *rendőrség*. If we make a misstep. If they imagine a misstep. They will turn."

"What are you talking about?"

"Nothing."

"Tell me."

Shorter than Dorján by nearly a foot, but János possessed something different. Occupied his compact space with more authority. "I want to know what happened to my fucking father," he yelled. "Did you know that? My mother lied to me for years. Years. Said he was sick. Died because he was sick. But, no. No! They took him away and beat him. Kept him for months, and no one knows where. They broke him, Dori. When they'd finished with their fun, they brought him home. Threw him into the road like a filthy parcel for my mother to find. I want to know why. Why, Dori? Why my father?"

Dorján looked down at the black earth, the soil marred by his footprints. He could think of no reply.

"I will force them. The *rendőrség* will have to answer me!"

Calmly, "No one will answer you, János. You know that."

"And that's all right for you, isn't it? Isn't it? Admit it to yourself. You are a coward. You close your eyes and think the world goes away."

"I never said—"

"Next thing you'll be telling me you want to be *Pionir*." He turned his head and spat. "Little red scarf tied around your neck and you're all set to follow them."

"Shut the hole in your face." Shot of anger, and he inhaled the smell of rotting humus. One hand gripped the other, and he shook this dual-fist in front of him. "You better shut it, shut it now, or you'll regret it."

"Shit, Dori." Casual laughter that was sitting on top of something else. "Did I tickle something?"

Hands formed into hammers, János bolted forward, slamming his puffed chest off Dorján's. And Dorján stumbled backwards, landing on his backside with a dull thud. Sticks prodded his thighs and backside, and pain moved up through his hips.

János spat again, looked down on him, said, "Why is your cock jammed in my ear?"

"Fuck. It's not."

"All I hear is the drumming of your piss. All I want to do is leave. Take Nevena with me. I love her, you know."

Scowling, Dorján rolled onto all fours, before he lumbered to his feet. Resisted the urge to rub his behind. He knew János loved Nevena. He loved her too, but not in the same way. He loved how she connected them. Balanced them, made them all equal. János wanted to pull her away, keep her for himself, and Dorján could feel something collapsing around him, his legs teetering.

János sat down then, putting his head in his hands. Spoke softly. "I hate it here, Dori. I hate Bregalnica. I walk in the street, and sometimes men scorn me. Račić always smiles. He smiles because he knows what happened to my father. Smiles to let me know it could happen to me. If I am not quiet. I am so filled with rage, it is choking me. Blinding me. You understand? Your father is gone, is he not?"

"Why do you ask me? You know the answer."

"Where is your hate, my friend? Where is your fury?"

Where is my fury? Where is it? Dorján sniffed. Placed his hand on the bark of the tree.

"I'm going."

"Shit. Where?"

"Nowhere. I'm going nowhere. I don't know."

"Come on, Dori. Why are you like that? I'm sorry, all right? I'm sorry. I don't want to fight. I don't know what is inside of me, anymore. So much. My heart is a fist. I can't trust myself."

"I'm cold. I'm going home."

"Can't you see this is our chance? This is what our fathers would've wanted. Hell, they probably helped us themselves."

"What? Told you where to poke the stick?" Roll of his eyes. "Dead men aren't in the helping business, János. Other than growing the bloody grass."

"This is our freedom, Dori. Right here. Can't you see that?"

::::

WEEPING WILLOWS WERE SWAYING, and the mouth of the path lay in moving shade. Dorján crossed the road, jumped the gutter, and waited on the other side. He watched the woods, expecting János to be close behind him, but his friend was taking his time. While he stood there, Dorján plucked sour apples from the low-lying branches, crunching through the flesh and core and seeds and all. Dropped the brown stems at his feet.

He leaned against the thin trunk of the tree, and as quickly as his anger had risen, it settled back down again. So many years they had been together, the three of them, leaning on each other. When had it started? Without a second passing, Dorján could pinpoint the very instant that bound them together. They were children, and after days of quiet skies, they were allowed outside again, meeting in the field behind the village. Though stark lines existed among them, Hungarians standing on one side, Serbians on the other, the children did not acknowledge it. They played war in the grass, and together they fought against a common unseen evil, tucked down among the blades of green.

The previous year, the field had been scraped, topsoil piled into a large hill. He could remember the digging machines with their clawed arms filling enormous trucks with the exposed clay. Bricks, they said. They would use the red clay to make bricks.

Though the surrounding area was practically barren, the mound had grown a fine coating of baby hair. Nevena was standing there, sun in her hair, squinting as she smiled. Her face was perfectly round, smooth like a white stone. János was beside her, his face pressed close to hers. When Dorján climbed the hill, he heard János whispering to her. Charming her.

"I'm going to marry you," he said. And then he jabbed the air with his small finger. "But first, I'll need a tie."

Dorján watched as Nevena giggled, and he turned his back to them, mouthed the words, "But first, I'll need a tie." Glanced over his shoulder at Nevena. What if he approached her, saying the same thing? He could never say it the same way as János had, like a sugar cube was melting on his tongue. Besides, she would know he was copying, stealing. And he was not a thief.

When she saw him standing there, she said, "Hi, Dori. You're visiting your *baka* today?"

Thoughts blank, and when he spoke, a string snapped, the sentence that had been circling was loose. "You have to marry both of us. To be fair."

János grabbed his stomach and roared with laughter.

Nevena was polite, eyes wide. "I'm sorry?"

There was no time to recover. His neck had begun to ache. He lifted his hands to his jaw.

Planes were coming from somewhere, and Dorján could feel them before he even saw them. Bones vibrating, tiniest hum in his teeth, his skull. Making him ever so slightly dizzy. Then there they were, passing right above them in a grand and beautiful assembly of grey bodies and wings, thin cloudy tails. If he could erase the fear, he would have been filled with boyish awe as he and János and Nevena scrambled to the very top of the mound. Close enough to touch the bright blue sky.

They stood side by side, three heads tilted backwards. The planes were travelling away from Drobnik, and Bregalnica, and toward the city in the distance. Dorján did not blink as they moved closer to the blur of buildings in the distance. When they reached the outskirts, they seemed to hover there, an obvious illusion, trapped inside blades of sunlight, something tumbling from their metal bellies. Something tumbling. Round and dark and dropping downward. Grey birds. Toward the streets and buildings and people. Air emitting a piercing wail as it was sliced and re-sealed.

The bombs disappeared into the landscape, and his heart beat a single hopeful note when nothing happened. Then his own ears and eyes, so cruel, refused to lie to him. Refused to shield him from the hollow crack, the layers of rippling dust. And next his legs, also traitors, standing on top of the knowledge that burrowed through the ground. Without a word from an adult's lips, Dorján sensed the target.

He felt Nevena's fingers knotting themselves into his left hand, and János's fingers knotting themselves into his right. They stood tall, the three of them, shafts of wheat, bound together and wavering as the air curdled. He would never be able to explain how he knew what he knew. The knowledge moved through the earth, rose up through his feet and legs, through his body, into awareness inside his mind.

Not a doubt. The hospital. Filled with Nazi soldiers. Exploded. And his father. The doctor. Dead.

:: ::

SHADOWS BEGAN TO DISSOLVE in the creeping darkness, but Dorján still watched the path. Pockets of people strolling out of the park, young people mostly, banging against each other with loud hoots. He saw a woman wearing a long skirt and moments later a wiry boy running along the path. Home to dinner, no doubt. As the time passed, an orange moon hung low in the sky. Dorján took a step toward the road. He should go back into the woods, find János, apologize for the fight. They would fix things. János would be calmed and everything would be all right.

A second step, and he stopped. A lone figure had appeared on the path. A man, young or old? Wearing the clothes of every other man, a long dark coat, navy or black, and a wide-brimmed gentleman's hat that covered his face. Dorján watched closely as the man paused just at the juncture where the path sloped downward. Bending his head slightly, the man raised his right hand so that his fingers were at the height of his temple. And slowly, he rotated those fingers in a clockwise circle. One, two, three times. Nothing more than a subtle flick of his wrist. He lifted his head, straightened his shoulders, and trotted forward.

The sight of that simple gesture blew dust from old places inside Dorján's mind, and he took a deep step backwards, tilting against the narrow tree. Rolled his body slightly so he was facing the opposite direction. Dorján was certain he had seen that man many times before. Somewhere. Somewhere. But he could not place him, even though the sight of that gesture made his throat seize, the blood pound behind his eyes.

He could hear the man's determined steps growing fainter and fainter on the gravel road, and only when the cricket song filled his ears did Dorján turn around. The man was gone. The path was empty. Cautious steps toward the gutter, and Dorján peered up and down the road. He heard horses trotting. And around the bend came Gazda László, Tibor's grandfather, asleep in his cart. His chin rested on his chest, and his tattered straw hat slipped from his bald head. The leather reins lay limp across the farmer's knee. The horses needed no guide.

That shaky feeling had returned, and Dorján brought his hand to his ribs, wished he had not eaten those sour apples. He bit his lip. Hard. János was nowhere to be seen, and Dorján could only assume he had taken a different path. Which was not surprising. If there was a straight line between two places, János would insist on creating a curve. They would catch up tomorrow after he swam. János would be there, standing next to Takáts, urging Dorján forward. They would talk then, make things better.

Dorján watched the back of Gazda's cart as it moved past him, rattling and groaning when it struck the ruts in the road. What a simple pleasure that must be, he thought. To know your way home. To know just where you belong.

Chapter 7

DARKNESS HAD BEGUN TO descend, and she could feel it brushing against the windows. Even though the moon was bright, when she glanced outside Gitta Kelemen saw only her hazy reflection. Thin face, thin lips, thin greying hair pulled and twisted at the back of her head. Empty pad of skin pooling underneath her bony chin. Grief had done that to her, she knew. Crept into her body and slowly consumed the sweet fat that plumped her up.

To cut the silence, she flicked on the radio, heard the stream of good news. Always good news. Stories that would make a person feel better, if only they allowed them to penetrate their hearts. Gitta could not abide it, twisting the dial with a harsh snap of her wrist. That is not real. That is not real. But to whom could she complain? No one was left untouched, and no one even talked about the war anymore. They ignored the homes that were filled with new families. Forgot about the faces that were missing, or failed to notice the pale outline where shop signs had been removed and hastily replaced. People tucked it all away, it seemed to Gitta, and stood on the edges of the street, smiling and waving as President Tito drove by in his shiny black car.

János was only sixteen and so much like his father. Infected with that same fiery righteousness. When she cautioned him, he would reply, "People should be able to stand up and say what they want. Speak their minds. Why not?" These innocent statements always alarmed Gitta. János did not realize he was only a boy, not an army, and that a public voice was a dangerous thing to use. When she tried to explain that to him, he only shrugged. He likely thought she was not to be taken seriously. "Believe it," she had said. "Your mouth serves you best when it is closed."

When he was younger, she often noticed his expression full of a strangely comforting sadness, though sometimes she found it a struggle to meet his dark eyes. Aware of the questions behind them. He never asked about that girl, Anneliese, after she had left. But that did not mean he had forgotten her. Imre had invited the *Schwab* to stay with them. And while the girl remained in their home for only a matter of weeks, she had taken up permanent residence in János's heart. His innocence was so blatant that Gitta knew she needed to protect him. She would be a strict mother and harden the parts of her son that the world would discover and joyfully destroy.

Folding her arms across her chest, Gitta leaned her hips against the counter. Then she heard it, a soft crunching sound, something moving on the stone outside the window. Her heart jumped, János was finally home, and she quickly picked up the white bowl, pulled out the cutlery drawer, clutched a fork in her hand. The stuffed peppers were still warm, and there was a heel of crusty bread in the cloth bag.

Tinkling of fingernails on the side window now, a crystal sound that made Gitta's hair stand upward. She held the fork against the top button of her dress, back of the tines pressing against her skin. "Who's there?" Trembling voice.

"Ah, just my old self, Gitta *néni*. Sorry to startle." Zsuzsi Szabó opened the back door, waddled across the kitchen, slid a bowl onto the counter.

"Ah no, no. Don't apologize. I've grown foolish being alone."

"That happens," she smiled, then lifted the dishcloth from the bowl. Inside there was a rounded pile of deep green pickles. Shiny and fat. "Are they not lovely?"

The odour of vinegar and dill had struck her already. "Yes, yes. Beautiful. But there are too many. We are only two, you remember."

"Ah—stupidity!" Put her palm to the back of her head. "And I am only two as well. Though some days I believe Dorján has someone else living inside of him. Or else he is hollow." She removed the top pickle from the pile, brought it to her nose, and sniffed. Closed her eyes for a moment before dropping it back into the bowl. "You have jars, of course."

"Of course."

"Save them. They are good for your boy. Good for digestion."

"Yes."

"You should smile more, Gitta *néni*. You are still on this side of the grass, and you should not put yourself elsewhere. You will find yourself there time enough."

Gitta nodded.

"Look at me. I sit and cook and eat and laugh and sew, and eat some more." She rubbed her midsection. "I am growing fatter still, yes?"

Gitta reached for a knitted shawl, covering her slender shoulders.

"Now you," Zsuzsi continued, "must wear heavy shoes. Otherwise the wind will steal you."

Thin smile. "Dorján is home, you said?"

"Yes, yes. Just now. János?"

"Not yet."

"Ah."

"Soon though, I am certain." She glanced at the tin pot on the stove. Steam no longer seeped around the edges of the lid. "He is often late. But today, more so than usual."

"This is the age," Zsuzsi said, one stump-like finger in the air, "where they wander and make us worry. More on their minds than a warm meal. Try not to worry, Gitta *néni*. Only serves to weaken your blood."

"I am not worried. Not at all." Though she was. Normally tardiness would have invoked a quivering anger, but today she felt empty. They had argued once again that morning. She never should have told him. Last spring. Fear led her to do it. Fear held her jaw open, shook her torso, words hopping from her throat.

They were eating a meal of stringy meat, boiled potatoes.

"I can't get my teeth through it," he complained. "This is not fit for the pig."

She pushed the food around her plate. Quietly, "It is all that we have."

"Others have better."

"Yes. Yes, they do. But some have nothing. We must be grateful we have meat."

"No," he said, pushing back his chair. "Grateful for what? That men who are in the Party can eat like the president, while we fight with the dog for scraps? Who decides?"

"That is the way it is, *szívem*. Let it go. Let it be. It is not a fight for a child."

"If only I were bigger, I would go to their stores and take what I want. No one would keep me out."

A lump of dry food stuck behind her breastbone. She glanced at the window, saw that the wooden prop was removed, the window closed. "You cannot say that," she whispered.

"I can say what I want. And I will."

He was defiant. Like his father. And that single fact was what led her to tell him the truth. Explain that his father had not died from illness, as she had told him. Yes, she had lied, but it was easier that way. Easier for a child to understand death when it is nature stealing the soul. She told János that Imre was broken. Taken from their home and beaten. She even revealed how Gábriel, Imre's brother, had left the country after Imre had died. How he wanted to take János with him, but Gitta would not allow it. She told her son everything, and once it was outside of her, she felt relief. Now that he knew what the *rendőrség* were capable of, surely he would temper his words. Be more careful when he expressed his ideas.

"Do you understand the dangers?"

János lifted his head, and when she saw his full face, her heart fluttered, hands and feet went numb. While she had expected to see sorrow, awareness, resignation, instead he appeared older. His eyes were cold. Welling up with hatred. He wore the faintest smile around his lips.

"I understand," he had replied then. "I understand much better now."

Zsuzsi approached her and patted her shoulder. "You are concerned, Gitta *néni*. I can see worry on your face." The old woman walked toward the door. "He is on his way now. Of course he is! I am close if you need me," she said as she gently clicked the door shut behind her.

Gitta walked in a tight triangle around her kitchen. She would deal with the pickles tomorrow. They had survived a fortnight steeping in the sunshine; another evening resting on her countertop would make no difference.

Her shoes clacked on the floor, and whenever she stopped, she could not help but count the ticking sounds of the clock. Time seemed to spread like a spill as she waited and waited in the near darkness. A lamp was within her reach, but she did not want to turn it on. She did not want to change anything, until he was home. János was late. Really late. And as another hour closed, her worry caved into helpless anxiety. He was later than he had ever been before.

Gitta took an old bowl filled with stale bread, cold bean soup, a pinch of raw meat she had saved from the peppers, and put it on the floor. Then she went out through the gate of the first garden, past the barren cherry tree and wilting vegetables of the second garden, and into the third garden. Buksi was there in the darkness, panting and drooling. She untied the rope, gripped the chain around his neck, braced as it bucked. A sharp *kuss* from her throat, the dog calmed, and she led him up the path and into the house.

Surely people would think her unwell, letting a filthy dog into her home, allowing him to spatter water and devour scraps beside the very table where she and János dined. But, at that moment, Gitta needed to be close to another breathing creature. Days were growing shorter, and she missed Imre. His death still hurt like a festering tooth. Sour taste of rot curing her tongue. She felt alone, with the exception of a son who had skipped his meal, and a dog with torn ears and black gums. Besides those two, she had nothing else in this world.

Chapter 8

"DO YOU BELIEVE IN dragons?" Takáts said without smiling. He walked around the long wooden desks, tapping a metre stick on the wooden classroom floor. "Well, do you?" Lifting the stick, he pointed the damaged tip at a boy in the class.

"No, sir."

"No, sir, what?"

"No, sir. I don't believe in dragons. They're mythical creatures."

"Excellent answer." Tip of the stick slicing through the air. "And you, Szabó. What do you think?"

Dorján stammered, willing the last few moments to rewind so he could listen more closely. He had been examining the dirt still underneath his fingernails, the white lines near his nail bed, trying not to think about the faceless man he had seen last night. And at the same time trying to ignore the obvious gap in the desk behind him. János's chair was empty. "I—I…"

"Your answer now, Szabó."

"Yes, Takáts Úr. It's a possibility."

The classroom erupted in laughter, and Takáts lifted his long ruler, swung it hard. It whirred before slapping a desk. "Szabó! Has the pool water affected your brain today? Are your ears full?"

"Yes, sir. Ah, no, sir."

"If you find my company less than engaging, you're welcome to return home and work for your *nagyanya*. Learning to sew, perhaps?" Backside perched on the edge of the desk now, he leaned in closer, spoke slowly. Stench of digested onion on his breath. Dorján could see a faint green stain on his slender wrist when his watch shifted. "Your *nagyanya* has hemmed my trousers, you know."

"Yes?"

"She says you're quite good with a magnet. Down on all fours. Finding lost needles and such."

"Yes, Takáts Úr," Dorján croaked, handful of sand in his throat. "I mean, no, Takáts Úr." Cheeks throbbing, he lowered his head, sensed salt water rising in his eyes.

"Where is your associate today, Szabó?"

"János?"

"No, Szabó, President Tito himself. Who do you think?"

"He's…he's home. He's sick. I don't know."

Takáts smiled. "I don't understand your response, Szabó. He's home, he's sick, or you don't know?"

Breathing through his mouth, Dorján stared at the plaster wall of the classroom. Near the dusty chalkboards, someone had painted a life-sized mural of an older man. He stood tall and held a long-handled spade, the rounded end pushed into lines of earth. Behind him was a trail of faded sheep. Dorján knew all the others were watching him, and underneath the desk he pressed his knees together until the bones ached.

"Well?"

"I don't know, sir."

Takáts bowed his head, glared at Dorján over lowered black-rimmed glasses, then turned back to the class, clearing his throat. "One would think Szabó's observation is the product of an overactive imagination up to no good. But let's build on it for a moment. Consider that, at one point in our past, dragons were a possibility."

Several soft voices said, "Ahhh," as though ready to listen and accept this new concept.

"Let's talk for a moment about war. Wars have been fought on our soil, but the war to which I'm referring happened a long time ago. A fight for survival. More so. Against the elements."

Hand popping up. "Isn't all fighting about survival, sir?"

"Good point, young man, but this is a different story I'm telling. During a period in our prehistory, cave bears dwelled in the mountains around our fair country. These bears were quite distinct from the scrawny beasts you sometimes see in the square. Riddled with ticks. No, these bears were twenty feet long. Pack animals. Living in the best homes available."

"In homes, sir?"

"The caves. Where do you think men resided ten thousand years ago, *fiam*?"

"No, sir. In caves, sir."

"Exactly. Cave bears were deadly, deadly creatures. And the fight for a proper estate resulted in the loss of many men."

He turned quickly as he spoke, hunching his back.

"Now, let's fast forward a little time. Zip, zip. You have adventurers moving over the mountains, exploring our caves. Let's imagine what they found in our mountains—claw marks on those cave walls, enormous skulls with razor teeth." He opened his own mouth then, teeth narrow and yellow, but all still there. "Evidence of battle. Broken spearheads. Long-dead fire pits."

A rolled map hung from hooks behind Takáts's desk, and he moved toward it, fumbling with two clips. The map unfurled, and Takáts called a boy to the front, placed a loose arm over his shoulder, pointed with his stick, said, "Can you read this for everyone, *fiam*?"

A boy leaned forward, squinted. *"Zemlja zmajeva."*

"Well done, young man." Takáts rubbed the boy's back, then nudged him toward his seat. "Land of dragons. Land of dragons. Does anyone know what that means?"

Murmuring now, heads shaking left to right.

"The unknown." Tapping his stick again. "Ah, the unknown. These explorers were so certain of the existence of dragons, they recorded that knowledge on their maps."

"Are there still dragons, sir? I mean cave bears?"

"Interesting question, and one we can certainly consider. Within the comforts of our school. Where we are given the privilege of being permitted to think."

"Yes, sir."

"On a metaphorical level, of course. What is a dragon? A threat. Fear. What lurks beyond our borders? Where are we truly safe? Here, my young friends. Right here, exactly where you are."

"I don't understand, sir."

Takáts shook his head. "What is it that you do not understand, *fiam*? Your skull is too thick?"

"I guess so, sir."

"It's a simple lesson, *fiam*. We all know someone who has forsaken everything that is offered, yes? Who foolishly has chosen to walk into those hills and live with the dragons rather than work hard and live comfortably where he belongs."

The boy shifted in his seat, rubbing his nose.

"Of course we do," Takáts continued. "It's a dangerous thing to do, but there is no bravery in it. Not a single hair of bravery. Only cowardice, my friends. Bravery can be found right here at home. In our villages, our towns. People striving to make things better. So that we can witness our country growing stronger and stronger."

Dorján kept his head lowered, reached out, gripped the metal leg of the desk until his knuckles were pale. Takáts's lecture seemed especially designed for Dorján's ears, and the words dragged over his body, making his skin sore. He could not shake the sense that Takáts knew what they had stolen from the field, knew about János's plan to run away. More than ever before, Dorján wanted to see János. His best friend clamouring through the classroom door. Tension from their fight dissolved. He needed to see Nevena lift her eyes and smile, but when he *tss-tssed* quietly, she would not look at him.

"We will conclude now," Takáts announced. "Enough talk of dragons that don't even exist. Unless, that is, you're in conversation with Szabó."

Chapter 9

STANDING OUTSIDE THE ROUNDED wooden door, Gitta Kelemen looked upward. In the uppermost part of the curve, she saw the small plaque bearing an image of a two-headed eagle. Wings outstretched on either side, heads gazing off in opposite directions. Thick neck cleaved down the centre. Even though she had only been to the Komandant's home a handful of times, she always paused in the doorway and studied the eagle. Considered that the unnatural beast had two faces to present, two minds to make decisions. Two identities to offer the world.

She could not help but notice how different this home was from the one in which the Komandant grew up. When she was still a girl, she would visit his house to buy eggs for her aunt. His father was a farmer, raised goats to the north of his farm, and tended a cherry orchard to the south. Sometimes she would enter the home for a drink of water. The house had two rooms, maybe three, small windows that allowed little light, and she remembered that one of the mud walls was always damp, even in the heat of summer. Tiny rivulets of water trickled down from the thatched roof. But never a pool on the floor. A weeping wall, she always thought.

Now when she reflected on it, she realized that Dragan had loved her. She had not fully understood that at the time, had not cherished it, but years later she knew it to be true. They often sat in the orchard, beneath the trees, as far away from his father's goats as possible. She did not want to hear them making noises, tapping the earth, scraping their horns against wood or rock. Gitta was unable to look at a goat without thinking of her mother, and everything that had happened. Of course she could never mention this to Dragan, and as though instinctively, he led her in the opposite direction, fingers just above her elbow. They walked among the trees, found a place to sit, and ate sour cherries until their teeth and lips were stained.

During the springtime, the gnarled branches wore a shawl of blushing pink. Once Dragan struck the trunk with his open palm, the tree shivered, and a shower of petals fell down upon them. That was the only time that he had ever kissed her. A single brush to her neck, while they were lost inside that flurry of pink. Then he moved behind her, opened his legs, and cupped his body around hers. His knees bent, grazing her hips. And without speaking, he picked the petals from her hair. One by one by one.

She lifted the iron ring on the door, letting it drop against the metal frame beneath it. With dusty hands and pulsing heart, she pushed down on the handle and went inside. If Gitta could have thought of any alternative, she would not be asking for help. Not have scuttled through the village in the weak light of morning, ready to beg. Though she could point to nothing specifically, Gitta had never felt accepted in Bregalnica. She had arrived there as a girl, eleven years old, wearing the sordid story of her mother's illness like a black cloak. Everyone knew, and over the years the truth bouncing from village to village had become distorted, the story growing all the more fantastical. All the more surreal. But her mother's wrongs should not have clung to her like they did. The woman had been sick, sick inside her head. Nothing more, nothing less. And people do things, sometimes shocking things, when their brain is shrivelled and dry.

"Hello," she called out. "Hello?" The grand hallway was bright and orderly, not a single nick or streak of dirt in the white plaster. When she caught sight of herself in a spotless mirror, she very nearly turned and fled. Her scarf was hastily tied, and her eyes were red and dry. Like a rat's. Face gaunt, and her shiny, swollen nose appeared twice its natural size. She looked confused. Mad. She looked like her mother.

"In here," came a gruff voice. "Come through."

She removed her hand from the doorknob and wobbled into the home. Toward the smell of coffee and cigarettes, faint odour of burnt flour. Her legs were fluid, ankle bones no longer wanting to stay connected.

In the kitchen she found the Komandant and an officer seated at the table. The Komandant's wife was in a tall-backed chair, and she busied herself with needlework, did not budge. Acted as though Gitta had never entered the room.

"Ah, *Gospodo* Kelemen. Good morning."

"Komandant Dobrica." Gitta closed her eyes, took a breath. There was a familiar comfort in the sound of his voice, and she allowed it to wash over her. "I am terribly sorry to inconvenience you at such an early hour."

The Komandant waved his hand, left trails of cigarette smoke in the air. He placed his smoking hand on top of his narrow skull, his black hair full and slicked. "Not at all. Not at all." Nodding toward his company, he said, "Brigitta Kelemen, this is Oficir Račić."

Gitta nodded slightly, and Oficir Račić leaned his bulky frame back in his chair, rubbing his greasy chin, said, "Kelemen. Kelemen. Ah yes. I remember your husband." Then, with a wet grin, single eyebrow perked over a hooded eye, "He was a strong man."

The words slithered across the floor toward Gitta, and as they moved up her legs, her knees began to quiver. For a moment, she thought she might crumble at this mention of her dead husband. Subtle, no doubt, but Gitta knew what he meant. Those three months when Imre had disappeared. No one would answer her questions. When he returned, he could barely utter a word. Only told her the government would not accept his explanations. That he had no choice but to serve as he did. The country was at war; he did as he was told. Still, they damaged him. Damaged him so badly, they knocked his spirit loose from his bones. And then, with her hasty decisions, Gitta had lifted the latch and set it free.

She stood there, in the middle of the room, dull dress wrinkled. Pinched her leg until her brittle nails broke through the skin, and only then could she see straight.

"Will you take a chair, *Gospođo?*"

"No, no," she whispered, fists bunching the fabric of her dress. "No, no. No, no." Her head began to shake, and she wondered if it might ever stop. If somehow it could tumble from her body, roll across the floor, come to rest at his wife's feet. Gitta would look up at her, and with such a spectacle, she would have no choice but to look back. Would her eyes register surprise or satisfaction?

"What troubles you?"

His kindness calmed her. His neatness. "I—"

"Brigitta. Sit. Sit. Take a coffee." Jutting his chin toward his wife, he said, "Aliz, serve her something."

His wife flinched slightly, said, "Dragan," in a low, rolling voice, nearing laughter. But she never laid her work aside, never stood up.

Gitta was not surprised, nor did she care. After she married Imre, she had heard rumours that she had broken Dragan's heart. That afterwards, he plucked someone blindly from the collection of available girls, and selecting Aliz had been a hasty mistake. "Please, please. Thank you for the kind offer, Komandant. I won't…I won't take much of your time."

"Explain your troubles."

She blew air out through pursed lips. "It is János. He is not home. I spoke with his friend last night, our neighbour, another young boy, and he has not been seen since working in the field. The bus ride home."

"János. Your boy?"

"Yes, yes. My son."

The Komandant placed his small cup into its saucer, dropping his cigarette into the remaining grounds. Swirled the cup while the dying cigarette hissed. "Out to school, Brigitta?"

"No. Not out. I waited and waited, and I … I fell asleep." Her voice cracked and her hands shook, and she crossed her arms, gripping her elbows. Stared down at her worn shoes.

"Could he have come and gone?"

"No. I'm certain. How could I fall asleep?"

"Did you have an argument?"

Yes, of course they did. Since she had told him about Imre, János was unrelenting with his questions about Gábriel. About life in Stuttgart. Those questions made her nervous. What was he planning? What was he planning? She refused to answer, to offer a single detail to his hungry brain.

Again, that morning, he started with the questions. Gitta simply shook her head and looked away. "Eat and go," was all she said. "Or you will be late."

"Why won't you answer me?" he yelled and tossed his dishes into the sink, cracking the edge of the bowl. Then he told her she was stupid. "You are for nothing." After everything that happened to his father. To Imre. "For absolutely *nothing.*" He spoke through his teeth with such force, his spittle landed on her chin, and she raised her hand, striking him across his boyish cheek. "You should have let him take me. Why did you not let me go?" He did not wait for an answer. Slammed the door to their home.

János did not understand. Gábriel was so quiet, slipped away so easily. No one suspected he would abandon his country. Everyone who knew him had to answer questions. Even Gitta. She said she did not know where he was. He was a bachelor, a wanderer, and they had not spoken. Then, in what she knew was a warning to others, his home burned to the ground. Two properties on either side were also destroyed. Roofs for mothers and children, barns for the animals, vast numbers of hives filled with bees and honey. All gone. Smell of burnt sugar lingering in the air long after the rain. And they could do nothing, those neighbours, only press their round faces into their hands and weep.

"No, Komandant," she lied. "We did not argue. It was a morning like any other." After waiting a moment, she whispered, "I thought, perhaps, I could speak with your daughter."

"Nevena?" The Komandant frowned and tapped his watch. "But she has gone, of course. Class has already begun. You have lost track of time, *draga moja.* The morning is passing."

"She was home?"

Aliz Dobrica's lips split then, and she squawked. "What sort of question is that to ask? Yes, she was home. She is a good girl. Dragan, surely. This. Must we?"

"I did not mean—I never meant to suggest—I know they, they, they…János talked about her." A vein in Gitta's neck began to throb, blood squeezing through.

"She is young. And she is stupid." Gravel in the woman's throat. "But, ah. Not that stupid."

"Now, now," the Komandant said, lifting his hand, gently waving again. "All we do is wait, Brigitta. He is likely home this very moment. Rifling through your cupboards."

"Yes. Of course."

"You worry yourself too much. Sometimes they need to explore a little before they realize home is warmer."

"How could I fall asleep?" she moaned. "How could I let that happen?"

"I guarantee, *draga moja*. I know what it is like to be a young man. He will be back as soon as he is hungry."

Oficir Račić took two walnuts from a plate, cracking them in his hand. Brought his palm to his mouth and sorted withered nut from shell with his tongue. He smiled again, brown flesh in his teeth, mumbling, "And he will have a good story for his friends, no doubt."

A queer sound then, like funeral laughter, burst from Aliz Dobrica's lips. She quickly muffled it, and with mouth now tight, she nodded, drawing the black thread up through the fabric in her lap. Needle bending in her finger.

Chapter 10

"ICH WARTETE." I WAITED.

János leaned against a cement pillar just beneath a sign that said *Filmtheatre*. In the window to his left was a poster surrounded by soft lights, depicting a robust man with a curled moustache gripping a podium. A second man kneeling, washing a wooden floor with a small brush. *Der Untertan. Man of Straw.* János glanced at the poster, then back to Dorján, then to the poster. A cluster of filmgoers hustled past them, wool coats and neat hats, leather gloves and perfume, and Dorján could feel the itchy fabric on his cheeks.

"Was mit dir passiert?" What happened to you? János said, his German harsh and confident. *"Ich wartete."*

"I...I don't know." Dorján scratched his neck with unkempt fingernails.

"You don't know?" János spoke Hungarian now. "You don't know. Dorján, my friend, you've been sucking milk from a sour tit so long now, you're satisfied with the flavour."

A sparkle on the back of János's hand, and a single yellow coin appeared, royal head and laurel ring. János played with it, moving it across his knuckles. "We can go, you know," he said, nodding toward the film poster. Circle of bulbs flickered. "We don't have to stay."

"I don't want to go. I don't want things to change."

János laughed, and Dorján couldn't help but stare at his handsome face, unblemished skin, brown hair neatly combed. He wore ironed shorts, a matching suit coat, and shiny oxford shoes.

"But it must change. Once you understand something, you must change."

Then Dorján heard scraping behind him, turning to see an old woman in a pale dress and apron in the middle of the street. Her flabby arms jiggled as she brushed the damp cobblestone with a straw broom.

"It's already polished," Dorján called to her, waving. "Don't bother yourself."

"Was?" She lifted her head from the curl of her back, showed her face, a riddle of dark spots and soft creases. Her eyes were bright and wet. She frowned, shook her head, tapped her forehead with her index finger, then pointed at Dorján.

"Why does she do that? Use her broom when the street is clean?"

János lit a cigarette, letting it linger on his pink lips. "Why would she not? That's what she's told to do, and she does it. She is a listener."

"Ah."

"So. Shall we go in?" Smoke poured from his mouth.

Dorján replied, but his voice was drowned by the scraping, as though the sharpened tips of the bound straw scored the stone. And then a rattling sound rose above the movement of the old woman's broom, and Dorján looked upward, scanning the black sky for moving lights.

"There are no dragons here, my friend," János yelled above the drone. "None."

"I don't believe in dragons."

"Ah," he shouted, tossing the coin in the air, catching it. "But you do." János flicked his cigarette into the street, glowing tip rolling toward the old woman, and then he turned, striding though the wide open doors of the theatre.

As he reached out to touch his friend's back, Dorján jolted up in bed. Mouth already open, wanting to speak. Eyes blinking, blinking, in the bright morning light.

::::

DORJÁN ROLLED OVER ONTO his stomach, up on his elbows, and peered through the small window just above the wooden headboard. There he discovered the source of the noise that had seeped into his dream. Dozens of men, women, and children, brown faces and pure black eyes, meandered along the dirt road. Shaggy horses tugged a row of wheeled caravans, and a horn blew in a low moan over a base of tinny tambourine music. Several steps behind the group, an emaciated bear, leash around its neck, tottered along as a young boy struck its hind legs with a switch.

As he dressed, Dorján could hear his grandmother clacking plates and cups, bellowing into an empty room. "Ah, the *cigányok*. The useless racket. Like they are coming through the house."

He pulled on his clothes slowly, making his way outside. The long backyard was divided into three sections, one area where they sat and ate, a second area farther from the house where they grew vegetables and fruit trees, and a third area where the outhouse stood. He walked through the first gate and then the second gate into the last area. As he sat on the hole while his body drained a nighttime of water, he heard Buksi in Gitta *néni*'s backyard, throaty snarls as the dog ate. And then he heard a different sound, like air sucked through a tube.

He finished and buttoned his trousers, opened the door of the outhouse, crept into the garden. When he peered through a knothole in the fence, he saw János's mother kneeling on the soil beside the dog, her face pressed deep into his ribs, fingers knotted in his thick fur. He watched as her back rose and fell in sharp motions, and he realized she was sobbing. Two days had passed, and János still had not returned. Dorján turned his face, felt the secret of the coins curdling inside his stomach like a sickness. He had lied to Gitta about her son. Lied. Told her he had gone to swim, when instead they had stolen off into the woods. And now, Dorján had the dark thought that after they had fought, János had weighted his pockets and disappeared. He could barely admit it, but some thread of him no longer trusted his best friend.

When he returned to the kitchen, his grandmother placed a thick slab of bread on the table. Beside it, a large bowl of steaming milk. They both sat at the same time. She sipped from a cup, then swished the last of her coffee, dumping the liquid onto her saucer. Holding the cup close to her face, she scrutinized the wispy pattern formed by the remaining dregs. "Eat," she said. "Eat. You will need your strength. You have practice, yes? To swim?"

He nodded, then bowed his head and tore away chunks of hard crust, dipped it into the milk, and placed it in his mouth. Closing his eyes, he chewed and chewed, though the softened bread could have slid down his throat without him swallowing.

"You will make us proud. I am certain of it."

Avoiding his grandmother's gaze, he focused on the quarter loaf of bread lying on the cutting board. She noticed, said, "Yes, we will need more. On your way home?" She wobbled beside him, reached into her wide apron pocket to gather loose change, then dropped the money on the table beside him. Walking away, she lifted her foot slightly, twisting to inspect her shoe, the heel. As though something might be stuck to it.

He blinked as he watched her. The bread. The money. The heel of her shoe. And he felt a little rush of emptiness inside his chest. A bubble opening, that sudden awareness of something he had forgotten. His mind had been working on it for two days, and now it hurled the memory into consciousness. He remembered who the man was. The man who had paused just beyond the swaying willow and rolled his hand in the air.

He had been seven, maybe eight, years old and only saw him a handful of times. Sleeping in his small bed, Dorján heard strange sounds, and his body leapt up before his mind was barely awake. Blackness all around, his mother's husky wails frightening him, as though a stranger were kneeling on her chest. His father was dead, and Dorján knew he was the only protector in their house. He tiptoed to the hearth, took the poker in his hand, and crept along the wall. Heavy poker held aloft in his sliver of an arm.

His mother's door was ajar, and what he saw made him stop. A man, his face lost to the shadows. Body so big, a mass of flesh inside the room that did not belong. Covering his mother, pasty backside convulsing like a hairless mongrel's in heat. His hands reaching and squeezing, and his mother mewing, arching her spine. He saw her thick white leg dangling over the edge of the bed. When she straightened her knee, Dorján saw her shoe. She was wearing a high-heeled shoe.

At once, he felt the weight of the poker in his hand, metal shaking, ash-covered tip dotting the plaster wall. His father had made those heels as a hobby. Shaved and shaped and sanded those wooden heels with his very hands.

When he peered again into the dim light, the man was seated on the edge of the bed, his wide back to Dorján. He was wearing cotton underwear and a loose undershirt. After jamming his legs into trousers, he stood with an almost snap. Shoes on, and he leaned over, placing something on the painted night table. No conversation followed, and as the man left his mother's bedroom, Dorján scuttled across the floor and hid beside the miniature hutch with the doors made of wavy glass. He pressed his face against the cool wall and watched the man, back like an arrow, clip down the hallway.

The man opened the door and paused. Morning sunlight streamed in around his square frame, and the man lifted his hand, elbow to the height of a salute. But he did not touch his forehead with his finger; instead he twirled his hand around and around on a limp wrist as though in time to some internal music. He stepped out into the street, closed the heavy door, and took the brightness with him.

After several moments Dorján tiptoed into his mother's room, lifted the blanket, and lay down on the flattened mattress. He turned onto his side, facing away from her, and edged backwards on the damp sheet until he could feel her warm body pressed against his. A strange smell hovered over the bed, reminding Dorján of healing skin just freed from a bandage. He tried to ignore it, but the odour made an emptiness bloom within his heart. He wished she would dust the furniture or refill the pillows. Wash the yellowed sheet and hang it in the garden.

"No shoes in bed," he whispered.

She did not answer.

"*Apa* made those heels."

Her body straightened, thin air between them, and she nudged him with her thigh. "Go. You need to eat."

Dorján got to his feet, taking a handful of coins scattered beside the bills on the night table. He glanced at his mother, her stained lips, hollow black eyes. Her feet were bare now, the shoes fallen to the floor, tips of heels and soles touching. He moved his foot, knocking the shoes so their parts were no longer kissing. His mother did not seem to notice. Just lifted her arm, placing it over her eyes.

"How much?"

"Why do you always ask this same question?" she mumbled.

"Because."

She sighed, rolling over onto her side, one enormous breast sitting on top of the other. "Just half, Dorján. Just half. Nothing will ever change. We have no need for a whole."

He put his coat on over his pyjamas, buttoned up his hard leather shoes, and slipped out into the crisp early morning. Ran down a cobbled street in Drobnik toward the tiny shop where the fat lady with thick eyebrows cut a large circular loaf into two even pieces. Her arm waggled through her sleeves, and she asked after his mother, "How is Ilona *néni*?"

"In bed."

"Ah." After handing the half loaf to Dorján, she touched his cheek with her dusty hand, and said in a voice low and soft, "Ah, *kis szívem*. Someday she will smile again."

He walked home, not thinking of his mother or the man, but of those beautiful shoes. So out of place on her feet in the dirty bed. He tried to shake the image from his head and put his nose to the blackened bottom of the bread, pinching morsels of the dense loaf and holding it in his mouth until the starch tasted like sugar.

::::

"EAT," HIS GRANDMOTHER SAID again. "Nothing good ever came from hunger."

A ball of dampened dough sat on Dorján's tongue, and he could not swallow it.

"I know you worry about your friend. But you need not."

He looked up at her, pressing the hard ball into the roof of his mouth.

"So what?" she said. "He wanders a little here. A little there. His feet are not buried in this soil like mine are. Like yours are."

Dorján shook his head.

"János is only a boy, Dori." She shrugged. "Besides, he does not have the means to go far. What can he do with nothing?" An encouraging smile.

Those words moved through Dorján's body like noise through water, and the milk and bread in his stomach congealed, wanting out. He ran out the back door, through the first garden and into the second, where the fruit trees grew. Branches barren, the smell of rotting sweetness wafted up from the soil. Dorján held the trunk of an ancient apricot tree, bent at the waist, and vomited on the curling roots.

Chapter 11

SEVERAL DAYS LATER, KOMANDANT Dobrica stood in Gitta's kitchen. He pinched the legs of his dress pants and tugged lightly as he sat down. She had not scraped the coals in the stove, and the room was damp, his smell easily filling the room. A handsome smell. Cleaned skin, oiled hair, layer of smoke.

"I came to check on you," he said. "Have you heard any word of the boy?"

She shook her head. "No. Just silence."

"Silence is not necessarily a bad thing, do you agree? Noise could be far worse." He ignored the scattering of dried bread crumbs, placing his hat on the table.

Gitta bit her lip, staring at his hat. Deep black felt, brand new. Perched on top of crumbs and flour. A hardened drop of apricot jam. The hat appeared so foreign in her kitchen, his pale hands resting calmly on her table. So much like a dream, she could not decide whether she was awake or asleep.

"I do not know what to do," she whispered. "I am alone."

She sat in the chair opposite his, and when she laid her hand on the table, he reached for it.

"Of course you are not alone. Anything at all I can do to help. We can do to help. Tell us what you think, what you need."

"You will help?"

He laughed then, but only lightly. Not enough to disturb the crumbs. "Of course. I will ask some questions. Oficir Račić will ask as well."

She stood then, walked to the door, touched the handle, moved to the counter, leaned and breathed, fingers stroking the faucet, back to the table, and sat again in the same chair. How long could she exist inside her body, like a corpse that refused to move, yet refused to stay still? As she paced, she thought of Imre. Usually his memory filled her with longing, but at this moment, it swung on a hinge of resentment. How could he have drifted away from them? Selfish, selfish betrayal. Leaving Gitta to raise a child on her own.

"We will find him, Gitta. I promise."

"Yes." Those words should be coming from Imre's mouth. But instead he is dead. He chose to die, did he not? To make her a widow?

"And when he is home, your worry will soon turn to anger. Yes?"

"Ah."

"Do not be too hard on the child. He is a boy after all."

The stove was cold, but still she asked, "A coffee, Komandant?"

He pursed his lips. "No, no, Brigitta. Now is not the time to stretch for hospitality."

She stood again, leaning her back against the countertop. She felt lopsided, wondered if her stockings were missing, if perhaps she were wearing only a single shoe. A bare foot on cold floor, inviting illness to come up through the sole of her foot.

"Are you all right?"

She turned her head, looking out the window behind her. "It is me," she breathed. "He has left me."

"Why would you say that?" Head tilting.

"He told me, Komandant. Told me I was for nothing. That I should have—" She glanced at the window. "That I had made choices only with my own interests in mind."

"And what do you think?"

She bowed her head. "I did what I thought was right."

"Ah," he said, flicking his hat with his thumb. "I see." He reached into the pocket of his coat, retrieving cigarette and matches. Pushed the cigarette into his mouth, cupped the lit match even though there was no wind. "*Tetka* Zsuzsi," he said. "She is the best we have. For sewing. You agree?"

Gitta turned to face him again. "Yes, yes. She does fine work."

"Do you know there was a time when I would not go to her?"

"No?"

"Foolish, of course. I believed only a man truly knows the body of a man." He inhaled smoke, letting it exit through his nostrils. "I travelled to the tailor in Drobnik."

"I know the place."

"Remember me his name, will you?"

Gitta bent her head, closing her eyes. She knew the place, but she did not know the name. Strange how clearly she could picture the big glass window, several naked sewing dummies standing inside, one draped in fabric, thick black stitches, lines of chalk. Years ago she had stopped there in front of his store, staring at the fabric and metal frames. For a moment, she considered pausing, turning back. Waiting for Imre to return, to explain himself. A whisker of doubt was tickling her ear.

Jaunty music moved out through the glass, and the grey-haired man in shirt and vest sang as he worked. As she watched him, Gitta had the inexplicable sense that the tailor had never betrayed his wife. No, he had never fallen in love with another woman. He was content with his tiny shop, even though business had faltered. He was happy with his life. The sight of him made Gitta clench her jaw, and her moment of indecision quickly faded. Anger pushed her legs forward, and she had gripped her son by his tiny wrist, striding the rest of the block.

"I'm sorry. I do not recall his name."

"No matter. But I will tell you what I learned from this tailor. He was to make me a suit jacket, yes?"

She nodded.

"I visited twice, three times. He recorded his measurements on his papers. Very precise, or so he appeared to me." The paper on his cigarette crackled as it burned, and the smoke filled the room. He pulled a glass tray toward him, tapped. "Finally I try on my new jacket. The body fits like it should, yet the sleeves are confused. One sits just below my wrist as you would expect, and the other two inches too high." He smiled. "Do you know what he said to me?"

"He would fix it?"

"No, nothing of the kind. He said, 'Ah! I should have measured both arms.' And when I questioned him, he looked me straight in the eyes. Explained how I have one arm significantly longer than the other."

"Ah."

"'But no,' I replied. Then he gestured to the sleeves, and said to me, 'Isn't it clear? Can't you see? The problem is with you, sir.' For an instant, a single instant, I wondered how could I have gone through my life without realizing such a flaw in my form?"

Gitta glanced down at her feet then, discovering that both shoes were in place, stockings as well.

"I left the tailor," he continued and stood up. "I knew myself well, you see. I knew I was fine. The error was his to own, but he would not accept it. Do you understand?"

She nodded again. "I do."

"Things will be all right. You are raising your boy well, Brigitta. You are strong and capable."

As he moved past her toward the door, Komandant Dobrica briefly placed his hand on the curve of Gitta's back. The warmth of his open palm startled her, made her eyes close. She had not realized how cold she was, how empty. And she had so long ago forgotten what it was like to be touched by something alive.

Chapter 12

NEVENA TOOK THE SEWING shears and a handful of coins from her mother's hand.

"Have the old gypsy sharpen them," her mother said.

"Yes, *Majko*."

"And do not pay him until you get them back."

"Yes, *Majko*."

"And make sure the ones he gives you are actually mine. I don't want to see rusted handles, chipped blades."

As her mother spoke, Nevena narrowed her eyes ever so slightly, and her mother balked. "Do not look at me like that. Like you are not stupid."

"I never—"

"You are young. And there is no difference."

"Yes, *Majko*."

"And child. Take off your bracelet. Nothing but the wind on your wrist, or it will be gone. You will never see it again."

"Yes, *Majko*." She unsnapped the simple gold chain, laid it in a glass dish on a tall table, and then went out the door.

The open area just beyond the village square was crowded, the dark people peddling wares, and a few villagers shuffling about buying tin pans or having their pots repaired. Nevena stood just outside the cluster, watching the tired faces nod and smile. A young gypsy boy approached her, his slender arms saddled with a dusty watermelon, and she tried to wave him away. But he would not retreat. Instead he moved closer and pressed the melon into her stomach, until she stood back, yelled, "Neh," and shook her scissors in the air.

Beside her, a woman nodded at the boy, purchased the fruit, and in an instant Gazda László's grandson, Tibor, abandoned his garden stand and stood directly behind the boy to witness the exchange. And once the boy had money in his fist, he bowed and spoke to Tibor, smiling and laughing, moving his hands as though explaining how best to do business.

While Tibor's back was turned, attention diverted, tomatoes and carrots disappeared from the shiny mounds on his stand. The gypsy children, food stuffed underneath their winter clothes, rushed up the road leading away from Bregalnica, handing off their spoils.

The women kept their heads covered in colourful cloths, and their long skirts had the hems sewn shut between their ankles. Nevena's mother had told her the women closed the bottom of their skirts so they could slip items down through their waistbands, always appearing empty-handed. If she listened, she would surely hear the jingle as they walked. Nevena watched these women as they tended charcoal fires, dropping fresh vegetables into the pots, the smell of smoke and strange food carried away on the faint breeze.

She was about to call out to Tibor, tell him what had happened, when she caught sight of Dorján. He brushed past her, took several steps down the narrow pathway between two stores, and stopped. Leaned against the mud wall, legs and waist in a triangle of sunlight, chest and body lost in shadow. He cupped his hands against his face, and moments later she could see smoke billowing about his head.

She hesitated, her palms dampening. So rarely did she see Dorján without János, and the unnaturalness of it made her nervous. As though he were the soothing calm in the centre, and the location of the storm was unknown. Holding the scissors behind her back, she walked toward the passageway, and when she reached it, her feet remained on the cobblestone, not stepping onto the packed clay.

"János home yet?"

"No."

"Soon, I'm sure."

"I don't know." He smoked furiously.

"Well, you know him best."

Turning his face away from her, he spat on the ground, and said, "Perhaps you know him better than I."

She looked down then, embarrassed. Her mother was right. She was young and she was stupid. Dorján did not see her as she wanted to be seen. Free of insecurities, clever jokes tumbling from her mouth. Dorján did not recognize that János was like the gypsy boy with the watermelon, pressing, pressing something onto her. Something she may have wanted but did not necessarily need.

He pinched tufts of his hair with his hand, mumbling, "I don't feel well."

"You should be home, then. Not here."

"No," he said and threw down the cigarette. "I like the noise. The air is good."

She looked at the smoke curling out of his young nose and took a single step closer. Had the inclination to touch his arm, his shoulder.

"In case you're wondering," he said as he lit a second cigarette, "We threw them all in the river. Every last one of them."

She stared at the stones near her feet. On the edge of the stonework, near the passageway, the pattern was disrupted. "Really?"

"Do you think I am lying to you?"

"Of course not."

"I did it. I threw them away. János was furious." He bent slightly, placing a hand over his stomach. "But it would have been trouble. So much trouble."

After a moment, she laughed lightly. "Like Attila needs any more. Doesn't he have enough?" But he ignored her joke about the mysteries of the Hun rumoured to have treasure hidden beneath a tumbling river.

"I want you to forget we ever found them. Can you do that?"

"Of course. I had already forgotten."

"Really?"

"I mean I will. I will forget."

"Promise." For a fleeting instant, he looked at her, his eyes red and raw.

"I promise," she said, and her mouth went dry. Then she held up the scissors as a way of showing him she had something else to do. "You should go home. Go to bed. Have your *baka* make you a health soup. You'll feel better, Dori. Soon you will." She backed away, left him there, wavering inside of his sickness and his smoke.

:::::

WITH LITTLE PROBLEM, SHE found the old gypsy and waited while he sharpened three dull knives, handing them to a woman who quickly wrapped them in a cloth. Looking at his face and hands, Nevena could not tell how old he was. His skin looked like antique leather, but his eyes, though tired, were still wide and bright. When it was her turn, the gypsy gently took the scissors from her, spun the stone with a small foot pedal, and pressed the blades against the stone. Metal screeched and he worked both blades, slowly, carefully, swiped the metal in a dirty scrap of fabric, and held it up to the sunlight. Then he closed the scissors, grabbed the blades in his wrinkled hand, and returned them to her, handles first. She reached into her pocket, relieved to find the money still there, and placed it on his strangely white palm. She turned to leave, but he clucked in his throat, and she looked into his black eyes. His thick finger rooted through the money, and she expected him to demand more, but instead he pinched two coins from his palm and returned them to her. He bowed slightly from his shoulders, enough to show his gratitude, but not enough to threaten the balance of his tiny hat.

As she wandered through the crowd, she searched the faces for János. Somehow she expected to find him in the commotion, hiding like he would, in plain sight. But she did not see him. Only worn brown faces, black greasy hair, bodies covered in layers and layers of winter clothes even though the fall sun was high and warm.

In the hour before she left the house, she had overheard her parents arguing. About János. Her mother hissing about his family, his heritage, and her father insisting that János was a decent boy. "We should have put a stop to it years ago. Spending too much time with those two, ignoring girls her age." But her father disagreed. Said János was no different than he was as a young man. "A desire to see and to understand. He will be back soon enough." And her mother made a sound then like spitting, said, "So what if he is not? Too many years you have grown comfortable, Dragan. You may lead the village, but how well do you lead your family?"

Her father was right. She was certain of it. János would be back soon enough, and with a story of some wild adventure, thwarted plans, perhaps a mention of another girl, some poor peasant's daughter who had wanted nothing more than to run away with him. He would hope to make Nevena jealous, and he would stare at her as he spoke, and even though her mind would not permit it, pink would still rise in her cheeks. While she listened silently to his story, her heart would fill with oil and water, and she would wonder how she could be silently connected to someone who made her feel both admiration and irritation.

Nevena saw a cluster of onlookers and heard a "Haa! Haa!" followed by animated clapping, the sound of a shaking tambourine. She moved through the group to see a boy, not much older than her, his pants up over his ankles, hair stuck on end. There was a half ring of dried white paste near the side of his mouth, as though he had just awoken and wasn't given time to wash.

The boy held a chain and at the end was a skinny bear, now up on its hind legs. While hollering, he struck the bear on its back, and it danced from one hind leg to the next, front legs up, gentle paws limp. Turning, turning, leash chafing its neck. Nevena could see clumps of old excrement hanging near the tail. Its fur was straggly, and among the knots and burrs were hints of thin skin. As she stepped closer, a foul smell wrapped around her face, and Nevena darted forward, dropping her extra coins into the boy's painted wooden box.

The boy smiled and nodded, struck the bear again so that it lifted and batted its bony paws. She stepped back and looked at the boy's inviting face. In that instant, she had the desire to talk to him, ask him questions about himself. Did he like to roam from place to place? Did he play magical music, like some of the others? Was he hungry? But she heard her mother's voice, a bird's caw, telling her he was filthy. And if she looked him straight in his devil black eye, he might steal her soul.

The boy waved his hand and another gypsy took a few coins from the box, disappeared into the store, and returned with a dripping bottle of beer, offering it to the boy. First the boy drank heartily, then passed the remainder to the bear. It lifted the bottle in its paws to its chained mouth. Drank through its muzzle, beer sliding out its cheeks, caramel foam coursing through the fur on its neck. The gypsy boy leaned toward her and whispered something. His eyes wide. She did not understand the words, but his expression made her heart flutter, and she turned away. She ran past the passageway where Dorján had been standing, held her breath and glanced in, but he was gone.

Chapter 13

GITTA KELEMEN WANDERED FROM room to room. Waiting, waiting for something to happen. For news to arrive. For the cold silence inside the walls to be broken. But there was nothing, only the occasional visit from Zsuzsi and Dorján, which Gitta could have done without. Dorján was always quiet, would not look her in the eye, while Zsuzsi chattered non-stop, her words pleasant, foreign, barely registering over the dull drone inside Gitta's head. She could not understand anything and only smiled, sipped coffee, and smoked cigarette after cigarette until her throat and chest burned, the back of her tongue turning grey.

Her work was piling up around her. The cotton bags of laundry she accepted from families in Drobnik went unwashed and unironed. Just yesterday a woman arrived on her doorstep for her clean tablecloth, her husband's pressed shirts. Gitta had nothing to offer her. Faint chirping from her lips, and she sorted through the mound. Found the woman's belongings, loosened the knot, and peered inside. Her linens damp, smelling slightly of yeast. Word would soon circulate, and the work would stop coming. There was always another woman ready to take in laundry. Accept the extra money. And Gitta did not care.

One afternoon she fell into a hazy sleep on János's bed, but she soon awoke with cramped legs. Both knees sideways and bent, feet pressing against the lower board. She realized the child-sized bed must have been too small for her son's growing frame, and she left the small room, closing the door, could not allow those new realizations to settle on her skin. That she had not given him the things he needed, had not made him comfortable. That he had run away not just from Bregalnica, but from her as well.

He would have a new bed, the best she could manage. When he returned. When he returned. She gripped that thought inside her head until her skull ached.

Harsh tapping at the door, front this time, and Gitta assumed it was another woman. Looking for folded clothing. She counted to one hundred, but the incessant click of knuckles against wood did not stop. Somehow she managed to direct herself, on weak legs, toward the source of the knocking. When she opened the door, there was Gazda László's old wife, short and stout, the midsection of her dress filling the entire door frame. Gitta could not recall her name, but when she saw the woman's friendly expression, the basket hooked on her arm, she wanted nothing more than to close the door, retreat into her darkening home.

"I was just about to leave," the old woman said. "You took your time."

"I was... I—"

"No matter. These are for you." And she thrust the basket toward Gitta. "The sun has gone cold for the winter, and we have more than we can eat. More than we can sell."

Gitta held the handle, her mouth open but no words creeping out.

"I'll need that basket back," she continued, moving the tips of her shoes onto the strip of wood that separated outdoors and in. "I can wait."

In the kitchen, Gitta dumped the vegetables onto the table, carrots and cabbage and potatoes, all coated in a fine layer of dried clay. Went back to the open door and returned the empty basket.

"You were quick, quick."

Gitta nodded, her hand on the latch. "Thank you," she managed.

"Thank you. I'm grateful."

The woman waved her bloated fingers but did not step away. "I wanted to mention to you. Tibor is troubled over this."

"Tibor?"

"My grandson. You know him. He works in the square, yes?"

Gitta nodded.

"Of course I do not know for sure what thoughts rattle about in his head. He is a little, ah, what can I say? Difficult. But the two boys were the same age. He looked up to János, I believe. Misses him. When he learned that János was," hesitation then, "away, he became agitated. We could barely console him."

"Ah." Gitta's throat began to constrict, breathing slowed.

"We are here for you," the old woman said. "Even Tibor. He has his challenges, but he is a reliable boy. Can help you winter your garden."

"I can manage."

"Of course you can manage, Gitta," she said, and she reached up to touch the knot of her scarf. "No one thinks you cannot. But, you should understand, you do not have to."

"I…I understand."

Gitta closed the door softly, then peered through the thin drape, watching the hunched shadow glide over the road. She hoped Tibor would not be next in the alcove. Surely the presence of that child would push her over the edge. Gentle, no doubt, but his grunts and hacks would torment her, when the only noises she craved were those originating from her son. She would be satisfied with another argument, yes, an argument. János's anger spewing out onto the floor. Rising up over their shoes, touching their ankles, and connecting them. Even that.

Eleven days and still no sign of him. She went back to the kitchen, saw the dusty heap of generosity on the table, on the floor. A sickly frustration mounted in her limbs, and she kicked a fallen cabbage as hard as her skinny leg would allow. But the cabbage did not move. Instead it spun several times, then squeaked to sudden stillness. "Where are you?" she whispered, and her hands formed fists, struck her skinny thighs. Heel of her shoe coming down onto a yellow root, smashing it. "Where are you? Where are you? Where are you?"

Every moment she thought of her son. She was twirling, her insides like an aimless dervish, whether she was actually moving or not. Sometimes she would allow herself to imagine him rushing through the door, and light would flood her body, carrying her across the floor toward him. A long, tight hug. And other times, she would see herself through a more honest eye, beating him with a wooden spoon, striking him until the wood cracked and splintered, and her son shrunk back into a child, a tiny boy who feared her and loved her. Who promised, just after they had buried Imre, that he would never abandon her. No matter what. He would never leave.

"You will keep your promise," she had told him.

Yes, Anyu. Forever.

Forever had not lasted nearly long enough.

She could not fathom life without him. Her mind could not go forward, and instead she spent the long waiting hours, going back. Reviewing chapters, trying to piece together the twists and turns in their lives. And though she tried not to, when she felt as though she would lose her mind, she could not help but remember her mother. The few words the sick woman had hissed into her face a month before János was born. A phrase that penetrated her, left a mark on her mind like an old scar.

:: ::

SINCE GITTA WAS NINE years old, she had only seen her mother a single time. Growing up, her aunt would allow no mention of the woman, and after Gitta married, Imre also forbade it. But still, one afternoon she defied everyone, took the train, travelled to the northern border of Komarovo where the *elmegyógyintézet* stood like a fortress.

It had stone walls, a black iron fence, tangles of lush vines weaving in and out of sharpened pickets. As she passed through a gate and walked up the bend toward the entrance, she considered that the structure could easily have housed a wealthy family rather than a collection of misplaced souls. Mostly adult females lived there, and a handful of large-headed children.

With proper papers, Gitta gained admittance to the asylum. She reached up to remove her hat, but a heavy nurse said, "Leave it. You won't be long here." A second nurse, younger with red cheeks, guided her out of the atrium and down a long marble hallway. Gitta saw a toothless woman pacing, counting her steps, another standing, skeletal body pressed against the wall, rocking left to right. In an open space to her left, perhaps once a ballroom where couples had danced, a woman crouched on the floor, plucking bits of nothing from the air with stick fingers. A man, perhaps her son, in a brown suit and glossy shoes looked down at her. Gitta shuddered, and the nurse cleared her throat, saying in a masculine voice, "This way." She resisted the urge to look behind her, to soothe herself with the knowledge that the front door still existed.

Two dozen or more women and children populated a large courtyard. Some swaying, some standing still as though rooted to the spot, staring up at the sky like withering flowers. In the very centre stood an old woman in bare feet, shuffling along, following the pattern of chipped bricks, crossing over patches of unevenly packed earth. As she moved, dozens of shiny black birds lifted off the ground around her, and perched on the edges of the slate roof, cocking their heads. Gitta paused in the door frame, "There?"

"Yes, there," the nurse said.

"Are you sure?" The woman was squat in her body, and her flat head was covered in grey stubble. She looked nothing at all like Gitta remembered.

"Quite certain, *Gospođo* Kelemen." And the nurse nodded at the round lump underneath Gitta's dress, said, "Touch nothing. And wash your hands and face thoroughly before you go."

Then she left Gitta alone.

Gitta took a deep breath and stepped forward. Too late to turn back now. She couldn't understand her sudden desire to see her mother. A desire that had overtaken her mind, allowing her to think of nothing else. Even though Imre had made her promise not to visit, for weeks she felt dizzy, disconnected, and she conjured this idea that being close to her mother was the only thing that would make it stop. She so badly wanted to show her mother her grown body, her full, round face, the burgeoning weight nestled inside the cradle of her hips. And just what did she hope for in return? Something, something, some small acknowledgement. A smile or glint in her mother's eyes. A single moment of joy or recognition that Gitta could grasp and carry forward while she birthed and raised this baby. If only her mother might meet her gaze and tell her, *You are my daughter, and I am proud I brought you to this world.*

The afternoon was dull and grey, damp cold wafting up from the ground, but Gitta's mother was draped in only a sheer cotton gown. When she was close enough, she could see her mother's limbs were pale purple, and her knees and elbows white with blistering scale. Humming, she teetered back and forth on a single spot now, feet planted a distance apart, her hands lifted upward. Gitta could make out her mother's dark nipples grazing the papery fabric and the triangle of hair between her legs.

Reaching her hand out, she stopped short just before she touched the hump on her mother's back. "It is me, *Anyu*. It is me, Brigitta."

Her mother lifted her bent neck, staring at Gitta with wet eyes. Mouth falling open, her face narrow, blue flesh drooping on the bone.

"*Anyu?*"

Nothing but a groan from that lipless hole.

"Are you cold, *Anyu?* Would you like a shawl? Something woollen?"

Her mother blinked but still no sign of awareness. No fear or sadness in those hazy eyes. The woman began her shuffle again, moving her dirty feet, blackened toenails, tracing the broken curve of the laid brickwork. Ambling around like something dead but still fed by warm blood from a stubborn heart.

On rubbery legs, Gitta took several steps, following her mother, but when she saw the nurse watching her from the doorway, she stopped and straightened her coat.

"*Anyu,*" she whispered. "Please, *Anyu*. Please know me. I belong to you."

The old woman froze, and Gitta was startled to see her turn, move toward her with such speed. Before Gitta knew what was happening, there was a flurry of white and blue, a sour wind, and her mother was before her, clutching at her pregnant stomach with ice fingers, face pushed into hers. Her breath cut through the air, the stench of gangrene, and she cawed, "It is not yours. Not yours. Not yours. Not yours. Not yours." The phrase a circling chant.

And then, the pretty nurse with the man's voice appeared, bending her mother's fingers backwards until they cracked, yelling, "Let go, you imbecile, let go," pressing hand to wrist, arm folding like a wing until her mother fell to her knees, cowering on the ground. Firm hand on Gitta's elbow then, guiding her away, away, so quickly that Gitta did not have a moment to gather herself. They strode across the courtyard, down the hallway, and the nurse nudged her toward a door.

"In there. You may wash." It was not a suggestion.

Gitta entered the closet space, and went to the stained sink. Running hot water from the tap, she scrubbed her hands with the brown cake of soap, splashing her face and neck. She wanted to lift her dress, cup warm water in her palms, and let it roll over her stomach. But she didn't. Just dried herself with the roll of towel, buttoned her coat, covering the crease marks in the fabric left by her mother's grip.

"You cannot understand," the older nurse said in Serbian when Gitta returned to the atrium. "You would like to reason. Would like to draw them out. But you cannot."

"Her clothes? A coat?"

"She has everything she needs, *Gospođo* Kelemen."

"She does?"

"We've tried. Surely you must know this. But the woman refuses any comfort at all."

Gitta brought her hands to her stomach.

"You must not concern yourself, madam. They are well provided for." The nurse glanced at her shoes. "Considering, well, the conditions that led to their arrival."

Gitta nodded. "Do you—do you know what she meant when she said—"

"I am quite certain she meant nothing. A confusion."

"Nothing?"

"We want to attribute meaning, do we not? It is human nature." Then she paused, considered her words. "A healthy human nature, I should say. But you have to accept that some things mean nothing. Some words mean nothing."

"Yes."

"Forget this," the nurse said. "Go home and forget this. Your son is coming soon."

"My son?"

"I am never wrong," she said with a wide smile. "Sons bring much happiness to a family. Unless, that is, they fall in love with the wrong woman." Those words, even though they were whispered with light-ness, echoed off the arched ceiling.

At home, when Gitta lay down to rest, arms over her swollen ab-domen, she would hear the squeal of rubber soles, bare feet padding, all those murmurs and moans. Noises that should be held within the confines of a human skull were out in the open. Pinging off the flaking domes and rough plaster walls. Then her mother's song, the sand-paper slish of cold naked thighs rubbing against one another. Brittle nails scratching dead skin. All that desolation trapped inside stone walls, but Gitta had helped some of it escape. Those sounds, gathered up, packaged inside her mind. She accepted it. What else could she do but bring the parcel home?

And in the days leading up to her child's birth, her son's birth, she played it over and over again. Heard the sounds sneaking out of her mouth. Nothing she could do to control it, even though she was mortified her baby's first lullaby was the confused wail of human dis-content.

::::

SHE COULD WAIT NO longer. Gitta took up her pen and wrote the let-ter. Addressed it. Held it aloft and spat a little on the sealed envelope.

Next she slipped the letter into a larger envelope, writing a second address. Once the gossiping women left Zsuzsi's home, she would bring it to the old woman. For the letter to have any chance of reaching its destination, Gitta could not dare mail it herself.

Chapter 14

"YOU ARE SWIMMING THESE days? Working hard?"

"Not so much."

"Not so much? What stupidity."

Oficir Račić fished out a chunk of egg from the thick soup, shovelled the spoonful into his mouth. "Ah," he said, revealing yellow yolk paste on his tongue. "How I long for my mother." He wiped his face on the inside of his wrist, tapped the side of his empty bowl with the spoon. Zsuzsi Szabó was quick to her feet, scooping another ladle of the thick broth.

Dorján wrapped his hand around his bowl, pulling it closer.

His grandmother dipped her head, stared into his bowl, confused at the contents. "*Szívem*, if you do not eat, you will turn to dust."

"I'm not hungry."

Oficir Račić sat back in his chair, pushing away his empty bowl. "No appetite, *dečko*?"

Dorján shook his head. "I think … I think my stomach is sick."

For a moment, Oficir Račić lowered his head, staring at Dorján through his bushy eyebrows. Then he shifted his attention to the dirty fabric of his blue shirt and wiped a streak of soup from his belly, licking the residue from his plump finger.

"Did you know," the Oficir said, "that guilt likes to make its home in the gut?"

"No, sir," Dorján managed, then sipped the soup. A broth his grandmother had made especially for him, meant to bring health and energy to an ailing body.

"You look at the stomach of a cow. The inside. And it is so clean and pure and perfect. Not a single stain." His tongue flicked over his lips. "Now a man's stomach. By the time he has reached middle age, it is nothing but a lacerated mess. Sores and scars and damaged flesh."

Dorján swallowed the morsel of carrot he had been chewing for far too long. "You've seen a man's stomach?"

"Ah," he replied, laughing lightly. "I have seen so many things. I cannot even begin to tell you."

Zsuzsi removed his bowl, said, "You will take a coffee, sir?"

"No, no, no. The soup was enough. You are too kind, *Gospođo* Szabó." Then he turned to Dorján again. "What was I saying? Ah yes. You see the cow feels no guilt, only gratitude for the warm sky and supply of grass. No guilt. But a man, all his secrets are stored in the pot of his belly. And those secrets try to work their way out through the puckers and folds. Destroy the pot."

"Ah."

"Do you understand what I'm trying to say, *dečko*?"

"Are you certain, Oficir Račić? You have no desire for a coffee?" Zsuzsi's voice was tight, and she stood close to him, leaning slightly, blocking his view of Dorján. "I will grind the beans. I have, yes." Nodding at the heap of peelings, pile of soaked bones from the broth. "They are there, ah, somewhere."

"I said no, woman." He patted his police hat lying on the table, twisting the rim so that the emblem was now facing her. "You will leave the room now."

Dorján watched his grandmother clasp her hands, nod ever so slightly, her compliance almost imperceptible because of the stores of fat underneath her chin. Then she left him alone with Oficir Račić.

"You were friends, yes?"

"Yes."

"Good friends?"

"I think we were."

"You were? You are no longer?"

Dorján's leg jiggled underneath the table. "We are. We are."

"But you clearly said you thought your friendship was in the past."

"I … I wasn't thinking."

"Ah."

"I misspoke."

Oficir Račić scratched his silver stubble and smiled. "Sometimes terrible confusions rise up from misspoken words. You should be careful of your language."

"I'm sorry."

"You needn't be. Were you fighting perhaps?"

Dorján watched him closely. How his hands fluttered in the air, the way he tilted his smooth oversized head. But there was nothing familiar about this man.

"No," he replied. "We didn't fight."

"I've been told something different. From your teacher, *Gospodin* Takáts. Said there was an altercation in the field."

Dorján shook his head.

"Said you injured your friend. Knocked him to the ground."

"No, sir."

"No?"

"That was an accident. We were—we were joking around. János said so himself."

"Joking around. You are not lying to me?"

"No, sir."

Oficir Račić scratched at his left breast, then gently cupping his hand around the flab, smiled again. Two teeth were missing. "Did he have a girl here?"

"No."

"Ah. You have little hesitation this time."

"He didn't. Not that I know."

"In Drobnik, then?"

Counting seconds before he spoke. One. Two. Three. "No."

And Oficir Račić laughed. "Of course not. The girls in Drobnik would not look at us, no?"

Dorján shook his head, tried to grin.

"No different when I was a boy." Oficir Račić pressed his body forward, wooden table cutting into his gut. Lowered his voice. "Whores. All of them. Think the slit between their legs is lined with gold." He sat back then, tapped his fingernails on the edge of the ashtray. "There is rumour," he said casually, "that János Kelemen has abandoned his country."

Both legs jiggling now. Dorján tried to breathe slowly.

"There is no shame in telling the truth, dečko. But to lie casts a shadow on your family. Your father's name."

Dorján stirred his soup, the spoon rattling on the edge of his bowl.

"Your father was a good man, you know. A good doctor. Once he operated on me, did you know that?"

Dorján shook his head.

"My gallbladder. Ah, the pain I was in! And he split me open," thumb sliding sharply up his midsection. "Cut the filthy bastard out." He pushed his fist into his stomach and belched. "I have never missed it. No. Not a single day."

"That's good."

"Yes, yes it is. Do you want to see the scar?" Hand touching the stressed buttons on his shirt.

"No, sir. No, no. I don't."

He laughed, nodded. "No more than a white hair on an otherwise perfect body." Then he stood and pointed to Dorján's full bowl. "Am I to blame for your turn of appetite?"

"No, sir."

"I only do my job, you see."

When the Oficir smiled this time, his eyes crinkled, and Dorján relaxed slightly. Acid shuttled downward, away from his throat.

"Oficir Račić?"

"Yes, dečko?"

"He did talk about going."

"Ah. I thought as much. One look at your face, and I know what time it is. Good man for telling me."

"But he's not serious. You have to believe me. He's always talking about something when he should be quiet. That's the way he is."

"Of course. The boy is probably chasing a warm tail." A moan of pleasure drove his eyes up into his head, and his great frame quivered slightly. "I was young once, you know. So many women. He'll be back when he's satisfied."

"I think so too, sir. He'll be back."

Chapter 15

TIBOR JUST APPEARED. GITTA had not expected him, and he had not knocked on her door to announce himself. Instead he must have crept through the back gate, down the slender walkway, through the fence and into the area where the cherry tree shed its leaves, worn stalks lying limp on the ground.

When she stepped outside to shake crumbs from a cloth, she heard someone moving about behind the fence. Then she heard Buksi growling, an angry rumble, and she imagined the dog's mouth full of froth. She had assumed an animal was rummaging, but when she peered through a crack in the wood, she discovered Tibor. Vines and dead foliage in a mound on the side. His pitchfork held aloft, and he stabbed the cool soil, lifted and turned. Working the stumps and shrivelled roots down through the earth so they might decay over the winter months.

She pulled open the second gate. "Tibor!"

He did not flinch at the sound of her voice. Never slowed his work.

"I did not know you were coming. I did not expect it. You do not need to." She knew she was rambling. "I…I just have not found the time. But I can do. I can manage, you see."

Of course he did not respond, other than casting a sideways glance through slit eyes.

"Did your *nagyanya* send you? I know she has sent you here. I understand. Do not feel you must, Tibor. You have other things to occupy your time." Even though she knew his hearing was fine, her voice was growing louder. "This is my work, my task. Tibor, I—"

She wanted to, but she could not ask him to leave.

He removed his sweater, throwing it behind him. Began digging again at a fevered rate. The afternoon was especially cold, and Gitta thought she saw steam rising from the back of his neck, his armpits when he raised his hands.

"I am pleased to see your face has healed. It must have been a terrible accident. To hurt yourself like that."

Something in what she said made him hesitate, and he spat on her garden. Next a string of guttural, popping sounds straight out of his stomach.

"Well," she said lightly and took a step backwards. "A drink. You will take a drink of something. Water. Coffee."

When he shook his head, she heard his jaw snap, teeth clank together.

She said nothing else, beginning to work alongside him. Picked up the broom, swept leaves. Yet this only seemed to provoke him. He stopped moving the soil, and with his head pressed forward on his neck, he stared at her, then at the gate, making a straining sound. She was the one to shake her head this time. She would not be urged out of her own garden by a boy no older than her son. Instead, she would remain quietly beside him and watch. She did not trust Tibor to do his work diligently, properly.

Only after he had finished would she admit she had been wrong. Tibor continued tirelessly, as though his body were made of machine parts. Once done, he gathered his few tools, wiped his forehead with a scrap of fabric, and without so much as a nod to say goodbye, he picked up his sweater and left her yard.

The next day he returned with a bale of hay, dragging it through the gate. Cut the thin rope and spread the hay over her soil. Unnecessary, she thought, as her garden was not large, not warranting such meticulous preparations. But she said nothing and allowed him to do the work.

Over two weeks, he came several more times. Painted the trunk of the tree near her front door, repaired spider cracks in her exterior plaster, replaced rotted boards in the fence bordering her and Zsuzsi's land.

If she was out of sight, she could hear his noises, rasping, choking sounds. Angry sounds. He fell silent if she came into view but never looked at her. Except for that one time. When she had offered him a small amount of money. He froze, midstroke with his brush. He turned and met her gaze, his paint-speckled face lifting toward her. Nothing for a moment, but then he opened his mouth and out rolled brittle laughter. Not what she had expected. The sound, so thin and fragile, frightened her. It could crack and cut.

She kept her distance after that, though when she could, she watched him through the windows. She wished he would stop and felt deep relief when his visits ended. Everything outside her home was prepared for the oncoming winter. The thought of it made her nervous. It did not seem right to have the appearance of order when her insides were churning. Her mind was full of jagged, misplaced phrases. Sentences of nonsense and confusion. No meaning to her story.

Chapter 16

"AUF WAS WARTEST DU noch?" What are you waiting for? Standing on the front steps of the *Filmtheatre,* János lifted one foot, then the other, soggy red carpet beneath his feet. He wore crisply ironed pants and shoes, but his shoes were dull and the shoelaces were untied. The poster for *Der Untertan* was skewed in the window, and half of the surrounding lights had failed. "Well? I'm freezing. Let's go in," he said, and he hunched over, arms close to his body as he smoked.

"Me too," Dorján replied. He stood there in nothing but a cotton nightshirt. Behind him, a thin mist snaked over the road.

János threw down his cigarette, a faint sizzle rising from the wet carpet. "Come inside with me."

"I don't want to see that movie."

"It'd be good for you."

"Going home would be better."

János laughed. "You've been a coward since we were boys."

"That's a lie."

He laughed again, but this time he placed his hand on his jaw as though something pained him. "It's not your fault, Dori. Can you name a single man who's not?"

"My father wasn't a coward."

"He treated the Nazis."

"He treated anyone who was sick."

"Ah, yes. So he was a good man, just not very smart."

Dorján felt anger bubble up inside of him, and his hands closed into fists. He would pound that slender smirk from János's face.

"Calm down, Dori. I was only joking."

"I don't think you're funny."

"You used to."

János brought his hand to his jaw again, and began to laugh. His laughter splintered into a hundred children's voices, all giggling in unison. The street behind them was empty, but Dorján could hear those children playing, the sound of shoes running through dirt, tired lungs gasping for air. Then a wheezing sound above, high-pitched and desperate. Dorján looked up into the pale sky, saw a formation of black metal birds gliding through the air. Felt a vibration in his calves. When he lowered his face, János was gone, but he could still hear him, words spiralling out from a long, long hallway inside the theatre. "Hurry, my friend. Hurry and find me."

:::::

HE AWOKE SUDDENLY IN the darkness, his heart beating rapidly inside his chest. He sat up, placed his soles on the cold floor, and for a moment listened to the soft snores of his grandmother sleeping in the adjacent room. The old clock just outside his door ticked and ticked, and then chimed a single soft note.

Three weeks had passed since Dorján had seen his best friend, and the questions were slowly making him ill. His appetite had drifted away, though his body was still stretching ever upward, thinning out. He found it difficult to swim for any length of time, his performance suffering. He realized now there was no excuse for not checking, for not going back into those woods. For letting the days pass, one after the other. He could no longer defend his shaky logic, believing that if he did not know the truth, the best possible outcome was still wide open. János would come home.

Dorján got out of bed, and coat covering his back, he took the lantern from the hook, slipping out the back door. He went through the courtyard and out onto the mucky road. Icy November rain spat down from the sky, and in the glow of the flickering street lights, he could see the cloudy water racing through the gutters. He turned the collar of his coat upward, pressing forward into the night.

As he reached the edge of the village, he heard the rumble of a car. At this hour of night, the sound made his spine tighten, and he hurried off the road, slipping behind a tree. Stood straight like an iron rod, waited as the car rolled slowly past. Only once did he open his eyes to peek. A spark of light illuminated the inside of the car, and he saw two men. The driver with his head bent, lighting a cigarette. The passenger, laughing, the barrel of a long gun resting on his shoulder.

Finally the car disappeared around a curve in the road. Dorján waited for a second vehicle to follow, but when none came, he stepped out from behind the tree, continuing walking. Kept his head turned slightly, so as to listen. There would be questions if someone saw him alone at night. Questions he would not know how to answer.

Along the way he passed a work site on the outskirts of Bregalnica. A large unfinished building that had the potential to be a prosperous bracket on the edge of the village. He stopped and looked at the shell, wide and square and flat in the face. He was much younger when work had started, a flurry of young men and equally sturdy women using wheelbarrows to move and position blocks. Not much he could do, other than bring cold water or a glass of *pálinka* to the workers during lunchtime. But work soon slowed, then gradually halted. No one knew what the building was meant to be, and now it was nothing but a criss-cross of joists and mortared supports, floor still strewn with gravel. It appeared abandoned, except for a pristine white sign with the red words Long Live Tito hanging skewed over the gaping hole where the door might be.

Once, Tito came through the village in his shiny black car. The door opened, and the man rose up and out of his car as though his body were made of sharp creases, and here was the practised unfolding. Dusty workers took a break, and most everyone was there, cheering and clapping. Dorján could feel the crowd flush with pride and hope, and he climbed onto the pile of cinder blocks, craning his neck as Tito moved like fluid through a sloping cylinder.

No one might have noticed, but from his vantage point, Dorján was able to see Tito and his hands. A farmer reached out to touch Tito, but the president first slipped his fingers into the tight pocket on his coat, removing a pair of crisp white gloves. Barely a shift in his smile or his words, and he quickly tucked his clean fingers into the gloves. Then shook hands vigorously, nodded. Up on the cinder blocks, János balanced on one foot beside him. "Did you see that?" he whispered. "Won't even touch his own people."

Dorján shook his head, feeling both excited and uneasy as the great man moved closer. Strong jaw and blue hat with the red and gold band. So close now, Dorján could see the circular mole over his lip, the shine on his neck from a recent shave. He wore dark glasses, with silver rims, and even though there was no telling, Dorján had the distinct impression that Tito was staring not at him, but at János.

Dorján walked onward through the village, wiping the rain from his forehead. He pushed his wet hair away from his eyes. Once the street lights ended, he laid the lantern in the muck, dug matches from his pocket, and curled his back while he lit the strip of braided rope. Eyes barely adjusted to the darkness, he could not see the deep potholes, and several times his feet sank into freezing water. A shock of liquid seeping in through his shoes dampened his socks, wet wool chafing his heels.

He stopped just outside the wooded path that led over the hill and into the park. Instead of crossing the road and passing underneath the drooping willows, he hopped the gutter and stood beside the sour apple tree. Tonight it offered no shelter; the leaves had all fallen, matted and rotting, plastered to the hard earth. He stepped on the dead blanket, fermenting apples flattening beneath his shoes.

Just a few minutes. Nothing longer. Then he would go and check the tin box. He laid the lantern near his feet and lit a cigarette. Brought it to his lips but barely pulled on it. Wanted the cigarette to burn as slowly as possible. While he smoked, the rain petered out, but the sky was no brighter.

In the farmer's field behind him, he heard rustling, and he turned to see a stray goat a short distance away. It had long curling horns and twisted its head to scratch its back. Then it rubbed its wet sides against the fence. Yellow eyes reflected in the light from the lantern, and Dorján had the sense the animal was spying on him through those split pupils. Wondering why he was standing there in the middle of the night.

Dorján stared back at the creature and spat. He could be asking the beast the same question.

The goat made no utterances but stood there, pawing the earth as Dorján smoked. When the ember threatened to burn his fingers, he threw the cigarette into the mess of decaying leaves and wormy apples, and waited. Still his legs did not feel strong enough to cross the road, pass underneath the near-naked willows. If the situation were reversed, if Dorján were missing, there would be no hesitation. János would have stomped into the woods, seen what there was to be seen. Dorján brought the back of his hand to his mouth, nipping the skin of his knuckles between his teeth. He could not explain his deep reluctance. Perhaps his dream was correct, and he was nothing more than a coward. He decided to turn and go home. As that thought flitted through his mind, the old goat bent its head and raked its hard horns over the wooden slats. Again and again. "Fine," Dorján whispered. "Fine."

He picked up the lantern, leaping over the gutter and onto the road. Once deep inside the woods, he laid the lantern on the sodden earth, lifted the glass, and lit it. The light it offered was pale and uneven.

Even in the dimness, their secret place was not difficult to find. Just before the trail began to dip downward, he passed the thickest maple tree on his left. Lifting his lantern, he looked both ways and then abandoned the path. Nearly a hundred steps, one straight in front of the other. Marching, marching, before he located the area. He stood still and held the lantern in front of him, dripping trees and heavy branches glistening in the yellow light. At this hour in the woods, Dorján expected silence. But in addition to the thump of his heart, he heard constant movement as unseen creatures skittered through the brush.

Kneeling down, he reached between Root Rock, and his fingers located the tin container. What would he find inside? Neither answer would be pleasant. If only a little money was missing, then his friend was likely gallivanting close by. Making everyone worry while he played in neighbouring villages. If half the coins were taken, then he might be gone for a very long time. Travelling far away from Bregalnica. Following his dangerous dream.

He took a deep breath. They should not have fought. They should not have fought. Dorján had pressed against János's plan like a stone wall, and there was nothing for his friend to do but bounce away. Leave him. Desert their childhood plans. Dorján should have been patient, listened. Maybe over time, he could have dissuaded János. Turned things around, back to the way they should have been.

The tin was not tucked behind the rock as he had predicted but was lying on the ground. When Dorján picked it up, holding it in his hands, it was impossibly light. He shook it, shook it again, and heard not a single clink or jingle. There was no need to open it, but still he did, pulling back the lid and stared inside. At the emptiness. The absolute emptiness. Every coin was gone. Even the few bills and scattered change they had stored were missing.

He shoulders slumped, and he slid his hand behind the rock. Explored the crooks and crannies, patted the ground and the surrounding area. Dove his fingers in through the moss and the humus and the animal waste. Nothing. Nothing. Nothing. And in a flash, fury erupted in his chest. His rage, rising up. A childhood glued side by side, promises to each other. *The little engineers.* How could he know so little about János Kelemen? The depth of that boy's cunning.

Dorján took the tin in his fist, drew his arm backwards, and threw it with all the force he could muster. An echo of metal striking wood, a feathery plop as the cheap tin landed on the forest floor.

"Stole it all, you filthy prick. You stole it all."

Chapter 17

"SUCH A NEAT HEM on your skirt, Mila." Aliz Dobrica crossed her legs at the ankle, sipping her coffee from a thin white cup.

"Zsuzsi Szabó," Mila replied. "Her house is like a chicken coop in spring, but she works wonders with the needle. I was there once with the baby and would not let her down from my lap."

"The pins and things."

"No, no. Not even. Afraid I would lose her in the mess." The women laughed, and Mila continued, "She is so quiet, my girl. I might have been a month finding her."

Nevena did not look up as the women spoke, keeping her head bent, eyes focused on the messy clump of fabric in her lap. The threads were knotted and snarled, and she yanked at the floss, making a small hole in her practice piece. She smoothed the fabric with her thumb, then bunched the torn portion into her fist.

Mila, her mother's closest friend, was beside her now, holding a silver-handled tray piled high with *medenjaci*. Nevena took two of the honey spice cookies, and when Mila jiggled her loose chin, she took two more. Slid them into the pocket of her skirt. "*Hvala, Tetka* Mila," she said, and the woman replied, "Take as many as you want."

Nevena smiled. She did not tell Mila that these *medenjaci* tasted so much better than her mother's did. Always too much spice. But when Nevena had mentioned this to her mother, Aliz had scowled. "Why not? We want others to know we have, right? That we do not struggle."

"For spices?"

"Of course not." Shaking her head. "You do not understand these ways."

No, she did not. She did not understand how putting too much spice into a cookie and ruining the flavour could mean anything at all.

"They are fresh," Mila said. "Tough now, but they soften as they age. Something like a man."

Nevena nodded, blushed slightly, and with her finger traced the circle of the cookie in her pocket.

Turning, Mila laid the tray on the table, then said to Nevena, *"Slatko?"* She took a small spoonful of the berry preserve from the crystal bowl, washing it down with water from a miniature glass.

"I don't like it."

The woman flounced down on the seat next to her, and Nevena smelled perfume billowing off her clothes. Reminded her of dying gardenias, just before they let loose from the stems, fell to the ground.

"Me neither," Mila whispered. "I do believe wild strawberries make me itch." Red nails scratching the flesh on her neck. "But I must taste, at least. Otherwise I insult your mother."

"She doesn't care."

"Ah, but she does. She knows who samples her *slatko,* who has a second or third taste, and whose spoon is dry."

"Really?"

"I have known Aliz since I was a young *devojka,* and even when she is fast asleep, she is watching everything."

Nevena sighed, starting to bring her needlepoint closer to her body. But Mila picked it up, placing the fabric on her wide lap. "Did you know the underside should be as neat as the side everyone sees? There is pride in that."

"Well, both sides are an equal mess, *Tetka* Mila. There's no pride in that. When *Majko* sees, she'll be furious I wasted the thread."

"No, no. She will understand." Gentle clucking in her throat. "Listen, listen. Your mother likes to think she is a spider." Mila leaned closer to her, sugary breath. "Can you imagine? Born with the knowledge to fashion a web. But, ah, she also had to learn."

Nevena frowned, looked at the floral plates decorating the wall between the two tall windows, the brass cross nailed above the closed door. Sometimes she imagined what life might be like if she had Mila for a mother. Calm and easy. Perhaps she could even talk to her about Dorján, and how to fix the problem that felt as snarled as those threads. Nevena relaxed as the woman took the needle in her fingers, beginning to pick at a strand of floss, drawing it backwards through the fabric.

"You do not help her, do you, Mila?" Aliz clacked her cup against the saucer. "The child will never learn to walk if you keep holding her wrists."

"Nonsense. And you know it."

Another woman, Snežana, stood beside the back of the stove. In early November, extra rugs had been mounted on the walls, but still the room was cooled by drafts. "I am surprised," Snežana said, "that Zsuzsi Szabó still sews. I thought she lost her means."

"Ah, yes." Aliz straightened her back. "There was a whisper of that. A wife whose husband was in the Party. She needed a new machine. There was talk of taking Zsuzsi's and giving it to her."

"Ah. That is the way, sometimes."

"I said to Dragan, I will not hear of it. She is the only reliable seamstress we have for miles."

"Agreed."

"And did he take?"

Aliz smiled and shook her head. "He knows what is good for him. She is the best in the village, yes?"

Snežana nodded and sipped her coffee. "*Tetka* Zsuzsi is making the dress for Jovana, and we could not ask for better."

"Ah, your girl will be a lovely bride."

"Yes, like her mother once was," Snežana replied, grinning. She reached up, patting her burgundy hair.

Aliz yawned, brought the inside of her wrist to her mouth.

"You are tired."

"Sleep did not want me last night."

"Dragan, then?" Shrill chirp.

"No, no." Aliz glared at Snežana, lowered her eyebrows, and angled her head toward Nevena. "My head was aching. I could not rest."

"Ah."

"I was wandering about the house. Looking out at the darkness. And I—I saw something in the road."

"What do you mean? Something."

"Did you see it?"

The women glanced at each other. "See what?"

"The light last night. The light in the road."

"During the storm?"

"Yes, exactly. I had a terrible pain behind my eyes."

"The red river coming?" Mila.

"Ne." Aliz shook her head, brought her hand to her white cheek. "How I wish it away. But it does not listen."

"Surely it was just your head. No one who is right would be out so late."

"No. I do not know. I had such a shiver move right through me. Had the sense it was not from this world. And I started to think of that boy."

Nevena's teeth, which were moving through a cookie, stopped. She stared at her mother, eyes wide.

"You know, the boy who is missing."

"Gitta Kelemen's son?"

"Yes, he." Aliz slid her empty cup and saucer onto the table, glanced at her daughter, then removed her work from the wooden pedestal beside her.

"I heard he is wild. Making his poor mother sick with worry, while he runs around like a heated dog off its chain."

"I heard the very same, Mila."

Mouth suddenly dry, Nevena reached forward for her glass of water, gulped.

"I had this curious sense it was him."

"On the road?"

"Yes. Moving along there." Aliz licked the thread, rolled it between flattened thumb and forefinger. "Searching for something he has lost."

Coughing, coughing now, face pulsing, and Mila patted Nevena's back. "Take it easy, *draga*. Did I not say my *medenjaci* were dry?"

Nevena wiped her watering eyes, stammered, "You can't say that, *Majko*."

"Neva?"

"You can't. You just can't. János is not a thing. He's not a ghost. A dead ghost."

"Well, how do you explain my feeling? You, a foolish child with only sixteen years."

"I don't know." She bit down on her tongue, staring at the curving leg of the table, the tiny wooden claw holding the wooden ball.

"There. You do not know."

Hand in front of her mouth, and she spoke. "Perhaps Gazda László was missing an animal. He was searching the roads."

Thread snapping in her mother's fingers. "Neva, *draga*." Sharp smile. "Please do not challenge me in front of my friends. Is there a reason why you are so adamant? Have you seen the boy since?"

"No, *Majko*."

"Now, now, Aliz. She is so young."

"And there is nothing more offensive, is there? To be young?"

"It is not her fault."

"No, but how it makes me suffer."

Snežana giggled, said, "Soon she will be married off, Aliz. And you will be more than lonely."

The conversation whirled around her, and Nevena was light-headed. She wanted to stand up and walk away, but she felt as if all the water in her body had shifted downward, pooling in her feet, and she was weighted to the spot. When she glanced about the room, none of the women would look her in the eye, and she understood then that this was not the first discussion involving her. Involving János. Likely they spoke of Dorján as well. She could only imagine what they were saying. A tangled line between the daughter of the Komandant and two fatherless Hungarian boys. Now János was missing, and like everyone else, she heard the rumours. Shrunk inside her skin whenever she caught her mother staring at her. Questions on her white tongue that the woman would never ask. Asking would have made things easier. Nevena knew nothing, knew nothing, and would admit that. Could her mother not sense her sadness, her confusion?

"He was a"—Mila cleared her throat, touching Nevena's thigh with warm fingers—"a friend, *draga*?"

"I knew him."

"Of course." Then she moved her hand through the air, cupping it quickly as though catching a fly. "I have a nice boy for you. Someone to meet, that is all."

Nevena shook her head, felt heat in her ears. "I don't want to meet anyone."

"Aliz?"

"You will be respectful, Nevena. When someone extends you an invitation."

"But—"

"Ah, do not fret, *draga moja*. He will take you into Drobnik. You can go to the shops. Eat something tasty. Walk over the bridge. He is a nice Serbian boy, *draga*. Very nice."

Nevena smiled, said, "*Hvala, Tetka* Mila."

"And you will forget all about the other one. He is not for you, that boy. Your mother has told me."

She opened her mouth to reply, but nothing came out. It was useless to try to make them understand when she did not even understand herself. She pictured János, standing in the mouth of a cave. A fire crackled near his feet, and his damp clothes hung to dry on a stick. His grinning face marked with soot. He would be there for an hour or two, enough time to rest. Before he pressed onward, going wherever he wanted to go. That was a possibility. A possibility he owned because he had no father. And because he was a boy.

"I see the problem," Mila said, holding up Nevena's sample. "Your stitches are too tight. You fight the fabric, *draga,* when the fabric is insignificant."

Chapter 18

SKY LIKE BUCKLING STEEL, but Gitta did not stay inside. In fact, the threatening clouds drew her out from her home. She wrapped a shawl over her coat, tying a black scarf over her head. As she walked the road, she passed not a single soul. Which was a reprieve. She would not have had the strength to lift her face, to show her eyes. Those expressions of kindness, words of comfort. Little blasts of sand against her skin. Too many, and she was raw.

She did not rush, maintaining a leisurely gait. Anything at all to nudge time forward. As she walked, she imagined herself moving over time, pushing it backwards with the ball of her foot, leaving it behind her. Since János had left, minutes and seconds had adopted a drunken rhythm. A skipping dance, twirling or waltzing. Stumbling over themselves. No longer could she trust in time's linear reliability. Instead, she was certain, it enjoyed torturing her.

Once she reached the cemetery on the edge of the village, she stopped. It had been months since her last visit. She was not a woman who made a habit of visiting the dead.

The cemetery was a gently sloping hill covered in grass. Even though the grass was pale and stunted, she could clearly tell that it had been cut in recent weeks. People still tended to the grounds.

There were rows and rows of crosses, once neat, but no longer. As the ground froze and thawed over the years, many of the older ones had shifted, leaning their heads this way and that. Gitta had the impression that several of them were peeking out from behind their sisters, young children wanting to be seen.

Imre's marker, still relatively new compared with many others, stood defiant and upright. Even though every monument was essentially the same, she found it easily. Eighteen steps north, six west, thirteen north again. His place was directly to her left.

She did not bend onto her knees or lower her head. If someone were to see her, she did not want to appear as though she were praying. Instead she stood quietly, brushing his engraved name with her gloved hands.

She thought she had grown used to Imre's absence, but it was only delusion. With János gone, the desire to have her husband home was so commanding, it might well have possessed her. As she cleaned the cross, she imagined it, the evening her son had not returned, playing out so differently.

As she paced, Imre would have slid behind her. Used his wide hands to grapple the worry seated on her back. Settled her in a chair, something sweet sitting on the arm. Then he would have gone to search, cutting through the night, holding a wide bowl to the rain the next day, mirroring the afternoon sunlight back to its glowing face. No force of nature would have prevented him from finding János. The child would have been home before Imre would rest.

How cruel her mind could be. Offering translucent fantasy, a soothing imposter. Imre had given up on his own life. Why did she think he would fight for her son when he had been unwilling to fight for himself? He had left her alone. And now her dead husband lay sleeping beneath her feet.

::::

DURING THE WAR, IMRE was required to leave his work at the sausage shop. He never admitted how much he missed working there, with the *Schwabs,* Frederic and his brother. Preparing cuts of meat, making sausages. There was joy in those simple tasks. Honourable, honest work.

She could not remember the exact date when he began working for the Nazis. One day seemed to flow into the next, and when he arrived home, his face held a smile. He was happy to be home with his wife and son. When she questioned him, he only told her he was aiding in translation. Nothing sinister, he insisted. Just one meeting after the other. Helping them with investigations. Making sure information they retrieved was accurate. The Nazis wanted nothing more from him than his proficient language skills. With the blink of an eye, he could twist one language into another. So many tongues inside a single mouth. All learned when he was a boy, as he moved through the village listening closely as groups of men spoke. Words, sticking to him, like metal shavings to a magnet.

He maintained a proud front at the beginning, but gradually fatigue crept into his bones, and his face grew gaunt as his appetite diminished. She began to notice grey whiskers sprouting from his moustache, and almost overnight his hair had thinned. When he stood directly underneath a light, she could see the greasy skin of his scalp. He stopped playing with János, tossing the boy in the air or pinning him to the ground with a single large hand. And when János tormented him, he gazed at the boy through moist eyes, said, "Another time, *szívem. Apa* is tired."

"Talk to me," she would say, and he would only shake his head, replying, "I talk enough," and stare at the blackened glass in the door of the stove. Imre was good at keeping secrets.

She remembered only a single time when he confessed to the hardship.

She had baked beets in the oven, and when they cooled, she peeled the skin onto a piece of brown paper. Rinsing each globe under water, she chopped it coarsely in her hand, the knife coming through the flesh of the vegetable, pressing against her palm. The deep blue-red colour coated her fingers, the skin of her hands, bright spatter on her wrists and forearms. Surely there must be magic inside something that pulls this colour from brown earth.

Imre came up behind her, and she swayed her hips from side to side, expecting him to notice. Hoping he would reach out and grab her backside, pinch just to the point of pain. She waited to feel his mouth on the back of her neck, hands roaming over her hip bones, dipping downward, rubbing her through her dress like he used to do. But instead he drew in a sharp breath. And she dropped the knife into the bowl.

Eyelids rimmed with pink, mouth hanging open. "What are you doing?" He blinked and blinked, but never closed his mouth.

"Beet root. A salad. Something to make you strong."

"I…I—" Stammering. "I do not want it in the house. I do not want this coming into the house."

"A salad?"

"Throw it out," he said.

"Imre, you are crazy. Of course I will not. If you do not care for what I prepare, János and I will eat it ourselves."

"Get it out," he repeated. Words squeaking out through clenched jaw. "Wash it off your hands."

She laughed a little. "You have grown stranger and stranger, *kedvesem*." Then she picked up the knife from the bowl, began slicing through another root. "Since you took that job."

"Have I," he replied, but it was not a question.

"Yes. Why do you not quit?"

"Quit."

"Yes. Go back to Frederic. At the store. Surely he still has a place for you. Let the soldiers find someone else who speaks every language so perfectly."

He was quiet behind her, and she could feel something building. Words rolling up from deep inside of him. Bursting outward into the room.

"I do not have a choice!" he screamed, and spittle struck her cheek. "Do you understand me? I do not have a choice. I listen and I tell them what is said. That is all I do. But I have to watch. You know that? I have to watch how they tear the words from mouths. Mouths that do not want to co-operate. Mouths that are clamped shut. Mouths that are wet with fear. They will do anything, do you hear me? To get those words. I watch, I watch, I watch. Gitta. I wait for the words. I plead inside my head, just speak, please, just speak. Just speak. Just speak! Stop the screaming. The crying. Give me your words. Your words. And let it be over."

"Imre!"

"I do not have a soul for this. To witness this suffering. I am slowly, slowly, slowly going insane."

Then his hand whipped around her, into the sink, and he gripped the full bowl and threw it into the room. Splintering porcelain, neat red cubes in flight, striking wall and floor and stovetop, liquid spray reaching every corner.

Shock made her bring her hands to her face, leaving brilliant stains on her cheeks and lips. Imre stared at her, confused eyebrows pressed together, eyes narrowed in a nest of wrinkles. Fingers shaking, and ignoring the mess on her own skin, she reached out to grasp him. To hold him and calm him. But he backed away from her, shards of the broken bowl sticking into the soles of his shoes, and his reverse steps scraping and crunching all the way down the hallway.

"Imre," she called, as she tiptoed through the mess. "Wait, Imre." Even when she heard the front door open and close, she did not stop calling to him. "Please, Imre. Please, my love. Let me listen. To you, Imre. To your words. Let me listen to you."

:::::

SHE GLANCED UPWARD, THE sky continuing to darken over the cemetery. She could not grasp if it was morning or afternoon, or if evening was about to descend. Yes, her suspicions were right. Time was playing with her. Taunting her.

A deal, she thought. Could she manage it? She stomped her feet gently, soft grass beneath the soles of her shoes. If she admitted everything that pushed her husband to his grave, maybe she could make a deal. A handful of miniscule changes. That was all she was asking. The slightest of alterations. *Kérlek?*

In an instant, her world would involute, then unfurl, a tongue of spring green. She would no longer be there, icy drops striking the top of her head. Alone and standing on top of her dead husband. Pretending to tidy his grave, pulling long grass, while Guilt wrapped his fingers around her chest, squeezed. Ah, Guilt. Oldest man, but his spindly strength never faded.

"I lost him, Imre," she whispered. "How could I lose our son?"

She was aware of her voice in her ears and looked about. Noticed someone much farther back in the cemetery. Standing there, dressed in funeral tones. Nearly invisible against the dull sky.

She pinched the arm of the cross. "It did not happen overnight, Imre. No, no. I lost him long before he ran away."

A pause. She had not expected a reply, had she? Some sort of sign to say he was listening and that he was with her? She was not surprised by his blaming silence. Imre had not spoken a word to her since he had died.

Glancing up again, she saw that the person, a man, had begun weaving through the markers. This way and that. Stepping lightly on the grass, crossing over the dead. Coming toward her. Or so she believed.

She guessed it was the Komandant, but Gitta did not wait to greet him. She knew he would offer to help. He would be willing to lift some of the burden from her bones, and at this moment, she could not allow that. That burden was the only thing weighing her down.

Lowering her head, she turned on her heel and exited the cemetery. Rushed home and when she checked the rooms, discovering them quiet, she moved toward the clock. While she was away, the hands had been sleeping. Time, that indolent bastard, had barely moved.

Chapter 19

HE DID NOT COME to their house as her father might have wanted. Instead Nevena took a bus from Bregalnica and met the boy in front of the shop in Drobnik that sold fine-grained breads and *dobos torta* and nut roll and cherry *piskóta*. She had been to *Branka Poslastačarnica* many times before with her mother, and when she was younger, her mother always bought her a small drink of apple juice sold by a brown-skinned vendor on the street. Served from a wooden cask, contents warmed by the summer sun.

Nose kissing the window, she looked at everything displayed on metal shelves. Swirls of chocolate, tawny layers of hardened sugar sliced into neat triangles, golden sponge with vanilla cream. Her mouth watered. So long since they had purchased from this store, and her mother in their kitchen was unable to replicate the flavours. Nevena, of course, was helpless. Having failed continually on nearly every domestic chore.

"What do you like?"

A voice in her ear, deeper than was natural. She straightened, turned, and touched the tip of her cold nose.

"My name's Petar," he said. Here he was, the Serbian boy.

"I know." Acidic squirt in her stomach. "I mean, *zdravo*, I'm Nevena."

"Such a beautiful name. A marigold."

"How do you know that?"

"My *baka*'s also a Nevena."

"Strange."

"Not really. It's not an uncommon name."

"Ah, I guess." Another squirt, central nerve tingling.

"Well," he gestured to the glowing windows, "what do you like? *Branka* is the best."

"Nothing. No. Nothing." Her mother had warned her to be polite and personable. "Trust me," she had said, "if *Tetka* Mila says he is a nice boy, he is a nice boy." Then as she rubbed colour into Nevena's thin lips and tugged a frumpy felt hat onto her head, she hissed, "Do not embarrass me. A good family from Drobnik."

Though he looked at her as if he had never seen her, she recognized him. They went to the same school, but he was a class ahead. Up close, he was more handsome than she had expected. Cold blue eyes, narrow face, and a tall, slender body. He had black hair that, curiously, did not move in the wind, as though he had combed sugar water through it. He grinned at her, revealing crowded teeth. When he dove his hands into the pockets of his ironed trousers, she could hear change jingling.

Finger in the air. "Well, in that case I will buy two hot *čokolade*, and if you don't want, I will drink them both."

Inside the store, the smell of melted chocolate was too much. She stood behind Petar as a young woman in a stained apron barked orders and ladled two spoonfuls of hot chocolate into white cups. He carried the miniature cups to a small table, marble top, and instead of sitting across from her, he pulled his wobbly chair closer. If they were the arms on a stopped clock, they would be separated by only a couple of hours.

Removing her hat from her head, she tucked it underneath the table onto another chair.

"So," he said. "You are here." He bit the fingertips of his gloves, tugged them off, and arranged them neatly on the table. He seemed to take some satisfaction when one leather hand rested precisely on top of the other.

"Yes, of course." She sipped the drink. It was sweet and almost pudding thickness, so much flavour she nearly sneezed.

"You have *čokolade* on your nose."

"Sorry," she replied, blushing.

He laughed, then ran a single finger, thin like an insect's leg, over her hand. "My mother told me you were pretty, but I didn't believe her."

"Ah." She did not know how to respond, and she wiped the tip of her nose, glancing into her cup. Felt ashamed she had finished the drink so quickly. In a tumbling blurt, she announced, "I can't cook and I can't do crewel. I don't see why I need to know how. I plan to work at a real job. Not roll around inside a house all day long."

Another laugh, somehow muffled inside his mouth. "Pretty and opinionated. My mother is prone to exaggeration, but for once she was accurate."

Redness staining her cheeks and neck again. Her skin barely had a moment to lose the heat before he said something else to coax it back. But she did not find the attention unpleasant. Not like János, full of boyish antics and false charm. Launching into a back flip to slow her walking, or bringing her limp flowers stolen from the cemetery. Over the summer he had pleaded with her, "Let me sketch you," pad and pencil in hand, his hat skewed on his head. Finally she agreed, and he positioned her over a small puddle. Midafternoon, and the sun was bright and angled, and he stood a few feet ahead of her, pencil barely gracing the page. She was flattered but could not understand why he never examined her face, instead focusing on the still water of the puddle. "Are you almost finished?" she had growled, and he had replied, "Ah yes, ah yes." Only when she bowed her head did she see the reflection. The crystal clear water like a mirror, showing her skinny thighs and strip of beige underwear. Everything revealed, the summer heat having driven the damp cotton fabric into the various folds between her legs. She ran at him, tore the pad from his hands, saw the meaningless squiggles, and flung the paper into the puddle.

Petar acted like a young man, not a boy being dragged toward adulthood. He moved with precise and natural gestures. Confident in himself, but not cocky. She straightened her back, lifting her head. "Thank you."

He yawned slightly, looking out the window at the people milling past, children pausing to stare in at the desserts. "I'm going soon."

"Going?"

"Of course. I am nearly eighteen."

"Ah, yes. I forgot. Are you nervous?" She had altered her voice ever so slightly, slowing her speech, pronouncing her words with extra care.

"Don't be silly. It's my duty to serve my country, and I'm as able as anyone."

When he reached to hold the edge of the table, she saw his wrist, white and slender. Feminine, almost. She could imagine it snapping under the weight of a shovel of gravel. Calluses quickly making homes on his hands.

"When do you leave?"

"Late spring. After I finish the year of school. I received my letter only yesterday."

"Ah."

Tugging at the cuff of his sweater, he murmured, "It's only a year, and then my service is over. It'd be nice to know someone was waiting for me."

Not knowing what else to do, she smiled. Then, without hesitation, he took her hand in his, and as he held it in his lap, he flicked her short thumbnail with his own. Clicking, clicking. As if testing its strength. *Do not embarrass me.* Her mother's words inside her head, and she let him hold her hand, felt the warm sweat on his palm. When her nail began to ache, she smiled again and eased her hand out from underneath his. She picked up her cup, nearly empty, and without considering her appearance, she pushed the tiny cup to her face, licked away the sweetness that clung to the sides. When she caught him staring at her with amusement, he smirked, said, "Ah, you like it after all."

"Yes, yes. Very much." Cup clanging to the table. "Bad habit."

He pointed to the edge of his jaw, brushed away nothing. Perhaps an itch. She did not understand why he was patting his face while staring at hers. At once, he was incredibly close, she was able to see flaking skin inside his wrinkled ear. Before she could lean away, his mouth was on her chin, lips open, sucking slightly on her flesh. A cleaning prod of his tongue, and she froze in place, squeaked, "Ah."

"No need for a napkin," he said as he sat back.

With the sudden surprise, warmth rushed in contrary directions, to her cheeks and between her legs. Unexpected wetness. She crossed her legs, squeezed, then peeked at the other patrons, but no one seemed to care. As her chin dried, she caught the faint smell of his saliva on her face. Sour and sugary at the same time. "Thanks?" she managed, noticed his lips were slightly puckered, as though he was ready to do it again.

"Are you ready?"

She hesitated. The strange knot lodged between her legs had not yet unravelled. And she was nervous it might show. Just last week she had heard a discussion on that very predicament. Her mother had nagged her to spend more time with other girls, and with a little ef-fort she fell in with a group led by Jasna Ković. A short girl with curly hair and a chest wide enough to hold a shelf of figurines. Jasna's father was an electrician, but he was in possession of a wide selection of university texts. Some biology books contained detailed descriptions of body parts, accompanying photos of naked adults with black bars over their eyes.

A thick stench of bleach, but four or five of them jammed into the wooden stall of the washroom, while Jasna explained in technical terms the physical properties of lust. Swellings and protrusions. Oils and human spice that soap won't remove. Boys know, she had ex-plained to those gathered. "If your knees don't touch when you walk, they know you're ready." "Ready for what?" another asked shyly. "To be mounted, stupid." A chorus of "Ahs." Then a tiny voice, "What if your legs are bowed?" And Jasna replied, "Then you're probably a whore. Wanting it all the time." As this newfound knowledge was ac-cepted, several girls had begun to snicker, and one had begun to cry.

"Well?" Petar said. "Are you waiting for someone better looking to come along?"

In spite of her nervousness, she giggled and stood up slowly. She smoothed the back of her long coat, and she was grateful for the cover. She tugged the hat on over her hair and slid by his chest as he held open the door. Bell jingling above her head.

As the afternoon passed, they strolled in and out of many stores. The stock was sparse, but there were still women milling about, touching the bolts of damask or purchasing stockings. In a clothing store, Petar selected a thin red scarf, finely knit, and wrapped it around Nevena's neck. "Something to remind you of me," he said as he pulled his wallet from his back pocket, silver chain linking it to his belt. She picked up the end of the scarf, bringing it to her nose. The fabric smelled of smoke and dust, and it had likely been hanging on the rack forever. Most people could not afford a single luxury, and here she was with something new and beautiful wrapped around her neck.

Back in the street, a light snow began to fall. Petar reached into his pocket, pulled his gloves onto his hands, looked at the sky. Shrugged. "What to do now?"

"How about the bridge?"

"For?"

"To stand there, so high up. Nothing beneath us."

He frowned, folding his arms over his chest. "The point?"

"No point. Come on," she said, her confidence building. "The view is beautiful. You'll see."

They walked through narrow streets, passing old buildings with clean windows and arched frames. In places, bullet wounds still marred the plaster, dark holes surrounded by a web of cracks. Glowing storefronts, men crowding the door of the snack shop, the chemical smell of liquor mingling with their joviality, billowing out on the air. On the outskirts of Drobnik, they passed block housing, still under construction, simple flat facades, cement cubes. Snowflakes fell, stuck to her coat and hat.

"Let's race," she said and dashed ahead. She expected him to follow, but as she neared the bridge, she turned and saw him lagging behind. Watching him dragging his feet tightened a stitch in her heart. She suddenly thought of János. Where was he now? He would have raced with her. Yes. Right up to the end. And then he would have let her win.

Chapter 20

STANDING IN FRONT OF the *Schuster*'s shop in Drobnik, Dorján watched the man fix a lady's shoe into place, then tap, tap, tap a replacement heel onto the base with an undersized hammer. The store seemed oddly empty, no shoes on the shelves, no cuts of leather piled on the table. But still the man worked steadily, his fingers rough and knobby from years of pinching leather. On his wide back he wore a brindled sheepskin vest.

Flecks of snow fell onto Dorján's black hair, his winter coat, and he brought a bare hand, numb from the cold, up to the glass. The man heard the faint squeak when he touched the window, looking up from his work, grinning. "Come in, come in," he mouthed, brown cigarette dancing on his bottom lip. But Dorján shook his head, turned, and walked away.

Though he had spent hours in the shop when he was young, Dorján did not want to talk to the shoemaker. He did not want those simple memories to be tainted by another layer, by a more mature understanding of the man and his work. As it was, when Dorján held those moments aloft, they were perfection. Just the three of them— Dorján, his father, and the *Schuster*. Once his father was gone, Dorján did his best to avoid the shoemaker. If his toes pressed against the front of his shoes, he traced his feet on pattern paper, giving it to his grandmother. He had the sense that continuing the relationship would only poison the past. What if the shoemaker was dull or belligerent? The magic would quickly dissipate.

Every month it was the same. As soon as he could toddle, Dorján followed behind his father, walking the narrow stone streets through Drobnik. Before they left, his mother always kissed his father full on the lips, saying, "Something nice. Yes, something nice for my feet." Inside the shop, his father hoisted him onto the high stool near the massive machine that sewed leather, and Dorján sat still while the two men laughed, talked about women and work, raised their thumb-sized glasses into the air. A light clink, and they threw back their heads, drank colourless liquor. *"Prost,"* they said, smacking their stomachs. Whenever Dorján eyed the bottle, the shoemaker reached over with his bear hand, ruffled Dorján's hair. "One sip and you will not grow another inch, *fiam!*" Then, every single visit, the old shoemaker reached into the chest pocket of his leather apron, feigning surprise when he discovered a piece of chewing gum wrapped in waxed paper. Dorján would settle on the stool, gnawing and gnawing on the gum until his jaw throbbed and the gum eventually disintegrated, fragments lost in his cheeks, underneath his tongue.

Over the years, as Dorján grew older, the laughter slowly receded. His father and the shoemaker began to talk more often in hushed tones, and as one visit turned into the next, their conversations grew more furtive and mysterious. Dorján longed to somehow be enveloped into their discussions. He could not understand the topics, but he was certain those words resided entirely within the male domain. No mention of such things when friends met in the streets or around the dinner table while they ate goulash and *nokedli* by the spoonful. The murmurs remained exclusively inside the small shop, and though Dorján wanted to speak, he had nothing to say about the strange countries they discussed, different sides of an enormous fight, a man named Hitler.

Those visits with the shoemaker arose from a curious hobby. When his father was not at the hospital, he haunted the dimly lit shed behind their home. In his free time, the slender man glued and scraped and sanded wooden high heels. He would hold them up to the window, a heel in either hand, to compare. And then he would close his eyes and stroke them, telling Dorján, "Light may lie, my son. But touch knows the truth." If he was not satisfied, he would re-clamp the form of wood, and whittle and sand until both heels were identical. Careful not to soil his clothing, his father would dip each heel in stain, rubbing it with a cloth until it shone. Then lay it on the bench, next to its curving sister. A neat row, delicate heels that always reminded Dorján of eagles' claws.

During the summer months, Dorján and his father sold the high heels directly to customers at a booth in the market in Drobnik. Women would come from all over and, with flapping arms, describe the shoe and the colour of the leather, buttons or no buttons, strap or strapless. His father would exit the booth, examining each lady's leg. They would murmur, "Ah, Dr. Szabó," and with a subtle pinch of wool, hike their skirts ever so slightly so that he might appreciate their particular calves. Back in the booth, his surgeon's fingers slid over the neatly arranged heels, each pair bound together by a bow of beige yarn, until he announced the appropriate match.

In the winter, the temporary stands were dismantled, the stone street empty. But the women still craved their shoes, and Dr. Szabó had made a bargain with the cobbler. He would supply an abundance of heels, if the cobbler would produce beautiful shoes for his wife. Once a month, Dorján and his father would arrive with a small sack of heels. Sometimes a pair or two, sometimes more. And they would stay and visit, and occasionally, his father would leave with a cardboard box under his arm. Jauntily strolling home, he would say to Dorján, "Now that, my son, that is a man you can trust."

Right before they arrived, he would hand the parcel to Dorján. In through the door, Dorján would press his knees together, hold it out to her, and without even glancing into his wide eyes, she would tug the box from his hands, tear it open. Slide her long toes into the openings and dance about the room. Squealing, squealing, hugging his father, while Dorján stood waiting, his legs aching as the bones tried to touch. "My feet," she would cry, "will have the envy of every woman in Drobnik." And Dorján wished his father had never made him carry in the gift, had never inserted him into their ritual. He recognized his parents as a nicely balanced married couple, and he, an extra weight.

After his father died, his mother wore the same pair of shoes over and over again. She tossed the others into the cupboard, and whenever the door swung on its hinge, she cursed them quietly. Stared at the heap of shoes as though she resented them. Hated them, almost. As though they were withholding something that could not be returned. He wondered if she somehow blamed them for his father's death. The plane, whirring overhead, letting loose a dark mass that sailed through the warm air without a sound, spinning, spinning, and landing so cleverly on the marked spot. Partly that, perhaps, but later Dorján realized it was money. Money spent on frivolities instead of saved. His mother tumbled, a painful and depressing fall from shaky privilege toward abject poverty. He quickly went from living a comfortable life in Drobnik with his parents to being an orphaned boy, holding his grandmother's fat elbow as the two of them waited in long lines for coffee and low-grade meat.

Dorján now looked down at his shoes, laces tattered and knotted and ready to burst. But he would not trouble his grandmother for new ones. Besides, these days such things as laces and buttons were hard to come by. He thought of the coins then. And János, with his greedy, selfish dreams. Even a fraction of those riches could have made his life easier. Made his grandmother's life easier. She was a woman who had always made do with next to nothing. Would accept what was left at the bottom of a bag or barrel. When was the last time she held something new in her hands? After so many years of being almost-brothers, how could János do that to him?

With angry strides, Dorján walked through the town square, crossing behind the enormous statue of a dragon. Head gazing toward the sky, discolouration streaking away from its eyes as though the coppery creature had been weeping. He passed the storefronts, some glowing, some darkened and closed. Several of the buildings were degrading, painted plaster curling away from the structures, flakes of yellow or orange or dirty white.

At the edge of town, he stepped onto the bridge, gripped the icy rails and peered over into the dark blue water. Tumbling and foaming, the river cut a sharp trail through the land, slowly dissolving the pale walls of limestone that bordered each side. Dorján could not recall the old bridge, the one that had been destroyed. This one had been constructed almost overnight, and it looked practically identical to the old one. If evidence of the debris did not linger below, sticking out of the sandy shores of the river, a newcomer might never know the difference.

All the walking helped. During the past couple of weeks, when he was not in school or helping his grandmother, he walked into Drobnik every afternoon and wandered along the narrow streets. He passed many people wearing grey and black wool, hunched against the cold wind, but he did not look anyone in the eye. Not trusting his tongue, he spoke to no one, keeping his knitted hat tugged down to just above his eyes.

His legs were tired now, and he had walked the anger out of them. Sour sadness was beginning to settle in its place. For the first time in his life, Dorján understood what János meant when he said he could not think. Though János claimed the barriers came from the outside world, Dorján had fashioned his own brick walls inside his head. All he could do was slam against them, and they would not budge. He could not fathom his friend's betrayal. Could not find a way to accept it. Dorján did not really care about the coins, the money. That was nothing more than a skin on the surface. No, it was so much more. By leaving, János had cleared his throat of any connection and spat on the plans they had forged in their youth. They were to surge into adulthood as a team. They had promised each other they would stand strong together. Getting a solid education. Everyone would know them. Two engineers. Gitta *néni* and his *nagyanya* would marvel at their sons. Dorján and János. Contributing more than anyone might have expected from two poor village boys without fathers.

Dorján leaned back against the railing, lit a cigarette, and pulled the heat into his chest. Dry snow twisted over the bridge, gathering in crooks and corners and against the sides of his shoes. Slowly a car moved past him, an old metal horse driving off the bridge and onto the road. Dorján strained to see the faces of each occupant. A man in a rounded hat driving, a female passenger with dark red lips, a fur collar on her coat and a beige hat, an older man in the backseat, and a young boy with his feet up, sleeping on a blanket beside him. For some silly reason, he thought that János would be tucked inside the warm car, on his way home. Back to his aching mother, ready to push putty into the cracks of her heart.

He tossed the stub of his cigarette over the bridge, and the wind sucked it in through the arches. In the corner of his eye, he saw a flicker of red, then turned to find Nevena walking toward him. Scarf wrapped around her neck the colour of poppies. Her head was bent against the cold, and her hands were deep in the pockets of her coat. He noticed she was wearing a proper hat, something he had not seen before. Murky green felt. And he wondered if it was new. Like the scarf.

As she approached, his body lightened, and his mouth soon sported a sheepish grin. In school, he had barely spoken to her. Felt as though the squinting eyes of Takáts and Beštić were watching him. Waiting for him to falter and tell them everything about János and the coins. So he simply swam in the mornings, did his work, passed in his assignments, disappeared during the morning recess and the short break for lunch, and swam again in the afternoons. He avoided everyone, even Nevena.

But here she was, heading straight toward him. Had she followed him? That would be just like her, he assumed. Quietly keeping track of his wanderings, waiting for the right time to say hello. He could talk to her now. Out here, standing on this bridge. Nothing but a lazy river tumbling beneath him, and the dreary sky above. There was air to breathe and space to move his arms and legs, and he could look her in the face now and speak.

Chapter 21

GITTA NEVER TOLD ANYONE, not even the Komandant when he came to see her the second time. He asked her if she had noticed anything strange about János, and she flushed at the thought of it, but shook her head. Said, "I am a weary woman, Komandant, and he is a sixteen-year-old boy. Everything he does is strange."

"Of course," he replied. "I remember well those days." Then he patted her hand gently.

She noticed the softness of his fingers and brought her hands to her lap, rolling them inside the fabric of her apron. "You are very kind."

"It will get easier," he said. "It really will. We eventually grow up."

He stood, insisted she remain in her chair, and she did. Some part of her wanted him to return to his seat, sit with her in silence. Hold the ache together. It was so heavy and damp, this unknown. Worse than any pain she had ever experienced before. Witnessing her mother's illness. Losing Imre. Betraying Anneliese. Nothing could compare.

The Komandant would stay with her if she asked. Help her. But she could not open her mouth.

As he walked toward the door, he glanced over his shoulder. Nodded. She would not meet his eyes, instead staring at the window.

Remembered that last morning. Watching János getting ready for school.

He had left his bedroom door open while he washed. She was about to reprimand him over his lack of modesty, but when she saw his naked body, she seized. He stood on a towel near his table, dipped a cloth into a bowl and moved it into his armpit, up over his shoulder. She breathed through her mouth, slowly took the picture in. Cloth slid over his neck, drips of water falling down his pale back. How his shape was identical to Imre's, his trim waist, broad back, short, strong legs. Even though he never trained a day, he had still grown the body of a gymnast. She stared at him, her son, standing there inside the body of her late husband. And she felt such a confusing desire boil inside her lower stomach. Not for what others might imagine. No, no, nothing of the sort. Just a simple wish, a rancid wish, to be loved.

He moved the cloth, dropping it into the bowl. Then in the bright light, she noticed a mark on his back, just below his shoulder blade. Red and swollen, two C shapes, one hovering above the other. She recognized it instantly. A bite mark. When she and Imre were much, much younger, he often pushed his teeth into her shoulder while he rocked on top of her. Not so powerful as to break the skin, but enough to frighten and excite her. Drive her toward that sweaty spasm. For a day or two, she would be aware of that sore place underneath her dress. Something exotic on her body, a sort of gypsy tattoo. Until it faded, and she could tempt Imre into marking her again.

But now, here was a sign on her son's back. And Gitta could only imagine it had come from a girlfriend or perhaps a woman. She was certain someone had done that to him during a moment of entanglement. What other explanation could there be? The very sight of it sent a shock to her wrists and ankles, making those clusters of bones vibrate unpleasantly. She stepped away from the open door, floated down the hallway, and leaned against the wall. Turned her face so the plaster cooled her cheek.

She realized something at that moment. That her son was no longer a boy. In the days that followed, she realized something else. Outside of what he ate for dinner and what he wore to school, she knew practically nothing at all about his life.

:::::

BARELY A BRUSH AT the front door. Even though it happened many years ago, Gitta remembered that sound so clearly. It had pricked her ears, a rustling, like a fresh straw broom against dry wood. When she looked back on it now, she could still recall standing behind the door. Hearing that sound. And she was filled with the eerie sense that whoever was on the other side was going to do her harm. Was going to change everything. But of course she did not listen to her nerves, her stomach. She chastised herself for being foolish. The war had ended, and she reasoned her stomach was unaware of these changes, had not had time to settle. She hauled open the door, morning sunlight striking her eyes. Mist rose off the damp dirt road.

A girl stood there, dressed in too many layers, small leather suitcase and a longer wooden box near her feet. Her mouth smiled, but her blue eyes were flat and nervous. Gitta felt an unnatural warmth rolling off the girl, only eighteen or nineteen years old. She knew the girl was a *Schwab,* and she wondered why the girl had not gone, had not left Bregalnica like so many other German families had done when the Nazis retreated. Gitta had the sudden urge to close the door, pretend she had seen nobody, but instead she leaned her head toward the *Schwab,* said, "Yes?"

The war was over, but there was no return to normal. No one even remembered normal. How they had all lived together, worked together, before lines were scraped in the earth. And now, everything was shifting, so quietly. A different kind of uncertainty. It was happening mostly at night. Many of the *Schwabs* who owned land and stores and homes, handed down to them by their father's fathers. Women who had been born in those homes, grown up and given birth in those homes to sons and daughters. Deep, deep roots, hacked off at the surface. So many gone. Still more leaving. Some disappearing. Fields unharvested, tools still hanging in the sheds, supplies left in the cellar barrels. Meat turned to string in iron pots, infant clothes folded on shelves, sewing machines abandoned, fabric still underneath the needles. Gitta saw ghosts moving along the streets in the blackness of night. Many evenings it rained, and sitting inside her home, window cracked an inch, she could hear no voices, just the soles of shoes gathering up the muck.

At least they were not forced from Bregalnica. They were not pushed out. Not like in the cities. Gathered up and shipped out like mislabelled parcels. They had the choice to stay if they wished. But still, many neighbours left quietly. Receded with the Nazi soldiers as they returned home.

Soon, she was aware of the whispers, other faces, other families slipping quietly into place. Picking up the shovels and the unmade dresses, and without hesitation living inside these pre-made lives. Balance, someone with authority explained. *You will forget what is gone.* Newcomers will help to achieve a balance to our population.

"Ist Imre zu Hause?"

At the mention of her husband's given name, Gitta bit her lip. "Imre?"

"Ja."

There was still time. She could lie, turn the girl away. Surely this pretty ghost was lost. Did not belong at her door. But again, Gitta's mouth did not obey, and she said, "Kelemen Úr is here, yes. Come in." She stepped aside then, and the girl plucked her case and box from the stone step, entering Gitta's home.

Imre was behind Gitta then, his face serious, and he ushered the girl into the front room, closing the door. Gitta pressed her ear against the wood, but they spoke in rapid-fire German and the language, once erotic when whispered by Imre, now sounded guttural and foreign. The girl was pleading, crying slightly. But everything was muffled, and Gitta was able to understand close to nothing.

Movement in the room, chair legs scraping. Gitta rushed down the hallway into the kitchen, plunged her hands into the sink's icy water, busied herself by washing the same dish over and over. She did not have to turn around to know Imre was leaning against the door frame.

"Gitta," he said. "Listen."

"To what?" She turned the plate over, running a knitted cloth over the rim.

"To me."

She paused before she said, "Why is she here, Imre? Where is her family?"

"They have gone."

"And she has not?"

A moment stretched. Then, "She will stay with us. For a short time. She will help with the boy. With the kitchen. Whatever you need."

Gitta held the plate with both hands then, pressing her wide thumbs into the porcelain. Pictured it snapping with the force. "I need no help. Now or ever."

"You will find something for her. You will."

"Imre! Who is she?"

"We will talk later."

She released the plate, let it clang on the bottom of the basin, and turned to face him. "Later? What stupidity. Please, Imre."

"Let me think, will you?"

"Think? You have brought a stranger into our home and ask for time to think? Am I not your wife?"

But he raised his hands, letting them drop. She saw the thinness in his arms. Frame of a skeleton now, when once he could hold all his weight upside down on a single gymnast's palm. "Enough," he said softly. "That is enough." Then without looking her in the eye, he turned and walked away.

Gitta leaned against the counter, folded one arm across her waist, brought the nails on her other hand to her teeth. How much longer would she have to feel like this? That the outside was no longer the outside. Walls and doors and sealed windows meant nothing. Sorrow would always find the crack, in roofs or door frames or human hearts. And whittle its way inward.

Yet she had invited the girl in, hadn't she? Stepped aside and allowed her passage.

The girl crouched now on the floor with János. Her coat removed, folded over the arm of a chair. An old wooden puzzle spread on the floor between them, a simple puzzle the boy had done a thousand times. Outgrown years ago. Ridiculous girl, trying to cajole him into play. But Gitta soon realized it was not the girl who was cajoling, but

János, mugging for attention. He grinned at her, waiting for her to feign surprise each time he placed one correctly.

She plucked up a piece, shook it inside the ball of her two palms, handed it to him.

He slid it easily into its spot, told her quietly in practised German, "I am not easily fooled."

"I can only assume," she replied and touched the fringe of his hair just above his ear.

:::

THAT NIGHT GITTA SLID across the sheet toward her husband, fluffed straw crinkling beneath her. She slid her leg against his, ran the tip of her finger over his chest, felt his nipples harden against the cloth of his pajamas. Then she pressed herself into his side, and moved her hand downward, reaching and cupping him between his legs, rocking her strong hand gently back and forth until she felt him beginning to change.

"Imre," she whispered.

"I know, I know." His voice low and deep and soft.

"We are together."

"Yes, yes. I'm sorry for that, *szívem*. I needed time to think."

"Have I broken your trust? Ever?" She shifted her hand, allowing her fingers to glide from hip bone to hip bone, rising and dipping over the hardness.

"Of course not."

"Who is she?"

"She is Anneliese. Frederic's daughter."

"From the store? Where you worked before the war?"

"Yes."

"I would not have recognized her. She has grown."

"Fifteen years. Still a child."

"But they have left, Imre. They've closed the store and gone. Why is she still here?"

He turned toward her, brushed the hair from her face. "Love."

"What do you mean?"

"She is in love."

"With?"

"Sàndor's son. Tomi."

"Ah," Gitta said, her hand stilled. A *Schwab* in love with a Hungarian boy. "That will be difficult now."

"Yes."

"But why not go to him? Why here?"

"I do not know everything. She was very upset when we spoke. She just wants a chance, she says. To see what will happen. To see if it will work."

"Ah."

"But do not you remember, Gitta? Don't you remember those days? You and me and there was nothing else? So young, so young, almost without skin, we were. Everything was simple then." His fingers moved over her collarbones, and he unbuttoned her nightdress.

"I remember, Imre. I do."

He pulled her nightdress up over her thighs, while she undid the bow just below his navel, tugging at the cord to loosen the band of his bottoms. He moved onto her, and she opened her legs, bent her knees upward, and angled her hips. Slowly he found her, and she touched the length of his spine, pressing her heels into the backs of his legs. They were nearly the same height, a perfect fit, but in the months that had passed he had grown slimmer, weaker. His body felt a little unfamiliar, but still, it was his. It was his. As he pushed, he held his weight on his elbows, and she felt his shoulders shaking.

Even though everything had changed, was still changing, they were still essentially the same. He was the boy who had danced among the gypsies, and she was the girl who had wished for a kiss. Such pure joy inside that moment, she very nearly cried out.

That night they slept back to back, soles of her feet pressed against the dry soles of his. In some girlish way, an immature way, she would imagine that they lived like that as well. Feet pressed together. He was the landscape upon which she walked. And she, his.

A perfect image of balance and support, but it crumbled when she remembered the young girl, a stranger, sleeping in the narrow room beside their own.

::::

SHORTLY AFTER ANNELIESE ARRIVED, Gitta noticed music in her home and did not like it. A strange underlying harmony that had not been there before. The girl hummed and sang quietly, and more than once she had noticed the girl's wavy hair on the floor, loosely curled into the beguiling shape of a treble clef.

On a cool afternoon she discovered Anneliese teaching young János to dance in the front garden. Gitta held her breath, as the girl moved in light circles, laughing, her arms up and out, tight hands twisting at the wrist. *He will run away*, Gitta whispered. *He will run from you*. But no, she was wrong again. Instead János mimicked her movements, shyly and awkwardly, swirling on a single foot, waiting for her smile. Gaping at her, as though everything was held in the curve of her two lips. Unfettered pleasure making his young face wide and shiny.

Gitta moved away, could watch them no more. In all these years, how could she never have thought to dance with her son? There was no place for it, no place for it. Not these past months. Years. So much struggle and uncertainty. And besides, János was a different boy with her, a boar, often wild and surly, in need of shaping. Firm hand, wooden spoon, clear directions, stark borders of right and wrong.

She heard him giggling. She peeked to see Anneliese bend at the waist while János placed his palms on her flushed cheeks. Gitta felt the sting of it. She did not recognize her own son.

::::

138

"SHE PLAYS BEAUTIFULLY," IMRE said. "Gitta! Ah! You will not believe."

Gitta frowned slightly at the pride in his tone, consistently brighter since the girl had arrived. "I am sure. She played when you worked at the store?"

"No, no, of course not. A violin among the sausages?" He laughed, slapping his thigh.

Where then? Where did you hear her play?

"You embarrass me, Imre," Anneliese protested, turned her head to the side, lowered her eyes.

Hearing the girl say her husband's name made Gitta frown more deeply. Too little time between them for such casualness. The two of them shifted to German, but Gitta was able to grasp enough words to follow along.

"You are modest when there is no room for modesty."

"Come, Imre. You like to play jokes."

"You will play for my family. I insist. There is never music in this house."

"Never?"

"We are poorer because of it. It is not what I wanted for my son. To grow up in a home without music pouring into his ears. A house without music is like a home without life."

"I see."

"Something no one can take. No one can silence."

Both Imre and Anneliese sighed together, staring at the streaked glass door of the stove. Gitta was not sure where to look. The words had been batted back and forth so quickly, she had grown confused. She must have misunderstood. Surely Imre would never say something so cold about the home she had created for them. Surely she had made a mistake.

"*Kave?*" she asked. "I can make it."

"Later, Gitta. Now play something," he said to the girl. "Play for my son." Though János was too big for it, Imre scooped him up from the floor, securing him on his lap. "Clap for Anneliese," he told him. And János clapped.

Anneliese went to her room and returned with the narrow box.

In the dim light of candles and fire she opened it, withdrew a violin, wood the glossy colour of burnt sugar. Heel of the instrument tucked underneath her delicate chin, feet spaced, and she closed her eyes, pulling the horsehair across the strings. A haunting minor key, the violin's human voice, smooth strands of melancholy filling the room. The girl swayed her body back and forth, elbow gliding in and out, effortlessly, her curls falling over her shoulder.

Gitta watched Imre closely as his face softened, back relaxed, his lips parting ever so slightly. She could easily identify the emotion in her husband's eyes. Even she was not immune to it. Music slipping in around her, making her helpless. She could feel it in her own flesh, nudging her sadness, like two fingers pressed across her throat.

She now understood Imre's desire to help the girl, to shield her. Something so fragile in her manner, her movements. Gitta had the urge to consume her beauty, her innocence. Hide the girl's youth inside her stomach, wrapped tightly in a protective coat of Gitta's own acidity.

Chapter 22

NEARING THE BRIDGE, NEVENA was stomping, glancing behind her as she approached Dorján. He recognized her coat and the shape of her body, but her face was not quite the same. With that hat, a woman's hat, she appeared older. She had shed some element of childishness and now moved with some certainty. Of what he had no idea.

He took a deep breath, said, "Hey," when she was practically beside him.

"Ah!" Her head bobbed upward, and she jumped back slightly. "Ah," she said again.

At once they spoke together. "Were you following me?" and "What are you doing here?" collided mid-air, and Dorján's hope was rapidly nullified by Nevena's confused expression.

Both floundered. "No, no. Of course not." "I'm just, you know, just, you know—"

Embarrassment flared in his ears, and he scratched his forehead, lit a cigarette. "I'm surprised to see you here."

"Um. I'm just walking. My mother. Her friend. I mean." Glancing over her shoulder. "Have you heard anything?"

"Not a word."

She kept reaching up and touching the knot on her scarf. He could smell chocolate on her breath, and he noticed a faint trace of brown near one corner of her lips.

"I don't understand it," she said. "I don't understand where he went, and why he's not coming back."

He took deep drags on his cigarette, and though he felt sweat trickling down underneath his arms, he tried to appear unconcerned. Opening his mouth, he let the smoke emerge gradually, covering his face like the hand of a ghost. His vision grew blurry.

"What do you think happened, Dori?"

"I don't know anything." An unintentional snap.

"Sorry. I never thought you did."

"Listen," he said, but he had no idea how to finish. He clenched his jaw, waiting for words to come to him. "That's a new hat?"

"No. It's my mother's. She made me wear it."

"Ah."

"I know. It looks stupid."

"No, it doesn't. You look nice." And heat punched his ears again, making him aware of the deepening chill in his spine, his limbs.

"I should go."

"We could, you know, walk home together."

"I would but—um …"

And then another boy was beside her. Black hair and a juvenile moustache. Unbuttoned coat free of lint and hitches, and the flaps swung open as though the cold never touched his skinny frame. He wore creased pants, high on his waist, cinched tightly with a belt. His shoelaces looked brand new.

"Hey," he said, his leather-gloved hand jutting out toward Dorján. "Vuković, Petar."

Dorján shook his hand but did not announce his own name. He could smell the same sweetness on this boy's breath.

"This girl does not waste time." He grinned, touching Nevena's shoulder. "Had to move to catch up with her."

"Really."

Paw on her elbow. "Do you see the bridge?"

"I remember them building it up again," Nevena said.

"Shit," he said. "We all do. And it looks exactly the same."

"Well. Kind of."

"All right, you've seen it. Now let's go."

"I wanted to look at the river, too."

He held out his hand, pointing the way, and Nevena stepped onto the bridge. Leaning over the edge, she stared at the rolling river. Petar darted up behind her, hands on her hips, and shoved. Playfully, but Nevena screamed when her hands slipped from the railing, and her body fell forward, metal banging just below her breasts. Even though there was no danger, Dorján jumped toward her, but Petar quickly wrapped his arm, a skinny tentacle, around her waist, lifted her from the ground, spun her around. "Don't jump," he cried. Even his laughter was lean.

Feet on the ground, she shook her head, rubbing her stomach.

"That's not a funny joke," Dorján said, and he stepped toward Petar. Spat on the ground near Petar's new shoes. New shoelaces. "You don't know what can happen."

"What?" He scowled, turning his innocent face left to right. "What?"

"Too late if she gets hurt." He tried to grab the sleeve of her coat, but she evaded him. "Nevena!" He wanted to ask her, *Who is this chicken's ass*? But from her sudden shyness, he could easily tell she was there by choice. Petar was not someone from the street, tailing her. More likely an invited guest.

"You should go in for the films." With thumb and forefinger Petar smoothed his patchy moustache.

"What?"

"Drama suits you."

Cigarette clamped in his teeth, his feet and hands began to tingle, and Dorján knew he was going to strike Petar. Rapidly, his fists calculated the amount of force that would injure that turned-up nose but not force shards of bone into the front lobe of his brain. Just as he was about to swing, a gust of wind struck him in the back, then came round and plucked Nevena's green hat from her head. The errant hat rolled over the stone on its brim, jumping and dancing, and Dorján was momentarily distracted. Petar did not leap after the hat, but instead he grinned, saying, "Your hair looks much better without a frog shitting on it." Then she bolted, stretching both arms just as it skittered away, yelling, "My mother will murder me."

"And that ugly hat decides," he said, both hands palms upward. He laughed, nudging Dorján's shoulder as though they were old friends. "Guess that means we're heading somewhere more private."

Dorján reached up, took the cigarette from his mouth, and flicked it into the space between them. Petar crushed it with the heel of his shoe, turned, and followed Nevena. Legs like stilts, his steps wide and deliberate, no suggestion of rushing. When he reached her, he took the recaptured hat from her, crushing it under his elbow. Grabbed her hand, leading her toward town, strands of her loose hair kicking in the wind.

Damp air rose from the river and Dorján's skin shrunk. At once he realized how cold he was; ice had crystallized into his bones. He watched Nevena and Petar, joined at the shoulder, disappearing around a corner of a mustard-coloured shop. Not once did she turn her head and glance back at him. He was dismissed.

How quickly she seemed to have forgotten about everything. Those long summer days when he and János would chase her through the woods, when they would pause by the stream to capture frogs or sing black snails out of their shells. They would pretend they were a wild family, the three of them, no parents, no authority, no limits. In their muddy kitchen surrounded by trees, she would prepare mud wrapped in leaves, and they would pretend to eat with enthusiasm. She had forgotten how János would fight any boys who ridiculed her. Fight them until they were bloody.

He stopped himself. What was the point in travelling backwards? Her interests lay somewhere else now. A scrawny *seggfej* from Drobnik who dressed like an American.

Another few minutes and he would leave. He did not want to risk running into them again. While he waited, he lit another cigarette and surveyed the expanse of land on the other side of the bridge. Tucked away in the hills were several buildings, blocks of concrete that matched the drab colour of the sky.

Dorján stared at the horizon as his palm and fingers blocked the sight of the factories. Now he could see nothing but rolling hills, naked trees, and yellowed grass, a sleeping landscape, workers absent. But as he looked at the surrounding area, he could not help but notice several lines creeping up from behind the fleshy part of his hand. Unnatural snakes curling around. He lowered his arm, once again revealing the factories and the thick pipes jutting out from the flat rooftops. Pristine hills ruined. The sight of it bothered him, even though he understood there was hope and promise in that black smoke.

This last cigarette made him feel nauseated, as though tar coated his empty stomach. To soothe himself, he pretended that János was just behind him. Just out of his line of vision. But when he glanced, there was only another car cutting across the bridge, a single man this time, rounded glasses, both hands gripping the very top of the steering wheel, knuckles white. Appearing anxious that his automobile was no longer on the earth. Instead gliding over something sturdy but entirely breakable. Something man-made.

"Please come home, my friend," Dorján whispered, and wiped his chapped hands over his face. Their argument over Nevena was such a waste. Her bright eyes, her beguiling smile, nothing more than a chisel to their alliance. But was it really about Nevena? No, he could admit to himself. Something inside of János had changed. Dorján had not known about János's father. He thought about Tibor then. Why had János selected the mute boy? Perhaps János felt helpless. And what better way to ease that discomfort than to sting the foot of someone who is even more helpless? If only Dorján had known the flailing thoughts trapped inside his best friend's mind. They should have never fought. He missed his friend. Missed him. Missed him. Missed him.

Then he remembered the coins again. Saw the empty tin in his mind. There was no ignoring it, and Dorján made a mental correction. He missed one side of János. The boy who sat with him in the courtyard, sharing bites from the same crust of bread, sipping from the same bottle of lemon soda. The boy who began calling Buksi *their* dog, when Dorján lamented not having an animal. That was the boy he missed. A brother and, in small ways, a father to him. Not the angry thief. Not the young man who stole what they had found in the field. And ran away from home.

Chapter 23

"WHO WAS THE FLEA?"

"What?"

"On the bridge."

"Ah, him."

"Well?"

"Just a friend. He lives near me."

"What kind of friend?"

Nevena crinkled her nose, said, "I don't know what you mean."

Petar laughed, and his laughter clung to the air long after he had closed his mouth.

Gripping her wrist, he opened a low wooden door, pulling her through ropes of tangled ivy into a hidden courtyard. A perfect square made of cracked plaster walls, mustard-coloured paint, roofs of pink tile. On the stone, a carpet of dried leaves, broken glass, and sheets of yellowed paper, headlines faded.

He leaned against one of the walls, pulling her to face him. "Do you like your gift?"

"Yes, yes. It's nice."

"I thought we could go to my house. But my mother is home."

"I could meet her?"

"No."

"Ah."

"Trust me. You wouldn't want to." Petar reached behind his head, gripped a handful of ivy, and stripped a length of dried leaves. "I wonder, could we climb it?"

Nevena giggled and considered for a moment why ivy held its leaves, even after they had died. Sometimes even until the spring, new ones arriving, pushing the dead ones aside. She thought to mention this to Petar but decided against it.

She glanced about the courtyard. In the very centre stood an old iron bench, rust crawling up the legs. Petar was still holding her mother's hat, and he gripped the brim, spinning it through the air, and it settled lightly on the seat of the bench.

"Come here," he whispered, and she stepped forward. "Are you cold?"

"A bit."

He hugged her and enveloped her inside his coat. She placed her head against his flat chest, could hear the thrum of his heartbeat. He lifted her face, bent her head backwards, and brought his open mouth to her lips. Mind calculating quickly the polite moves, *Do not embarrass me,* she lifted herself onto the balls of her feet, tilting her head left to right. His mouth covered hers, and she could feel his tongue circling her lips, darting inward, running over her teeth and gums. She moved her head to the side, suction broken, and he smiled. Again, those long teeth.

"Funny," she said, as she scanned the walls. "The door has disappeared." At one point someone had painted the wood to match the plaster.

"That's how I wanted it. There's no way out." Milk on his laughing breath had grown stale.

"I'm sure I can find it." A joke. She felt safe, didn't she? Petar was a nice boy from a good family in Drobnik. Her mother had repeated those words over and over again.

Innocent expression. "Do you want to try?"

She shook her head.

His forearm rested across the small of her back. He clutched her hand, slid it between their bodies, and brought her fingers to his crotch. She felt the hardened mass to the side of his zipper and squirmed, tugging her hand away.

"Why not?" he whispered. "There's no one here. No one will see."

"I...I don't know."

He took her hand a second time, pressing it against him. Pressure on her wrist making her fingers weak, but she managed to close her hand into a fist. Another moment of useless effort, and he threw her hand, the force making her arm swing.

Sliding sideways, he moved away from her, glaring at her from the corner of his eyes. "My mother's friend said you were a smart girl."

Rubbing her wrist. "I am. I am smart."

"I don't think so. A smart girl understands how to get along with people. Knows how to be friends." He walked to the bench, placed one foot on the seat, spat, lit a cigarette.

"I do know how." She had few other girls in her life, but she had János and she had Dorján. Though they were very different, she knew what it meant to be a friend.

At once she longed to run back to the bridge. To see if Dorján was still there. Someone familiar and easy. No confusing expectations. They could walk home together. Side by side.

"So you say." Tone high and feminine.

"Petar?" She took two steps toward him, was about to tell him she was leaving, when he reached toward her, tugging both ends of the scarf. Loop of fabric tightening, tightening around her neck. A gasp, and he let go. She sank her fingers between the scarf and her skin, worked to loosen it. "That hurt!"

"I have to go now." Voice calm as he pushed back the sleeve of his coat, checked his silver watch. "But I'm going to think about you this evening." He tapped the face of his watch with two bent fingers. "Before I go to sleep."

She blushed again, against her will.

"There's a bus. Somewhere." Digging into his deep pockets, he pulled out loose change, tossing it at her knees. Coins rolling, one spinning. A stomp, coin stilled, tip of his boot just missing her toes.

She stared at the money, then watched Petar stroll toward the painted door. Pull it open, slam it shut.

She waited. How long she could not be sure, but the light was changing. When the vines of ivy turned blue in the shadows, she left the courtyard. Walked through the streets, back toward the bridge. What were the chances Dorján might still be there?

Of course he had already left.

Nevena walked onto the bridge, held the railing, and peered over into the rushing river. The old bridge, broken but defiant, jutting up through the water. Snap of fabric, she removed the scarf from her neck, held it out in front of her. Empty wind teasing it from her grasp.

She released it, watching it dance in the air. She expected it to kiss the surface of the river, spread over it, submit to the water, but on its descent it snagged on a portion of the abutment. Nevena sighed, her mind a clump of frustration and confusion. This meeting was not what she had expected, and she understood her mother would be dis-appointed if she knew.

As she walked away, she turned once to see the scarf. The wind had not recaptured it. Instead, a woman in a thin coat lay on her stom-ach, in the middle of the bridge, her arm stretched through the metal grille, trying to catch its red tail.

:::::

"MY HAT?"

Nevena closed her eyes, saw it sitting on the bench in Drobnik. Waiting. "It blew off my head."

"How could you let that happen?"

"At the bridge. He took me for a walk on the bridge to see the water. It was windy, *Majko*. An accident."

"He took you for a walk? Really." Flick of her wrist, a one-hand clap. "No matter, *draga moja*. We will not mention it again. I am cer-tain he feels badly."

"Yes, yes. I'm sure. He said so."

"He did?"

"He liked the hat."

Aliz Dobrica smiled widely, her golden glint. "Of course he would. I am not surprised. Tell me everything." She took Nevena's hand, made her sit. "I want to know exactly what he said."

She began to tell her bits and pieces. Every sentence cleaned and checked. As they were speaking, Nevena heard the front door open and close. Her father, returning home from several days away. Aliz, like a broom, swept out of the room and across the floor toward him, and Nevena overheard the woman chirping excitedly.

"A nice boy. A strong Serbian family. Nearly eighteen. But he is going away this spring. To the base north of us. The same as you did." Her father mumbled something. Then, her mother again, voice like a tightening wire. "And why not talk? She is a young woman, after all. I was her age myself. She is growing up, Dragan. What is wrong with promises?"

At dinner that evening, her father wiped his mouth on his napkin, tossing the cloth onto his plate. "So he tried to buy you with a shoddy scarf?"

"Of course not!" A burst from Nevena's mouth. But her voice lacked strength, and when she placed her hand on her lap, she had the sudden sensation of that lump against her palm.

Her father bent his head and folded his arms across his chest. "You do not know the mind of a young man like I know the mind of a young man. He is from a fine family, yes. His father is in the Party, yes. But what does that say about him? Nothing. He is not a man. He is only seventeen."

"He wasn't like that."

"You made no offer to him?"

"Offer?"

"To wait for him. To wait and carry on when he returns."

"Of course not." She stared at the corner of the napkin, watching the fabric draw up the liquid from the plate, oil and paprika staining the cloth.

"Good. Then there is no word to break."

"Dragan!"

"I have met the boy. Seen his face. Have you?"

"Of course not. Mila knows the mother."

"Ah, Mila. Another one."

"She knows, Dragan."

"Well, he has the chin of a coward. Nose like an emaciated rat. If he were seated at my table, my appetite would hurry out the door. Zip. Goodbye."

"Ah, such cruelty!"

"That is it. Not another word. It is finished."

"Dra—"

Nevena bowed her head, pinching her thigh. While her mother shifted in her seat, a bound chicken being plucked, her father had scraped away the threat. If she were not far too old, she would have jumped up and kissed him.

Hand up, toward his wife. "Where is this scarf now?"

"I lost it."

"Like my hat?"

"Well done. You threw it away, yes?"

"It was an accident."

"A smart accident, my young girl. Come talk to me when someone offers a life. Something real. Until then I will hear nothing else."

:::::

WHEN HER FATHER ENTERED her room, Nevena pretended she was asleep. He often did this after a trip away, surprising her by placing a trinket or a charm on her bedside table. In the morning when she awoke, she brought it from her room and asked where it came from. But her father would only smile and say nothing. "Well," she always joked. "Seems I have a suitor coming in the evening." And he would reply, "Never!"

This night, though, she heard the wooden chair beside her bed squeak. His breathing. A slight wheeze of fatigue. And he began to whisper. "I am sorry," he said. "Sorry for being so harsh. I embarrassed you."

Air moving over her cheek, and she felt his hand touch her hair. Lift a length of it, bouncing, as though he were weighing it. She opened and closed her mouth, moved her eyes beneath her lids, feigning a dream.

Hand withdrawn, and he said, "I see you unfolding every day. So slowly becoming what you will be." He took several deep breaths. "I do not understand how something so beautiful came from that woman."

Saliva began to pool in Nevena's mouth, but she feared swallowing would reveal her wakefulness. She heard a tiny clink, and the chair sighed as her father stood. When his footsteps had receded into the hallway, she slit her eyes, saw an animal, cut from crystal. Even in the dim moonlight from the window, it glittered. A doe, head lowered, neck reaching. And Nevena imagined that if the creature were alive, it would be seeking strands of grass through the snow.

Chapter 24

THOUGH IT MADE GITTA unhappy, Anneliese did not leave. The rhythm of their lives shifted, but Gitta managed. The girl worked quietly, completing chores without complaint. A moment of free time, and she sought out János. Touched his hair and his face, and with her money she bought him small gifts from the market. A white shirt. Leather lederhosen. A set of painted trains that connected with metal hooks.

"How long will she stay, Imre?"

"Until."

"Until is not an answer."

"We will see. We will see. Why do you keep spitting in my ears?"

Gitta had no choice but to believe her husband. That when her family gathered their belongings, Anneliese stayed behind because of love. For a boy named Tomi Pástor. A boy she had not once mentioned in all these weeks.

She was certain Imre was holding something away from her. Some details she did not understand. Thinking back on it, Gitta wondered if she should have pushed harder. Asked more questions.

She had not. Thought her silence reflected her strength. Besides, her husband had been this way for several years, and she had grown used to it. Accepted it, even. As long as they were together, some part of them would remain strangers.

::::

GITTA WAS FOLDING SOFTENED cabbage leaves around ground meat when she heard a gentle tapping on the front door. Barely audible, almost like a young child with a soft fist. She wiped her hands on her apron, went to the door, opened it to find two officers standing on the cobblestones. They were unfamiliar, both older men, tall with clean-shaven faces and wearing crisp uniforms. One of them smiled at her, said, *"Dobro jutro. Da li je vaš muž kući?"* Good morning. Is your husband home? The other said nothing, sharp mouth turned down, a rusty sickle fallen on its side.

Gitta nodded, tried to reply, but her breath stalled in her lungs when she noticed their belt buckles, square and silver, the letters JNA on a gold star in the middle and the words *Vojna Policija* flanking the star. She put her hand on her chest, patted herself, then stepped aside, whispering, "Yes. He is. He is here."

They removed their hats, held them underneath their arms, front rims facing forward, bending slightly as they came through the low doorway.

"Please," she said, gesturing toward the front room. "This way."

"Thank you," the smiling one said. "If you could tell your husband we are here. He is expecting us."

The scowling one cleared phlegm from his throat, spat into a folded handkerchief.

Gitta rushed down the hallway, past the mess in the kitchen, and out through the back door. In the yard, she found Imre, seated at the small table with Anneliese, heads together, talking. His hand was covering hers, and he said, "You must. Soon." Anneliese was weeping silently, saying, *"Nein, nein, nein."* When she lifted her face, her eyes were swollen, nose red and greasy.

"Imre!"

He leaned back in his chair.

"They are here for you," she hissed.

A slow, deep breath, and he rubbed his hands over his face, his eyes aging by the minute. "I know."

"How can you know?"

"I knew they would come for me. They came for others. You did not think?"

"No, of course not. I am stupid, yes? I thought the war was over."

"The war is over. And the war will never be over."

"Riddles. You keep your riddles, Imre. For once!"

"It is nothing. I will not be long, Gitta. Just a requirement, you see. I am certain they want nothing from me."

"Nothing? *Vojna Policija,* and you say it is nothing?"

"They have a few questions." He shrugged. "About my position. I did what I was told. I listened, I explained what I heard. I did not have a choice. That is all there is to it."

"And you are not afraid?"

When she asked that, he lowered his eyes, blinking, but only for a moment.

"No." His hand formed a fist. "This is not an unreasonable request given the circumstances. They want to know what I did. I will tell them the truth. Give them the words they want to hear. I will be okay. I am strong with my languages, and I helped to translate. I did what I was told to do. Everything else I have forgotten."

Gitta brought her hand to her mouth, could smell the earthy stench of cabbage. "Well, go answer their questions. Before they come through the house."

He stood slowly, as though his muscles were weak on his bones. Said to Anneliese, "Wait in the back garden. There is no trouble for you, of course. There are others like you in the village, but why announce yourself?"

When Anneliese stood, Imre reached out, touched her elbow, whispered, *"Alles wird gut. Mach Dir keine Sorgen."* Everything will be fine. Do not worry. Then he turned, placed a hand on his wife's shoulder for a moment, and strode into the house.

:::

"GOOD THAT YOU ARE here." The smiling one said and clapped Imre gently on the back.

"Of course. This is my home."

"You look well."

"As do you."

"The end of fighting, it is good for our health, is it not?"

"Yes. Yes, it is."

Sighing, Gitta sat down. All that cordiality slowed her heart rate, helping her to grow calm.

"You received a notification from us?"

"Yes, sir."

"I will give you a moment to get your coat, *Gospodin* Kelemen."

Gitta jumped up, said, "You leave? Could you not ask your questions here?" She knotted her fingers together, pressing her arms against her sides. Calm veneer disintegrated. "You may have this room. It is quiet. You will take a coffee. Yes. A coffee."

"Not to worry, *Gospodo*. We will not be long at all. I will have him home before dinner." He leaned his head forward, still accommodating and friendly.

"Then you will stay?" Gitta asked.

"Stay?"

"For dinner. Both of you. When you bring my husband."

The irritated one cleared his throat again, making another fold in his handkerchief.

"That is very gracious of you, *Gospodo*." More pleasantries.

And Gitta tried to mimic his congenial expression, until she realized he had not answered her question.

Imre appeared in the doorway wearing his long brown coat, his hat. "I am ready."

"Good!" The smiling one clapped his hands together again.

Imre turned toward his wife, saying, "Gitta?"

"Yes."

"You will look after the children today."

"The children?"

"The boy. And yes, the girl."

"Ah."

"While I am away."

"You will not be away long."

"No. But say it."

"Of course, *kedvesem*. Of course."

"They are perfect. Both of them."

"Do not worry your wife," the policeman said as he pulled on his gloves. Tight black leather. "Your children are thriving. Such fortune to live on good soil and be provided with so much."

"Yes, yes, yes." Imre walked ahead of them, hands at his sides. His coat, once a handsome fit on his wide back, now hung limply. Cuffs covering much of his fists.

:::::

FOR A LONG WHILE, Gitta sat on the wooden bench just outside her front door. Watching the road for a vehicle to appear. Eventually, when the sky became murky and the air cooled, she went inside. Anneliese already had János washed, hair combed, nightclothes on, and she sat in a chair, the boy tucked in beside her, reading a book about animals. Wild animals that lived all around the world.

Gitta went to the stove, lifting the lid on the pot of the cabbage rolls. Enough food to feed a small contingent. She stroked the *töltött káposzta,* their tight translucent skins, nestled safely in the salty liquid. Darkness had already crept into the warm room, and she knew they would not be eaten tonight.

Chapter 25

SHE WATCHED HIM CROSS the courtyard between their homes. Body like a curved wire. For a moment she closed her eyes, hearing the heavy scuff of his shoes over the icy stone. Without seeing him, Gitta could imagine it was János, moving in that lazy way young boys, nearly men, often did. Not lifting their feet, shoulders hunched, shy hands hidden inside pockets. She would allow herself this moment. Believing that figure coming closer to be her missing son. For a split second she dozed, dreaming János had grown, taller and skinnier. Her heart flooding with a purposeful thought. She would need to gather his clothes and bring them to Zsuzsi for adjustment.

Light tapping on the wood frame, and Gitta was awake again, aware. She opened the door for Dorján, and he lowered his head to avoid the door frame. A breath of early winter came in with him; hard grains of snow soon beaded into water on the knotted rug.

"I have something for you."

"Yes?"

In his hand he held a letter, and before his arm was fully extended, she grabbed it. Peered underneath the rim of her glasses to read the label.

"It doesn't make sense." He ran his hand through his hair, wiping the moisture on his pants. "It's addressed to my *nagyanya*. I have never heard this name."

"Easier that way."

"What way?"

"To have a letter come to her. A stranger's name as the sender."

"From Würzburg? We don't know anyone in Würzburg."

"Neither do I."

"You don't?"

"More chance to reach me this way. Otherwise it might get, well, lost."

He shrugged, and she saw a confused innocence in his expression. She knew he understood something of the war, as it had taken his father and consumed his mother. But still, his face was open, an unscarred palm.

Though her dry hands shook with anticipation, she slid the letter onto the windowsill, tucking it among the limp leaves of a spider plant. "Leave your boots on," she said to Dorján and gestured toward the table. "Come, and—" She was tempted to say *wait with me*, but the words would not emerge. Of course he would not understand that her life had become nothing more than one continuous wait.

He moved to the table, lifted the chair, and sat.

"Did you swim this morning?"

Nodding, "Yes. Every morning. And most afternoons."

"Good, good," she said. "It is good for you. To do that."

He smiled.

"I have nothing to offer you."

"I just ate."

He coughed into his sleeve, and she stopped herself from pacing. They had always had a comfortable relationship, not particularly close, but close enough. She was the mother of his best friend and over the years had always maintained a safe and sturdy distance from the boys. But now she wanted to be near him, wanted to touch his hair and his cheek. Wanted to hear every detail of every story. Absorb some weighty element of his youth to keep her airy body from floating away.

"I can make a coffee."

"All right," he said, smiling. "A coffee."

She placed a small tin *kávéfőző* filled with water on the stove, poured the greasy beans into the funnel, cranked the handle. In the past she had passed the grounds through the grinder twice, pulverizing the beans into near powder. But Imre did not like the black dust that floated on the foamy head of his coffee. Grounds too light to settle to the bottom of his cup. Said he would rather drink nothing at all if he could not drink it properly.

After placing the *kávéfőző* on the stove, she slid into a chair opposite him.

"I have been meaning to ask you, Dorján. How well did you and János know that boy from the square?"

"What boy?"

"You know, the one who sells the vegetables for Gazda László. His grandson. Tibor is his name. Yes, Tibor."

Hesitation, and she noticed it. A shift in his chair, flush of heat in his face, as though the name unsettled him and he were suddenly aware of the temperature. Perhaps just his winter coat. He never took it off.

"I don't—I mean, not really. Sometimes I see him there. That's all. Nothing else."

"I know he does not go to the school."

"No."

"So you would not see him much."

A shrug. He rubbed his nose so forcefully, she heard the cartilage snapping back and forth.

"Did János know him?"

"Same as me."

"Strange," she said. "Yes. Strange." She expected Dorján to question her, but he was silent, leg jiggling. She could feel the slight vibration moving over the floor. And so she continued. "Sometimes he is waiting outside my door. I see him through the glass. Standing there. Wants to help, I suspect. Perhaps his *nagyanya* is forcing him. She says he is a friend to János."

"Help?"

"I have given him work. Some days he has found his own."

"What work?"

"Nothing really. Just a couple of things, to be rid of him. Cleared some dead vines from the back garden. Turned the soil. Painted here and there. All outside. He does not talk, you know."

Careful nodding.

"László's wife came to the door once. Said a change has come over the boy since János… since János left. She believes Tibor misses him."

Dorján sucked air in through his teeth. "Misses him?"

"Yes."

"You don't need him. I could do those things."

"As could I."

"Why didn't you ask me?"

"I do not have the mind to ask after anything."

"I wouldn't have him here, Gitta *néni*."

"No?"

"He's simple."

"Yes."

Biting his lip, then he said, "And he's not so simple."

"Ah."

Spitting from behind her. An angry sound. Water bubbled in the tin pot, flying drops sizzling as they landed on the hot stove. She jumped up, scooped a large spoonful of coffee into the *kávéfőző*, and stirred. Removed it from the heat. Holding the *kávéfőző* by the long, thin handle, slowly pouring coffee into the little cup. Placed the hot pot on the wooden board, and gripping the edge of the saucer, she brought the drink to Dorján. He reached for it immediately, but she said, "Wait, wait. You will burn yourself."

"If you need help, I can do things."

She glanced at the letter, propped against the window. "János will be back," she said. "Soon he will come home." *To me.*

"He'll have a long list, then."

"Yes, yes. I'm sure he'll be after you to do half of it."

"I'd gladly do it, Gitta *néni*. You know that."

"I do."

Without thinking, she went to the window. Then she went to the windowsill and gently withdrew the letter from the curling clutches of the plant. She dug her thumb underneath the flap of the envelope, then dragged across, heavy paper peeling away on either side. Took a deep breath before she unfolded the note. This would bring immediate relief; she sensed it as she pinched the paper. She would finally be able to draw air into the lower portion of her lungs, instead of continually panting.

"News?"

"Yes. I cannot wait. I must open it."

Hesitation, but he ventured. "János?"

"I believe." She skimmed the note, catching all the important phrases. Her shoulders fell, mouth open. "Ah," she whispered. "Ah."

"Gitta *néni*?"

She turned, held the edge of the sink. "He—he's there," she said.

"There?"

"The letter. It is from my brother-in-law. János is with him." Her voice choked.

"In Stuttgart?"

She began to shake, emotion bubbling outward. But inside her head, she spoke to herself. *Wait. Wait. Don't do it. Do not break. Not with the boy watching.* She heard his chair move over the floor, he was about to get up, but she turned back, put up her hand. "I am fine, Dori. He is safe. Not home, but he is safe."

She sat back down, smiled.

"I knew it. I just knew it." He slapped the table, and the foam on his coffee leaped and landed. Splattered on the wood.

"I assumed the same."

"I don't know how. I don't know how he was able. To do what he did."

Gitta's eyes blinked slowly, and she could not focus.

"You know what I was thinking about yesterday? When we were children, and the Heerführer was here. Do you remember?"

"Yes, yes. When the Germans moved through our village, so many people housed the soldiers. János thought we were more important as we offered a roof to the Heerführer." She drew in a deep breath through her mouth. "He liked János. He liked you too, but János would not leave the man alone."

"I know exactly what he said."

"Tell me," she whispered. "*Kérlek*, Dorján. Let me close my eyes for just a moment and listen to you talk."

::::

HE WAS A THREE-STAR general of the Wehrmacht, and during the early 1940s, he stayed with János and his family as long as was necessary. Dorján, when he visited their house, could barely move in the presence of such a formidable man, with his massive frame, curling moustache, crisp belted coat, and gold bird sewn above his left breast. At the kitchen table, János's father and the Heerführer conversed easily in German and drank shots of strong *szilvapálinka*.

The boys were permitted to play quietly in the kitchen, and Dorján held a tiny tank in his lap, spun the wheels gently, moved the hull back and forth without making a sound. But János lunged forward, scraped his wooden tank over the cool floor, made popping noises as imaginary cannons flew from the main gun. While Dorján did not budge, János drove his tank around the legs of the table, let it smash into the Heerführer's black shoe. Dorján watched in surprise as the Heerführer said nothing, smirked, and moved his leg so his shoe protruded a little farther into their play space.

"Do you use the periscope?" János yelled as the tank crawled over a pair of boots placed beside the Heerführer's chair. "How far can you see?"

"*So schlau*," the Heerführer said, voice filling the small room. "At such a young age."

"János, János! Do not disturb the Heerführer with your childishness."

The Heerführer waved his hand. "Not at all. I know they have many questions. My Hungarian for you is weak, but I will see. Come," he said and opened his arms to the boy.

Dorján's narrow jaw dropped, and he stared as János climbed into the man's wide lap, fiddling with the brass buttons of his coat.

"Back straight." The Heerführer stroked János's back, and the child automatically obeyed. "Strong men have strong backs."

Dorján longed to be beside his friend, dandled on the other knee. He would hold his spine like a healthy tree.

"At home, in my village, I have a son about your age."

"Clever like me?"

Laughter. "Very much so. I think that." The Heerführer leaned forward, pressed his sharp nose just behind János's earlobe, sniffed. "And you smell like him too. A little sour behind the ear."

"What? Like rotten milk?"

"János!" Bellow from his father. "Your tongue needs a spoon across it."

"Let me see," the German said, and he gripped the boy's cheeks, squeezed. Mouth split, János stuck his tongue out as far as he could, loud *Ahhh*. "No such discipline required, sir. A perfect tongue."

"You are too gracious, Heerführer," Imre said. "Your tolerance is impressive."

"Nonsense. It is my delight. He is a taste of my home."

János brought his arms close to his body, fists underneath his chin. "You're going to eat me?"

More laughter. An endless pit of it.

Sighing, Dorján slouched on the floor. If only the Heerführer wanted to eat him. He'd allow him to take a bite. Surely, without doubt. His leg, his side. To draw out such delight, Dorján would offer up a finger or a shoulder blade.

"No, no. I would need ten of you to fill my stomach."

János relaxed, fiddling again with the brass buttons.

"I would like to teach you something. Both of you." And he lowered his head, staring at Dorján.

Dorján inched closer until his face was close to the Heerführer's knee.

"You hear the sounds from the skies, yes?"

Dorján nodded, and János raised a finger, said, "They are fighting up there."

Another smile. "Fighting, yes. But we must!" The Heerführer looked about the room, gaze settling on the shiny boots next to his chair. "Do you see these boots?"

Both boys nodded.

"Well, what if I told you those *Armeestiefel* are growing stronger, and they will move."

"By themselves?" Dorján croaked, then sat on his hands.

"Exactly. They seem innocent enough, yes?"

"They're just boots," János said, frowning. "They don't move by themselves."

"Ah, but imagine those boots could, and soon, if there is nothing to stop them, they would trample all over your clean house and cover your floors and tabletops with dirty footprints. On your clothes and your skin. Boot marks on everything. Filthy stains your tired mother cannot wash. She would cry, your mother. What would you do?"

Dorján felt a rush of righteousness and courage flood his body, and he leapt up, skinny arms waving in the air. "I'd put a tank there. Right there! Stop those boots forever."

"Very good!"

Praise absorbed, Dorján instantly grew an inch. He crouched down in front of the boots, sized them up through squinting eyes. His tongue stuck out between his lips.

"What can you report, soldier?"

Eyes wide, Dorján exclaimed, "They moved, Heerführer! I saw them! Just a tiny bit, but they moved."

"Ha! And you, János Kelemen? What can you say?"

János slid off the German's lap, picked up his wooden tank from the floor, then scowled at the Heerführer. "Boots don't move. That is a silly story to tell."

Dorján held his breath, Imre Kelemen frowned, but the Heerführer threw back his head, loudest laughter blooming in the room. "Ah! Silly, yes. Your father has overfed me on his *likör*." He seized the glass and drank the remainder. Hands on his knees, he leaned toward the boys, speaking first to Dorján, "When you are grown, you will be of good service to your country." And then he peered over his glasses at János, smacked him gently on his back, murmuring, "And you, my young friend. One day you will be big trouble."

::::

WHAT IF SHE COLLAPSED? The dog would know what to do. The dog would know.

After Dorján left, Gitta went to the back garden, untied Buksi, and brought him into the house. As the dog did each time, he balked at the threshold, remembering, no doubt, the only time he had tried to creep in when Imre was alive. Dogs did not have a place in the home, and when Imre saw him poking his nose inside the kitchen, he took a handful of ground pepper, pushed his palm into the dog's muzzle. The dog snorted and sneezed, clawed at his face, but never again did he try to enter their home. Gitta did not think it cruel, really. That was how it was. But now, as she urged the dog in through the door, pleaded with him, she could not imagine. Would never allow anyone to cause the old dog distress.

The dog sniffed and sighed and turned around, then lay on the warmed floor just in front of the stove. Gitta sat on the floor next to him, leaned her body against his thick fur, and pulled the letter from her pocket. Addressed to Zsuzsi Szabó. Originating in Würzburg.

Though Dorján was confused, she knew instantly that the letter was from her brother-in-law in Stuttgart. Over the past few years she rarely received a letter from him, but that did not mean he had rarely written. Letters were lost, seized, destroyed. Especially when sent by someone like Gábriel Kelemen.

This one was too important to leave to chance, and he wrote an unknown name on the envelope, postmarked it from another city, sent it to her neighbour. An innocent white envelope with no connection to a man who had claimed he was leaving for a visit but instead forfeited his country.

Surely, if she read the letter a second time, the message would be different. The words would be kind to her and alter themselves. They would give her the story she wanted.

Quickly she scanned over the news of another baby, a huge daughter, 4,100 grams, details of his growing business, his wife making draperies, knitting sweaters. Then the shock of the final paragraph.

Really striking her this time, not just fluttering about her head. Several sentences, a jumble of letters spelling all the wrong words. "János is not here. But he is welcome, of course," it said. He had plenty of work for his nephew. "Tell him to be careful. Very careful. The risk might be too much."

At once, the weight of her own skin was too much for her frail bones. The note was still the same. The same.

Those lies she had spoken to Dorján—they slid from her lips so easily. Why had she done that? She could not explain it. Other than a simple need to have those wishes outside of her body. If she heard them, even if they originated from her own throat, they had to be true.

But no. The lies only offered a few moments of self-deception.

She slumped near the dog, and the room began to spin around her, walls and painted clay figurines and decorative plates blurring in the air. Sharp stab to her intestines, she bent at the waist, reached up, and clutched the carved armrests of the chair. The note tumbled to the floor, and the dog stood, nudging the papers away with his muzzle. A high-pitched squealing sound arrived in the room that made the dog whine, and he stepped lightly over her limbs, licked the veins in her forehead, trying to calm her, to quiet her.

No easy way to allow this information in. It moved through her like a plague, her organs bulging, straining with the load. She had been certain. So, so certain. Though she had based her assumptions not on evidence, but on pithy hope. And she was wrong.

Her son was still lost.

Chapter 26

HE WAS FINE. FINE. He had made it safely to wherever he was. A house in Stuttgart. An apartment? How he had managed the journey with no documents and a pocketful of gold coins, Dorján could not fathom. The thought of it filled him with both relief and a spiralling rage. Relief, János was safe; fury, everything was ruined. All those promises that had glued them together as children were meaningless.

Dorján paced up and down the walkway between the homes and the road. Snow was falling, flakes gliding through the naked trees, landing on his head. He stomped his feet so hard his shins ached. Then he leaned his head against a cold tree, wanting to slam the trunk.

Deep breaths, and gradually the spiral loosened, weakened, the end letting go, flapping. When it collapsed on itself, Dorján recognized a hole, burnt clear through him. An emptiness, sides smooth and dull. János was gone. There was a chance, more than a chance, that Dorján might never see him again. Over the years János had always been his voice, filling his mind with the right thoughts. And now Dorján did not know what to say. Did not know what to think.

Did not know what to do about Tibor. After what had happened between them, Tibor should not have the will to help Gitta *néni*. Perhaps it was only his grandparents who forced him to do so. Or perhaps the boy had a plan.

Winter was here, and the local market had been closed for well over six weeks. Tibor would be at home with Gazda and his wife. Even if Dorján ran there right now, what could he do? Could he tell the boy to leave Gitta *néni* alone? To never set foot on her land again?

Just thinking about it forced the spiral to reverse, anger twirling around and around again. Biting down, he felt the faint snap in his teeth. He pulled away a fingernail, spat it in the street.

Everything had started out as a joke. Or so Dorján had thought. Funny at first, and he had laughed along with János when they tricked Tibor. Only later, when he turned it over in his mind, Dorján found it had lost its humour, replaced by prickly shame. Tibor did not deserve it; of course he did not. But once the process had been set in motion, Dorján was unable to stop it. Or perhaps he was unwilling, if he was completely honest with himself, to stand in János's way. To challenge him and his choppy proposal.

Until the time János pointed him out, Dorján had barely noticed Tibor in the village square. He was simply a structure that Dorján saw so often, the farmer's grandson who registered no more than the chipped stones or the constant smell of cigarette smoke in the air. Occasionally Dorján had to purchase vegetables from the stand, but even then the transaction was wordless, and he cannot say he ever actually looked Tibor in the eye.

Early summer of last year, he and János were sitting on the low stone wall, drinking *limonádé*, and János pointed at Tibor, saying, "Look at him. Doesn't he look like a bird?"

Dorján angled his head, frowned.

"Come on. Look at his fingers."

Even from a distance, Tibor's fingers appeared extraordinarily long and slender. They moved over the fruits and vegetables, touching and tapping. Perhaps the backdrop of bright red peppers and tomatoes caused his fingers to look ghostly white.

"Birds have wings, not fingers."

"That's not what I meant."

"But, you said—"

"I don't know. He just reminds me of a bird. He shouldn't be there. A filthy pest."

"Where else should he be? That's his work."

"Yes, yes. I know," János said, but Dorján could tell the agreement came only from his friend's mouth and that his mind was working on something else.

Many afternoons they sat on the stone wall and watched Tibor. Dorján asked the reason, but János only scratched his chin, said, "I don't know yet, but we'll see."

"We'll see? I see nothing. He knows how to count. He keeps the cart clean."

"I think he's lost his brain. Goat shit in his head."

"Of course he has."

"But even so. Look at him. He knows what's going on."

"He doesn't know anything, János."

"Do you want to make a bet, my friend?"

On another day, they had watched as Tibor interacted with a man clearly sent on an errand from his wife. Two eggplants in his basket. Then a scrawny girl, simple dress, body like thin vines. Tibor acted exactly the same as he always did. "Can I be more bored?" Dorján asked, and he lay down on the stone wall, lit another cigarette. "I'd rather find pins with a magnet."

"Something new," János whispered as an older woman approached the cart, full red lips, low-cut buttoned dress revealing powdery mounds. Her hips were wide, and she swivelled as she walked, basket swinging. Dorján sat up, stared. He guessed she was one of those ladies from Drobnik. The waiting ladies, they called them. Clusters of them standing in the doorway of a home, stained plaster, disintegrating curtains in the window, fanning themselves and pulling at the neck of their dresses even though there was an adequate breeze.

Dorján could hear her breathy voice. The sound of it made him quiver, and he spaced his feet farther apart, letting his heels bang against the wall. Tibor fluttered as he served her, tapped the carrots, caressed the furry apricots with his white bird fingers. But his eyes never wavered from her breasts, and as he gaped, she casually brought her hand to her chest, slipping a thumb in and out of the softness. When the woman's order was finished, she stepped around the cart, dropped the money into Tibor's shirt pocket, and touched his face. Rubbed her thumb, that same thumb, on his cheek. "Such a darling boy," she murmured. His mouth hung open, as did Dorján's, and Tibor grunted in a way that made Dorján flush.

As soon as she walked away, Tibor made a series of curious dance movements. "Ah," János said. "I knew it. He liked what he saw." Then Tibor turned on his heel, and shoulders hunched, he scuttled away in a half walk, half run, eyes darting left and right. Around the stone wall, down the narrow passageway beside the coffee house, and he disappeared.

"Let's follow him," János said, and he leapt off the wall.

Let's not, Dorján thought, but still he trailed behind János.

They found Tibor standing in the deep yellow grass that brushed up against the back of the church. No one came back here unless it was to check the foundation after the spring thaw. Tibor had his forehead pressed against the rough stone of the structure, one hand, fingers spread, against the church wall. He was gasping, back shaking, as though he were crying. Lost in a tangle of emotion, he never heard them approaching.

"He's upset," Dorján said. "We should leave him alone."

"Wait."

The wind shuddered through the grass, revealing scrawny legs, bent knees, a bare backside, shorts in a puddle around his ankles. Dorján halted, feeling his stomach flop over behind his ribs.

"Tibor!" János called in a friendly tone. The boy started, scrambled to haul up his clothes, tried to run but tumbled. Sound of a cat crying, he rolled onto his stomach and wriggled up and down, flattening a circle of long grass, but managed to contain himself and fasten his button. Dorján looked down at him. Though his eyes were wide and afraid, he had pretty features, unblemished and practically hairless, curling eyelashes, and thin pink lips.

"Tibor, Tibor, Tibor," János continued. "No need to be shamed. Right, Dorján?"

"Uh—" Dorján could not speak. Sure, he had handled himself in the outhouse many mornings, rushing, rushing, jaw clenched, so his grandmother would only have the bread sliced, hot milk just poured into his bowl when he returned. Occasionally, if he took longer, she would pat herself down low, saying, "Your stomach is mad with you today, *szívem*?" And he would mumble, "Yes, *nagyanya*, a little."

"That's the domain of boys, isn't it, Dorján?" János said.

"Domain?"

"We're all waiting for a woman, aren't we? Ah, yes, they make us wait. But well worth it."

Well worth it? Dorján shook his head slightly. He had no idea what János meant. As far as he knew, both he and his best friend had never even had a girlfriend. They had danced with girls, kissed cheeks and held hands. Four times Dorján had seen a woman in nothing more than her slip and brassiere in his grandmother's kitchen. One of those times being his own mother, but he would not think about that. Think about the perfect curves of her grown body. No woman could be as beautiful as she was. Those months before she wilted and died. But never anything beyond that. No, never.

Dorján missed something then. While his mind raced, a deal had already been established between János and Tibor. Nothing more than a few dinar here and there, skimmed off the top of Tibor's sales. His grandfather would not miss a single coin. "I guarantee it," János said. Tibor would hand the money over, and when it seemed enough, János would help him find a girl. Buy him an hour with one of the waiting ladies.

"You deserve it, do you not?"

Tibor nodded, wiping his hands on his shirt over and over again.

"This will be our secret. No one will ever know about the stain you planned to leave on our village."

And that was how it began. János sought out an opening, and an opening he found. Over the months, Tibor stole small amounts of change from the purse tied to his belt. Every day, János would pass through the village square, pause a moment beside Tibor, and inside a simple handshake, money would pass from one person to another. Never much. Never enough for it to mean anything. But over the days, the collection grew. Bit by bit. János stole an empty tin from his mother, and together they hid their bounty in the woods. Jammed behind Root Rock.

It might have gone on like that forever, at least until winter arrived and Gazda László dismantled his stand. But one day, without warning, Tibor decided he had offered enough. He had given the boys enough money and would give no more.

He followed them into the woods. Phantom footsteps, making not a single sound. Dorján had not realized the boy was behind them, not until he stepped out from behind a thick trunk. The tin was open, János kneeling, poking his fingers through the coins.

János sprang up, greeted Tibor like an old schoolmate, clapped him on his bony back. "Good to see you. Who is watching the stand, my friend?"

Gesturing then at the money, arms spinning, furious air passing out from his tightened throat.

"Don't worry, Tibor. Your time will come. It will." So soothing, his words. Butter melting, sliding over a tilted pan. "We are not there yet, my friend. Not even close. We have the whole future ahead of us, yes?" János turned his back to Tibor, took several steps and lit a cigarette. "All the time in the world."

Tibor became still, and Dorján thought he would back down. His face appeared deflated; surely he would walk away from them. Leaving Dorján to straighten everything out with János. Enough was enough. This little game would have to end.

Arms and legs flailing, wide ribbons of pale skin, Tibor bolted forward. Muscles constricted, Tibor appeared to be tripping, tumbling over his oversized shoes, head forward. His face struck János first, mouth wide open, and when he made contact, his jaw closed. Teeth clamped down on wool and cotton, and skin.

Dorján rushed to help János, but his friend had already flipped, straddling Tibor. Fists flying, János striking Tibor's face. Flesh growing pulpy, smears of blood. "János, stop!"

Tibor held his hands to his slippery cheeks, but János scratched them away, pinned left then right underneath his knees. "Stop! János, stop!" Another smack. Knuckles to a weeping eye.

Dorján dove toward them, tackling János. Rolled over, losing his grip, the three boys now split apart. János leapt to his feet, bounced in place, shook his bright red fists. "*Az Isten faszát!* Bit me, the *balfasz* bit me!"

"We should just give it back."

"What?" Finger stuck deep in his ear, shaking.

"It's not worth it."

Mad laughter next, riding up and down a rickety ladder. "Did someone pick out your brain, leave shit in its place?"

Dorján said nothing. Could not think of a single word. Everything between them was different, in only a matter of months. János so agitated. So full of fury. And their friendship no longer calming him. This leaky, leaky friendship.

Lighting a cigarette, Dorján looked around the clearing. Tibor was gone. He had left as quietly as he had arrived.

That was it, then. Right? That was the last time they had seen Tibor, with the exception of that single moment on the bus. Passing through Bregalnica on their way to harvest corn. János had peered out the glass, placing a finger to his lips. Taunting him. And now, he was skulking around János's home, acting the repairman.

What sort of game was Tibor playing? Was he planning to do something to right the wrongs Dorján and János had committed against him? Dorján scratched his head, chewed another fingernail. Then again, maybe he was playing no game at all.

Chapter 27

THE SHORTEST DAYS OF the year, and Gitta was grateful for the darkness. She slept as many hours as she could, taking sips of *pálinka* when she was aware of her wakefulness. Most days Buksi slept in the kitchen, and Gitta often dozed in the chair beside the stove, her feet slipped from her shoes, lying underneath the dog's stomach. When the dog whined at the door, she walked outside with him. Kept him on a rope. Could not stand the thought of losing him, even though the dog had never once run off.

Zsuzsi came with food. Dorján filled her empty box with coal.

"I don't understand," she heard him whisper. "János is all right. Why is she worse?"

Zsuzsi shook her head. "I do not know, *szívem*. I do not know."

The Komandant came to see her again, asking gentle questions. What could she say to him? Admitting she had no idea what had happened to her child was far too painful to repeat. And she was unable to share her lie, of course. Very few people would ever hear it. Such a statement could have far-reaching consequences, and even if he wished, the Komandant would be unable to alter them.

He handed her a large paper-wrapped parcel, soft and cold in her hands. "It is nothing," he said. "Nothing at all."

"I remember. The last time you brought me this."

"Yes, yes." He reached out, but his hand circled back, and he did not touch her. "As do I."

:: ::

ONE NIGHT SEVERAL WEEKS after they had taken Imre, the Komandant came to her door. He was not the Komandant at that time, but he was rising through the ranks, she had heard. His contributions recognized. Soon, he would be rewarded.

The hour was late, full darkness, both János and Anneliese were already sleeping. There was a small package tucked into the crook of his elbow, and his shy eyes would not meet hers. She moved aside, but he would not enter her home.

"You have word of his circumstances?" she had asked, but he shook his head. The silence hung between them, cut only by the gentle call of a nesting owl. The sound floating on the air like an old memory. She closed her eyes. "Then?"

Finally, he said, "I know nothing." His voice was a murmur, and Gitta could barely hear him.

"Nothing?"

"I should not share this."

She gripped the door handle, edges of metal pressing into her palms. "Of course you must share."

"I knew they wished to discuss your husband's work. I heard rumblings, and I tried to dissuade them, Brigitta. They would not listen to me."

"I do not understand."

"I have no control over such things."

"No."

"I ... I considered you had thought about me. I mean, that I might have some knowledge for you."

Gitta folded her arms across her chest. "You have not entered my mind, sir," she said. That was untrue, of course. She had thought of him often, wondering if he had tried to intervene. For her sake. From his expression, she was certain he still cared for her. Would never wish to see her suffer.

He pouted slightly, nodded. Then said, "He is safe. I know that much. Just do not worry."

"How might I not worry? Tell me? My husband has been removed from our home by the military police for an afternoon of questioning and has not returned. Fifteen days have passed since."

"I know. I know." Wrist pressed to his forehead. "I am stupid to say such a thing. Of course you are full of worry."

As his face sank, she regretted snapping at him. He had come to her home to offer some soothing words, and instead of gratitude, she had shown him coldness. "Yes."

"These things take time, Brigitta. To understand everything. To draw out the right answers. Your husband assisted the Nazis, you will remember."

The war is over, she thought.

He nodded gently. "I understand. I do. Our country was divided then. So many of your people offered a roof to the Germans while they occupied our little village. How do we come together now, when men in our own village fought on opposite sides? How do we face each other in the street?"

"Imre did not want this fight. He had no sympathies to either side. He has done nothing wrong."

A step closer. Voice lower. "I have said more than I should have."

"Ah."

"Brigitta?"

"Yes."

"I have never wished sadness on your home. You must trust that."

She lowered her head, looked at his shiny shoes, undamaged heels. His feet shuffled as he spoke. His voice was sincere, and she knew he was telling the truth.

"Never," he repeated. "Even though. When we were young."

His tone made her feel first comfort, then shame. He had not even crossed the threshold of her home, but she could sense him inside of it, lacing the air with hope. Then the shame arrived inside her heart as the sight of him, the smell of him, made her wish for simpler times. An easier life. "I...I did not mean to imply."

"Not to worry. I understand. Of course I do." And he pushed the soft parcel into her hands, glancing at her for only a moment. His eyes were wet and dark.

"I need nothing," she said, crinkling the paper.

"Everyone wants for something, do they not? A warm home, a nice meal, another's hand inside their own." He squinted, revealing faint wrinkles around his eyes.

"I want my husband to come home."

"Ah," he said, and he raised both hands, showing her his palms. "If only I could, Brigitta."

When he left, she closed the door and carried the parcel to the kitchen. Cut the knotted beige string and opened the paper. Meat. Pink and milky and soft with delicate strands of fat. A young calf slaughtered, no doubt. On her own, Gitta could purchase nothing as fine as that. She lifted the paper and brought the meat closer to her nose, inhaling the raw smell. Felt the weight of the flesh pressing against her palms, two kilograms, maybe more. She would make a goulash, taking half to Zsuzsi. Like her, the old woman was trying to feed a boy who was always hungry. And besides, that would assuage the trickle of guilt inside her throat. Even though she loved her husband, she had just pulled a steely thread of strength from Dragan Dobrica.

∷∷

PAPRIKA. FORGOTTEN FROM THE short list. Gitta had sent Anneliese to the market to buy a small bag of coffee beans and half a round of bread. But as soon as the girl had closed the door, Gitta saw the empty jar. The sight of it made her dizzy, and she realized the rooms in her home were hot and stale, with not a breeze through the open window. She reached into the cupboard, pulled out the jar, and held it in her hand. Stared at the glass streaked with pale red dust. None of it quite made sense. How her kitchen could be missing something so basic. So ordinary. She could vaguely remember using the last spoonful of it, but still, she had the notion that someone was stealing from her. Robbing her of an item so fundamental to creating a decent meal; it was criminal.

She placed the jar on the counter, trying to straighten her thoughts. Her head was sore from all the shrinking and stretching, trying to accommodate an impossible coupling of hope and despair. The constant worry over Imre. Lies flying into the face of her son. "Your father is involved in important business. Any day, he'll return. Any day. No doubt with a surprise for you, *szívem*." Five weeks gone and not a word. Not a whisper. Questions she was unable to ask, and even if she could, there was no mouth willing to answer. It was as though he had disappeared into a crack. Never existed at all.

The day before Imre left, he had given her a small amount of money. "For the kitchen," he had said. "Buy food to make a child strong. Yes, yes?" "Of course," she had replied, and the image of János's bones growing straight and tall made her smile at her husband. He did not return her expression but instead gave her a long, hard look.

She knew the money was from the girl, but Gitta would never have accepted it directly. Still, she was grateful for it and was able to purchase items that normally they would have forgone. Besides, the girl was an extra plate, was she not? And she certainly was not timid at the table. In the weeks since she had arrived, her jaw had already grown thicker with Gitta's meals.

That afternoon, Gitta would prepare a goulash in the summer kitchen to the side of the property. She would have to cook it slowly with onions and stock and two handfuls of sweet paprika. She found a basket, placed a container of lard, the meat, and three onions into it, ready to carry out to the garden. Then she noticed the empty jar on the counter. Ah, yes. The paprika. How had her mind wandered so quickly? So quickly. The spice was nearly gone. And Anneliese had just left. The girl could purchase a packet of it in a shop in the square.

Gitta rushed out the door, small change jingling in the pocket of her apron. "Anneliese," she called, but with younger legs moving at a steady pace, the girl was already a good distance away. Gitta tried to skip a little, "Anneliese!" But she could not catch her. She would have to go to the market herself or borrow some paprika from Zsuzsi.

Gitta began to walk down the road. It had been several weeks since she had been away from her home, and the openness was a welcome relief. She felt the warm, packed dirt beneath her shoes and heard last night's rain moving along the slender ditches that lined the edges of the road. Gitta breathed. Once. Then again. The late summer air was sweet and ripe. Harvest was near. She turned her head, saw a cluster of old neighbourhood women sitting on weathered chairs, stockings rolled to thick knees, chirping and laughing. Sunlight caught in one of their mouths. A gold tooth.

"Gitta!" one called. "You are keeping your hands busy?"

"I am," she replied, holding up her fingers. Yes, they were her fingers, red and chapped from soaking and scrubbing the stains from collared shirts. Her washing work was steady and monotonous, but making something clean gave her a sense of direction.

"That is the best way, yes?"

She nodded, stumbled over a small stone, caught herself. She had not noticed the horse and cart, the sound of the wheels groaning, until it was right in front of her. The horse bucked its head, snorted, spray landing on her cheek. "One side or the other," the farmer said as he pulled the reins, veering the cart around her.

"Yes," she replied and moved out of the way. She straightened her back, smoothed her hair, and fixed the metal clips that had come loose, hanging behind her ears.

"You see?" the farmer called over his sloping shoulder. "A small step will do."

A small step will do. She lifted her arms away from her sides, and the breeze spread around her sticky neck, up her dress. Cooling her legs and trunk. Her eyelids fluttered, and for the first time in ages, she felt real. Hazy edges of herself sharpened, and she could define where her body ended and the rest of the world began. She would walk. Yes, she would walk to the market and buy the paprika herself. She was not a widow and should not be carrying herself in such a way. Imre was working, and surely he would return eventually. He had done nothing wrong. They would understand that.

When she saw his face again, she would pull out his secrets. Force him to tell her everything. About his nightmares. About Anneliese. So many thin layers between them. Not one very strong on its own, but together they formed a wall.

As Gitta strolled behind Anneliese, she caught the girl's song trailing in the air. And it annoyed her, that foreign music, like a lullaby. Then, as she stared at the girl's back, she saw a young boy run out from a courtyard, catching hold of her hand. János. Fingers locked, their double fist swung between them, and now Gitta could hear two voices on the wind. The girl's, of course, and her son's. A child who never sang a note in his life. Now singing.

Gitta held her lips tightly, and with each step, the heels of her shoes pressed more deeply into the road. She did not understand this girl, why she was sleeping under Gitta's roof. Surely there were other families. Imre would offer no explanation, and whenever she gently asked Anneliese a question or two, the girl would only smile faintly and retreat to her room or the back garden. If love was keeping her in Bregalnica, it existed in curious form. Why not go and visit with the subject of her admiration? Why would she not even speak his name? Whenever Gitta dared to mention him, the girl's pleasant appearance drained, and she blushed, shook her head. Looked at the floor or walls or ceiling, with a gaze that Gitta could only describe as deceitful.

They were skipping now, Anneliese and János. And laughing. Her brown hair glowed as she danced over the road. From behind, she might look like a foolish gypsy, except her dress was made of rich silver damask, too fine for a walk to the market. She said something and reached around to poke János in the ribs. He threw his round head back, then jumped. He clutched her hand with both of his and brought it to his cheek.

Gitta's eyes widened as she focused on her son, caressing a stranger, and then, then, he brought her hand to his boyish lips and kissed it. Another squeeze, and he broke away, turned and bolted back to the courtyard where a clump of boys was screaming and driving wooden tanks through heaps of pebbles.

Gitta waved as he passed in front of her, but he did not pause. No wonder. Her dress was similar in colour to the road, and likely he never noticed her. She bit her lip, knew she was lying to herself, and irritation bubbled up and burned. For a reason she could not explain, her mother's face kept arriving inside her head. The grave expression that day at the institution, her mother's claws gripping her pregnant stomach. "It is not yours," she had cawed. "Not yours." She had meant the child. Had meant János.

No, Gitta thought to herself. *He is not mine. His teacup heart belongs to a Schwab thief named Anneliese.* A woman who did not belong in their lives.

Enough. Even though Imre had forbidden it, Gitta would take matters into her own hands. She would find an excuse to have the Pástor boy come to her home. Something related to Imre. Everyone knew he was away, and though Gitta never asked for help, the notion of it was not unlikely. She would have to pretend she was incapable of a task, some sort of male chore. A tiny pinch at her sensibilities, but she would suffer that if it might shake Anneliese, force her to face the papery love that kept her here. Foolish as it was. A girlish crush should never have tethered her to a village when her parents had collected their belongings and left. The family should have stayed together.

For the first time in many months, Gitta felt a glimmer of hope. Imre simply did not have the insight to handle the issues of a delicate female heart. But she did. She had never shied away from difficult decisions. If everything went according to her plan, when Imre returned, as the Komandant assured her he would, things would be moving along. Rim of the stagnant pool broken. Either the connection between Tomi Pástor and Anneliese would flourish, or Anneliese would recognize the inanity of it. Abandon her childish pursuit and seek out a reunion with her family.

Gitta followed many steps behind Anneliese. If she called to her now, the girl would likely hear her, but Gitta remained silent. The weather was beautiful, and she felt heartened by the sunlight on her thin cheeks. She had the distinct sense that Imre was near, that soon he would return. She just had to be patient.

As she rounded a corner, only a handful of steps behind Anneliese, Gitta saw a familiar face walking toward them. It took her a moment to recognize him, but sure enough, it was Tomi Pástor. He appeared as though he had been working in the fields. His face and arms tanned, shoulders wide and strong. He was tall, his limbs a little too long for his skinny trunk.

Perhaps Gitta did not need to create a flimsy excuse after all. Here he was, and in a moment Anneliese would see him as well. Gitta tipped her head to the right, squinting in the sunlight. Why had not the girl noticed him already?

She watched Anneliese carefully as the two passed each other in the road. Passed each other! The girl did not slow down; in fact her steps seemed to quicken. Anneliese had greeted so many people as she walked, but yet she made no attempt to nod or smile at Tomi. Instead it was as though a lanky ghost had passed her on the road, and she turned her head. And when Tomi passed Gitta, so close she could have touched the dusty fabric of his shirt, he stared straight ahead. His face scrunched, a puzzled expression, as if a math problem with long figures was working its way through his mind. Anneliese at his back, still strolling toward the market, straw basket swinging loosely in her fist.

Gitta's legs stopped moving. Awareness flooding into her. It took several moments to grasp everything. So simple. So much suddenly made sense. She felt naked, a thousand cold hands smacking her awake. Startlingly aware, confused crickets scraping out sounds, breeze moving through dried leaves, the scent of the dirt road, foul and sweet at the same time.

She saw them now, the secrets between her husband and that girl. The warm looks that Gitta continually ignored.

In the middle of the road, her legs and heart began to melt. She had to move quickly, or would have to be carried. Eleven deep strides, and she stood on the packed mud of a courtyard next to a home. Wild vines and tiny pink flowers clinging to the walls. Laughter through an open window, the smell of cooked fruit in the air. The door swung open, held by a shoed foot, and a woman scooped the air with flour-coated hands, said, "Ah, Gitta. Come, come." And without thinking,

Gitta stepped into the dimly lit home, sat on a hard chair, and said, *"Jó reggelt."* Good morning.

"A minute," the woman said, "and we will take a coffee together, yes?"

Gitta nodded.

The woman stood on one side of a long wooden table, her daughter on the other, dough stretched to the thinness of skin covering the surface, hanging over the edges. Underneath the table, the woman's toddler son crouched, occasionally pressing a hand through the membrane, the shape of a rounded mouth.

"Tomi!" the woman bellowed, and Gitta jumped, shaking her head before she realized the young child bore the same name. "Out!" Bite in the dough, and Gitta saw the boy's eye peering through the circular hole. Then he skittered away on all fours like half a spider.

The woman sighed, called after him, "Do not bother me when your stomach seizes, Tomi. You will not eat for a week." Then, to Gitta, "He is a chicken catcher, like I have never seen!"

Gitta nodded again, watched as the woman and her daughter coated the dough with melted butter until it glistened, folded and folded, with practised steps. Then the woman gripped an enormous pot with both hands, shook the softened fruit along the centre of the dough, a sprinkling of dried bread crumbs, folded again until she had a fat log the length of the table.

"We will leave it," she said to her daughter. "It deserves a rest, yes?" Then, to Gitta, "Tomorrow we make soup noodles. Enough to last the winter. You are welcome to join us, and we will share."

"No," Gitta said. "Thank you. I will be—will be going out tomorrow. To Drobnik." The words surprised her, as she was not aware her mind had already made a decision.

"Yes?"

"I promised János I would take him. He had need of something."

"Ah." She washed her hands, drying them on a cloth. Even though it was nearly noon, a rooster began its hoarse *koo-koo-ri-koo,* and the woman leaned her head out the window, laughing. "He is old and demented. Nothing but milk between his ears. But I have not the heart to choke his neck; he has too much passion."

"I understand."

"Yes, yes. A coffee, then."

"A glass of water? I was on my way to the market, and the sun overtook me."

"Of course. I know, Gitta. We cannot deny we are getting older. Our youth is slipping away."

Gitta looked at her shoes, leather worn and stretched, revealing the strain on her bones beneath. She thought of Anneliese, of her pretty, open face. Not a mole or a scar. Gitta thought of the girl's hair, no trace of coarseness. Remembered, then, the easy bend of her shoulders and back as she moved the bow across the wires on her violin. Her hips, her trim calves, the flesh draped so perfectly over her young frame. Covered in fabrics Gitta could never afford.

Imre had seen it all as well. Had been drawn to it, enough to betray her. In the worst way possible. Right underneath her very own nose.

She would not allow her neighbour to see how much she carried inside. To see her mouth twist or her eyes weep. She sipped the water and spoke about pleasant things. There was nothing to do but wait until a reasonable amount of time had passed, then lift herself off the chair, praying her body did not burst in this woman's sweetly scented kitchen. Or on her short walk home.

::::

GITTA CLOSED THE DOOR to the Komandant and went to the kitchen. Laid the package on the countertop and sat down. How could she look at his rich gift and not remember those weeks when Imre was gone? The strange man who returned. Her husband and no longer her husband. The Komandant never meant to remind her of that sadness, of course he had not. He was trying to help her, to find a way to fill her up from the inside. With food. A simple meal. The weight of his kindness nearly made her weep.

With János missing, she had no intention of preparing the meat. Could not envision a single meal. Food that she would eat alone. Perhaps she might give it to Zsuzsi. The old woman and her grandson had done so much for her. Too much. She did not enjoy the debt she was creating but did not argue over it. No opportunity to help was missed. Yesterday, Dorján even spent the better part of the afternoon picking grass burrs from Buksi's back.

As the dipping hand of the clock knocked forward and forward, she thought about her aunt and uncle. Relatives who still lived in a neighbouring village but had not spoken to Gitta since she had left as a teenager. Moved to Bregalnica. When her mother had been committed, they had taken Gitta into their home. Never welcomed her, though. Instead they watched her with suspicion, as though they believed she contained a spoiled seed. Swollen skin. Convinced in due time it would split and bloom.

Not that she blamed them.

She stared at the parcel on the countertop. Near her feet, Buksi lifted his thick tail, let it slap the floor. An effort to distract her. The dog's fur was neat and shiny, clean of all the burrs that had marked it only yesterday. They had arrived on the wind, with their spiny spurs, tumbling over and under the fences, tangling into his fur. She was certain they meant something, but she was unable to decipher it. They were not just fleeting moments of life. They could not be. She thought she could have told the Komandant. He would have understood what she meant, offered his opinion.

Her eyelids lowered, and she wore a sedate smile. The answer would come to her, yes, in time. And she waited, listening to the clock, watched liquid redness move out through the paper, pool on the countertop, and patiently drip onto the floor.

Chapter 28

THROUGH THE GLASS PANE, Nevena saw Dorján swimming. Not a formal practice, she guessed, as the entire team was not there. Just Dorján and some others boys in the water. Takáts pacing on the brown tile, shouting orders. She saw Dorján stand on the edge, toes hooked, arms back, and then a hiccup on the surface. He was beneath the water, gliding through, shoulders first then arms lifting, propelling him forward. His upper body forming the sharp lines of a triangle.

She had not stopped thinking about him since she had seen him on the bridge. When Takáts had his back turned during class, she tried to say hello. But he ignored her. A result of her afternoon with Petar, no doubt. Not just the afternoon, but the rumours that followed. In the washroom she had heard the girls talking. One stall over, saying coarse things, describing events and circumstances that made her stomach knot. She heard Jasna Ković. Sound of pages flitting. "There," she said. "I told you I had a photo."

Somehow the rumours leaked out through the school doors, hobbled along the cobblestone, out of the town and through the village. A lengthy journey, but her mother heard everything, confronting Nevena.

"Were you alone with him?"

"Well, yes, for a—"

"Then it is your own fault. You should never have been alone with him."

"But I did nothing."

"Who is to say?"

"I say!"

"And that is good enough?"

"If he lied, he lied. He could have lied about anything."

"Ah! Why does your father insist we remain here? We could have a home in Drobnik." She laughed, rolled her eyes, talking to herself now. "Why do I even ask the question? He thinks I do not know. That I am so, so stupid."

Though it was Nevena who felt stupid. Why did nobody care for her? Not her mother, not János, not Petar, and certainly not Dorján. Even the girls, Jasna and the others, offered her no time. In some ways, she decided, her father was the only person who loved her. Who thought she was remarkable simply because she existed. He was pleased the moment she was born, he told her, and she need do nothing more than be present. His adoration was such a constant, somehow it no longer seemed to count.

Just before his head would strike the wall, Dorján broke the surface. Palms slapping the tile, his body appeared to fly up and out of the water. He wiped his hands over his face and crossed his arms over his dripping torso. Takáts was frowning, coming close to him. Even through the glass, Nevena could hear his words. "A fail. A complete fail."

Dorján mumbled something, but Takáts sliced through the air with his hand. "You have been asked to work. Not splash in your *nagyanya*'s sink."

When Dorján lowered his wet head, Nevena turned away. She could watch him no longer. The sight of his broad shoulders curling inward made her sigh. They were the same somehow. She and Dorján. Neither one of them knew how to fight back.

:: ::

DORJÁN STAYED UNDERWATER LONGER than he should have. Lungs about to explode, and he opened his mouth, pushing air through the water. An explosion of wobbly bubbles all around his face. A pleasant disorientation.

As he emerged, gasping for air, he thought of his mother. Only her this time. Not the man who visited her after his father had died. The man who always paused at the doorway, twisting his hand near his temple.

He replayed her death. Over and over again. Occasionally he discovered something new. A portion of a faded memory, and he would polish it up, put it in its place. Someday, he was certain, if he remembered every detail, he would understand. Realize what his role had been. And what he could have done to stop her.

Once when they were together in the little shed in the backyard, he asked his father, "Why did you marry *Anyu*?"

"Your mother," he replied, holding up a wooden heel to assess the curve, "is beautiful."

"And?"

"And nothing. She is a beautiful woman."

Dorján waited, watched as his father dipped a rag into the tin container of stain, daubed the heel. But he did not elaborate. That was it.

Dorján coursed through the water in the pool, came to the wall, flipped, and pushed off from the tile. Perhaps that was a portion of the problem. His father's callous assessment. He often wondered if once the appraiser had died, the value of the object had plummeted. With no one to care for it, eventually it would decay.

He remembered the morning after the explosion. Seeing his mother spread out on the bed in the warmth of the afternoon. The curtain above her head lifted and fell as though it were breathing air into the stale room. She did not move, lay there, strap of her nightgown fallen, large breast exposed. He started to hum, hoping his tiny voice would make her lift a hand, cover herself, but she never did. Her eyes were open and did not move. She murmured in a leaden tone, "Close the door."

People said her death was an accident. But Dorján knew differently. The evening before she died he had seen her crouched on the blue and white tiles in the kitchen, mound of shoes piled next to her. In one hand, she held a small hammer, and she took each shoe, gently placed it on its side, tap-tapped until the heel let go. Then she opened the door to the furnace, placed in one perfect heel after another. Slowly and carefully. She lay down, and Dorján could see the fire reflected on her sweating face. When she stood and walked away, he went to the furnace, peering through the little door. Nothing was left but a handful of embers, like blackened stones.

He crawled into bed with her that night, surprised by the plumpness of the mattress, sweet smell of wind trapped in the cotton sheet. His head grew woozy with hopefulness, and he moved his young bones backwards until he was lost in her clean folds. As her hand stroked his skinny arm, he dozed, imagined them on the water somewhere. A gentle river, a basic raft he could build himself. She would rest on the raft, letting the sun darken her skin, and he would leap off the side, a cooling splash, swim only a few metres before her voice called him. "Come back. Come back, *kis szívem*."

He was hardly aware of slipping across that threshold of sleep, never felt her hand glide over his folded elbow, up his forearm, wrist, hand, over his ribs. Tips of her fingers skimming the skin of his neck, and finally, her plump, damp palm pressing over his mouth and nose.

Breathing muffled and his eyes burst open, body stiff. He waited, waited for her to realize, and he could not move, could not fight her, his mother, her hand still blocking his air. Surely a mistake, a mistake, but her rose-scented hand did not shift.

Ice cracking inside his neck, Dorján thrust his head upward, struck his mother's chin, teeth clanking. Then a noise erupted in the room, blocked out the sucking sound as Dorján choked on air. Though he heard the animal wail come from his mother's throat, he knew it originated in her heart. Silence followed, until she whispered in a flat voice, "I thought, I thought, I thought we could drift away together."

She drowned in a bathhouse the very next day. Other women were also bathing, barely noticed she was beside them one moment, vanished the next. Her breasts were first to break the smooth surface. Dorján had heard that part of the story more than once. The beautiful Ilona Szabó fished from the bath. Dead, yes, but siren body naked and glistening with a thin coating of the charcoal-coloured mud.

Dorján pulled himself from the warm water, coming face to face with Takáts. His teacher was shrieking, mouth ragged, a rip in his face. "You fail. You are a complete failure."

Though Dorján willed the words to skim over his wet skin, fly off his back in a spray of fine droplets, they did not. Instead, they stuck to him, irritated him. Made him wonder why he was doing what he was doing. For what?

He thought of those burrs adhering to Gitta *néni*'s dog. When he had spent an afternoon removing them, Gitta had a look of confusion on her face. Why was he so patient?

He could not explain it to her. He did not fully understand it himself.

Chapter 29

"JÁNOS!" SHE CRIED. "COME help me, *szívem*."

Her little boy appeared around the corner of her bedroom door, ran to her. Wormed his strong fingers in through the knot on her apron strings, loosening it.

"Fine?"

"Yes, *köszönöm*." The apron fell away from her shoulders. "Ready yourself. We are leaving. We are going out today. To Drobnik."

Gitta laid the apron on the dresser and stared at herself in the mirror. Her face was pale, her lips thin and hard, surrounded by fine wrinkles. Leaning in closer, she smoothed the few errant hairs that refused to lie flat. These last years had marked her body.

For a moment, she imagined her skin peeled away, muscles and tendons disintegrated, revealing the greasy bones hidden beneath. Her skeleton resting on top of the earth, picked clean. Someone might think her skull delicate, her gently sloping forehead, narrow nose, small feminine holes that now held watery eyes. And if a man might see beauty in such things, perhaps he would consider her skull pretty. The hands, though, would make him gasp. She held them up to the mirror, turning them front to back. They surely did not belong with the other bones. So large and knobby, like the mitts of a dancing bear. He would assume an error. A grisly trick.

But her hands had served her well. They were the hands of a soldier, capable of doing necessary things. Things that made a typical woman squirm. Not so, for Gitta.

She washed her face in the basin and then changed her clothes. She put on stockings and a pale blue dress with tiny flowers buttoned up to her neck. While she was cooking, she removed her wedding ring, thought to leave it on the windowsill. But she plucked it up now, slid the large band onto her finger. A knitted sweater and, finally, her best scarf, tied at the nape of her neck. János was in the kitchen, eating *pogácsa,* and she called to him. It was time to go.

They did not take the bus but walked through the village, up the sloping road toward town. Through the gap in the stone wall, on tired cobblestone streets. She hurried up the steps toward city hall, tugging János by his wrist. Armed guards stood on either side of the double doors, the shafts of their dull black guns against their shoulders. As she passed between them her heart began to clang, an angry ram beating against the base of her throat. She glanced down at János, saw her hand holding his. Relaxed her grip when she noticed his fingers were blue.

Inside the building, she leaned forward, whispering to János, "Stand over there." She pointed to a distant but still visible corner. "Stand over there and do not move." She flushed when her voice carried up to the high ceiling, falling back to the glossy floor like empty shells.

She expected him to complain or to argue, but he did neither. Listened to what she said, marched to the corner, faced her, and clasped his young hands together. A childish smile on his face, "See, *Anyu*?" the smile said. "I can take orders. When I choose."

A sharp nod, he was a strong boy, and then she approached a man in uniform sitting behind an organized desk. His eyes were black and shiny, and his expression did not shift.

She leaned toward him, "I need to talk to someone." She handed him her papers, and he smoothed them on the table, studying them.

Subtle adjustment in the position of his head, an invitation to proceed.

Gitta inhaled deeply, but her lungs would not fill. The hurt was still there, swaddled in a bandage of anger, taking up too much space in her chest. "About a girl. She has been in my home. A *Schwab*. Her family left the village."

His wiry eyebrows lifted, slight crinkling of his smooth forehead. "She lives with you?"

"No, no, no."

"Then why is she in your home?"

Gitta paused, uncertain about what to say. "I am a stupid woman, sir." She glanced at János and nodded. "Soft in my heart. But I made a mistake, and now I must do what is right."

"You do not answer my question."

Another moment, teeth opened, but her lips closed. Then, "A juvenile crush on a local boy, sir. He does not even know her. Good parents would not have allowed the girl to stay alone."

"Some have remained in the village. So? I do not understand your issue."

"Well, yes."

"She is causing problems?"

Gitta told the officer a weighted story about Anneliese. That her face was that of an innocent, but her soul did not belong to the country. She had betrayed the goodness of the people with her words and with her actions, spreading lies to whoever will listen. Speaking out against the government, the Party. She does not recognize that we who live here want nothing more than to rebuild. Make ourselves strong. "She is a dark one, Oficir. And if she is left to flourish, with her appealing face, she will grow against us. Others will follow her lead. Follow her way of thinking."

Gitta did not know where the words were formed. But they poured from her face, spilling down over her ribs, like infected water.

The man lifted his hand. She need say nothing more.

On the way home, they stopped at a *kávéház*. She bought herself a small Turkish coffee and a pot of liquid chocolate for János. He gulped it, staring at her suspiciously. "We are the same, you and I. Strong. Strong." She pinched his chin, shook it slightly. "You have my hands."

::::

GITTA PLACED A SUGAR cube on her tongue, closed her mouth around it. Pushing the sharp edges against the back of her front teeth, she brought her cup to her lips, pulled coffee in through the cube. She shivered as heavy sweetness slid back over her tongue and down her throat. The thick drink rolled down her chest, coating her stomach, and she accepted the simple pleasure of it. Bitterness disguised, nothing but warmth and sweetness entering her body.

János was running in the street, and for the first time in so long, the house was calm, quiet. Both fingers holding the tiny cup, she took another sip of coffee. She closed her eyes, then pressed the cube against the roof of her mouth, crunching it in her teeth when it did not crumble. She tried not to think about the girl, where she might be, what was happening to her. But it was difficult to erase the image from the insides of her eyelids.

That gentle tapping on the front door. Always gentle tapping. The two tall men standing there when Gitta opened it. "We only want to talk," they said. "A question or two. No need for alarm." Hairy hands gripping Anneliese's upper arms, backs of their knuckles joggling her breasts, and they made no effort to stop. No effort. She had wept, pleaded, and that only brought faint smiles to their mouths. When they reached the door, she pushed back against them, like a stubborn puppy not wanting to go through a gate. "Gitta *néni*," she cried in broken Hungarian. "Tell them. *Kérlek*, Gitta *néni. Kérlek, kérlek.*"

But Gitta said nothing. Until János appeared in the hallway. And she growled at him to stay put, or he would feel the wooden spoon across the backs of his legs. Still, her threats did nothing, and he rushed forward to save the girl. "Anneliese," he screamed. *"Mein schönes Mädchen!"* My pretty girl!

And the men turned their faces down toward this child who spoke clear German, until Gitta grabbed his shoulders, yanked, saying, "What is wrong with your brain? You stupid *fiam.*"

When she looked up, she met a pair of curious eyes, staring into her face. His head cocked slightly. *"Ki ő?"*

"He is mine, sir. Mine. Yes, yes."

"*Lügner!*" Liar! János whispered, and Gitta slapped his face, held him by his ear.

"Are you certain?"

"Very much so. He is my son. Do you not recognize his eyes are drawn from my own head? His chin pulled from here?" With her free hand, she gripped her jaw, left streaks of red on her skin.

Gaze flitting from mother to son to mother to son, but János curled his mouth, crossed his eyes. He pushed his knuckles into her hand, the one that pinched his ear, and stuck out his tongue.

"Show me."

Gitta released her grip, knocked János backwards, stepped over his small body as she rushed to her wardrobe. Found the yellowed envelope with the family papers, and she gripped the documents, brought them back, passed them over with shaking hands.

The man let go of Anneliese, studying the papers slowly.

"You see, you see?" Gitta said, trying to sound calm, though her words quavered in the air. "He is mine. Mine." János belonged to her. Solely to her.

He took his time, licking his lips. Picked bits of dried skin from the corners of his mouth.

Finally, a word. "Good."

Gitta nodded, head not stopping.

Pleasant then. "I have a son. His age. Hard for a woman to control a boy, yes? But you must manage. Obedience begins at home."

Gitta watched the man's fingers curl into a fist. "Yes, yes," she said brightly. "Of course."

Anneliese had watched the exchange quietly, misunderstanding. Wailed again when they clasped her arms, pushing her out through the door. To Gitta, her crying face appeared younger than fifteen years. János rushed toward her a last time, but Gitta caught the collar of his shirt, would not let go. Shiny buttons popped and rolled over the floor.

"We are done with her," she spoke into the cup of his ear. "Finished. It is over. Do you hear me, *szívem*? It is done."

A FINAL PROBLEM. THE girl had not time to collect her belongings.

Once János was asleep, Gitta took the girl's bag and opened it. A handful of fine clothes, which burned very nicely. Her shoes were still beside the front door. Gitta collected them, placed them on top of the flames. Stabbed the leather soles with the iron poker.

She took the travelling bag, walked to the back garden. Buksi was asleep in his basket, gentle snoring. Up and over the fence went the bag, into the field behind the homes. Someone might find it, but likely not.

Gitta returned to the warm kitchen and sat down in the chair next to the stove. Thought to close her eyes, rest a moment, when she spied a wooden case balanced on a table in the corner. The violin.

Ah. Inside of her, a special reserve of hatred had developed especially for that violin. She would never forget the way its music wound around her husband's head, turning his eyes toward the girl. Lured him away. Like a charm. Like witchery.

It would give Gitta joy to destroy it.

She stood and went to the table. Fumbled with the tiny metal clasps, no doubt made for delicate fingers. Once the case was opened, she withdrew the violin, grasped it in two hands, and lifted it above her head. She could envision it smashed, splinters of wood skittering across the floor. Strings singing as pressure released.

So light in her hands, air and thinnest wood. She hesitated. Looked at it more closely. Fine construction, beautifully polished, remnants of rosin dust on the strings. The bow made of dark wood and white horsehair. Gitta twisted the screw, watched the hair tighten, the back on the bow strain slightly with the stress.

She understood the strain. Understood the stress. Could not bring herself to break the instrument.

In the early morning, the world still awash in shades of grey, she awoke to hear the moving music of the gypsies. She went to the front door, opened it, and at that moment a small boy was passing in the street. No larger than János, dark face, sleepy eyes. Stretched sweater with holes on the elbows, missing a coat. His feet wrapped in mucky rags.

She rushed to find the violin and bow, and brought it to him. His walking barely slowed, but he accepted it without looking at her, taking it into his hands. Scratched his back with the tip of the bow, pushed the violin under his chin.

Gitta watched him as he continued his walk through the village. His arms swung loosely at his sides, but the violin remained clenched between chin and shoulder. A strange sight. A boy with a wooden extension near his neck. No reluctance in his stride. He moved as though the curving body and intricate scroll had always been there. Was part of him.

There was nothing to question.

Chapter 30

"I'D FORGOTTEN," DORJÁN SAID, "that you were waiting for me."

Cigarette to his mouth, János sucked in smoke with his thin cheeks. His skin appeared dull, did not reflect the few remaining lights surrounding the movie poster. The poster itself was torn and faded, and the curled edges fluttered in the wind. "Yes, Dori. You left me in the woods."

"I shouldn't have." Dorján looked down at the red carpet lining the steps and platform. Once plush and bright, it was now threadbare in places. Dingy yellow mesh showing through. As he stared at the landing, he saw a gold coin just sitting there. Barely recognizable. Worthless.

"You could have come back. Why didn't you come back?"

Dorján finished the crabapple cupped in his palm, skin and flesh and seeds and all. Went to flick the stem into the empty road, but it struck an approaching man, clung to his wool coat. The man never noticed. Instead he rushed up the stairs of the movie theatre, jostling past them. Dried leaves were stuck in the band of his hat, around his scarf. The uppers of his shoes were shiny, but the bottoms were caked in mud.

He glanced quickly at both boys, but his face was a blur. Nose and mouth and two eyes jumbled, unrecognizable. With swift and practised movements, he bent, plucking the coin from the carpet, pocketing it. Then he turned his back to them and lifted his right hand close to his temple, limp at the wrist. Slowly he twisted his hand around. One. Two. Three times. Deep breath, fabric of his coat expanding and contracting, and then he disappeared inside.

"Him," Dorján cried. "Because of him. I was going to come back. To find you. I promise I was."

János shuffled forward, upper body stiff and awkward. He bent from his hips to look into the decrepit building, and he laughed, only lightly, as though the movement of his chest caused him pain.

"Because of who? You dream of ghosts, Dori."

"Do I?"

"Yes. Your eyes are closed."

"Yes, I know. My eyes are closed. I am sleeping, you see."

Wind slid down the cobblestone street, handfuls of dead leaves singing, a chorus of dry notes. János moved into the shadows by a cracked pillar and shivered. Dorján had not noticed before, but now he saw that his best friend wore nothing but shorts and a beige shirt, a single tattered shoe. That shoe was wet and the leather swollen on his foot.

"What happened to you, János?"

"I'm cold, my friend," he replied, and the blue smoke from his cigarette clouded the air between them. Air that stank. "It's no fun without you. Will you hurry up?"

"I will. This time."

"Ah. It's nearly over, and I'm tired of waiting."

Dorján began to shiver as well, and as he rolled, he felt the sheets and woollen blanket falling off his body. Heard them tumble to the tile with a soft thump. He opened his eyes and sat up. Cold and confused and coverless in his own bed.

::::

"IT IS THERE, I tell you. It is there."

Dorján was in the attic of the home he shared with his grandmother, and she was calling up to him from the hole in floor.

"Behind the wooden boxes. The head is there. I know it."

As he moved over the boards, dust billowed around him. Slits of sunlight streamed into the warm space through cracks in the straw roof.

"Anything yet? I am too old to be holding my breath."

He opened the brass latch on a trunk. He moved aside letters and documents, lifted a layer of paper, found a yellowed gown neatly folded.

"I said behind the boxes, Dori. Not in my trunk!"

"Fine, all right," he called to her. Then, to himself, "Nothing wrong with her hearing."

"I heard that." A squeal.

In the very corner of the attic, three boxes sat on top of one another, and Dorján had to lean on his stomach to peer over them. When he saw the head, he jumped slightly. A red-faced mask carved from hardwood, high cheekbones and drooping wooden flesh underneath yellow eyes. Long wild hair covered the crown, and when he lifted the mask, fingers stuck in the snarl of wool, he felt the softness, lanolin still hidden there. He brought the mask into a strip of sunlight, touched the sharp nose, a stringy grey moustache hanging beneath it. Bright white teeth and red lips. Fixed near the temples were two curling horns from an old dead goat.

"I've got it. I've got it." He slipped it on over his head. He could see through the drilled holes perfectly, and it moved as it should when he looked left and right.

"Quickly. Come down, *szívem*. Before you crash through the ceiling and flatten me."

Watching his step, he backed out of the attic, careful not to strike the dry horns on the beams that crossed overhead.

"Wonderful!" she exclaimed after Dorján had descended the ladder. "So much like your grandfather. He would be proud!"

:::

GITTA WOULD NOT LEAVE her home. She heard the children screaming, running about like birds with clipped wings. Free to flail about as they shook socks filled with sawdust. Through the window over her sink, she saw Dorján emerge from Zsuzsi's house, baggy white pants, tight cuffs around his ankles, wool skins laced together, covering his shoulders, making him broader than a full-grown man. For a moment, he turned to face her, and he wore a horned mask. He raised a paw, shook it, and she lifted her hand to him in return.

He would join the others, and if János were here, he would be among them. Acting like animals, beating drums, striking the ground with sticks. Shrieking and punching their padded woollen chests. When she was younger, she believed in this spirited fight against nature. She always imagined winter fighting back, icy gales rippling the beards and wild hair. Straining, straining against the weight of spring. How the men and boys, so much larger than life itself, would frighten it into submission. Warmth would rise, and winter, shamed and tired, would scurry away on all fours, its frosty tail tucked between dirty white hind legs.

But no, she decided. Winter was not a young man and likely left on its own. Gave up with barely any fight at all. Quietly retreating to a place where peace might be found. Why would it stay? Exposed to such torture.

She boiled water and coffee grounds in the *kávéfőző*, poured the black liquid and creamy foam into her cup, brought it to the table. She did not drink it, though, just used her finger to twirl the cup round and round by the undersized handle. Last curls of steam, and she stopped, laid her hand on the photo sitting next to the mug. When she could resist no longer, she turned it over. Brought it closer to her face.

Earlier that day, Gitta had found this photograph of János. Tucked between leaves of paper, recipes her aunt had long ago scrawled, ink faded. A series of photos had arrived in the mail, sent by her brother-in-law, and while most of them appeared damaged by water, this one was intact. She remembered the very instant it was taken. János had just turned four, and Gábriel had come to visit. Those days were heavy with grey, everyone taking light steps. Thinking a jump or a stomp might cause so many cracks in so many countries to unite, a massive fissure to open and take them all. But that afternoon, Imre and Gábriel laughed and drank *pálinka,* and there was never a single mention of the hollowness outside the doors of their home. They looked backwards and backwards, but never a day ahead.

"Show me," Gábriel said, clapping his hands. "Show me what you were."

Enough liquor sloshing in his stomach, and Imre jumped up from the table, trying to stand on his hands. Elbows buckled, and he came down on the kitchen floor in a clump.

"Ah, you are so soft now. Strength of a baby, young brother."

"Nothing of the sort." Sticking out his barrel chest. "You just need to hold my feet."

"Do you know you could have been one of the greats? You could stay in the rings all day long. You had it, my brother. You had it."

Gitta remembered that Gábriel's suggestion had burned her. Imre had made his choice. He could not do both. He could either stop training and have a family, or remain a bachelor, as Gábriel had, and chase slippery dreams.

"For what? And lose what I have now?"

Imre defended himself, and even though her heart swelled, her face did not change as she placed a plate of sour cherry pastry between them.

Imre grabbed János, the boy's small head pinched inside the crook of Imre's elbow. Clutched his ear and tugged, and János yipped and struggled, arms winding in the air, fists punching Imre's meaty forearm. Twisted free, expression of success on the child's chubby face.

"This is all I need, Gabi. Everything is right, and everything is right here."

Later, Gábriel unpacked his camera, a black sheet, and a flash bulb that he held in his hand. He took Imre's photograph, and then her photograph, and then the two of them together, boy perched on her knee. Their faces sharp and stern. Then Imre pressed János against the wall, spit in his palm, swiped the boy's hair. János made a toothy smile, but Imre pinched his lips, "We want to see your face, not your teeth. Keep your grin for another day."

So clearly Gitta could recall Imre yelling, "Show me your strength!" And János placed one laced shoe in front of the other, lifted his fat fists, held them underneath his chin. Angry snarl. All there inside the picture. But it was his four-year-old eyes that hurt Gitta the most. She could barely look at the photo without a solid mass inside her splitting right in two. Her son's eyes were watery innocence. Pure and still open to wonder. Why had his expression frightened her? Frightened her more than anything else in the world? Why had she worked so hard to eliminate that soft innocence? Replace it with fortitude and resilience. Fix something that was already perfect.

She went to a front window, watching the procession. Creatures larger than life. Red and brown and black faces. Nearly all of them painted with otherworldly smiles, rows of teeth even but incomplete. The sun was dropping in the sky now, goblin shadows dancing in the street. Soon they would light the fire, flames licking up around the enormous puppet. The masked men would roar and clap as winter's constructed body and head were eaten by orange flames. Pointless display, Gitta knew. Winter was already long, long gone. She drew the curtains, staying in the darkness.

Gábriel came to visit one more time, shortly after Imre died, and he told her that he was leaving. Going away and not coming back. Asked her, begged her to join him. They would cross the border together and start a new life. Completely fresh. He would help her, whatever he could manage. They were family, after all.

"You have to be strong, Gitta. For the boy."

She glanced down at her large hands, the cuffs of her dress. She wore dull colours now, as she would for the remainder of her life. "This is our home. Imre is here."

Gábriel tugged hard on his cigarette. "No. Imre is not here. Imre is dead."

"He…he—"

As Gitta stuttered, Gábriel took her cold hands in his. The skin around her nails was ragged and dry. He brought her fingers to his mouth, blew on them. "You are not taking care of yourself."

"No."

"A poor choice."

"I cannot. Not these days."

"And János? Does he not deserve a mother who is dedicated to him?"

"He will survive. Surely I can fade just a little. For today."

Gábriel released her hands, began to pace the floor, weight on his heels. "Let me have him."

She closed her eyes, laughing ever so slightly. Lately her eyes had been tormenting her, and now another sense was joining the game. "My ears," she said. "Ah, the tricks."

Rainy sheets of words flew out of Gábriel's mouth. "Take him with me. It will be a better life, Gitta. I make that promise to you. I do. He will have a better life. I know where to cross, where to take him. We will not have a single issue. It will be safe. We will be safe. Someone is waiting for me. For us. Trust me, Gitta. You have to trust me. I am Imre's blood. I loved my brother and I love his son. I know what is best."

His request, spoken so politely, landed in her legs first. Sharp smack, like a piece of wood hitting those curving tendons just behind her knees. The burden of her hips and torso and head was nearly too much, and she almost crumpled. But she was not made that way. Would not give him the satisfaction of exposing her weakness. Shock pressed backwards, she formed her hands into mallets. Would use them. Would use them if he so much as brushed a hair on her son's pink cheek. Never would she lose him. Gábriel Kelemen would have to take an axe to her ribs, remove her heart first.

"I see you are upset. But think for a moment."

The back door opened and closed, the sound of clomping shoes, boyish skipping. János was in the kitchen. She could hear him rummaging around, looking for food in empty cupboards. He was growing and needed more. More than they had.

Narrowing her eyes, she smiled at her brother-in-law. Spoke calmly and quietly so as not to alert János of her distress. "That is why you have travelled here. With your filthy thoughts and beggar's smile. You only want to slide into his life and steal his son.

Steal my son. Another thief! Ah, jealousy. How come I never saw it before?"

"No, Gitta. I want to help you. Come with me. Please."

"I will not bend," she snarled, saliva pooling behind her teeth. "I will not bend."

"If you cannot bend, then you will soon break, Gitta."

"Then I will break. I will break, but I will be with my child."

She was ready to fight, but Gábriel simply frowned and removed his coat from the arm of the chair. Slipped it over his shoulders. Dipped into his pocket and placed a neat pile of bills on the round table. "All I can manage."

"I want nothing."

"Burn them, then." Rubbed his face, rims of his small eyes on fire. "No. I am sorry. Use it for the boy. I know you will look after him."

Even now, all these years later, she could picture him so clearly. Walking toward the door, out of her house, out of their lives. Imre and Gábriel had never spent much time together in those last years, too much distance, and the road toward each other was troubled. Still, she recognized Gábriel as a part of her family. But that day, her anger had been a blade through her vision. She could not see him. Could not grasp his intentions.

She let her head fall backwards, mouth open. The evening Gábriel left had been quiet. Not like this night. With the skittering madness, men dancing in furs and masks, monsters from a child's dreams. The squalor grew louder, and she could smell the faintest smoke seeping in around the window.

Gábriel stood in the empty road. "My offer is always open to you."

"I cannot. I cannot leave everything."

"Maybe one day you will understand," he said as he stepped backwards into the shadows. His soft voice still floating through the night, becoming fainter and fainter. Until his final sentence arrived, and she was uncertain whether it was his words or her imagination. "Sometimes," she thought she heard, "the best way to stand your ground is to walk. And to walk. And to walk away from it."

:::

DORJÁN MOVED THROUGH THE crowd, looking for her.

A goat-man bent and brought a flame to the kindling, and when the crackling began, he turned to the crowd, lifting his triumphant fists toward the starry sky. Winter burned on its stick, flames disintegrating the fabric, the ancient wooden face. Reek of burnt wool as the body curled inward on itself. Men drunk and happily releasing all the energy they had stored throughout the winter.

Then he saw her, on the other side of the ring. He wanted to move closer, to stand beside her, but did not dare. Instead he watched her through two perfect circles drilled in the mask. Her hair was loose and over her shoulders, and she wore a dark scarf, dark skirt that covered her knees, and heavy stockings. She lowered her face into the knot of her scarf but lifted her eyes toward the fire.

He considered the distance between them. Just a handful of metres. And he whispered to her, the heaviest thoughts inside his head. He needed to look at her and tell her. Even though she would never hear. He was sorry for the fighting. Sorry for turning his back, even though she had turned hers. Sorry for keeping the coins, for lying about it.

At the moment he told her he missed her, missed their friendship, she turned, faced him, and angled her head. Of course she could not know it was him. Hidden behind wood and animal fur. Could she?

The wind changed, blew a mouthful of smoke in through the eyeholes, and he blinked. Brought his hands to his mask, rubbed his wooden eyes with his fists. When he looked back at her, he was certain she was watching him, with the faintest smile on her face.

Chapter 31

THROUGH AN OPEN WINDOW Gitta could hear the old women in the street, chattering in rapid fire. A row of them, and she could imagine them clearly, seated on chairs or benches, or leaning against the plaster walls of their homes, skein of wool tucked into an armpit, sweaters or baby trousers growing underneath the needles. They watched each passerby; they watched the children, János among them. Their voices were happy, light, like young birds stretching out from warm nests.

At once, the crows grew quiet, and Gitta straightened her spine, angling her head to listen more carefully. She heard a car, idling close by, then a metal door opening, the sound of a package dropping on the road, door slamming shut. The car sputtered, changing gears, and the engine faded away. Then the women began to squawk, words indecipherable, and underneath it a frightening silence. Gitta was up at once, tearing down the hallway, fingers pressing against the cool walls, chest and head pressing forward.

She had no idea today would be the day Imre came home.

She found him lying on the wooden walkway above the gutter. The women had pulled him from the middle of the road. His body was nothing more than a pile of thin sticks draped in filthy fabric. No sign of those who had delivered him. "They just threw him there. "Ah, ah, ah, threw him like garbage," Zsuzsi cried, then covered her mouth with the back of her spotted fist.

Imre's skinny face was ashen, with slit eyes like scabs, clothes caked in dirt, both legs bent at unnatural angles. She dropped onto the slats of wood, cupping his head in her hands. Hot and dry. She was not prepared for this moment, had pushed it from her mind. Easier to reside inside that hazy limbo, bitter seed of anger hard beneath her tongue. She had convinced herself that she and Imre had already fought. And shame forced him to avoid her, late every evening, already gone before she awoke. He was like that, worked so hard, the effort of two, even three men. But now he was here, he was home. Brown blood in his moustache, lower lip with a ragged split, yellow scum inside the crevice.

She touched his hair, matted to his crown, and then opened her mouth, seed tumbling out. She would forgive everything, she knew she would. Without a second thought, she would forgive his betrayals. His love for another woman. A mistake, a brush of stupidity, and here he was. Here he was. He was still hers. He was still hers. Alive. She brought her lips to his right ear, puffed and closed. "Imre," she whispered. "Imre, my heart, can you hear me?"

"Air, Gitta. Give him a little." Zsuzsi.

Whether inside of her home or out, Gitta had always kept herself tightly bound. Movements and expression carefully controlled. But when she saw her husband open and close his mouth, upper and lower jaw misaligned, several teeth cracked, she broke. Belts loosened, and her voice bounced into the road, shrill and accusatory. "What have they done to him?" she yelled at the circle of women, who stood there, staring, fingers to their cheeks. "Three months. Three months. The animals took three months to ask him a question. He had no choice. Did what he was told to do. Never injured a soul. And look, look what they return to me. Is this my husband? Tell me!"

Swiftly, Zsuzsi pushed her face into Gitta's, and the old woman nodded slightly, pinched her own lips, twisted. "We have said enough, my friend. We would do well to work harder, complain less."

Imre never made a sound as the women lifted him, easing him backwards in through the door. Carrying the pieces of him, still

joined to his trunk, down the hallway and into the bedroom. Zsuzsi stayed, helped Gitta to remove his clothes and wash his withered
flesh, wrap his wounds. Sour smell that made their eyes weep. Two
other women rushed away to find the doctor. Gitta gripped the metal
footboard, swaying on her feet as she stood before her naked husband, flesh she no longer recognized. "Do not worry, you. Do not
worry," Zsuzsi sang softly as she dressed him with practised movements. Clean cotton nightclothes, stiff sheets folded around him.

Catastrophe of his body under blankets, and Gitta released her
hold on the footboard of the bed, held one of his feet. "Can you say
something, my love?"

"*Tss-tss,*" Zsuzsi whispered. "Let him be. Let him remember the
smell of his own home."

But in the days that followed, as Gitta sat in the room beside her
husband, all she wanted was to hear a sound. Any sound coming out
through the wires that now tied his jaws together. A moan or a whimper, a garbled cuss or a cry. Something to let her know he was not lost.
He was hidden, yes, but still inside of himself. With patience and with
forgiveness, she would love him enough, and he would emerge again.

::::

EVERY MORNING, GITTA BROUGHT a bowlful of warm milk to his
mouth, and he pulled the liquid in through his teeth. After he had
eaten, she moved him this way and that, gathering the sheet from
beneath him. She carried the sheet to the front garden, gripped the
edges of it, and snapped it several times. On sunny days, she saw the
cloud of dust rising up from the cotton, tiny particles of skin and
scab lifting into the breeze. Blown up and over the fruit trees, invisible against the sky. This sight filled her with some small pleasure. She
imagined the damaged parts of Imre's skin gradually peeling away,
and she captured those injuries, released them back into the world.
Slowly but surely he was returning to her. Soon the sheet would be
clean, and Imre would be home.

::::

"WHERE IS ANNELIESE?"

Gitta stood in the hallway outside the bedroom, ironing shirts and dresses and linens that belonged to other people. The doctor had removed the wires three days ago, and though she gently coaxed him every day, this was the first time he had spoken. The sound of it, stone scraping against stone, made her jump, and she burned herself. Shaking her hand, she stared at her husband's chin. "What did you say?"

"I ask where is the girl?"

"The girl?"

"Yes, the girl. Where is she?"

Gitta studied her palm. A red triangle from the tip of the iron's face. Weeks since he had returned, and she had waited patiently. Assumed he needed rest, to be alone inside his head, when instead he was thinking, thinking. Not of her and János and how to reconstruct their lives, but of the toxin he had introduced to their family. Forced her to take a knife to the root of it. Cut it out. Calmly, she replied, "Gone, Imre. Gone. Left."

"How can she leave?"

"I do not know, Imre." Gitta pressed the iron down on the starched cloth. "She simply left."

"What did she say?"

The iron hissed, steam rising up around Gitta's face. Her palm throbbed, and when she made a fist, she could feel the welt crinkle. "She believed you were not coming back." She laid the iron to the side, folding an embroidered cloth into a neat square.

"Why would she care if I came back?"

"Why?"

"Yes. What difference would that make?"

This response confused Gitta, but she ignored it. Of course the girl would care. Imre was the only reason she was here. Casually she added, "Do not ask the boy about it. Only now has he stopped crying."

"János."

"She did that to him. Insinuated herself into his life." Gitta measured her words, let them tiptoe into the room, lie next to him in the bed. She was taking a chance, she realized, hacking through the girl's intentions, but Gitta held this string of hope that Imre would agree with her. Would be grateful for the girl's absence. Then somehow Gitta could forget what he had done. His horrible slip. She would explain to him it was easier if they could agree to a clean floor. Scoured and spotless. Place everything, everything in the past.

Imre was silent, and Gitta cut the girl again. "She thought nothing of abandoning him. The poor child."

"*Kuss!*" Imre hollered. "*Kuss!*"

Twice he used it, that guttural reproach reserved for wayward dogs. Gitta did not jump. This was the first time she had heard his full voice, but it was not intimidating. Instead his attempt to create silence only served to infuriate her. The anger she had thought drained away was still there. Full black bruise inside her chest.

"I know what you did, Imre. I know."

"What I did? What I did? I did what I was told."

"I am not talking about the Nazis, Imre. I am talking about this girl."

"Anneliese."

"Do you think I am so stupid? Do you really think I would not understand? I saw how you looked at her, saw it with my own eyes." A long hiss. "Want all over your face. And then the lies. Dragging the poor Pástor boy into your story. What does Tomi Pástor have to do with anything?"

"You have water in your head."

"You think? He was in the street. She walked right past him. I was only a few steps behind her. The whore. And not a word, Imre, not a word. He never so much as looked at your lover. She was that, was she not? Your lover." Her voice spiralled higher, her muscles growing tenser. "How could you deceive me?" Words pressed out through grinding teeth, and her feet pushed into the floor. "How—how could you do that to me?" Whole body like a tightened knot, and at once she felt a trickle of hot water running down the insides of her thighs. She turned away from her husband as tears sprang from her eyes.

Even her bladder, tasked with nothing more than being a simple container, was betraying her.

"What have you done?"

"What do you think?" She gripped the hem of her skirt and wiped her legs. "That I would sleep under the same roof as a thief? A girl who had stolen my husband?"

"Gitta. Stop. Stop. You are lying to me."

"I am not a liar, no. I turned her out. Onto the street. That is where a dog belongs. A mongrel."

She waited then. Only silence behind her, with the exception of his breathing. Moments passed, hours, days, a lifetime. Finally he spoke.

"Damn you," he whispered. "Her father asked me. That is all. To keep her here, care for her, while they walked away from the lives they had known. I wanted them to stay, like some of the others. Keep working, I said. Time will ease these tensions. Surely time would make things better. The village is small. Neighbours forget. You are a friend to me, I said. You are my friend.

"But he refused, said he was no longer comfortable in his own home. His cousins in the city were dug out, forced onto trains, shipped like rotten meat. Years they had grown on this soil. How could he stay in a country that treated his blood like that? But, Anneliese, she is so strong in the head and the heart. She is in love, he said, in love, and would not leave with them."

"In love with you, Imre. Are you trying to torment me with your story?"

"Fool woman," he spat. "Look at me. Do you see me? What girl would feel for me? A scrap of a man, dried and useless." He coughed into the hollow of his upper arm. "No, it was Tomi. She wanted a chance to win his heart. But you do not remember that, do you? What it was like to be young and so full of someone else. You choose not to remember."

String in her throat pulled, vibrating. "But Imre. He never looked at her. He never spoke."

"She was—she was. He was—he was her. He was angry with her. I promised to tell no one."

"Not even your wife?"

"It seemed so small. Frederic asked me for that kindness, and I had to oblige. I had not expected to keep it from you for long."

"That makes no sense."

"She was shamed, Gitta. Did not want you to know. I had to keep my word."

"Shamed? Shamed?" Gitta remembered her own shame when she saw Tomi stroll past. Not even a glance. "You make no sense. Your mind is working hard. Mumbling idiot. You are as creative as ever."

"Damn you, damn you." He sighed. "How cold you have gone. I barely recognize you."

"What do you expect?"

"Anneliese was to have a child. His child. And he, a black dog, wanted no more of her."

Those few words fluttered out of his mouth, landing on her shoulder. She tried to flick them off, but they would not budge. A baby. Her eyes closed, and she saw the police with their hands on her. Her clothes, loose layers, their hands gripping her arms, fingers grazing her heavy breasts, clothes pulled taut and the thickness in her waist was there. The girl hunching, curling around her abdomen. Gitta could see it clearly, the knowledge already tucked inside her memory.

How it made sense. Sharp, desperate sense. How wrong she had been. "Imre."

"I was to help her. To keep her until she was able to find her way back into Tomi's heart. She was my chance, do you not see that? To do something good. And you. My wife. You are no different than those men who did this to me. But you are crafty, and you hide your face. Which makes you even worse."

"Imre!"

"Is this life nothing more than a joke? A game? *Ist dieses leben nicht mehr lebens wert?*"

Breath collapsing. "Don't. Please."

"He was a decent father, Frederic. A good, honest man. I made a promise to look after her as though she were my own. A small sacrifice to restore my soul."

Gitta cried out, covering her gaping mouth.

"There is no honour left in this world. Do you hear me? No honour left."

::::

IN THE MONTHS THAT followed, Imre walked about the house, back bent, as though a stone lay against his spine. Gradually his feet slowed. A shuffle. Old shoes over the floor. The stone moving inward, fusing with his back. Though the men who beat him had placed it there, it was Gitta who sat upon it. Her weight causing him to continue bending, bleeding. He never looked over his shoulder to see her remorseful face.

"Will you take a meal?" she would ask him.

He would not respond. Instead he moved silently about the kitchen, filling a glass with *pálinka*. Returning time after time to refill it. Until he collapsed, each night, and Gitta would drag him to bed or cover him with a woven blanket.

"A coffee, Imre? Zsuzsi made a *torta*. You must eat something."

Silence.

For hours he lay in bed. Gitta would often catch János sitting in a chair beside him, listening as Imre spoke softly. Strained words agitating the air, leaving it heavy with the stench of digesting of liquor. The sight of them, heads together, made Gitta cringe.

"There are some thoughts you must remember. Long after I've left."

"Leaving, *Apa*?"

"Yes, yes. I believe so."

"To where?"

"Ah. No man can answer such a question."

As she listened just outside the door, her mouth went dry. Panic burst from her stomach, coursed down her limbs, made her hands and feet numb. His words. So dire. Did he really mean them?

"You will bring me something, *Apa*. A gift when you return."

A demand, not a question, and Imre laughed. János, deaf to the bitterness in his father's voice, laughed as well.

"You are to listen, *bogárkám*." My little bug.

"Yes, *Apa*."

"They will give a little, you see. And while you say thank you, they will slip behind your back and take everything."

"What can they take from me?"

"Nothing. Unless you let them."

"I won't let them."

"It is all a dream, *bogárkám*. All a dream."

"But I'm awake, *Apa*." Gitta heard a soft sound, the boy slapping his own cheek.

Irritation now. "You're not listening. You don't understand."

Gitta wanted to storm into the room, scream at him. Stop this madness. Of course, he does not understand. What do you think? He is a child. He exists today. Not in the war. Not in tomorrow. He is a casualty of nothing.

"You think the anger goes? You think hatred disappears?"

"Yes, *Apa*."

"Do not be a fool, my little son."

"No, *Apa*." Trying to appease.

"Nothing stays in the soil. Nothing. No man, with strong heart and strong mind, will ever truly lie down and sleep."

:::::

EVEN THOUGH SOME PART of her expected it, the sight of him was still a shock. She had told herself over and over again that everything would turn around. The sadness was temporary and would eventually lift, and life would return to what it was before. Every day she told János that his father was ill. Had caught a sickness when he was away. Soon he would be better. This was not her husband. This was not her husband. She had nearly convinced herself and ignored the tiny fissures along his seams. Faint sound of cracks and snaps as he surrendered each day. Struggled to stand, slurring his words, sleeping in his soiled clothes. Yes, she had denied he was really breaking until he was before her in pieces. His spirit split in two.

She found him in the bed, spine curled, free from the weight. Sick smell of yeasty vomit clouding the air. His stomach was sucked inward so tightly, she had the thought that part of him had wanted to survive, the part that was a father to János. But his mouth and nostrils would not co-operate.

Gitta walked to the doorway, leaned against the frame. She would catch the boy before he saw his father. It was not good for a child to see a broken man. The very sight of destruction could ignite something in a young heart. There was no nobility in allowing life to drift away.

No, János would not witness this finality. Would not be marked by it. She would not move from the room, would wait in the doorway, the floor like sponge beneath her feet. At some point he would dart down the hallway, and she would catch him. Catch him by the arm, before he entered the room.

She waited forever, wavering back and forth, Imre's emptiness pushing against her. Making her feel as if she was there, and at the same time, she was not. She did not recognize her own legs. Her arms. Toes and fingers so far away and foreign. They did not belong to her. She was nothing more than two sets of limbs and a bobbing head, stubbornly held in place. Adhering to the gaping hole that was once her insides.

Chapter 32

GITTA KNEW THE SMELLS of spring were driving Buksi crazy. During these warm days, the soil had awoken, and everything held frozen over the winter had begun to thaw. Liquid trickled down through the compost. Cabbage stumps and potato stalks, left sitting on top of the earth, turned to paste. Humble snowdrops wriggled up through the remaining frost. The ground had begun to breathe again, exhaling its stench, before new life wound its way toward the sunlight.

Each March she would witness the change. A week prior, Buksi was a sleepy old dog who spent most of his hours curled in the soft straw of his basket. Now, he acted like a lively mutt, barking and barking, straining against his chain, wanting nothing more than to find some soft, sweet rot and to roll in it. But this year, the dog was even more frantic. Even from the house, she could hear him. Scratching the garden, yanking his tether, throttling himself. Probably torturing Zsuzsi with his urgent whines. She ignored the sounds, and soon enough the dog fell silent, finally giving up his fruitless struggle for freedom.

When she brought out a plate of scraps, Buksi was gone. She blinked, looked again, her gaze following the metal chain, an erratic curl of metal, as though it had snapped back from the pressure of being broken. She saw the claw marks in the moist soil and a small hole underneath the fence. She bent, ran her hand under the boards, and in her fist she collected bits of tawny fur that clung to the nails.

She sighed, looked up into the blue sky, crushed the fur against her palm. Buksi had never broken away before, and she feared for him. No one would have planted yet, but there was still much a large animal could destroy. She prayed whoever captured the dog would not strike him. Or worse, shoot him.

Lifting her hand, she let the breeze steal the puff of fur and carry it away.

:::::

"DORI!" HIS GRANDMOTHER CRIED, her feet frozen just above the paddles of her sewing machine.

Dorján jolted upright, striking his head on the underside of the table. He had been crawling around on the rug, moving a large magnet back and forth over the carpet. Every now and again he heard a weak clink. Lost pins and needles rising up from the flattened tufts of wool, adhering to the iron.

"Why do you shriek like that?" Rubbing the top of his head.

"I just saw some type of animal. A beast. Before the window."

He backed out from underneath the table, went to the window. In the distance, he saw the dog bounding down the street.

"Just Buksi."

"Ah! I am getting old."

"He broke free."

"Stupid me." Heels of her hands to her temples. "I thought it was something from the hills."

Dorján smiled. Whenever a sound or a sight frightened her, his grandmother would suggest it had somehow emerged from a cluster of hills just beyond the village.

"Perhaps it wasn't Buksi at all."

"Now you tease me. An old woman. The shame of it." Only half a smile breaking her round face. "Go. Get him. Gitta has enough worry in her head."

Dorján rushed outside, through the courtyard, stones still damp and slippery from the morning dew. He ran out from underneath the budding trees, hand to his eyes in the bright sunlight, peering up and down the street. The dog was long gone.

Even though the earth continued to throw off cold air, the sun was unexpectedly warm, and he lifted his face to it. If he went inside now, his grandmother would chastise him for not trying. So, he clapped his hands together, called to the dog, and headed in the direction he had seen him running. Toward the square. Toward the woods. He wandered for nearly an hour, whistling. "Buksi! *Gyere ide,* Buksi!" But the dog did not appear.

Dorján stopped at the path that led through the woods to the park. He had not walked down that path in months. Since that night he had left his home in complete blackness, a lantern in his hand. He had found the tin empty, the coins stolen. The small amount of money they had pilfered from Tibor. Gone.

"Buksi!" he called. He wanted to yell, *I'm not going in there after you,* but those words stayed in his stomach. Poking little holes in its rippled lining. "Ah! Why am I worrying about a dog?" The pair of willows that guarded the path was flushed with yellow buds, and the drooping branches waved back and forth. Lazily beckoning him to move closer. *Come in.* He thought of János then, imagining his laughter as he and his uncle counted their fortune.

Dorján turned, and walked away from the woods. *If the dog has a brain, he will find his own way.*

On his way home, he passed the village square. Saw an excited commotion of young boys and girls, husky voices, loud squealing. Ah yes, he had forgotten. Little reason to remember—he had not participated in the sprinkling for several years. But once he had. Both he and János had stood with the other boys on the stone wall. Waited with cupfuls of cold water. Pails filled and tucked away in the tall grass on the other side of the wall. They never knew when they would arrive, but sometime in the morning, the girls began to race. All of them dressed in brightly coloured clothes. Red skirts, white blouses, every edge embroidered with flowers and leaves and twirling vines. Early blooms in their hair.

They ran in zigzags before them, and while most of the boys threw water haphazardly, he and János always waited. For Nevena. The most beautiful girl of them all. Weaving in and out of the splashes. Barely a drop touching her. Until she slowed in front of them, making it easy. Shower over her head as her hair and clothes stuck to her. Her high-pitched laughter as she ran toward them, trying to push them from the wall.

Though Dorján never understood the reason behind the sprinkling tradition, he always imagined it connected both János and him to Nevena. By allowing herself to be drenched, she was showing everyone, including her frowning mother, that she belonged to them.

Dorján noticed Tibor working on the opposite side of the square, hammering the wooden slats of his stand together. Too early yet for any fresh fruit or vegetables, but once the weather was comfortable, Tibor would sell his grandmother's bottled jams or pickles. A few handicrafts she had sewn over the winter.

One side of Dorján's mind asked to walk in the opposite direction, but the pushier side brought him straight to the rickety stand. Lifted his hands to the slats, shook the stand slightly. Even said, "Looks sturdy, Tibor."

When he realized he was before Tibor and actually speaking, Dorján swallowed a bubble of air. Pushed his hand into his chest, belched quietly.

He had rarely spoken to Tibor. It was always János who did the talking. All the swindling. Not a lot of money, but that was beside the point. It was still stealing, and he could not forget the vicious fight. Tibor's bloodied face.

"I'll pay you back. I will," Dorján said.

Again, the words firing out from his left cheek. His right. Double barrels.

"We were wrong. A stupid deal we made. So stupid."

Tibor kept his back to him, kneeling on the ground. Dorján could see the curve of his backbone through his shirt. Perhaps he could not hear him above the shrieking clusters of boys and girls. Perhaps he was simply ignoring him. Counting the seconds as he tapped thin nails into the old wood.

"You don't want to sprinkle the girls?" Not a jab. Honestly. He meant nothing by it.

But Tibor's head snapped around, eyes narrow and angry. He did not look directly at Dorján but close enough.

Dorján opened his mouth again but was unsure of what he should say. Likely he was making things worse, and he should just pretend none of it ever happened. He glanced at his hand, and for a moment, he recalled dirty coins sitting there. Pulled from a cool pocket of air, an arm's stretch beneath the surface of the ground. If only they had left them. Nothing good came from digging. When the past was sleeping, why poke it with a sharpened stick?

Tibor began hammering in another thin nail, ignoring him. Dorján glanced up and down the street. He had no wish to join the sprinkling, and he certainly did not want to return home and search for more needles. Or sit beside his grandmother while her feet worked the paddles. Sometimes he found the clack-clack sound soothing but not today. The sound only served to remind him that time was passing.

He took the narrow pathway between two buildings and strode out into the field behind the village. All of the grass was yellow and bent, but he could see slivers of bright green peering up through the dead layer. Beneath his feet the ground was soft.

He walked to the middle of the field and climbed the mound. Once he reached the top, he sat down. Since the weather had turned, he had been going out there a lot. At first it made his throat narrow, but gradually he drew some comfort from the solitude. He was able to sit and think. Both Drobnik and Bregalnica were at his back. In the distance he saw the city where his father once worked. In the hospital.

Even though he traced every rise and dip, Dorján could identify not a single hole in the horizon. What had been destroyed had risen up again, so everything appeared unchanged. His eye took it in, offering his mind a pleasant deception. Nothing really happened. Believe it. Your father is still there. Somewhere working. Bent over wounded soldiers, sewing together their skin and souls.

Dorján remembered an argument when he was a child. In the streets of Drobnik. His father stood on one side of an imperceptible line, an incensed man on the other. Cursing him for doing the work of a doctor. The man spat, and the yellow wad landed near his father's shoe. Afterwards, Dorján had asked the reason for the fight, and his father said, "The man does not understand something very simple. When a boy is dying, he has no origin. He has no country, no history. He is only a boy."

Short as it was, that was the last conversation Dorján had with his father.

::::

"AH, MY LOYAL FRIEND," she said when she heard scratching at her back door. "You have returned from your travels."

Buksi bounded into the kitchen, circling, circling, throat emitting a penetrating whine. Wet muck clung to its paws and muzzle and the matted fur underneath his neck and body. But Gitta barely noticed the spatter as the dog shook. Barely noticed because she could not take her eyes off the item clamped between Buksi's sharp teeth.

"Drop it," she breathed. Only when she spoke did she realize she had been holding her breath, and the sulphurous wave hit her, making her fall to her knees. "Please, Buksi. Let it go."

The dog opened his mouth, and a flattened object slipped from his teeth, landing on the floor with a dull thud.

"A shoe," she said. "Why do you bring me a shoe?"

Buksi barked, then backed away, bent his head, mouth open, snarling. Not at Gitta, but at the shoe. Clumps of hair along his spine stood straight up.

"It is not, it is not, no, no, no, it is not." Gitta's voice sounded like someone else's, and she shook her head. "Garbage. That is it. Just trash."

Gitta knelt and edged closer. She could not look directly at the swollen shoe but examined the space around it, the space that had been displaced by its presence. She was certain, in that moment, that it demanded far too much room to ever house her child's boyish foot.

Her hand darted out, clutching the soaked leather. Slippery and icy cold, she brought the heavy thing to her face. Her nose met the opening where toes would slide underneath the tongue.

Unmistakable.

The stench of something dead.

Chapter 33

"IF HE IS IN there, we will find him, Gitta," the Komandant said, placing a hand on her back. "Do not worry until there is need to worry."

First light of morning, and dozens stood at the base of the hill, waiting for direction. They were dressed against the springtime chill, fur vests over shirts, trousers belted high around their waists. Even a handful of women arrived. Scarves knotted tightly over their full faces. Wrinkles of concern marking their expressions.

"Come," the Komandant said to the crowd, clapping his hands in the air. "Let us work together. We will cover every inch of the hill between here and the park."

"Thank you, Komandant," Gitta said.

"Yes," Zsuzsi said, her stout fingers gripping Gitta's upper arm. "It was just a shoe, my friend. A lost shoe. No reason to believe it belonged to János."

"No, no. You are correct. Of course."

"Dori would be here for you. To help. But he went to swim. Too late to call him back."

"I do not want him here."

"No?"

"No, no. What if?"

"Foolishness."

"Yes. I allow myself too much of it."

"I will be here, Gitta *néni*. You should go home. Wait for word. As soon as they reach the park with empty hands, I will come for you."

Gitta noticed Gazda László and his grandchildren were among the group. While his granddaughter stood there, arms folded, ready to search, Tibor scuffed his feet, let his head loll back. Gazda twisted a piece of skin on the boy's neck and spoke into his ear. Sharp clucks. Tibor winced, slumping his shoulders.

Turning to Zsuzsi, Gitta shook her head. "No, I will go."

"Where is the dog?" the Komandant asked gently, touching her other elbow.

"Tethered."

"But why waste our time?" Oficir Račić stepped toward them, threw up his hands, snarled. "When an animal could do the work?"

Gitta swallowed. "The dog would not go in. I tried. He refused to move." She had taken Buksi there with a rope tied around his neck. Stood at the edge of the dark woods that very evening. Urged the dog forward, then yanked. Rope cutting across his throat until the dog opened his mouth and hacked. Yellow foam, strings of saliva flying.

She had knelt beside Buksi, lifted his ear with her fingers, and in short whispery bursts, begged the dog to show her the way. To guide her to the place where he had discovered the shoe. *"Kérlek, kérlek, kérlek,"* she said over and over again. But "please" made no difference, and Buksi edged backwards, emitting a low, sad whine. Gitta walked home, the rope wrapped tightly around her wrist, hand and fingers gone cold and numb.

"Stupid beast."

"Nonsense, Račić," the Komandant said. "No one will ever negotiate with a frightened dog."

Gitta looked down, feeling the need to weep flapping in her chest.

"Calm your heart," the Komandant said, touching her shoulder. "We will find nothing. Not a single thing. You will see."

His voice, so strong and deep, did relax her. And as the villagers set off, crawling over the hill, she chastised herself for causing all the bother. She would do the same, of course, for any of them. Men and women she had known for years. Her countrymen. Bound together by both the hardships and the joys.

In something of a line, they marched through the brush, tromping over pale hints of new growth, stepping around sleepy trees, buds just beginning to open. Many people held sticks, moved branches, poking the earth. Gitta trailed behind, pausing often to smell the air.

Her direction felt aimless, and she had not realized she was following Tibor. Had not intended to. Somehow, as she searched the woods, her steps had fallen in line with his. When she looked up, she saw him glancing back at her, and by the time he reached a clearing, he was only steps ahead of her. She paused for a moment. A strange sight on the ground. An old tin she owned, rusted and lid open. Lying there. Not really big enough to store anything other than thread or buttons or loose change.

She was about to pick it up when she noticed Tibor turning to look at her again. Anxious or irritated, she was not certain. But stepping forward, head twisted, he soon tripped over a root and tumbled down. His hands sinking into soft earth, knees coming next. Her first urge was to rush forward and help him to his feet, but when he stayed in that position, down on all fours, Gitta stopped walking. Somehow he reminded her of Buksi, the way he had slowly lowered his face as if a crawling bug had caught his attention.

Then he sprang backwards, as though someone had grabbed his nubby sweater and yanked him to his feet. Elbows pinned to his sides, hands flip-flapping, watery yelps coming from some part of his face. He skipped sideways, away from the place where he fell, away from Gitta, and started smacking his head with his fists. The sound, Gitta thought, very much like small bird after small bird banging into glass.

She hurried past him. Saw it immediately. Stained and sockless, poking up from black dirt.

Only a mother can recognize her child by nothing more than an ear or a finger or a knee. A foot or a toe.

Next female gasps and male mumbling. The gritty hum of dirt moving away from dirt.

And she stood, rooted to the spot, no different from the old trees beside her. Witnessing, but unable to move or speak or collapse.

Neighbours around her, stroking her bark, patting her trunk, her branches, but she could not feel it through the stiffness, could not hear the words inside her pulpy ears. Soil pushed aside, the sight of his face, still young but sunken and stained from packed earth. His cheeks, his chin, eyelids not touching. So pretty. Even though he was still and quiet, he could be moving, could be rising up through black water.

She watched without blinking. Men scraping soil from his ears, lifting his head slightly, his body easing upward from a shallow grave. The icy winter having held him together, given him a home. His arms. Loosened and free, the men working to bring him upward, and before Zsuzsi stood to block her view, she saw. The stumps at the end of his wrists. Both his hands were missing.

Truth moved through her, drawn up by her roots, through narrow channels, contaminated moisture from the ground. And when she found her mouth, she opened it. Out rolled a moan, a hollow vibration. Tearing her with its barbed tail. Not coming from her head or her lungs or her stomach. But originating deep within her body, between her two bony hips, the barren place where her son had once thrived.

:::::

SHE REMEMBERED LITTLE AFTER that. Could not explain how she went from standing beside her dead son to returning home. There were people there. The stove was working. It was too warm. Coal nearly gone. Sides of the wooden box dusty and black. Too much light. Broom scraping the floor. Someone bending to collect pieces of loose straw. Smells of food. Flour sprinkled on the countertop. Shaved purple cabbage. Grease smoking in a pan. Spices and meat and onions and peppers.

In the past, no matter the damage that existed within her, somehow she could worm up through the middle of it and gradually press it outward through her skin. But this. This. There was no moving through it, no burrowing into it, no finding a weak spot and breaking it up. This type of hurt would live within her, tendrils of it growing outward, invading her organs and her blood, tainting everything. And she would give herself over to it, allowing it free access to every part of her body, until her entire insides were a dull, pale grey. Until there was nothing left but a shell full of sadness.

Her body propelled to the front room. Door closed. Clean and empty. Two little figurines nailed to the wall, red outfits, smiling faces. Still smiling now, even when they should not. Sounds muffled. Sitting on the lounger. Someone next to her. Zsuzsi. Fat and warm. Holding her waist. Tugging her handkerchief off her head, fabric crinkling on her shoulders. Could she pull her roots from this soil, from her home, and die? Could she do that? What was left? She was a widow, and now she was a mother without a child.

An old hand sliding over her spine, up and down, and Gitta closed her eyes as Zsuzsi gently patted her back. Patted her back over and over again. In time with the seconds of the clock. Until her ticking heart slowed to match it.

Chapter 34

EVEN THOUGH IT HAD been nearly a year since fire had eaten away the inside of the mortuary, the sweet smell of smoke still hung in the damp air. The interior was blackened, the roof destroyed. Lightning, people believed. A strange, dry storm. Dorján stepped over the charred debris, ran his hand along the mud walls. His fingers came away covered in soot.

Occasionally, his father would spend his nights there. More often during the war. During those final months of his life. Dorján was never allowed in the building, but if he had slept at his grandmother's the night before, he would rush over, wait outside until his father emerged in the bright morning. Face bloated and eyes watering from difficult work and lack of sleep. His black hair stood upright. Dorján would run to his father, clutch his cold hand, and bring it to his nose. Those hands always smelled like chemicals.

"Why do you stay there all night? That is not your work, *Apa*."

"There is too much to do and not enough help. Therefore I must. It is my duty."

"But why?"

"These days, I seem to care mostly for the dying, *bogárkám*. The dead."

"But why? You are a doctor."

"There are so many dead." His father bent then, pinching Dorján's chin with thumb and forefinger. "But we still care for them to ease the sorrow of the living. Do you understand?"

"*Nem.*"

He laughed a deep laugh that echoed through Dorján's bones. "Ah!" he said. "I am glad to hear that. Good, good. Now, let us find your mother, so I can see something wide awake and beautiful."

A defiant square of sunlight marked the floor of the burnt building, and Dorján stepped over it, leaned against the wall, lit a cigarette. After he inhaled, he held his hand aloft, turned it over, inspected the knuckles on his right hand. They were blue and swollen, and he struggled to unclench the muscles. This would affect his stroke, weaken his speed, but right now, he did not care.

Only hours ago, Takáts had signalled for him to come out of the pool, and Dorján finished his lap, lifted himself from the water. Stood on the edge.

His teacher approached him, eyes wide and excited. Head nodding, limbs moving faster than they should. Before he opened his mouth, Dorján knew he had important news of some sort. Something had happened.

"They found him."

He did not need to ask, knew Takáts meant János. He swallowed, arched his feet so that his soles lifted off the tile. What was happening now? What might they do with him? Though he was standing still, his racing heart did not slow.

"In the woods."

The woods? What woods?

"Near the park. In Bregalnica."

Dorján shook his head. He was confused.

"Dead."

The word. Released so gently through thin lips, but it struck Dorján's naked chest. Pushed him backwards, and he fell, arms out, his entire body touching the icy water at the same time. And the pool welcomed him, blanketed him, held him together, held him down. He sank to the bottom like a black stone.

Takáts peered down at him, still talking, and from underwater, Dorján studied the quavering form. By the way Takáts's fingers flickered as he spoke, this was no joke.

Dorján lay on the floor of the pool, unmoving, but slowly exploding inside.

When he could lie on the bottom no longer, he pulsed forward. Struck the wall of the pool. The water offered no resistance, did nothing to absorb the force. His fist cut right through it, and a cloud of blood burst outward. He clung to the wall, trying to stay beneath the surface, but eventually it pushed him upward. Pushed him toward the truth.

János dead. His best friend gone. Not gone away. But gone forever. Gone.

In the mortuary, Dorján opened his hand, winced at the pain. He hung his head and brought his cigarette to his mouth. Trapped the smoke inside his lungs until his throat was raw. In all his life he had never felt this empty. Not even when his father and mother had died. Those situations had been outside of him, beyond his control. But this. He had played a hand in this. He had fought with János. He had walked away and left him alone.

Oficir Račić was at his home when he had arrived after swimming. Dorján braced himself for an interrogation, but the Oficir was surprisingly gentle.

"When was the last time you saw your friend?"

Dorján's face began to crack, and his eyes burned. So many lies inside his stomach. So much guilt. "On the bus. After we harvested." Another lie. It did not matter. His stomach was red and ragged. *If only you could see, Oficir. It holds all my guilt. You would know the truth.*

"Ah, yes. You have lost your friend. I have no need to push you." Oficir Račić had smiled, poppy seeds trapped between his teeth.

Dorján held the cigarette with his teeth, curls of smoke making his eyes sting. He paced about inside the mortuary, caught himself mumbling questions to János. Questions that would never be answered.

He did not understand what had happened. When he left, János had been angry, yes, but alive. How could Dorján have walked right into the clearing, sought out the coins, and felt nothing. Did greed make him unaware? Numb to the strange circumstances? Make him ignore the cold hands on his back? Telling him, *Turn around, turn around, my friend. Hold up the lantern and see me.* What was there? Would he have even noticed? Dorján shuddered. What had the winter done to his friend's body?

From corner to corner, he walked. Lifting his feet over broken clay tiles, the remains of shelving, tables. Dirt crunching underneath his dusty boots. János would have been brought here if the building had not been lost to fire. Instead they took him to the city. To the hospital. A new structure, risen from the ground after the bombed earth had been smoothed. Dorján often imagined his father was still there, down a tunnelled hallway, in a room with bright lights. Tending to people with ailments. A row that was never-ending, and his father, dedicated as he was, simply forgot to come home.

But today, Dorján could not think about his father. Instead he pictured the building in which he was standing to be whole again. The shattered glass pieced together, panes back in their frames, tiles lifted, roof recovered, charred interior clean and scrubbed, fresh paint on the mud walls. János would be there, lying down, a hint of a smirk on his dirt-stained lips.

Inside Dorján's chest, a wave rolled forward, receded, rolled forward. He took shallow breaths, then hiccupped. His mouth opened, but the wave receded again. He wove his fingers in his hair, gripped and squeezed until his scalp threatened to separate from his skull. A sharp stench of scorched hair filled his nostrils, and Dorján relaxed his fingers, the cigarette rolling from his head to his shoulder, dropping to the floor. He had forgotten he was holding it. Forgotten he was trying to smoke.

When he heard footsteps on the road outside, he stood up straight. Lifted the loose tail of his shirt, wiped his damp eyes. As he watched the doorway, the sounds grew louder, and he realized who was coming closer. Knew it without a doubt. He could identify the sound of her gait from miles away.

Nevena stepped into the room, her cheeks flushed. She wore her hair pulled back from her face, and when he glanced at her legs, he saw that both of her black socks were pulled up to her knees. Anger jolted through his body as he remembered János in the field, tugging up a sock, his fingers dancing just behind her knee. Senseless anger. Idiotic anger. János was gone.

"How did you find me?" he said, as his mind spat out a simultaneous thought, *Maybe she wasn't looking for you.*

"I don't know. I knew you came here sometimes. I thought maybe you might be here today."

He lit another cigarette, puffed rapidly. Drove his free hand into the pocket of his pants. New pants his grandmother had sewn for him from leftover fabric.

"And so you find me." Jutted his head in her direction, widened his eyes.

He had not meant for those words to erupt, to sound so hurtful. Regretted them instantly as she turned her head, tears streaking her face. "I'm sorry."

"I'm sorry, too," she said. "I was mad, and then you were mad, and I just kept pretending that János was … was—I don't even know. And that everything would fix itself. How could this happen?"

He dropped his cigarette and went to her. Put his arm around her. Over the winter he must have grown, as Nevena's shoulder tucked right into his armpit. He pressed his face into her hair, and it smelled nothing like soap or a kitchen or fresh air. It simply smelled the same as it had since she was a girl. He inhaled deeply and closed his eyes.

"My father was close by. Said he didn't look hurt or injured."

Dorján nodded. Could not think.

"He believes perhaps a seizure. When János was alone. That happened to someone he knew when he was a boy."

Throat suddenly dry. Dorján felt himself beneath that apple tree, eating skin and flesh and seeds and dropping the wooden stems at his feet. He had left János by himself. He had abandoned him.

"Is that what—" Dorján could not finish the question. The idea of it made no sense. The coins were missing, and that would not happen if János had a seizure. He hoped more than anything she would not mention them. The coins.

"It could happen to anyone." Her voice climbed up an octave, and she was crying again. Though she was practically silent, he felt it through his ribs. The sense of it, the sense of sadness, made him want to destroy something. To injure himself.

He hugged Nevena closer, stared into the centre of the room. He could not remember being alone with her. It was always the three of them. Some part of him was ashamed, as though he were doing something wrong. Going behind János's back. Touching Nevena.

Staring into the centre of the room, he tried to envision János there. All three of them together. Yet, when János appeared inside his mind, he was lying on a table. Soil falling from his mouth.

Tell me. Tell me what happened. I need to know.

At that thought, the dream János bolted upright. *"Koo-koo-ri-koo!"* A rooster's crow from his mouth. Then laughter. "I fooled everyone this time, didn't I? Fooled the whole world!"

"I wish," Dorján whispered, and he blinked back tears. "I wish."

Nevena twisted her head, staring up at him. "What do you wish?"

Except for the two of them, the room was empty. The János of his imagination lay back down, pulled the sheet over his sunken frame, and slept. "The same as you," Dorján said. "The same as you."

Chapter 35

TWO WEEKS SINCE THEY had buried János next to his father. In a wooden box, nailed shut.

Two weeks of silence, of blur, empty pockets of misery inside her home. The pockets moved and she moved, and occasionally, they collided. Zsuzsi told her to rest, to rest, to rest. She tried, but whenever she fell into a light sleep, grief arrived, bent back her fingernails, and pulled her forward.

During the third week, a rumour slid into her house. She could not explain how it arrived, or why it thought itself welcome. Perhaps it was left by a visitor or slipped underneath the door jamb, inching across the floor. No matter. The rumour did not rush; it moved so gradually, she had not even noticed it. Until the evening it crawled into her bedroom as she slept, and when she awoke, it had germinated inside her head. A sunflower face, open and nodding, leaning toward her like something sincere, honest.

The next morning, Gitta wasted no time. She dressed, splashing cold water on her face. With a mechanical loop and twist, she tied her scarf under her chin. She stumbled out the front door and into the sunlight. Beyond the cobblestone strip near the homes, the streets were damp and shiny. Lurching forward, she gripped the knob of her front door, steadied herself, fingers of her right hand fanning through the air, trying to find substance where there was none.

Her legs felt as though the bones and skin had merged into a single pole, with a rounded end, and she could not balance, could not balance out in the open. Head drooping, she closed her eyes, glancing through a slit in her puffy lids. She checked her feet. Still two poking out from beneath the hem of her dull dress.

The clacking of knitting stopped and several women surrounded her. "Gitta *néni*. For your sake. Sit." A wooden chair, now, pressing against the backs of her knees, but she could not fall into it. Could not sit. She would face him today, look into his black eyes, and hear the truth. She released her grip on the knob.

"Leave her be." Zsuzsi.

"But, she is *részeg*!" Drunk. "Stench so strong, she could catch fire."

"Goat shit!" Zsuzsi hissed. "Do you hear me? Goat shit."

The ladies hushed, puckered lips closed.

"Ah, ah, the weight of it," Zsuzsi said softly now. She bowed her head, clasped her hands, and pressed them between her breasts. "Your knees would buckle too."

::::

THAT MORNING, GITTA HAD not touched the *palinká*. None of it remained, if she were to tell the truth. Only a single dust-covered bottle of *tokai*. She had no reason to save it, other than the hazy notion that perhaps one day, János would be a man. There would be achievements to toast. But now, but now, but now.

Feet tripping, a shoe slipped from her heel. She stepped out of it, left it upside down on the road, kept moving until she reached the village square. Eyes red and glazed, everything was distorted. Floating under a cold sea. Shop windows waving in and out, clumps of laughing men seated beside small tables, hands drifting, bodies and voices vibrating in time with her heartbeat. Other women beside her, hovering on legless trunks.

She stopped, pulling her handkerchief from inside her pocket. The heat threatened to puncture her. She pressed hard on her brow, her quavering throat. But she was dry, dry, dry. Her soul, nothing more than crumbs, held together by thin skin.

She waited behind another woman, jostling her basket, purchasing a bottle of apricot preserves. Staring at the women's violet hair, a half inch of white roots, Gitta had the impression that the hair was lifting off, leaving. Going away. The sight of it made Gitta feel a terrible weight inside her chest.

And then, Tibor, straight ahead of her now. He turned his head, one eye watching her, the other eye hidden behind the bony bridge of his nose. She could barely breathe, began to pant through her open mouth. Spread her feet on the bricks, so she would not topple over. Slowly, she pointed to the jars of sour cherries. Faded bodies floating in brilliant liquid. She held up one, then two fingers.

In that instant, when his palm hovered over the bottles, she thrust her own hand forward, seized his fingers, tightened, tightened, every wispy strand of strength riding down her arm and into her clenching fist, a man's fist, until she heard bones crack and pop.

"Tell me," she spat. "Tell me."

She turned more, did not abate as he wailed, body twisting, his free fist striking her fingers, her forearm. He flexed his back, spine pressing against the thin cotton of his shirt, unbroken blemishes marring the smoothness of the fabric. Foot kicking outward, cart shifting, and a bottle of cherries tipping and rolling and toppling toward the stone. A spray of glass and fruit and liquid spreading outward. Not stopping until the sole of her shoe was surrounded.

She dropped Tibor's hand.

The boy fell to the ground, sharp screams escaping through gaps in his clenched teeth. Hand pulled to his chest, he curled his shoulders inward, chin down. His legs thrashed, knocking the wooden cart again, other bottles raining down. As they smashed, the sweet smell of a busy kitchen filled the air.

She stood there, unable to recognize Tibor, nothing in her vision but the silvery glint of the scale. Blinding her. A man came behind her now. She did not see him, but felt his chest cupping her back. The odour of cigarette smoke and coffee and skin balm, like lemons, fine bristles on his chin catching in her hair. A smooth hand slipped into hers, butter voice coating her ear, "Gitta. This is not the way. This is not our way."

And she blinked, drew in a breath. The first in hours.

"Komandant." Dragan.

He let go of her, said, "You are fine. You are fine? Yes, yes."

A slow nod.

"Leave this mess, Gitta. Leave this to me." Then over his shoulder, "See her to her home, Račić."

The Oficir stretched his back, yawned. "Of course, Komandant. My pleasure."

Račić gripped Gitta's upper arm, pinching with his meaty grip. "Go," he muttered. "Move."

Gitta could not remember how to walk, and she experienced a brief moment of surprise when her left knee lifted, the light stretch of leg, one foot shifted in front of the other, propelling her forward. She opened her mouth, wanted to cry, tell him she could manage on her own, but her windpipe seized, and only choking sounds emerged.

As they reached the edge of the square, he growled, "Do you see that table? Do you see? That is my cup. I have yet to touch it." Speaking into the air above her head. "My coffee grows cold while I cart a fucking chicken to its fucking coop." He pinched her skin harder, cleared brown scum from his throat, spat into Gitta's path. "Stupid whore."

Gitta glanced behind her, looking toward the stand, toward Tibor, who remained curled beside it. An emaciated dog stood over the mess, bent its head, and wolfed cherries from among the glass. Carefully working the juice from the stone with its tongue.

"Move. Move!"

They walked away from the bustle of the village square and started down the street where Gitta lived. As they approached her home, the women leaning against the plaster walls stood up straight and stopped talking. When Gitta and Oficir Račić stopped in the shadow of Gitta's house, Zsuzsi edged forward on the bench, the ball of wool nestled in her lap rolled onto the cobblestone, came to rest near Račić's black boot. Zsuzsi moved to collect it, but he snarled, "Stay!" She descended the few inches until her backside once again spread over the bench.

Assisted by a slight shove, Gitta stumbled forward, pressed the latch, and opened the door. Clean, cool air wafted outward, like liquid passing over her. She entered her home, took two steps, her juice-covered shoe sticking to the floor. She was about to lie down in the hallway when she heard a soft click behind her. Heard laboured breathing. Oficir Račić had followed her inside.

"You will make me a coffee," he said. "With much sugar."

Gitta's aching heart began to quiver inside her chest cavity, and a rush of adrenalin pushed the air from her flimsy limbs, her hollow core. She reached out, fingernails striking the wall. She was home again and felt the full weight of existing.

"Today," he growled.

She never turned, never spoke, just walked down the hallway. Clouds had covered the sun, and her kitchen was now dreary and full of shadows. She lifted the grinder down from the shelf, did not wipe away the layer of dust. Dumping old beans in the cup, she turned the handle until they disappeared and opened the small drawer on the box to remove the grounds. After filling the brass *cezve* halfway with cold water, she placed it on the stove, waited for it to boil, then poured a spoonful of grounds into the pot and stirred.

As she prepared a Turkish coffee, she could hear Račić moving through her house, in the rooms, rummaging. Glasses clinked, wood slid against wood as drawers were opened. She could imagine his discoloured fingers pawing her clothes, touching her nightdress. Then she caught the distinct crunch of straw, creak of her bed frame, and the artery in her neck began to pulse, walls in the kitchen knocking ever so slightly as the force of blood moved her head. Račić left the bedroom, wandered down the hallway. She heard the sandy sound of his hand sliding along the plaster walls.

She saw him in the doorway next, smiling. He pulled out a chair, sat, and lifted his stout arms, clasping his hands behind his head. Dark circles of sweat marked the armpits of his light blue shirt.

"Your home is orderly, yes?"

Again, she said nothing.

"Not quite what I expected from a woman so, so *gyengeelméjű*." Weak-minded. "Is that what you say? I am not familiar with these parts of your language."

He gazed at her, mouth open, revealing bright gums, yellow teeth like a rat's. The skin on his cheeks appeared sore, as though his razor was blunt.

Coffee sputtered in the *kávéfőző*, foam bubbling up and spilling over on the stove.

"*Kérlek,*" she whispered when the smoke touched her nose.

"Ah," he said, laughing. "The hen has a tongue."

Deep breath, and she lifted the *kávéfőző* by its long handle, tipping and pouring thick coffee into a white cup. Two sugar cubes disappearing through the foam. Then she laid it on the table before him.

"There," she said. "Now drink it."

He smiled again, lifting his blue cap so it balanced on the back of his head. "Ah, but it is so hot, *srce*. Do you want me to burn myself?"

She looked at her feet.

"We will wait," he said. "You are alone now, are you not? You have time."

She could manage it. She would wait until he left before she allowed yet another knife of sadness to puncture her stomach.

"And I am alone, too." Removing his cap, he placed it on the table beside the coffee. Then he licked his thumb, rubbing it across the red star on the brim. Cleaned away the dust. "Did you realize I grew up near you? In the hills?"

"No," she said. "How might I know that?"

"You women. So much talk. I assume a collective knowledge."

"You assume improperly, Oficir."

"We have something in common, *srce*."

Gitta stared at him, saw a smile curl the corners of his thin lips.

"My mother too had trouble with a baby."

At the sound of those words, the air stood up, left the room. Gitta panted, haze around the edges of her vision. "My mother?" she breathed.

"Yes, yes. We all know her story. Did you think something so tasty would stay in the pot?"

"She was a sick woman. She was ill."

"Ill? Ill?" Oficir Račić slapped the table and snorted. "A woman who is ill. Find me one who is not, I say. Find me one who is not."

"You are a cruel man."

"No, *srce*. Not cruel. I am wise." He ran his clipped fingernails up and down the sides of his bulbous stomach. "You see, that is why I never married. Does every wife not have a hand in her husband's death? Whether by blade or tongue, they are both sharp and equally capable of cutting."

"Wise, indeed."

"I keep a knife on my windowsill, you know."

"Ah."

"Do you know why? Keeps the witches away." He slurped his coffee, murmuring, "Lovely," and licked the caramel foam from the long strands of his moustache. "Refresh my memory, *srce*. What was your late husband's name?"

"I see you are nearly finished, Oficir."

"Yes, yes. I am slow. And it is so comfortable here. I see now some of the things I have missed. Warm coffee made by a warm woman."

"I have things to do, Oficir. You can believe."

He stood up and moved closer, stared at her chest, her hips, as he flicked open his belt. "After," he whispered. "After." He unfastened the button, allowed his navy trousers to drop. Buckle clinking against the floor. Stains on the front of his knitted briefs, fabric straining.

"You knew to keep your husband pleased, yes?"

Gitta pushed her back into the countertop. "You have taken your coffee, Oficir. And you will leave."

"You have a nice face. A little ragged, but nice enough." He laughed, squeezed his crotch, snapped the stretched elastic on his waistband. "I will make you smile."

There was nowhere to go. Gitta's spine was against wood. "*Kérlek, kérlek*, Oficir Račić." Please, please. She had been saying that so often these days, it fell from her mouth with no effort. "You—you confuse me for another sort of woman."

Another step. His eyes were glossy. The colour of wet metal. He laughed again. Another step, dragging his pants with him. "I am no fool, *srce*. There is only one sort of woman. If you really want to bury something, any hole will do."

She could smell his body. Unwashed and stale. Sweat clinging to him like a fleece.

"There is no one here to watch after you now. Your men are gone."

With that phrase, something unscrewed inside of her. Her fear dissipated, prickles of hatred leaching in to replace it. Behind her back, her fingers tapped over the countertop. Tapped through the mess of withered cabbage. Tapped metal. She flicked it, turned the knife, and gripped the handle. Her hand, as big as his. It could do what was needed. What was necessary.

Oblige me, she thought. *Just one more inch. I will slice you from your clump of coarse hair to your fat throat. Piece by piece, I will feed you to my dog. Starting with your tongue. No one will ever miss you.*

Banging in her ear, then. A pulpy fist against warm glass. Knob rattling, and the door to the backyard swung open, grey light filling the room. A gust of damp air.

Gitta blinked, dropping the knife. There on the step stood Zsuzsi, her eyes fixed on Oficir Račić, lines of her lips turned down. Without a trace of uncertainty, she stepped over the threshold, wobbled into the kitchen.

"Are you having trouble with the fit of your trousers, Oficir?" Zsuzsi tilted her head and rolled her fingertip over the mole on her chin. "I am pleased to look after you."

"Ah," he said, bending to pull up the fabric. "You are a dense horse to interrupt us."

"Very dense, Oficir. But forgive me, I am old. If you are blessed, one day you will be too."

Chapter 36

WHEN GITTA WAS YOUNG, she had assumed her mother had told her a fable. A sinister narrative meant both to warn and to delight the listener. But when she was older, her aunt offered her the truth. Explained that the story was rooted in a tormented reality. Her mother's mind had been deteriorating for some time, but no one imagined the childlike woman would ever do such a thing. A woman who, in adulthood, had grown afraid of darkness, had served coffee and *torta* to imaginary visitors. After it happened there was no choice but to report it, have her removed from her home, her village. Taken to the *elmegyógyintézet*.

The story her mother told involved Gitta's young cousin, Jola. In the thatched-roof house right next door, the girl was about to give birth. Gitta had not understood how Jola's girlish body had changed so rapidly. The hard lump growing underneath her dress. At first Gitta tried to ignore it, but soon it became difficult. All she could do was stare at it, asking questions, until Jola became irritated and stopped coming to visit.

Just months earlier they had been playing in the attic, hiding underneath the hay, laughing and rolling in the dusty heat as late spring sunlight found its way through gaps in the roof. And now she could hear Jola crying, and the women moving about with an anxious speed. Shooing chickens out of the yard, sheep into the barn. Bottom doors latched. A single cow tied to the fence. Jobs completed, the women nodded to themselves. As though agreeing birth would be made easier if everything loose was caged.

Gitta was not permitted to attend. She stayed at home, in the kitchen, peeling and chopping onions until her eyes wept and the bowl overflowed.

Even though the sun was shining, Gitta could feel a change in the air. Something had clouded over. And then she saw her mother's face, realizing that it was her expression that had darkened. She was coming toward the house, not cutting across the garden as she normally did, instead walking along the road. Head bent, yellow scarf fallen from the top of her head, tied beneath her neck. Gitta had been told not to leave the house, but Gitta swung open the door, running to meet her mother.

"A girl? Is it a girl baby?"

Her mother's mouth was tight, and she never spoke. "Inside," she said. "Keep your eyes down."

They rushed back to the house, and Gitta's mother went to the cupboard, took out the bag of salt. A handful, and she walked from room to room, sprinkling it in the corners. Once finished with her efforts, she told Gitta everything that had happened. How Jola was too young to have a baby. How she was too beautiful, and with just her open face, she had lured the Devil right into the village. Not her fault, but that is the nature of such things. The Devil sees what he wants and finds a way to take it.

Jola writhed and moaned, and Gitta's mother and aunt had to grip her flailing arms and legs, holding her down as she tried to escape her own body. Between her legs they saw something emerging, not the wet crown of a baby's head, as they'd both expected, but a foot. Bloody and toeless, gnarled, more akin to the hoof of an animal than of a newborn. Then the second hoof slid out, a pair of legs with a curiously matted covering.

A pair of legs. Backwards knees drawn up and kicking, kicking, full of angry life, as Jola's own legs went limp. Flopped outward, soles almost touching, blood still glugging out into the jiggling pool. She told Gitta how her sister held Jola and lifted her upper body from the damp sheets, and how she had calmly gripped those two kicking limbs and tugged. Turned, revealing a tiny nub that could be the tuft of a tail. Blood up to her elbows, Gitta's mother had wrenched the baby free, sound of pulling stones from mud, and then came the sudden flood of water and little clumps of cream.

Her mother swaddled the newborn and left the room. Brought it out into brighter light to see if her eyes were fooling her. But there was no mistake. This was the child of the Devil. No smooth mottled skin, pink and blue and warm, of a baby. Instead in her arms she held a creature with a covering of wet tawny fur, a pink and black nose, slit yellow eyes, barely open. No cries, just a hoarse *ma-aa-ah* from its newborn throat. Jola had given birth to a goat.

Gently, gently, her mother described how she placed the side of her hand on the goat's neck. Pushed ever so slightly, held it there. Mouth wide, hard head knocking. But she held tight, did not waver. Minutes passed, and the goat stopped straining against the blankets, and the chore was complete. Just a job like any other.

"Why did you not let it into the yard?" Gitta asked.

"Should I have offered it feed, too?"

Gitta was uncertain but nodded.

"Did you not hear my explanation? He would have grown up. Looked like any other boy. Any other man."

"Ah."

"If a weed grows in the corn, do you leave it, just because it flowers?"

"No."

"Do not worry, *szívem*. It is over now. We will not see the Devil tonight."

Her cousin and the baby were dead. A pair of additional humps in the cemetery. Too late to plant a covering, and the soil dried and crumbled. When the autumn wind blew over it, it carried away the golden dust.

Afterwards, Gitta's mother went back to work. A solid woman with meaty hands, just like Gitta's, who toiled from first rays until the evening meal. She remained in their home for four weeks. Living as she had been living. A lantern burning to cut through the darkness, and the front room clean and ready for visitors that no one else could see.

::::

MORE AND MORE OFTEN these days, Gitta thought of her mother. Not with sadness or regret or longing, but with simple envy. Her mother was convinced of her actions. Led a guiltless life. And Gitta now viewed that as a rare treasure. Something made of pure gold. She wished for it herself. Wished for the release of madness. Wished, when she stared into a mirror, to see her mother's hoary face pressing out through her own.

Chapter 37

"YOU SHOULD KNOW," HE said.

Yes.

"I thought it better you hear directly. Rather than a story handed around."

She nodded.

The Komandant stood in her kitchen, hat in his hands, gentle pity resting in the wrinkles around his eyes. His square shoulders filled out a new coat.

"We have dealt with it, Gitta. I don't know the circumstances, but it is clear something foul occurred. Very clear."

"Yes."

"You suspected him?"

"I—yes."

"I thought as much. When I saw you in the square. Why did you suspect his involvement?"

She closed her eyes. "I do not know, Komandant. My mind is too full. I cannot think."

"You do not need to think. I am here."

"Köszönöm." Thank you.

"They believe…those who examined your son, they believe he

must have stolen something. Stolen from Tibor."

Again, the image she had tried so hard to erase was thrown up behind her eyes. Hovering there, the shock of it. The shock. Her son's arms. Ending before they should. She felt the tingle of it in her own hands. Ache in the bones of her wrists.

"My son is not a thief."

The Komandant looked downward, pinched one side of his moustache. "No, no. Brigitta, I did not mean to suggest. Tibor is a confused young man."

"Where is he?" She held the edge of the counter, closing her eyes. Saw Tibor behind the wooden structure, his fingers up and swaying, ready to tap the perfect melon or drop dusty apples in a basket.

"He will reside at the *elmegyógyintézet*. In Komarovo."

"Komarovo, you said?" The same place her mother had lived for many years. A keeping place for women and children who were not of sound mind.

"Yes. It is decent and clean with doctors and nurses. And others like him. He will stay there for three years, until he is eighteen, and then they will move him to a permanent place."

"Ah."

"Do not concern yourself with details. Račić has made all the arrangements."

"Oficir Račić?"

"Yes." The Komandant smiled and nodded. "He is coarse, I know, but I trust him. He is competent. Reliable."

The mention of Račić made her turn away, and she looked out the window. Saw Dorján in the courtyard, smoking. "Will they hurt him?"

A pause. "Do you want that?"

Her heart began to knock. Did she want that? "I…I cannot answer that."

"I am sorry, Gitta."

"Sorry?"

"We are not barbaric. The boy cannot grasp his own intentions. We tried to communicate with him—I tried—but he does not understand what he has done. No grip on this world."

She placed her hand on her neck, feeling the sharp points of her spine beneath her fingertips.

"A country is defined by how they treat their sick, are they not? I know you are familiar with that."

A second. Two. "Yes," she replied.

"Are you comfortable then? With everything?"

His words brushed over her, and she swallowed the air in her mouth. "I am, Komandant," she replied, though she had no idea what she was. She was not even certain she existed; if the walls and stove and coal in the wooden box were real. She glanced about through sagging eyelids, and everything appeared to be moving ever so slightly. Inanimate objects pulsing with a secret life she had never noticed before. *I am drunk,* she thought. *I am drunk on despair.*

"I should go," he said. "But I will visit later. To see that you are all right."

"Please."

"You will be fine, Brigitta. I will make certain of it. You are not so different from when you were a girl." He reached his hand toward her, running a single curled finger over the skin just above her elbow.

Gitta drew in her breath. The lightest stroke, barely more than a tickle, kicking up all kinds of dust. Dust from her youth. Urgent dust. And she clutched the Komandant's hand, leaned closer, stared at his neatly trimmed moustache, and for a single moment, she could imagine, if she did not look into his eyes, she could imagine. That she was not alone. That they were together and were sharing this devastation, balancing each other on their open palms. Lifting each other as they collapsed. In turn. Sharing, sharing. *Please, please help me. Kérlek, kérlek. I cannot breathe. I am suffocating here.* She slid his hand down her side, rippling over her ribs, held it there, pushing it into her. But he pressed upward, he did, gripping her breast with sudden force. His face in hers, mouth on hers, and she felt it between her legs. A painful opening of her pores. Desire in her muscles. Needing to be consumed, to be destroyed, her skeleton broken into bits. Irreparable damage. *Ruin me. I need that, I need that.* Down on the hard floor in the hallway, clothed and tangled, parts exposed. And she pulled up her black dress; he pushed himself into her. Several short thrusts. No questions. Her head struck the plaster wall, pinprick stars on her lids. Her eyes squeezed shut.

When they finished, she did not get up. She just edged onto the icy floor and lay still. Near her face, she saw shoe prints on the plaster wall.

Behind her, the Komandant was standing, fixing his clothes. He coughed. Then bent over her, gently tucked her breast back inside the stretched fabric, slipped her undergarments out of her creases. Tugged her dress down over her knees. From his pocket he pulled a handkerchief, patted her face, even though her skin was dry.

"I am sorry, Gitta," he said. "This was not my intent." He placed two warm palms on the top of her head, pressed tightly, held her thoughts gently in place.

::::

ONE MORE TIME, SHE told herself. One more time she would look into his eyes. Earlier, in her haze, she had been convinced. But time had caused her certainty to degrade. Had János stolen something? She could not believe it. It made no sense. Tibor owned nothing of value, and besides, how could a boy who would fret over a blemish on a tomato have killed her only son?

Gitta took a train to Komarovo. The journey was familiar, tracing the same path she had made years ago when she had gone to see her mother. She entered the high-ceilinged room and lied to the woman, a heavy nurse wearing a soft yellow uniform, brown laced shoes. Explained she was Tibor's aunt, had travelled a great, great distance to see her only nephew. She knew he was very distraught in his mind. Might they oblige her? A short visit, only to see his young face.

"Wait. Please."

The noises tickled Gitta, made her grasp her ribs, her stomach. Weeping and moaning, and prickly laughter. A lullaby of insanity. When she had last stood in this atrium, last stared up at the peeling ceiling, János had been so full of life, twisting and kicking inside of her. "It is not yours," her mother had hissed as she clutched Gitta's lump. If the nurses had not pulled them apart, what else might the old woman have said? "If you try to keep it, it will destroy you."

"Family name, again? *Gospođo?*"

Gitta blinked, stepped backwards. The nurse stood too close, clipboard pressed against her breasts. She eyed Gitta as though assessing her stability.

Once again, she offered Tibor's full name.

The nurse frowned, shook her head. "We have no record of any such patient."

"I am sorry? He has been moved already?"

"No, not moved. Never assigned to us."

"This is Komarovo."

"Yes, yes, of course it is." Narrowing of the nurse's eyes. "Do you think you are somewhere else?"

"Komarovo," Gitta whispered. She suddenly felt light-headed.

"You have made a simple mistake. Would you like to talk to someone else? A doctor, perhaps?"

"No, no. No, no." Gitta blinked again, running her fingers across her dry forehead.

"*Gospođo?* Do you need something sweet?"

Gitta waved her hands, "*Hvala, hvala.* I am fine," and turned on her heel. She heard the Komandant's soft voice in her ear. Telling her that Oficir Račić had made the arrangements. Oficir Račić. *I trust him. He is competent. He is reliable.*

She rushed down the red brick drive and paused outside the peeling iron gates. While she stood there, a realization descended upon her, covering her chest, her face. Soft and subtle, like a thin white sheet. She was certain, even if she searched, even if she questioned, she would never find Tibor. Never be able to look him in his eyes and grasp his guilt. Or, she now presumed, his innocence.

Chapter 38

"I'VE NEVER LIKED TIBOR," she said between sips. "He's *tajanstven*."

The *limonádé* Dorján had purchased from the village store was warm. They sat on the grass near the edge of the park, Nevena seated on his flattened coat. Walking along the road, she had wanted to continue underneath those twin willow trees, take the path through the woods. But Dorján had refused. Could not pass by the place where János had died. And he insisted they continue, farther away from the village, to an area where the trees thinned.

"You think he's sneaky? Why would you say that?"

"He was a thief. Did I tell you that before?"

Even though he was chilled, a burst of heat shot out from his stomach. He brought his bottle to his mouth, tartness making his throat tighten. A belch rose up, his eyes stinging. She had once used that word to describe him and János—*thieves*. As he remembered that, an image of the coins pressed against his skull. He had been expecting her to ask about them, was dreading the lies he would have to form. But she had yet to do so. "A thief?"

"I know. You would never believe. But he wasn't a very good one."

"No?"

"Every time I went to him for something, he weighted the scale. Once he even slipped a stone in with the peppers. I carried it all the way home to my mother. She was furious. Said he had a gypsy's blood in his veins."

Another large swallow, stretching his neck. "Maybe he didn't realize," he replied.

"He realized. Time after time. A boy can only make so many mistakes."

"Ah."

"He pretended to be something he wasn't. There's nothing worse."

Dorján was happy for the blackness that surrounded them. The stars coming now, one at a time, as though someone were on the other side with a thin needle, poking the fabric. A seamstress. He thought of his grandmother, saw her wrinkled face in his mind. Her swollen calves, cloudy eyes, slow-moving body. She had grown old almost overnight, had begun to sleep during the afternoons. The very sight of her head nodding and dipping made him afraid.

One day she'll be up there, he wanted to say to Nevena. *Making stars.*

"Did you know him well?" she asked.

"Know him?"

"Tibor."

"No."

"Did János?"

"No. Not at all." He had explained that so often, there was a truthful consistency to his lie.

"Tibor always seemed so frustrated. Ready to explode."

"I don't know. I had no business with him."

"He told them he fought with János."

"Told them?"

"You know what I mean, Dori. He let them know."

Dorján turned his head away from her. He wanted to erase the entire conversation. Everything so casual, as though János had just tripped over an extended foot. Would bounce back up any moment.

"Maybe something small. You know János." *I knew János. Once. Now there is nothing left to know.*

"Sometimes I forget," she said, and she let her head hang backwards.

After a moment, "Me too. I forget too."

"I'm waiting. Just waiting for him to run to us. I'm annoyed because he's so late."

Empty laugh. "Yes."

"My head is tired. Tired of trying to remember what has happened. It doesn't want to."

He understood then, found her cold fingers, squeezed them. She had not meant her tone to be so indifferent. They were the same, hating to remember and at the same time trying not to forget.

They leaned against each other and drank warm lemon soda. The evenings were still cool, so there were very few young people in the park. Occasionally a shadow emerged from the woods, two, maybe three, people. Strings of laughter snaking through the air. Somehow the sound of it made him feel better.

Wind lifted, blew strands of her hair into his face. They caught between his lips. He brushed them away, angled his head, noticed her reach up, rub a section of her scalp. More shadows arrived, and he counted them. Groups of friends stumbling across the grass. Bottles striking bottles.

Sitting so close to Nevena was unfamiliar. Slightly uncomfortable. He had thought about it, but now that he was there, it was not quite what he had expected. It would take some time to get used to this. Being two. Instead of three.

::::

"I HAVE HEARD YOU are spending more time with him."

"How have you heard?"

"Račić. Occasionally he patrols around."

Nevena lowered her head, face hot. More than once she had seen Oficir Račić strolling around the edges of the park, walking through the village square after all the shops had closed. He should have been sending everyone home, but instead he stayed with them. Sharing whatever they had to drink, to eat, his voice growing louder and louder. His shouting harsher and harsher. He never acknowledged her, and she had wrongly assumed herself invisible.

"I'm sorry, *Tata*. You're angry."

"Of course not, *srce*. Jealous, yes, but not angry. I would like to keep you to myself. But, ah! I know it is an impossible wish."

She knotted her fingers together behind her back. "It's nothing. We're only friends."

"Are you certain? Sometimes such confusions cause a lot of discomfort."

"Why would you say that?"

"Perhaps it is something with which I was familiar. In my youth."

She sighed. It would be impossible to explain. Her father would find it girlish and amusing. On his own, János had been overwhelming, only tempered by the presence of Dorján. But without János, Dorján was nearly too soft, too subtle, too silent. All traits she had adored while János flailed about nearby, breaking sticks and lighting matches. Together, they had been perfect for her.

Still, she cared for Dorján. He had been a part of her life since she was a young girl. Dorján. Dorján and János.

"*Srce?*"

"*Da, Tata?*"

"I will spend an afternoon with this boy. I will do that. Why not?"

"You will?" Her voice quavered. It would hurt nothing to have him take time with Dorján.

"Soon. Račić and I will be friendly." Gentle laughter. "We will see if he is made of strong material."

Ever since she could remember, he had the ability to set her at ease. Nevena smiled at her father then opened her mouth and inhaled when she remembered her mother. "And *Majko?*"

"Not a word." He pinched his lips. "Do not worry, *srce*. If he is a nice boy, then we will talk to her. She will have to listen. You will keep your friend."

Air released from her lungs. "He is a nice boy, *Tata*. You will see. He is good."

Chapter 39

RARELY ONCE A WEEK at the beginning, but over time the frequency of his visits increased. By the time summer began, Komandant Dobrica arrived at Gitta's house every evening. Always after dark. At first he would knock lightly, and after a while he would simply let himself in. They did little together, only sitting in the front room, a single lamp glowing. Their sides touched, and gradually she began to lean on him ever so slightly. Her thin arm pressing into him. As more evenings passed, her head came to rest on his shoulder. She would fall asleep there, in the silence, and awake in the morning, alone, a small pillow beneath her head, blanket covering her, shoes removed, laid neatly side by side on the floor.

Occasionally he brought her a parcel. Fruit or meat. He would sit at the table in the kitchen and watch while she prepared plum dumplings. He asked her questions about the process, listening intently as she explained how to fold the dough around the fruit. Pinch it closed so it would not leak when she dropped it into boiling water. When she soaked liver in milk, he insisted on knowing the reason. One night she sliced through the soft mass of a pig's brain, and he stood beside her and breaded it.

As they ate, he would tell her stories. Of his youth, his time in the army. Mostly, he avoided his present life and also danced around the months he and Gitta had spent together. Never mentioned the long hours when they wandered on his father's farm.

While drinking a coffee after a small meal, he began to talk. His mood was jovial as he spoke, though she knew the words hurt him.

He had only been on the base for a month, not more, when they tasked him with guarding the ammunition dump. So young and nervous, he said, and his partner soon abandoned his post. Left Dragan alone. The wooden structure in which he stood was surrounded by a high wall of barbed wire and then a deep field of corn that went on for a kilometre. He stood and did not move from his post, his ears straining to hear above the wind rustling through the corn.

"As the night wore on, I heard many things. A mother singing to her child. Someone hammering. Your voice. Yes, your voice, climbing into my ears. Encouraging me. We had, you know, spent so much time together."

Gitta leaned back in her chair, clasping her hands in her lap. He had never mentioned her before.

After another sip of coffee, he lit a cigarette. "All my imagination, of course, but as I was pacing back and forth, I saw a ripple in the corn. An irregular line of movement. That is how I would describe it. Not close to the fence but not far off."

Gitta nodded. "Somebody?"

"Yes, yes. I thought. I cried out to him. 'Stop,' I said. 'Stop immediately.' But whoever it was did not stop. Kept stumbling through the corn." Long stream of smoke from his pursed lips. "The border was close by, of course. And there were traitors. Are traitors. I was afraid, I will admit that to you. I was scared, and as I was ordered to do, I lifted my gun."

Gitta nodded again, and she could not help but close her eyes and think of János. If things had been different, he might have been part of a similar situation. A boy, running through the corn as fast as a pair of legs might carry him. As she visualized it, she felt his disorientation, his confusion as the rows and rows of tall stalks blended together in the darkness. If he were there, he would be lost. He would be alone. A tangle of dried leaves, gripping his limbs, during a nighttime coloured black.

Even though János was already gone, envisioning this struggle made her wheeze. She wrapped one hand around a glass of water, brought the other to her chest, spread her fingers wide.

"Yes, I raised my gun. Aimed at nothingness. Bent stalks. I fired, and within moments, noise erupted," he said. His hands swooped through the air as though helping the story to emerge. "Every man was awake, crawling through the corn to find the wounded traitor. The sound he emitted was such misery. To me, it did not sound human."

At this point, the Komandant laughed, and Gitta pressed her spine into the chair.

"They soon discovered I had wounded not a traitor, not a traitor at all, but the farmer's cow."

"Ah."

"The men ate well the following week. Everyone was happy. But they did not trust me afterwards with a gun."

He laughed again, but it soon faded.

"I am sorry," he said and lowered his head. "That was not a story for you. I should not have told it."

"I understand."

"I believe you do, Brigitta. Though I pretend to find it humorous, the memory is painful to me. I have never taken pleasure in injuring anyone or anything. You know that, yes?" He scratched his head, and a strand of smoke trailed up behind his ear.

"Of course," she replied. "Of course I do."

"Sometimes it is difficult to be Komandant. I can say this to you because I trust you."

"Yes."

"I have tried to be fair when forces are pulling me in two directions. But I have also made mistakes."

"As have we all."

"I suppose. I suppose that is true." He inhaled deeply on his cigarette. "I am only a man."

She remembered him as a boy, having maybe fifteen or sixteen years, covering his eyes as his mother pinned a stretched neck to the round of wood, bringing the cleaver down on the fluttering chicken. Blood on her thumb and wrist. His mother did not scold him or belittle him, just chuckled at her son's softness. Chuckled and shook her head. Only now did Gitta wonder if such a reaction might have done more damage than a display of anger.

After stubbing his cigarette in the glass dish, he rubbed his hand over his mouth. Tilted his head slightly. "I hesitate to say this. It will make me sound like a boy."

"Tell me."

"I have tried many ways to forget you, Brigitta, but never have I managed. I believe you are the only person who truly knows me. The only person."

There was no reply to such a statement. In many ways, she thought, he was the same as he had been when he was young. And in other ways, when she noticed his practised movements, his confident smile, she realized he was completely different. An eagle with two heads. She did not have the energy or desire to pick through him, separate the two.

Gitta stood to make a second coffee. She rinsed the sediment from the bottom of the *kávéfőző*, adding clean water and fresh grounds. The hours had passed, and she was growing sleepy. Dragan would take this coffee with her in the front room.

"You are feeling better these days?"

I am feeling very little, she wanted to say, but instead she nodded.

"Ah. Good, good."

As Dragan spoke, occasionally Imre's voice would arrive inside her head. Her husband never liked the Komandant. Never trusted him. *He tells many stories, Gitta, with too much colour. The man is skilled at hiding the grey underneath.* But Gitta had known Dragan when he was a child. Once he had loved her. Deeply. She understood that now. Imre was mistaken about him. Like everyone else, his stories were only stories. And when he strung his words together, she heard no colour. She also heard no grey.

Chapter 40

OFICIR RAČIĆ'S BOOTS SANK into the mud, and with each step, the earth sucked at them. The Komandant let out a watery hiss. "What do you want today? You make more noise than the boar itself."

Dorján watched his feet, bringing his soles down onto soft earth or wet leaves. He did not want to be there, with Nevena's father and the Oficir. Did not want to hunt wild boar or pheasants or wiry rabbits that appeared fat only until the fur was peeled away.

"I do not like to hunt," the Komandant confided.

Dorján cleared his throat. "No?"

"Of course you wonder why I go."

No, I do not. "Yes, why?"

"A man must hunt, of course. It is expected. And for Račić, really. Company for my associate is all. Besides, the wood air is fine for my lungs."

"Ah."

"Where is the appeal, I ask myself. Most men I assume prefer the camaraderie, enjoy the chase. But they drink too much and will shoot at anything. Under those conditions, even I look like a pheasant." Thin smile. "And Račić, so much like the wild boar."

"The horse's dick!"

"You think I am lying? Račić. Please. I have seen you take aim at your own reflection."

Oficir Račić laughed, then took a deep breath, smacking himself on the cheek. His body appeared to vibrate ever so slightly.

"Ah, yes." The Komandant's gold ring clanged against the metal barrel on his shoulder. "I do not like to hunt."

Dorján coughed again.

"We will share," he then announced. "Three ways. I am certain your *baka* would appreciate some fresh meat. And not a single moment standing and waiting in line."

"Yes," Dorján whispered. "She would."

They had driven along the narrow dirt roads, pulling over near a barren field. Yellow stubs of last year's harvest stuck out of the earth, giving Dorján the impression of an ailing scalp. As they walked into the field, his legs recognized the little dip between the road and the field. He looked around, saw the thick woods at the other edge, but there were no other markers. Surely this could not be the same field where he and János and Nevena had worked? Where they had found the coins? His palms grew wet, and the double-barrelled shotgun that the Komandant asked him to carry felt heavier with each step.

"You are like the ghost," the Komandant said and took the gun from him. Rifling through his pocket, he pulled out something wrapped in waxy paper. "Take it."

Dorján opened it, a brown candy. Hard with sharp edges, and tasting like sugar, some sort of spice. He walked behind the Komandant now, noticing how the man's black hair was combed sharply to the side and how his head shone in the sunlight. Coat tightly belted, his waist was very narrow.

Over his shoulder, he spoke to Dorján. "Who gives you the history?"

"*Gospodin* Takáts?"

"You are not certain?"

Dorján cleared his throat, repeated himself, no question this time. "*Gospodin* Takáts."

"Ah. Takáts. Does he do a fine job?"

"I don't know, sir."

He stopped then, right in the middle of the field, and turned to face him. "You do not know?"

"I assume so, I meant."

"You are his student."

"I am."

"You must know your teacher. Trust him." He lifted both hands, pressing several fingers into his temples. "He has his mouth to your skull, does he not?"

"Yes, sir."

The Komandant sighed, lowering his hands. "Such a beautiful land, is it not?"

"Yes, sir."

"Looking today, you would never guess the bloodshed, would you? Never guess how many men have fought and died among our hills."

"No, sir."

"Did you know this was the frontier land for the Roman Empire? Roman soldiers built camps, may have stood in our exact footsteps." Tapped the earth with the tip of his boot. "Barbarians waiting in the woods. Until the soldiers' eyes grew heavy. Just a chance. A chance." He crouched, letting his white fingers hover just above a row.

"I...I did, sir."

"Good. Takáts is teaching you something at least."

"And did you know," Oficir Račić now, eyes wide and happy, "that barely yesterday, men would bury their detainees in such fields? Up to their necks, surrounded by dirt." Flattened hand cutting underneath his chin. "Not so bad, you think? The swine are hungry, my friend, and they smell very, very well." Tap to his porous nose. "Always hungry, and in the evening they arrive in search of a meal. And, ah, how convenient. To have it already prepared, still breathing even. Warm and waiting on this vast plate."

"Račić!" The Komandant stood, frowning, handle of the gun on the ground, left hand covering the mouth of the barrel. "Only a weak man finds humour in suffering."

"But can you imagine? What a sight that would be."

"You will frighten the boy," he said. "His memories of war are shallow. Besides, the past is only a black dog at our heels, is it not? And now our country is strong and only growing stronger. So many freedoms here."

Oficir Račić snorted, rolling his eyes. "Ah, you are ripe with shit today, Dragan."

"We are slaves to no one, and we think for ourselves. The future is full of promise. That's where our sights should be."

"Bloated with it." Oficir Račić moved toward the trees. "I will step to the side, Komandant. You are about to burst."

The Komandant lifted his chin toward Dorján. Time to walk again. The pause was over. "Nothing worthy comes out of his mouth, but Račić is loyal. That counts for something."

Dorján agreed, though he did not understand. He lingered a few paces behind the Komandant as they crossed the field. Once inside the woods, they stepped quietly through the underbrush. The air was thick and damp, and it wrapped around Dorján's neck, slid inside his coat. Chilled him so that he longed for home, where he would sit at the table and his grandmother would fill his stomach with bread and warm milk. Even longed for the pool where his muscles would ache from the work, his arms and legs pulsing his body back and forth in the water.

The venture had been Nevena's idea. Pressed upon her father, no doubt. He had come to Dorján's house, asking him to join the hunt. A morning together. "Perhaps we will find something for our tables?" Dorján had no choice but to say yes.

He never expected to find an animal. Others had been complaining about the scarcity this year. Even hares had been in short supply. Another hour of roaming, and surely they would give up. He could go home.

The Komandant stopped suddenly, lifting his hand. Dorján froze, moved only his eyes, but saw nothing. Fluid movements, and even though the Komandant held a gun, he motioned to Račić, tilting his head toward the barrel, low hum in his throat. And then, right in front of them, a shadow transformed into a deer.

The doe lowered her head, rooting through the dead leaves. Chewed, her jaw circling. Finger on the trigger, sliding. "One… two…thr—" And in the same moment that Račić fired, a wet cough erupted from his throat. The deer sprang forward. Disappeared again.

"*Govno jedno*, Račić!" *You piece of shit.* "You could not hold yourself for a single instant?"

"Yes, yes, I know. I could not help it. I fucked it, for sure."

"Almost. Almost."

Oficir Račić lit a cigarette, slid a fist inside his coat, and struck his chest. "She is here, though. We will find her."

They continued walking, and the Komandant fell in step with Dorján, saying, "The deer, you see, believes it owns the woods. Believes it is free. But, ah, it is just a convenient illusion, Dorján. An illusion of comfort and ignorance."

"Yes, sir."

"Is the deer free?"

"Yes, sir."

He laughed quietly. "Ah, to have youth again."

Minutes later, they trod lightly between a pair of oaks, and the doe was there again. Raising her head as a branch cracked beneath Oficir Račić's feet, but still, he wasted no time, lifted his gun, rapid adjustments of feet and neck and fingers.

A shot. A cry from the animal.

Dorján jumped at the sound, but the Komandant did not flinch. He turned to Dorján, said, "You are wrong, *dečko*. The deer is only as free as the hunter and good luck allows."

Račić rushed forward.

"Only a wound," the Komandant called. "No need to work yourself into a sweat. You have not killed her yet."

Her blood streaked the spongy earth, a spray over the coarse moss. They followed the red wetness on the leaves. An easy trail, broken branches, uneven hoofprints. Into a clearing where the doe stumbled, front knees buckling. Head and chest bent low to the ground in a weakened prayer. Back legs collapsed next, and the creature rolled onto her side, panting, panting. Fringed black eyes wide and frightened.

"It's suffering," Dorján said.

"Yes, yes, she is." The Komandant marched into the clearing, stepped over the doe, thick neck between his knees. "You must flatten the thought. Remove it from your mind." He gripped her chin, lifted her loose head, and let it drop again. Stepped backwards, then a nod toward Oficir Račić, who came toward the doe. One hand dipping behind his back, he unsnapped a case on his belt. She did not fight when he brought the knife to her throat. Made a deep, clean slit.

Blood rushed out, disguising Račić's hand, and Dorján emitted a grunt as though someone had knocked him in the stomach.

"I do not like to witness this," the Komandant said, looking up at the clean, clear sky. "The very act of existing is a savage thing, is it not? Savage, but necessary."

Then he walked to the edge of the clearing, took several deep breaths. And Dorján, following behind him, stopped when the Komandant stopped. Dorján wondered if he should help with the deer, do something, but he waited, watched. He sensed the Komandant needed to spend a moment alone. He stared at his back and then noticed him do something curious.

The Komandant bent his head, lifted his right hand to his temple, and fingers loose, he slowly, slowly turned his hand several times in a circular motion. Then he dropped his hand to his side, straightened his back, turned to Dorján with a pleasant expression, saying, "Ah. There now." *There now.* "We must prepare our kill."

Dorján stared at the Komandant. Straight at his shiny face.

"Why. Why did you do that?" Words like feathers drifting through windless air. "With your hand."

"Ah, you wonder about my foolish gesture. It is nothing, really. Something the Major General taught me while I served. To take a moment and erase the past. My heart is too soft, and the hand helps to trick the mind. It offers me some small opening. Back to the place I was before."

The Komandant's eyes were a perfect match to Nevena's. Beautiful and brown. Dorján pulled in his stomach, but the air would not leave his lungs.

"You look at me strangely," the Komandant said. "You are unwell?"

Dorján shook his head.

"You have seen too much?"

He nodded.

"I understand. It is not easy to see such things."

Such things. Too much was rushing at Dorján all at once. All of his questions, and the answers slamming into his head. Testing the strength of the bones in his skull, full of secret hollows, stretches of lacy thinness.

While there had been none moments ago, now a wind moved through the woods. It pulled dried leaves from the branches, a flurry of yellow and orange dropping down on their heads. Oficir Račić puppy-yelped as he sliced open the deer's belly, turning the innards out onto the grass. Dorján's nose began to leak, and he sniffed. The weighty smell of blood and the contents of the animal's bowel cut through the sweetness of wet spruce and balding oak trees. Too much, and he ran toward the woods, crouched, and heaved. He wanted to vomit, have his stomach and head and heart emptied, but everything held. Closing his eyes, he thought of the old apricot tree in his grandmother's backyard, summer sunlight streaming through its leaves. He thought of János and himself sweating in the warmth, plucking the ripe fruit, placing it into a basket. He thought of Nevena teasing them and stealing fruit from the basket. Streaks of juice on her chin, pinkish spatter on her shirt. She tossed sticky pits at them, the brazen evidence of her theft clinging to their hair, once to János's cheek.

Cracking of the deer's skeleton, a second yelp of delight, and the apricot tree faded. The laughter faded. In the corner of his eye he saw a creased pair of trousers, mucky laced boots.

"Stand up." The Komandant was beside him, nudging him with his leg. "You will get used to this. You must. As a man grows older, you will learn, he can get used to anything."

::::

"WINTER WILL SOON BE upon us."

"Yes," Gitta replied. "The sun is turning away."

She and Zsuzsi sat on the bench in front of their homes. Gitta was still, back straight, while Zsuzsi's fingers worked furiously to knit a woollen hat. Pale blue with a band of brown.

"I make three hats each autumn, and by spring they are donated to the wind."

Gitta smiled. "He loses them?"

"I do not know. Loses them by accident or loses them on purpose."

"I doubt it, Zsuzsi *néni*. Dorján is not that way. Not careless."

"Ah, but his hair is always damp. The swimming. The water. A chill will find his bones one day and not leave." She clacked her needles harder, feigning annoyance, "And then he will look to me with his big face for soup and bread and whatever else."

The image of Dorján sick and in bed pained Gitta, and she sighed. "Then you will give him soup and bread and whatever else."

Zsuzsi stopped for a moment. "Yes, yes. You are right. Of course, of course."

"Dorján is all right, though?"

"He is good. Just good. He is quiet. Too quiet some days."

"Do you worry?"

"Yes, of course. A little piece of me always worries."

"You hide it well."

Zsuzsi's needles stopped, and she laid a warm hand on Gitta's thigh. "There is hope, my friend. There is always hope. If you nurture it, it grows wide. Works to smother the suffering."

While offered in kindness, those words were difficult for Gitta to hear. She was not ready for hope to crawl up those layers of grief and attempt to muffle them. Right now grief was holding her together, those forces pushing out from her stomach equal to the reality pushing in. Hope would loosen her, oil in the cracks.

Needles blurring the air, snapping, and Gitta noticed the hat beginning to take shape. Each perfectly crafted stitch joined with the others, soon enough of them to cover the boy's round head.

"Tonight, we will have something good to eat. You will come sit with us."

Gitta nodded, crossing her ankles. "I have peppers in the jar. I will bring."

"I have, I have. Dorján will be home soon. He went to hunt with the Komandant. They will find a hare, I am guessing. Maybe a bird."

At the mention of the Komandant, Gitta's heart quivered slightly in her chest. Could that be a thin film of warmth? Of hope? "Ah," was all she said.

"And look," Zsuzsi said, laying her knitting in her lap. "Here he comes now. But his hands are empty. Still, you will come. Yes, you will come and eat with us. We will find something to share. Something…"

Zsuzsi's voice began to fade as Dorján approached. Gitta could not lower her head. Her face was locked forward, eyes staring at their chests. The two of them. Dorján, Zsuzsi's only grandson, walking side by side with Oficir Račić. As they approached, he was laughing, and he clapped Dorján on the back then held him tightly on the shoulder so that their bodies were fused. Closer, closer, Dorján's pained face, the smell of metal on the breeze. They had killed something. She could just make out stains on the Oficir's skin.

"Ah," Zsuzsi said, disgust on her tongue. "Is that Račić? My eyes are worth nothing. Go, Gitta. Go before he sees you."

Gitta stood casually and walked behind the bench, slipping inside her home. She had no concern for her own safety; Račić would not bother her again. But Dorján. Dorján. Seeing them side by side felt like a thin pin pushed into her abdomen. She had no doubt Račić was capable of… of what? She thought of Tibor. Tibor, who was nowhere. Tibor, who would never be seen again. Life would edge forward as though he never existed.

Could some harm come to Dorján? Did she misinterpret a simple display of camaraderie between men? *Račić is reliable. Competent.* The Komandant believed that. Trusted him. Gitta's hand formed a fist around the door handle.

There was nothing she could do. No direction to take her thoughts. The weight of helplessness forced her limbs, and she knelt on the floor, leaning her heavy head against her forearm.

Chapter 41

"YOU HAVE TO TELL me," she said. "What's wrong?"

They met in the field, at the top of the mound. The grass had grown prickly, irritated by the oncoming cold. Summer had passed so quickly, he could not comprehend the early bite of fall. Dorján stomped down a small circle, blades cracking, and placed his sweater on the ground.

"Sit down."

Nevena folded her arms across her chest. "I will not sit until you tell me why you are acting this way. What have I done?"

"Nothing. You've done nothing." And he knelt on the ground, put his hands in his face, and through his fingers, he whispered, "I don't know what to say."

She picked the sweater off the ground, placing it over his shoulders. "At the beginning. Always a good place."

"You don't understand. There is no beginning. There is only an end."

He was certain, he was certain that Nevena's father had been the man who had visited his mother in those early mornings. Left loose change on her night table. The change that Dorján then clutched in his fist, scrambled to the shop so he could buy a half loaf of bread.

And he was certain, he was certain that Nevena's father had been the man who walked out of the woods after János died. Paused at the mouth of the forest, bent his head, and erased some action with a flick of his wrist.

Dorján's shoulders started to shake, but he pinched back the desire to weep. Hidden inside the tall grass, he could see nothing, only the wide blue sky. But he did not trust his eyes, believing that any moment the grass or the sky might be peeled away, an ugly underside of decaying roots and swollen insects revealed.

"I can't see properly." Though he did not intend it, his voice was a whimper. "Nothing is the same anymore." Would ever be the same again. But they had tried. For months. Tried to be the way they once were. When János was still alive.

"Are you having trouble with your eyes? Is there something wrong with your sight?" Her hand rested on his shoulder. "Dorján, answer me."

He nodded.

"Is it serious?"

He bent his head.

She spoke rapidly now, a spray of simple solutions. "We will find a good doctor. The best doctor, Dori. In Drobnik. If not, we will travel to the city. My father will find someone. He will. I will ask him. He will find the right man, and that man will help you."

"Your father."

"You know what he can do. You know."

"I do. I believe I know." Dorján gripped a handful of dying blades, their sharp edges stinging his palms. "The coins."

"What coins?"

"The ones we found."

"Last year? In the field?"

"So long ago. You remember?"

"Yes, yes."

"We were to tell no one. No one. That was our agreement. Our promise to each other."

Her head snapped back slightly. "I remember. Of course I remember. I have not mentioned them since. Though I've wanted to."

"Did you keep your promise?"

"You threw them in the river."

"Did you keep your promise?"

"They are gone now, swallowed."

"Did you keep your promise?"

"János is gone. Why make ourselves sore?"

"Nevena. Answer me. Did you?"

She bent her legs, putting her mouth to her knees. "Yes."

"Yes?"

"Yes, I told. I was afraid, Dori. Afraid of what might happen. And then," her face twisted, lips crinkled, "the worst did."

"Your father?"

"Yes."

"Ah."

"He said I had done the right thing. What might have happened if we'd been discovered? To steal something so valuable from the country. Imagine! Like stealing from our mothers. We're given so much, and we spit in her face."

"It was a mistake."

"Then János disappeared. He was gone."

"Why didn't you tell me?"

"What good might it have done? Nothing. I tried to erase it all." Tears drained from her eyes, down over her cheeks. She scratched the wetness from her jaw, leaving red scrapes. "If only I had pushed him to go sooner."

"Pushed who?"

"My father. He said he would, but he never went to find you and János. That night. He never found you. He stayed at home, slept in his chair, while, while, Tibor—"

Dorján bit his tongue.

"If he had gone, everything would be different. He would have helped us. The boys would never have fought. János would not have died."

Dorján could not look at her for fear something might burst from him. Though he did not move, he sensed lead weights dropping onto his body, two on either side, one pushing straight up through his spine. Splitting him right down the centre. "It's not your fault," he said.

"Not my fault? How can you say that?"

"It's true."

"Of course it's my fault. I have a hand in it. I am trying to accept that."

"Neva." Her name, just a breath.

"Why do you dig at this now? Why can't you leave it?"

He shook his head, would never say. "I don't know. I don't know. My mind will not stop."

On the hill, they lay down on the dry earth. The wind whistled over the tips of the grass, and the sun shone down, warming the small room they had created. Side by side, length of his left arm pressing against the length of her right. Dorján was much taller, and they made an awkward line, and he pictured János as part of their formation. A strong triangle, obtuse, yes, but each of them looking outward, protecting the backs of the others.

She turned her head so that her mouth touched the sleeve of his shirt. He could feel her breath through the cotton. "We will fix your eyes," she whispered, but he knew that was impossible, the thin seal on his lids broken. He could not walk backwards. Walk backwards until he came to that field where they had tugged corn from the stalks. He could not stop his foot before it kicked the mound, and the rat hurried out from underneath it. Could not prevent János from trying to find a higher place to hang his lunch bag.

Locating her sweating fingers with his own, he squeezed. And after a while, she stopped crying, her breathing calmed. He brought his face close to hers, their temples touching. When they were younger, the three of them often stood with shoulders touching, heads bent. Eyes wide open, vision distorted, and Dorján could see only Nevena's left eye and János's right. Nothing else. That closeness, clean breath mingling, always filled him with thick comfort. He had two best friends who would be with him forever. Nothing could happen to them. They were children.

Dorján tilted his head so that his eyelashes brushed against Nevena's. When he looked at her, he saw her eye, wet and sore. That nearness made him feel both full and empty. Half of his sight was filled with Nevena. Yes. But János was missing. And through that other eye, he could see the whole world beyond.

Chapter 42

"I RECOGNIZE THE SERIOUSNESS on your face." The Komandant sat back in his chair, folded his fingers, and laid them against his stomach. "Is this about my daughter?"

"No, *Gospodin*."

"Ah, good! I did not want to shoot you." He threw his head back and laughed. "Sit," he said, open hand gesturing toward a second chair. He slid a plate across the table. Sliced cake, thick black swirl of poppy seeds in the centre. "Take something to eat."

Dorján stared at the chair, new and clean, not a single nick to the paint on the curving arms and slender legs. Knees quivering, he wanted to sink into it, but he stood, keeping his body stiff and tall. "I will stand."

As he had walked toward the Komandant's house, he was certain the road rolled beneath his feet, sliding him toward the home at such speed, he did not fully realize what he was doing. What he might say. As he faced the Komandant, the realization struck him in the stomach, making him instantly queasy.

"Ah. Young legs, I suppose. Do not need the consolation."

Several deep breaths, and Dorján spaced his feet apart even farther. Everything in the Komandant's room was in perfect order. Papers piled neatly, books in a straight line, not a particle of dust on the painting or the desk or the trio of bright blue pots in the corner. There was solitude. With the exception of Dorján. His insides were vibrating so fiercely, he thought his skin might loosen, fall to the floor in a pinkish heap.

The Komandant pushed crumbs from the plate onto his fingertips, chewing them away. "Why do you bring your darkness into my home?"

"I … I," he stammered. "I want to know the truth." He was uncertain how the words had emerged, but there they were. In the air between them. Dorján expected some sort of reaction to his statement, but the Komandant was silent.

Finally, he spoke. "Ah, the truth," he mused. "Such a complicated word these days, is it not?"

"I want to know."

"Our country has no need for philosophers, Dorján. They exist only in a time of luxury. Scarce even then."

Dorján clenched his teeth. "You know what I mean."

"No. I do not." A growl. "And you will hurry now with your little game. My daughter may find you pleasant on the eye, but I do not."

If only Dorján could push his hand into his throat, grip the dry words, and haul them out. Slam them onto the table, making plate and pencil and papers all leap. He closed his eyes, and when he could not see the Komandant's shiny face, he was able to say, "János. János Kelemen."

Again, the Komandant did not respond as Dorján expected. Again, there was silence.

Dorján opened his eyes, wondering if the chair might be empty. The man gone. But no, he was there, head slightly bowed, a finger running over his thick eyebrows. He wore a ring, a wide silver band, large amber stone in the centre. "Yes," he said. "Ah, yes."

"Tell me."

"We have taken care of it, have we not? The boy, what was his name? He is in the right place."

"No. Tibor did nothing wrong. I'm sure of it."

"Tibor. Yes, yes. Now I recall. How can you be so sure?"

"I saw you there." Words tumbling out now.

"You did, did you?"

"Yes. I saw you walking away."

Joints cracking, the Komandant stretched and yawned. "So stupid. I walk most evenings. Good for the vigour."

"And … and." He wanted to ask about his mother, but he could not tug that burr from his stomach. So much weight on him, so many layers binding him, holding things against him. He looked down at his feet. Dusty old boots, knots in the black laces.

After several moments Dorján peered at the Komandant. The man poured clear liquid into his glass. Sharp smell of plums leaking into the air.

"You have something else to ask me?"

"Did you see him?"

"Him?"

"My friend. János. That night."

Shot of liquor. "Surely you attempt a joke."

"No, sir."

The Komandant scraped his fingernail at the corner of his mouth, refilled his glass. "I will tell you this, *dečko*. Very little provokes me. But young minds, ah, young minds can push me toward the flame. So many ideas and ideals. So few years pushing down on your spine. Pushing your feet into the earth. You do your learning inside walls. The likes of Takáts and Beštić spewing lessons, filling your head with shit." A second shot of liquor into his mouth, swishing through his teeth. Another hiss. "Words will not make you grow. Make you understand this life."

Dorján stepped back. As he watched the Komandant's features tighten, the buzzing swarm inside his chest abandoned him, a sick, dank feeling rising up in its place. His conviction folded on itself over and over until the shape was unrecognizable. He did not know what was right anymore. How could he hope to find answers when now the questions were no longer clear?

Could he have been wrong? Could he have watched someone else coming out of those woods? A man on a simple walk? Yes. Likely Tibor had been involved all along. A boy covered with thorns of spite. Why would he think otherwise? A terrible fight. A push. A punch. An unfortunate accident. And his mother. Those memories were so hazy, edges blurring into childhood nightmares. Maybe there was no one at all, and he had only conjured the figure who had arrived before dawn a handful of times. Maybe he had wanted so desperately to meet the ghost of his father, he constructed the very shadows himself.

Everything would be so easy if he could simply accept those few thoughts. Believe them. Life would roll forward in a predictable, easy manner. School. Swimming. And Nevena.

Suddenly Dorján felt lighter than he had in an entire year. As though someone had unsnapped the rusty metal hinges binding his feet, and fresh air was lifting him upward, upward to the clean white ceiling. When he touched down, could speak again, he would apologize to the Komandant, then quietly drift out the door, let time pass before coming back. His accusations would be forgotten. And it would be fine. Yes, it would be fine.

The Komandant drank another shot. Wiped his mouth with the back of his hand, cocked his head to the side. "You are smiling at me, dečko."

Dorján shrugged, smiled wider. Would laugh out loud if he could.

The Komandant gripped the rim of his desk and stood. "Our visit has come to an end."

"I'm sorry, sir. So sorry to have taken your time."

::::

EVEN THOUGH A YEAR had passed, Dragan Dobrica remembered every moment of that evening. Nevena had come to him, fear making her face unpleasant. She described the afternoon of harvesting corn, the discovery, a hidden clearing, the roots of a tall tree tangled around a rock. He knew the exact location. When he was twelve, three bigger boys often pressed him against that same tree, two holding his hands, the third planting sharp pinches against his frame. He would have preferred to have been beaten, tight knots of knuckles driving into his cheeks or his soft stomach. He would have felt more like a man taking that, marks on his body he could display. But instead, they pinched him as though he were a girl. A weak girl. Pinched his cheeks and his arms and his ribs and his legs. Each twist of flesh a sting but not more. Red welt rising, two round dots. All too soon the redness faded to pink and then back to the normal colour of his skin.

But that did not matter. A childish memory, nothing more. He had long ago taken his glowing shame and hammered it into something workable. Into something cold and strong and pointed. Besides, those boys had all grown into men. Two had died, and the third was rarely out of Dragan's sight. Oficir Račić, a man who never owned a single thought, always followed three steps behind him. Dragan felt a pang of joy whenever he assigned Račić a task, and Račić obeyed like a slovenly soldier.

When he left his home, Dragan would admit, his intentions were not clear in his mind. He had assumed Nevena was exaggerating, as young girls tend to do, and that he would find the boys with nothing more than a handful of clay. Pieces of a broken vessel. Scraps of metal. But when he stepped into the clearing, he realized she had been telling the truth. There was only one boy there, crouched over a pile of dirty coins, a sewing tin opened, paper bills and loose change inside. His name eluded Dragan at the time, but he was the shorter and thicker of the two. Brigitta's son, he recognized that much, but his face was nothing like hers. He bore the rude expression of his father.

The boy did not twist his body, keeping his back to the tangled path through the brush. He said, "Ready to talk? I knew you'd come back, my friend."

"Your friend?" Dragan repeated, amusement in his tone.

The boy jumped, falling forward so his folded lower legs covered the coins.

"Yes," Dragan said. "You are right. It is time to talk. Give me your name."

The boy shuffled on the ground, pulling dead leaves toward his legs. Stared up at Dragan. "Kelemen, *Gospodin*," he said. "János Kelemen."

"Ah, yes. I remember now. The earth is cold to the touch, is it not?"

"Yes, sir."

Dragan wove his fingers together, cracking his knuckles. "Then stand up."

"I … I strained my ankle. It … it hurts."

"You are injured?"

"Yes, *Gospodin*."

Over his shoulder, Dragan *tss-tssed* twice in rapid succession, and Oficir Račić lumbered into the clearing. "The child struggles to walk," Dragan said, jutting out his chin. "Lift him."

Račić spat to the side, marched forward, meaty hands digging into the boy's armpits, hoisting the boy to his feet.

Silence then, as the three of them stared at the treasure he was hiding. One coin stuck to the dirty skin of the boy's leg, lingered there, then after a second peeled off, clinking when it struck the others.

"What have we here?"

"Nothing," the boy said. "Garbage."

Račić snorted, spat again. "Fine garbage, I would say."

Dragan lifted two fingers, and Račić stopped talking.

"You found these, yes?"

The boy lowered his head. "Yes."

"Where?"

"In the field."

"While you worked?"

A sigh. "Yes. While we worked."

"And your idea is to keep them?"

The boy straightened up, folding his arms across his chest. "No, *Gospodin*. Of course not."

"No?"

"We were only counting them. Counting."

"We?"

The boy glanced behind him. "Me. Just me."

"And then?"

He did not reply, just shuffled his feet, kept looking behind him.

"There is no one there," Dragan whispered. "We are alone."

Račić laughed.

"I am curious of your plans. Sometimes youth is pleasantly unpredictable."

"No plans, *Gospodin*."

"Ah, but you must tell me."

"We—I was only counting. Tomorrow, tomorrow, we—I was going to—"

"Enough!"

The boy was quiet, but Dragan could tell by the slant of his head that he did not like instruction.

"That is the danger of telling the truth first," Dragan told him. "A lie becomes obvious."

"I never lied."

"Have you thought of your mother? Do you not think she could do with more? Deserves more? Or others in our village?"

Dragan reached inside his coat, pulled out his metal case, opened it, and retrieved a cigarette. Struck a match, smoked slowly for several moments. Most people, Dragan knew, did not know what to do with silence. The boy was no different, staring at him, a pleasing mix of irritation and panic altering his features. Eventually, Dragan allowed the cigarette to fall from his grip, saying, "My patience is a string, *dečko*, and you are swinging on it."

"Just counting, sir. I swear."

"You do not understand your betrayal."

"No betrayal."

"My daughter tells me everything. Did you know that?"

"Nevena?"

"I ask you do not speak her name." Dragan watched with interest as the boy's expression shifted.

"She would never say anything."

"Such confident words for someone in such a weak position. I remember something similar with your father."

"My father?"

"You are like him. Very much."

Innocence. "I am?"

"As I recall, he took something from me. Someone." *Someone I loved.* "So many years ago. I have never forgotten that, you know."

And I let him take her. Still the weak boy, covered in red pinches. I did not fight.

"What? Who?"

"Father and son. Thieves. Both of you. Two. Filthy. Thieves."

And that was the hard crack the boy needed. Dragan had flipped the bug onto its back, located the abdomen. Lips curled, nostrils flaring, the boy charged Dragan. Struck him with his upper body. But Dragan stood tall, his weight balanced like a wall of cinder blocks. Force applied, force returned, and the boy bounced backwards.

Well, did he bounce? Or did Dragan push? Did he push the boy with all the power he had? The resentment that had festered for years. In that instant, did he feel a sugary sense of pleasure as the boy tripped over a looping root, then his own angry feet, fell straight, arms spinning? Nature offering no cushion between the bones of his neck and the edge of a rock. A gentle landing, the knock barely making a sound. Maybe he pushed. But it was not a thought upon which Dragan would dwell. He had already flattened it, slid it into a slot inside his mind. A slot he would never open again.

The boy did not move, slumped downward, and lay quietly with his chin pushed deep into his chest. Račić stepped closer, nudged the boy with his boot. Kicked him. Twice in the ribcage. Then cupped his fat hand over the boy's mouth and nose for several seconds, wiped his hand on his trousers, and spat again. "He will be quiet for some time."

Dragan waved Račić away, knelt down on one knee, leaned closer to János. As he examined the boy's young features, he inhaled until his chest was full, held it for a moment, and released the air in a slow stream. Some time ago, Dragan wondered how Death could be so creative when he came to steal a soul. Back of a skull dented by an explosion, green infection in a torn toenail swimming through the bloodstream, an open mouth choking on its own vomit. Creative, yet when Death took what he wanted, he left behind only a single expression. The faces of the deceased all looked precisely the same.

With that, Dragan could tell the boy was gone immediately. Not from his silence or the stillness of his chest. He simply had Death's expression. Flat and empty. Bored, almost. As though he were done, finished, ready to move on to something new. Death, Dragan thought, was a strong soldier. He did his job without mercy and never stayed around to play.

Dragan touched the boy's ear. As he looked down upon him, he swallowed a crystal of regret that clung to his throat. He allowed himself to feel something, yes, but it was murky and its boundaries were poorly defined. The boy, he realized, was a person who did not belong. A young man who slipped beneath the grinding wheels of eventuality. The boy was so much like his father. Each a grenade, attitude packed tightly inside a metallic body, split pin ring tucked up under the hair. Only a matter of time before someone slipped a finger along his damp scalp, yanked at the safety. Pin removed, spoon released, and a few paces backwards. A short count of six before the explosion.

A second breath, and this time Dragan blew it out. He had come as far as he had because he understood the position of his fuse. Knew how to control it. Knew to accept what needed to be accepted and to do what needed to be done. He was not void of passion, not in the least. But he was smarter than to be ruled by it. Would not be where he was if he had indulged that weakness.

Shifting his legs, Dragan reached across the rotting layer of leaves and collected the coins. Dropped them into the deep pockets of his coat. When he had gathered every one, he gestured toward the tin box, saying, "For you, Račić."

As he stood, he placed his hand on the rock, felt stickiness. Turned his palm over, brought it to his nose. Sweet odour of blood on his skin. Iron and dirt.

"Take it after you clean up."

Račić grunted. "How?"

"I trust you are an intelligent man." A smirk concealed by the shadows.

As Dragan walked away, he heard Račić grunt again as he dragged the boy down a small slope. Returning steps, then the sound of a zipper opening, a hiccup and a sigh. Thick stream of water spattering. Dragan nodded and walked on. Oficir Račić would complete his work. In the middle of the dark woods, he had already found a way to clean the rock.

:::::

"SOMETHING SMALL BEFORE YOU GO." Dragan turned toward the shelves behind him, reached for a wooden box, grasped the lid by the tiny knob. He removed an item, a yellow glow in his fist, and said, "I no longer want it in my house." Snap of wrist, flick of stained fingers.

Dorján saw it sailing through the air, decided not to catch it. Would let it fall, strike the rug, roll beneath table or chair. Though when it was overhead, he thrust his arm up, and it landed flat against his palm, a quiet slap. Fingers collapsing around it. He opened his hand, brought it closer to his face. There it was. The thirty-seventh coin, the one with the insect, a humble praying mantis, clinging to the side of a shaft of wheat. For a moment his vision blurred, and he saw the wheat swaying. The mantis moving its thread legs, stubborn and patient.

"The very last one," the Komandant said. "It belongs to you."

"No. It belongs to—"

"To?" He laughed. "Do not try to sound noble."

"I…I don't want it."

"You will take it," he said, snapping the lid of the box back in place. "And I will never see it again. You wanted to be a thief, did you not? Like your friend? Well, now you are the same."

"But, you said—"

"Tell me. Just what did I say?" The Komandant clapped his hands in front of him. "Do you even know?"

Dorján bowed his head, his thoughts no clearer than a smudge of grey.

"Life is full of little lessons, is it not?"

Chapter 43

"THANK YOU. IT IS more than I can handle, but I feel I cannot say no."

Backs curled, Gitta and Zsuzsi leaned over wooden barrels, steam from hot water rippling through the cool air of the yard. They worked wet laundry up and down over boards, then rinsed each garment in clean water, twisting and piling them into a basket.

Zsuzsi leaned backwards, panted, rubbed her forearms. "Sew, yes, but I was not made to wash. What I would not pay for a pair of hands like yours, Gitta."

"You can have them. I suspect they do not even belong to me. Otherwise I would be stronger."

Water splashing over the rim of the barrel. "What stupidity. You are as strong as you have to be."

"Not so." Gitta pressed the side of her wrinkled thumb to her upper lip. "I was in the square yesterday. Do you know what a woman said to me?"

"What woman?"

"I do not recall her name."

"Tell me."

The rapid movement of her arm slowed. A fistful of fabric sitting on the board. "Someday you will put him out of your mind, she said. I will put János out of my mind."

"She has a black tongue, Gitta. She was young, yes?"

Gitta continued, as though she had not heard the question. "What absurd talk, put him out of my mind. As though he were peelings from a root. He was my mind. My blood. No longer do I think in a straight line. Do you know that Zsuzsi? Most days I feel like a ghost, hovering in my own home. How can someone know?"

"I do." Softness. "I do know. I had a son, you remember, and I have a son no longer."

Gitta sighed, then lifted her apron, wiped her face, even though her skin was tight and dry. Two steps, and she sat on a wooden chair, staring at her palms. "Forgive me. My sadness is selfish, making me cold."

Zsuzsi shuffled toward her, reached for her wrists, gripped them. A mess of brilliant redness, fingers and hands.

"It took me some time to understand," Gitta said. "That I will never know. I will never know who took the life of my child."

"How might you know?"

"I should know. I should be able to look into the eye of every man in this village. And see. Would a good mother not feel such a thing?"

"Of course not. Why would you?"

"I realize now, though. I am so full of fault. With Imre, with János. Mistakes I have made, I cannot begin to tell you." She thought of the girl, then. The *Schwab*. Her innocent face. The swelling of her stomach, her shrill German, and Gitta knew she had been pleading, pleading. Gitta swallowed, took shallow breaths through her mouth. "Nothing is clear to me. I deserve no comfort. From you or anyone else."

"Ah, Gitta. You go back and back, and what good is in it?"

"Yes." She leaned her head to the side. "I am weak."

"I understand, my friend. I do. Ah, I wanted to shrivel up and disappear. Let every leaf fall from my branches and slip into a deep sleep. Like you, yes?" Zsuzsi placed one weathered hand over Gitta's and sighed. "We are widows. We are mothers. Above all, we are the women of our beautiful country, and we will endure. No matter what happens on the surface, beneath our roots are reaching, touching. We keep the soil from lifting up and blowing away."

"If only I could. How do we do that?"

"It is not easy. But we remind ourselves. No matter what we have lost, our husbands, our children, there is always more to lose. We must be grateful for what is left. For the small help we can be to others."

Gitta frowned, nodding slowly.

"Listen. We have lived many days the same. Have we not? Side by side. We both know there are no assurances, Gitta. Never. You step or you perish. Some days you want to perish, but still you must step. And my friend, as long as I am upright, we will step together."

"Zsuzsi, I...I—"

Zsuzsi shook a finger, "Enough chip-chipping. Enough! We make the hens jealous."

Boards on the fence groaned, as though someone were leaning against it, and Gitta looked up. She saw a crescent of brown hair, a fist lifting in the air and lightly pounding the top of the head. Lit cigarette locked inside the knot of fingers.

"Dori!" Zsuzsi straightened her spine, rubbed her lower back, joints cracking. "Do you think someone severed our noses? That we do not smell your exhaust?" She clucked her tongue. "Come. Now. How can you loiter while an old woman works?"

::::

THE BOARDS OF THE fence, spiteful from the oncoming cold, had given him away. He had been waiting there, listening to them talking. Had not the courage to step into the garden, to face Gitta, his best friend's mother. How could he tell her what she needed to know? The truth about János. The night he had died.

He threw his cigarette onto the stone, stepped onto it, entered through the gate. The hinges creaked, rust flaking.

"I was just—"

His grandmother stood before him, her head barely reaching the height of his armpit. "Tell me nothing. Looking for food, no doubt. If you do not stop this foolish growing, we will give you a basket next to Buksi."

"The dog?"

"A girl for you," she said, pushing Dorján slightly with her chest. "Her face may have fur, but she is lovely and loyal." Small pout, shoulders lifted, palms upward. "You could do worse."

He blushed, tripping over his feet as he stepped to the side.

His grandmother shook her head, clicking sound coming from her cheek. "Perhaps she is too fast and too smart for you."

"*Nagyanya*. Buksi is not a girl."

"Ah. I had forgotten. But I am only pulling at your hair. I know your heart has already been stolen."

He cleared his throat, absent-mindedly brought a hand to his chest. His heart—was it stolen? Perhaps it had been. Since János was found, they had grown closer. Some evenings, he could not shake the thoughts of her from his head. With innocence, she had owned his heart, had kept it, since they were children. Since she had woven her fingers through his on the mound as planes flew overhead, bombs dropped, bit pieces from the earth. Everything so confusing, yet so simple at the same time.

Of course, now that he knew the truth, it would not stay that way. Nothing existed purely on its own. Gradually at first, then with sudden swiftness, that childhood connection was encircled with lengths of dirty twine. Tightening until portions of the muscle turned blue, began to wither. Walk away or die. His heart had no choice but to stumble home, close the door to its cage. Huddle in the corner, beaten and bewildered. How he would explain this to Nevena, he did not know.

Pressing a hand into his pocket, he felt the thin silver tin containing his cigarettes. It had belonged to his father. He began to withdraw it, but his grandmother shook her head, saying, "You are too young to smell so much like a man. Now, take those shirts and twist them again. My shoulders are not made for the job. But do not break a thread, do you hear me. Not a single one."

"Yes, *nagyanya.*"

"And you know I will hear if you do. I can hear a snapped thread all the way from a kitchen in Drobnik."

"I will be careful." He pulled off his sweater, tossed it onto the table. Then reached into a bucket, retrieved a shirt, squeezed. Strings of water trailed down his forearms, making him itch.

"Now, Gitta. I will bring you water."

"No, no, Zsuzsi *néni.* I am fine."

"Good, then. I leave you my replacement." Little bow. "Tell him what you want, and he will do it. He is a good boy." Arm stretching, slap to his cheek.

"He is," Gitta replied. "So very good."

His grandmother wobbled through Gitta's gate, crossed the courtyard, and entered through her own gate. He could hear her rummaging around in the backyard, humming to herself. Sound of rustling leaves just on the other side of the fence, and she called out, "These old peppers hold to the vine." A darker voice then, "Winter is coming for you, my little friends! Is a warm pot not better?"

Gitta and Dorján looked up, smiling at each other. That was one of many things he adored about his grandmother. Never had she kept a secret. Never did you wonder what she was thinking. She talked nearly non-stop, whether it was to a person, a plant, or even the grit at the bottom of her coffee cup. Explaining life. Explaining how to live better. Explaining how to be.

"I can hear you smiling at me," she sang. Vines snapping. "Ah, you want to keep your seeds? I will grant you that courtesy."

Eventually his grandmother finished, and he heard her shoes scrape across the stone, the door of the house open and close. Silence between them, other than sloshing water. Dorján's bucket of clothes was empty, and he bit his lip, ran his fingertips over the cloudy water. Stared at the ripples, lines crossing, a puzzle, melting together. What was he going to say to her? Dread like a cold glove squeezing his windpipe.

"If you can shake them," Gitta said, "then hang them. So the arms reach toward the ground."

"All right." He took a breath, lifted a twisted mound, shook the fabric. Fine mist of water landed on his face. With worn wooden pins, he fixed the white cotton shirt to the line. Wind moved through it, opening the arms, pushing air into the back, and for a moment, Dorján thought it looked like a body. Hanging upside down.

Gitta stared at him.

"Good?"

"Good," she said, stopping her work. Stared at him. "Why is your face like that?"

He wanted to pace but kept his feet still. Today was the day, he had decided, he would tell her about the Komandant. About János. Not another afternoon would pass.

"Like what?"

"Like you have pain."

"Pain? I have no pain."

"Yes, you do. But not in your body. Do you want to go? I can finish."

"No, no. I want to help."

"Should I not find that strange? A boy your age wanting to do the wash?"

"My *nagyanya*—"

"Does not expect you to stay."

"I... I—" and he opened his throat, flexed his ribcage, the muscles in the back of his neck. He would not allow the words to hide in his lungs. "I need to tell you something. Something terrible."

She laughed a little, continued her work. "There is nothing terrible you can tell me, Dorján *básci*. You are too young to worry."

"Yes. There is. I—"

"Go ahead. Please. You can say what you wish."

"I was with him," he said. "That night in the woods."

Her hands stopped. "Tell me," she whispered. "Tell me. *Kérlek*."

Her eyes were wide, lips slightly parted. He realized that even after all that had happened, she was still open. She was still there to listen. And he faltered, faltered so badly, his courage skittered down the backs of his legs, across the cracked stone, disappeared among the sleeping fruit trees. There was no finding it now, lost in a tangle of dying vines and dried leaves.

Dorján swallowed again, opened his dry mouth, and exposed only his own guilt. His own culpability. "We were together. Fighting."

"Fighting?"

"I don't even remember what it was. Something stupid. János said so many things, and I said so many things. He wanted to leave. To leave everything behind. Thought life would be better."

"And?"

"And I was angry at him. I didn't understand. I remember that. And so I was angry. I yelled at him. I wanted us to grow up together." *The little engineers.*

"Dorján. Why ache over this? Men argue. Young men argue loudly."

He dropped his head. "You do not understand."

"No?"

"I left him. Left him there in the woods. I waited at the path. In the farm, under Gazda's apple tree. But he never followed me. I waited. And then I was hungry, you see." He pushed his hand into the tenderness underneath his ribs. "My stomach drove me home."

She dropped the shirt then, walked toward Dorján, and placed her dampened hands on his shoulders. His body slumped under the weight of them. "You were his friend. A brother to him."

"If only I stood beside him. Or forced him to come with me."

"Force him? Who could do that?" She frowned, glancing upward. "Your memory has shifted to suit your sadness, Dorján. It is time to loosen it, let it go."

He turned his face to look at her. János was there in her lopsided smile, in her brown eyes and the gentle arch of her brows. His features hidden in her face. The sight of it bored a hole straight through his centre.

"I made a mistake," he said.

"Show me a man who does not."

"I want to see him, Gitta *néni*. To talk to him."

She peered upward again, clouds gliding across the pale blue sky. "I know. I know. But he is gone."

She nodded slowly at him, and before he realized it, his head began to nod back at her. It was not enough. Of course, it was not. Nothing he would say to her would ever be enough. But still, her forgiveness pushed a little air into him. Shaved down the callus on his heart.

:: ::

WHEN HE RETURNED HOME, his grandmother was holding a letter. Torn edge.

"For you," she said. She scowled and shook the papers. "I opened already."

"What is it?"

Dorján reached out, but she skirted away from him, began to pace about the room. Knocking furniture with her soft girth, waving the letter in the air. "I do not understand," she bellowed. "This makes no sense. You are in school. You are sixteen. Sixteen. Are you eighteen? Two years you should wait."

He shook his head, felt ripples of wind coming off his grandmother as she waved her arms.

"Do I not remember the day you were born? Did I not watch you come out from underneath your mother? Did I not mark it down so carefully in my book? Tell me my brain has not turned to meal, *szívem*. Tell me."

"You know. Of course you know."

"Ah," she said, and her hand came down, knuckle striking the wooden table. Letter sliding out from her fingers. Then she rubbed her face, every inch creased with deep wrinkles. "You were the most beautiful baby. The most beautiful child, *szívem*." Her voice had changed, thin like thread. "You look just like your father. You wear his face. And I want you to know your smile has given me a hundred years of joy."

He picked up the letter but already knew what it said. The mark on the envelope explained everything. It was from the state. He was to serve in the *Jugoslavenska narodna armija*. Every man's duty to his country. He would depart in three weeks, the letter said, and not return home for a year. Travel to a base two hours north of Bregalnica, where soldiers trained, built roads, guarded an ammunition dump. There had been rumblings of an accident, a grader rolling over, crushing several soldiers. But Dorján had not expected to be asked to serve before he had finished school. There were others who could go. Others.

"Who brought this?"

"Oficir Račić. Carried it with him when he came. I had let out a pair of his trousers. His waist has grown."

"Račić?"

"I asked him. I asked him. Is there nothing he can do? How can we interrupt your schooling? I told him you are a good student. And your swimming. Ah! How can we ignore that? There are so many ways to work, to make the people proud."

"And?"

"He said work would strengthen your spine."

"I said, the Komandant? Surely, the Komandant! Can he do something? Of course not, he said. Nothing. And he smiled at me. Said, the paper is the paper."

"Ah."

She reached over the sink, lifted the wood holding the window, allowed it to slide shut. Then, two fingers touching her nose, she whispered, "But." Raising her voice. "But! I feel he is a liar. Yes, they are all liars!"

Rapping at the back door then. Knuckles against wood, and Dorján saw his grandmother jump. *"Ki ott van?"* Who is there? she said, her voice considerably quieter.

The door opened, a face peering in. "Just me, just me." Gitta slid into the room. "Dorján forgot his sweater." She stared first at his grandmother, then at him, and finally at the letter locked in his fist. Colour drained from her face. "What is it? What is wrong?"

"I cannot even speak!" his grandmother said, hands tossed into the air. "My head is about to catch fire, I am so angry."

He noticed thin strands had come loose from his grandmother's knot of hair, and the wildness of her usually calm face frightened him.

He brushed past Gitta and into the courtyard, but she rushed behind him, clutched his upper arm.

"What?"

"I am leaving," he said. "That is it."

"Leaving?"

He held up the envelope and showed her the stamp.

"Who gave this to you?"

"The Oficir. Račić. Brought it here."

Her eyes changed then, dissolved into glossiness. "Do not go," she said flatly. "You are too young. We will keep you."

"Keep me? Until they arrest me."

Fist formed, she pressed her knuckles into her teeth. Then, "When do you begin to serve?"

"As soon as I return from swimming. We have a competition. "

"Dorján." She came very close to him, and he could smell the dampness of her clothes, the soap from the laundry. Her breath in his ear. "I need you to listen, listen. When you leave to swim, you will stay. You will stay and not come home. Do you understand? There is nothing for you here. There was nothing for János. I see that now. It was selfish of me to hold him here. Do you understand? There was nothing for János, and there is nothing for you. You have no choice." Her voice cracked. "You must do this. For your friend. For János."

Dorján glanced into her eyes. They reminded him of an animal that had been prodded too many times.

He shook his head. He did not know what to think, what to say. Everything had changed. Everything. And so quickly. Had it been this way all along, while he slept with a stomach full of milk? Had János been awake, nudging him, nudging him? "Can't you see this is our chance?" he had said when they were in the woods. "This is what our fathers would've wanted."

Dorján stared at the letter for a long time. Eventually he folded it in three pieces, slid it into his back pocket. The same pocket that held the single gold coin. He looked down at his boots, lifted one, then the other, and inspected the heels. Worn and uneven. "Tell *nagyanya* I will be home later," he said, and crossed the courtyard, stepped out into the road. Empty and quiet, everyone tucked inside for the evening meal.

He turned left and began a long walk. At first he tried to convince himself he was only taking in air, but as he strode up the stone road to Drobnik, he could fool himself no longer. He was going to visit the *Schuster*. A man he had not seen since he was a child. His father often told him, "If you need something that no one else might give you, come here. The *Schuster* is a man you can trust."

Chapter 44

BLACK HANDKERCHIEF KNOTTED UNDERNEATH her chin, Gitta walked along the main street of Bregalnica. She passed near the village square, saw Oficir Račić seated with another man at a tiny table, a chess game between them. He did not lift his head toward her, nor did she turn hers. That painful moment between them was so far in the past, buried beneath so many other memories, it no longer scraped at her back.

She passed the last homes and then continued along the dirt road. Buksi followed her, sometimes bolting ahead, jumping in the air as though the old dog were a puppy. As Gitta walked, she surveyed the fields on either side of the road. Nothing appeared nearly as vast as it had when she was a girl. The fields had shrunk, and the bordering line of trees had crept closer. Harvest over, and the soil was stripped. The cornstalks were silent, and they lay on their sides in polite rows, yellowed and dying. Occasionally she stopped, closed her eyes, and brought her thin face upward. Red glow behind her eyelids, the sun shone down upon her but withheld its heat.

He has asked her to meet him there. When she arrived at the grove, the field was empty. The Komandant was nowhere to be seen.

She was hesitant but stepped over the ditch, stood on the tired grass at the edge of the field. Most of the cherry trees were now leafless, and the ground was littered with yellow and orange leaves. The branches were barren.

She placed her basket at her feet and shook her head slightly. She felt confused, could not quite understand how time had slipped by. How could she be aware and unaware at the same time? She had expected to pick fruit, the same chore she had done as a young girl. Passing the afternoons alongside Dragan. Climbing wooden ladders up into the trees, their heads lost. His easy laughter carrying through the leaves. Yet that seemed like such a strange notion now. Surely workers had plucked everything months ago, and whatever remained had already become food for the birds.

She stood in the field, staring down at her dusty shoes. Thought about János and his love of sour cherry soup. Whenever he had eaten it, she could see stains on his young tongue. He told her as long as she made it for him, he would never go away.

It had been over a year since he had left. Since they had fought over his naïveté. His purity. That was an odd word for her to consider, but that was what it was. He had not suffered enough to understand, not enough to rid his mind of ideas. Ideas that did not belong. He had thrown open the door, slammed it shut behind him. How hard he had tried to pretend he was not hers. That he had sprung up from the soft mud like the frogs and the toads. Connected to nothing and no one.

She had chased him outside, cried out to him as he crossed the courtyard. Telling him to stop, to stop. She wanted to explain things to him. He would not listen. Her patience evaporated, and, face contorted in anger, she called him names. Mean names. Spilling her fury into the street for everyone to hear. Surely those words had hurt him. Propelled him forward. Made him walk away from her.

There it was, the back of his boyish head, skewed on his wide shoulders. Out of all the images she retained, why did that have to be the last one? Whenever she dreamt of him, which was often, she told him to turn around. *Kérlek*, János. *Kérlek*. Turn around and let me see your handsome face. For months he ignored her. But finally he turned. Yes. And he was smiling.

Death had made him considerate.

Crouching underneath a tree, she dug into the dry dirt between two roots, held clumps of it in her fist until it crumbled. She brought the dirt to her nose, had the faintest desire to touch it with her lips. She would never forget how the soil, in its kindness, had kept János over the winter. Carefully holding him together and then, without balking, turned him over to her. Allowing his softened frame to be wrapped in arms and air and clean blankets. She had that time, so short, before she had to give him back. Return him to the soil so it could finish the job it had started.

When she emerged on the other side of the orchard, she saw the house. Straw roof fallen inward and rotted on the floor of the rooms. Beams collapsed, stone walls cracked and jagged and tumbling inward. Thick smell of loneliness. She entered through the doorway, torn hinges holding nothing. On the floor she noticed the fallen door, still bright blue from paint, and when she leaned closer, she could make out a muddy boot print that the rain had failed to erase. She touched the print and, in her mind, saw the foot raised, the sharp strike, the door ripped away and falling. Falling. She knew for certain there was joy there, behind the destruction.

Cautiously she stepped over the debris, moved farther into the abandoned home. The Komandant's childhood home. A place she had visited so many times when she was a young woman. She went to the stone wall of the kitchen, and even though it was partially ruined, she could still see dampness squeezing out from the mortar between the stones. Water formed into cloudy tears, trickled downward into the debris. Turning, she leaned her shoulder blades, the back of her head, against the cold stone. If she stayed here long enough, might it pull something from her?

Of course she knew her son was dead. She understood that. She had seen his toes sticking up through the soil, saw him lifted from the hole, face discoloured, hair matted against his scalp. It was him, and at the same time, it was not him. That corpse was so different from what he had been. Perhaps this was what led to her shift in thought. How over time, those memories had slipped, faded, dulled to grey. Though she would never deny those memories, she had stopped fully believing in them. Instead, she found herself waiting. Just waiting for something to happen.

Rustling then in the backyard, and Gitta lifted her back from the wall, stood straight. Touched the top of her handkerchief, tugged it slightly forward so it shaded her eyes. A face appeared in the broken window, framed by a square of glass teeth.

"Dragan." Even though he insisted time after time, she still found it difficult to speak his name. The simple familiarity carried her back to her youth, reminded her that beneath the man, he was still a boy.

"Come from there." A bark. He disappeared for a second, reappearing in the back doorway. He glanced at the ceiling, at the remaining pair of beams. "Could drop any moment, Brigitta. Quickly. Please. You should not be in there."

"I am sorry," she replied as she stepped over the rubble, emerged from the house. "I did not mean to. To go in."

He pointed. "If it comes down on you?" His mouth was tight, eyebrows knitted, but he said nothing more about it. Instead, "I found the dog but not you."

Buksi was on his back in the grass, body curling back and forth, thick tail lifting then slapping the ground. Gitta opened her mouth to admonish the dog, but the Komandant stopped her.

"It is something, yes? How a dog can find comfort anywhere."

She nodded. "What is happening here? To the house. Why is no one caring for it?"

He shook his head, lit a cigarette, pulled gently. "I did. But it no longer belongs to me. Our government made claim to it some time ago. I was no longer permitted to care for it. In weeks they will cut down every tree. I should be proud, they said. Proud to build a stronger country."

"Every tree?"

"Yes. And then they will level the house. Finish levelling, I should say. I see they have begun."

"Dragan. I am sorry." And she meant it. She could see from his expression that he was pained by his thoughts. His desire to support his country's growth tangled up with sadness over the destruction of his childhood home.

"It is not just the house," he said, turning his back to her. "When I think of you, when I think of us, we are here. On this land. Working together. I always wanted us here. One day, I thought." Light laughter. "Stupidity, I know."

Gitta said nothing. For a moment she closed her eyes, imagining her younger self surrounded by that vast orchard in springtime. Flower petals falling from the sky, like sweet snow, landing on her. Dragan just behind her, plucking them from her long hair. Then summertime. Each branch full of sharp-edged leaves, heavy with purple fruit. Any misery that ambled along the dusty roadway, looking for a place to rest its damaged feet, would not stop there. *No, it would not stop there.*

"Do you remember this one?" A dying tree stood just outside the back door of the house. He walked toward it, broke off a rotting branch, tossed it.

"I remember," she said. "I helped your mother with the fruit. Preserving them."

"The apricot tree my mother loved. When the wind blew in the summer, the fruit would bump against the kitchen window. I felt like a rich man then. I did. Those days when I could reach over the sink, pull an apricot straight from the tree.

"My mother. She thought it would live forever. That fruit was gold to her. Gold to me. The only gold that mattered. Life was simple then. Easy."

He stepped toward her, and his face was full of concern. Sunlight caught on his lapel, struck her eye. He was wearing a small metal pin, a two-headed eagle.

"Dragan. Do not worry for me."

"I cannot help myself, *ljubavi moja*." My love.

Looking over his shoulder, she focused on the neat rows of dozing cherry trees. She could picture the earth before they were there. Immense and empty and covered with a fine spray of green grass. Then the sight of a thousand gnarled fingers breaking through the surface, growing outward from skinny brown trunks. Maturing into trees, open and airy, honest and gullible. Soon they would arrive, severing each one at the wrist, leaving the roots to wither.

"Gitta?"

"Yes, Dragan."

"They will come this week to smooth the soil. Remove everything."

"Ah."

"Will you walk with me this afternoon? Around the property? Among the trees? It is cold, but not too cold."

She knew he was watching her. Staring at the darts in the waist of her dress, fabric sewn inward to accommodate her increasing thinness.

"Yes," she replied, "Of course I will."

Placing his fingers just above her elbow, he guided her away from the broken stone house and into the naked orchard. She remembered him touching her there when they were young, how he could guide her with only the slightest movement. How he had let go, that afternoon in the village square, while Imre danced with the gypsies. The feeling was so familiar, yet at the same time his touch felt new. Like a promise.

"Yes," she repeated. "Let us walk through the orchard while the trees still stand." *Still breathe.*

As they walked, Buksi bolted between them, raced up and down the lengths of the field, his four legs a blur. Gitta considered that the dog was also putting aside the pain of today, stiff joints and cracked paws, hollow stomach. Instead he chose to remember the energy he had as a puppy.

"You will miss it?"

"It is land, Brigitta. I should be ashamed to admit an attachment."

"Still."

"Yes, then. All right. I will miss it." His grip tightened on her skin, and she could feel his warmth through the fabric. "It is an end, Brigitta. But it is also a beginning."

Gitta nodded, considering the circle of everything. The field would once again be flat and barren and clean, as it had been in the past. Eventually something functional would rise up in place of the trees. A factory. Concrete blocks and mortar, producing something she did not need or could not afford. At some point that would crumble, and the grass would grow. Life coating everything, oblivious to the stories hidden in the soil. Branches would push through the soil, flowers blooming, fruit dropping. Nothing would really change, even though it might seem so for a moment. If they waited long enough, she was certain, everything would be back as it was before. János would turn around in the courtyard; he would turn around and come back home.

Chapter 45

DORJÁN CROUCHED, QUIETLY LACED his boots, then stood and looked about the room. Early morning, and the only light in the room was the faintest glow from the soot-covered window on the stove. As she did many nights, his grandmother slept in a chair in the corner, her face pushed into the worn wing, eyeglasses skewed on her forehead. Behind her was a display of last night's work. A row of large glass jars, packed tightly with fresh yellow peppers, carrots, thick slices of cabbage. All preserved in vinegar and sugar and salt.

He gently removed her glasses, placing them on the table. He touched the impression they left on her papery skin, touched her thinning hair. How old she appeared when he could not see her eyes.

Chin quivering, her mouth closed, and Dorján knew she had awoken. "I'm going now," he whispered.

She stirred, eyes blinking, hands coming up to her head, fingers moving through her thin hair. "My glasses." Crackling voice.

She pulled them from the table, and with sleepy fingers, she unfolded the glasses, pressed them onto her face. "Ah. Better." Tugging her lobes. "I cannot hear a sound without my glasses. What did you say?"

"I'm going to swim."

"Today?"

"Yes."

"I thought it was tomorrow."

"The train leaves shortly."

"Let me prepare a breakfast. Something warm."

"I don't have time, *nagyanya*. Or the stomach." Hand gliding over his rumbling midsection.

"Milk, then."

"No, no. Don't get up. Rest."

She adjusted her teeth. "Go, then. Make a fine start."

"Of course."

"*Szívem?*"

"Yes?"

She stood, two wobbly feet. Her breathing was heavy as she lifted her stout arms and held his face in her hands. "Let me—let me see your face before you leave."

He wanted to, but he did not fold under her glance. Behind her streaky glasses, her cloudy eyes were wet and kind. His throat knotted into an impossible tangle, and for a moment, he thought he would choke. "I have to go."

"Of course. The train does not wait." She clutched his hand, pressing it into the loose skin on her neck. He could feel her tendons and windpipe on his palm, her chest rising and falling. Her warmth. "Swim well," she said. "And swim strong, *szívem*." Then she brought his wrist to her nose and inhaled deeply. Puckering her tired face as though trying to hold in his scent.

:::::

AT THAT HOUR, THERE was no bus to Drobnik. He had to run the entire way, his small pack striking his back each time his feet touched the ground. As he approached the station, a mustard-coloured building with white doors, he could smell metal in the cold air, could hear the hum of an engine.

He was late. No one else was on the road or rushing through the doors. He saw his reflection in the glass and, at once, a second reflection standing behind his own.

"You're here?"

"A surprise," she said. "To say goodbye. I wanted to see you before you left."

"Thank you."

"For what?"

"I don't know. For getting up so early."

Nevena laughed. "I don't mind." Reaching for his hand, her fingers were icy cold, his sweating, and the connection was peculiar. Uncomfortable. Charged.

"I have to go," he said.

"All I wanted was a moment."

He closed his hand a single time, her fingernails pressing against his skin. "A moment is not very long." *Though sometimes it changes everything.*

"Yes," she said but did not move away.

"I really have to go. Takáts will hammer me."

"I know, I know. I just miss you, and you're not even gone."

She embraced him, and before he could turn his head, she stretched upward, kissed him on the mouth. He did not move, waiting until she pulled away.

He glanced at her quickly, as much as he could manage without buckling. Her face had grown more beautiful, almost overnight, pale skin, black pupils. Dark hair parted in the middle. Her smooth forehead shone in the yellow lamp beside the station door.

"Goodbye, Nevena."

Another grin, wide and toothy. "See you soon, yes?"

After he had stepped through the door of the station, he stopped, pinched his mouth with his hand. He blinked rapidly, so many coils inside of him, wanting to unfurl. He wiped his hand on the leg of his pants. An infantile motion, but he did not deserve her kiss and did not want the memory of it sitting on his lips.

Takáts's voice, then, bringing him forward. Snapping him awake. "About time, Szabó. I was about to send Beštić after you." His teacher's head was jutting out from an open window.

"I'm sorry to make you wait."

Dorján leapt up the two steps onto the train, walked down the narrow aisle, Beštić and the other boys staring at him. An empty seat, and he removed his pack, sat down. Leaned his head against the glass. The train groaned, began to spit and stutter, edging forward. The harsh movements, heavy odour of oil and machinery, made his stomach seize. He closed his eyes, heard Takáts moving toward him, counting the heads, *"Egy, kettő, három..."* The man's voice a constant, his irritation stable and predictable. Somehow it lulled Dorján to sleep.

:: ::

HE AWOKE AS THEY neared the border. The stretch of land was stark, the short grass dry and dead. Scattered trees stood alone, the leaves already stripped by the wind. The train rolled past a sign stuck in the earth, and Dorján turned his head, saw through the window. A tattered stretch of fabric, painted black letters *Jugoslavija*. In seconds it would disappear, the letters unrecognizable.

But the train bucked and stopped, releasing a hiss of pressure. Takáts stood up, yelling over their heads, "They want our papers. A moment, is all. We will be moving again." He smiled, but as he strode down the aisle, Dorján saw anxiety in his eyes.

Waiting, Dorján blew his breath onto the glass, ran his fingers through it. A misty jail. Near the platform, two beech trees rose up from the earth. A series of numbers carved into their skin, and he read each one as they wound up the trunk. He had seen it before, had asked his grandmother about it. "A count of days. They are men, too, *szívem*, and want to go home to their families."

Dorján held on to this sentiment as he watched Takáts approach the guards. *They are men. They have families. Maybe children. Maybe young sons.* Behind them was a three-tiered red brick tower. A wooden platform with a high railing circled the uppermost portion, and a guard strolled back and forth. The glassless windows offered no light to the interior of the tower. Instead they narrowed in concentric squares, until the openings were only large enough for the shaft of a gun, and a single sharp eye.

Beštić held the railing, leaning out the door, while Takáts passed the documents to the guards. He was talking rapidly, hands jerking through the air. On the train, the boys were silent. They were watching as well. Some of them had lowered their windows. The guard did not respond to Takáts, just scratched his stubble, stared at the train. "It is an honour for our students," Takáts said, and lowered his head, revealing a bald circle, "to be invited to such an event."

The guard had no reaction, acted as though he did not hear a word. Then he strode past Takáts, pushed Beštić, and stepped onto the train. "Off. Off. Off," he screeched, cat's voice. He stamped a foot, once, twice. "Now. Now. Now!"

In single file, Beštić and the boys exited the door, lined up shoulder to shoulder, the black train at their backs. Dorján's chest felt bound in rags. As the guard moved down the line, step by step by step, he opened his mouth for air. Tried not to pant but could not help it.

The guard was an inch past him, and Dorján exhaled. Louder than he had intended. A twist of his heel in the gravel, the guard turned, looked Dorján straight in the eyes. Did not blink. Dorján could not hold his stare. His tongue floated on a surge of saliva, and he kept swallowing. He glanced sideways, upward, then forward, focusing on the red star in the middle of the badge pinned to the man's chest.

"*Izujte svoje cipele*," the guard said. He tapped his fingers against his thigh.

Dorján swallowed. "My shoes?"

Takáts jumped forward. "Yes, *féleszű!* Your shoes. Your boots, your—" When the guard raised a gloved hand, the words stopped.

"Your boots, *dečko.*"

His first thought was to find János. He would know how to fix this, how to talk his way out of the line, and back onto the train. A loud clap on the back to say goodbye and good luck. But János was not among the boys who stood, arms locked at their sides, heads facing forward. Dorján was alone.

Squatting on the ground, he pushed his fingers into his knotted laces, pulled. They loosened, and he slowly pulled the boots from his feet, stood up with them tucked underneath his arm.

The guard held out his hand, and Dorján glanced up toward the sky, handing them over.

"I see you have had repairs," he said as he turned them over.

A rapid nod. Though Dorján had not asked, the *Schuster* had fixed the worn heels, shined the soft leather.

"You would like to look clever on your travels. Taller, yes?"

A shrug.

"No, then?" The guard smiled underneath his winged moustache. "Ah."

Deep breaths. His stupidity. His stupidity. How could he have even thought of it? He tried to focus on the rocks pricking the bottoms of his feet instead of the pangs in his empty stomach.

From his belt, the guard unsnapped a leather pouch, removed a blade. Pressed the metal to the heel of a boot, force in his elbow, and the knife slid straight through the heel. Several slices, and he had trimmed the heel right down to the leather bottom of the shoe. He tossed the first boot at Dorján, striking his shinbone, and proceeded to destroy the second heel. When he was finished, he threw that as well and replaced his blade in its case.

Hands clasped behind his back, he squinted at Dorján. Over his shoulder, he yelled to the other guards, "Nothing! My nose is off today. A rare occurrence, yes?"

They laughed, yelled, *"Da!"*

The other students marched silently, heads forward, a controlled line, and mounted the train. Dorján sat on the ground, struggled. His feet seemed to have swollen in those moments, did not want to enter the damaged boots. The guards were watching him, smirking as his toes buckled, his clumsy fingers knotting the laces.

"Today!" Takáts roared. "If you were not an eel in the water, I would leave you here."

He stumbled to his seat on uneven soles, his mind stunned. As the train lurched forward, something watery widened within him. Like the river that cut through Drobnik. When he was a boy, he often rode on his father's shoulders as they strolled onto the bridge. His father would sway back and forth, pretending to loosen his grip on Dorján's scraped knees. From up high, the sight of water had always made him nervous. Afraid. This feeling did not change as he grew up, saw the bridge destroyed, and then slowly rebuilt. Both sides reaching out to meet each other. When he stood on the newly built bridge, peered downward, the water rushed and foamed over the fallen debris. Expanding its edges as it coursed along, consuming the banks, plunging forward.

The sight had always filled him with dread. But today, this moment, the memory of it made him feel alive.

::::

HOURS LATER, THEY ARRIVED at their destination. The boys rolled off the bus, trailing behind Takáts and Beštić, but Dorján stepped slowly, squinting in the bright sunlight. He had been here in the past, but at the same time, he had never really been here. Not in a way where he might open his eyes and look around. At the buildings, the purposeful faces, the concrete platform beneath his ruined boots.

He crouched, squeezing the leather near his left ankle. He had asked the *Schuster* to hide the coin in his heel, but he had not listened. Instead, the man had sewn a thin piece of hide to the inside of the boot. After kissing the coin, he slid it into the newly formed pocket, saying, "You will be a man's future." Then he sealed it closed with strong black thread. Dorján felt the coin there, a hard mass against his bone. Patient and hidden from view. Could see it clearly, dull and scratched, the noble head with laurel on one side, the insect and the shaft of wheat on the other.

"I—" Dorján had started after the *Schuster* had completed his work. But he did not know what to say. He did not know what was going to happen. What he might do. If he would do anything at all.

The old *Schuster* had frowned, running a blackened brush over the toes of the boots. "You have nothing to explain." Before handing them back to Dorján, he spat on them lightly. "Only health and fortune to you, child."

"Iparkodás!" Takáts cried. *Hurry up!* His teacher's face was red, and underneath his arms, dark circles of sweat stained the fabric of his shirt. The boys circled around him. Beside them, Beštić was distracted by the display inside a bowed window. A sample of flaky pastries and dark chocolates sold to those arriving or those departing. Those staying.

"Yes, yes," Dorján replied, but he did not move.

A forest of women surrounded him in rustling dresses, talking loudly. Takáts's voice drowned in the din, and for a moment, he could only hear the joyful chatter, wind through soft leaves. If he lifted his foot away from the platform, he could fall in among them. Lost inside their branches, their crooked shadows, their flush of happiness. A single step to leave everything behind. He could. He could do it. Bury his feet in that loamy soil. Safe inside his damaged boots. A golden mantis praying against his heel.

Acknowledgements

I WOULD LIKE TO thank the Ontario Arts Council for supporting this project. Thank you to my agent, Hilary McMahon, and Chris Labonté (who acquired the manuscript) for their endless enthusiasm. Thank you to everyone at the new D&M, especially Anna Comfort O'Keeffe, for giving the novel a home. A special thank you to Carleton Wilson who took the words and put them in a beautiful package. I am deeply grateful to both my editors: Barbara Berson who guided me through the substantive edit, and Shirarose Wilensky, who helped to shape and polish the story. Thank you also to my copy-editor, Maureen Nicholson, and my proof reader, Lacey Decker, for their sharp eyes. A warm thank you to my publicist, Corina Eberle, for her tireless efforts and her exceptional wit. I appreciate the kind and wise words of my early readers, Sara McGuire and Sarah Weinman. Finally, a heartfelt thank you to Jozsef Deák, who provided the seed for this novel, and to Aniko Biber who not only answered a hundred questions, but gave me the courage to push forward.

NICOLE LUNDRIGAN IS THE author of four previous novels. *Glass Boys* was one of *Now* magazine's top ten books of the year and Amazon.ca's top 100 books of the year. *Unraveling Arva* was selected as a top ten pick by *The Globe and Mail, Thaw* was longlisted for the Relit Award, and *The Seary Line* was given an honourable mention for the Sunburst Award. She lives in Ontario.